THE
CELESTINE INSIGHTS

ALSO BY JAMES REDFIELD

The Celestine Prophecy
The Tenth Insight: Holding the Vision
The Celestine Vision: Living the New Spiritual Awareness

By James Redfield and Carol Adrienne

The Celestine Prophecy: An Experiential Guide
The Tenth Insight: Holding the Vision: An Experiential Guide

James Redfield's Web site:
www.celestinevision.com

THE
CELESTINE
INSIGHTS

The Celestine Prophecy
AND
The Tenth Insight

JAMES REDFIELD

WARNER BOOKS

A Time Warner Company

Warner Books, Inc., 1271 Avenue of the Americas,
New York, NY 10020
Visit our Web site at http://warnerbooks.com

W A Time Warner Company

Printed in the United States of America
First Printing: October 1997
10   9   8   7   6   5   4   3   2   1

ISBN: 0-446-52394-1
LC: 97-61850

THE
CELESTINE
PROPHECY

An Adventure

For
Sarah Virginia Redfield

ACKNOWLEDGMENTS

So many people influenced this book that it would be impossible to mention them all. But I must say special thanks to Alan Shields, Jim Gamble, Mark Lafountain, Marc and Debra McElhaney, Dan Questenberry, BJ Jones, Bobby Hudson, Joy and Bob Kwapien, Michael Ryce, author of the tape series "Why is this happening to me again," and most of all, to my wife, Salle.

AUTHOR'S NOTE

For half a century now, a new consciousness has been entering the human world, a new awareness that can only be called transcendent, spiritual. If you find yourself reading this book, then perhaps you already sense what is happening, already feel it inside.

It begins with a heightened perception of the way our lives move forward. We notice those chance events that occur at just the right moment, and bring forth just the right individuals, to suddenly send our lives in a new and important direction. Perhaps more than any other people in any other time, we intuit higher meaning in these mysterious happenings.

We know that life is really about a spiritual unfolding that is personal and enchanting—an unfolding that no science or philosophy or religion has yet fully clarified. And we know something else as well: we know that once we do understand what is happening, how to engage this allusive process and maximize its occurrence in our lives, human society will take a quantum leap into a whole new way of life—one that realizes the best of our tradition—and creates a culture that has been the goal of history all along.

The following story is offered toward this new understanding. If it touches you, if it crystalizes something that you perceive in life, then pass on what you see to another—for I think our new awareness of the spiritual is expanding in exactly this way, no longer through hype nor fad, but personally, through a kind of positive psychological contagion among people.

All that any of us have to do is suspend our doubts and distractions just long enough . . . and miraculously, this reality can be our own.

And those who have insight will
shine brightly like the brightness of
the expanse of Heaven, and those who
lead the many to righteousness, like the
stars forever and ever.
But for you, Daniel, conceal these
words and seal up the book until the end
of time. Many will go back and forth,
and knowledge will increase.

DANIEL 12:3-4

CONTENTS

A
CRITICAL
MASS

I drove up to the restaurant and parked, then leaned back in my seat to think for a moment. Charlene, I knew, would already be inside, waiting to talk with me. But why? I hadn't heard a word from her in six years. Why would she have shown up now, just when I had sequestered myself in the woods for a week?

I stepped out of the truck and walked toward the restaurant. Behind me, the last glow of a sunset sank in the west and cast highlights of golden amber across the wet parking lot. Everything had been drenched an hour earlier by a brief thunderstorm, and now the summer evening felt cool and renewed, and because of the fading light, almost surreal. A half moon hung overhead.

As I walked, old images of Charlene filled my mind. Was she still beautiful, intense? How would time have changed her? And what was I to think of this manuscript she had mentioned—this ancient artifact found in South America that she couldn't wait to tell me about?

"I have a two–hour layover at the airport," she had said on the telephone. "Can you meet me for dinner? You're going to love what this manuscript says—it's just your kind of mystery."

My kind of mystery? What did she mean by that?

Inside, the restaurant was crowded. Several couples waited for tables. When I found the hostess, she told me Charlene had already been seated

1

and directed me toward a terraced area above the main dining room.

I walked up the steps and became aware of a crowd of people surrounding one of the tables. The crowd included two policemen. Suddenly, the policemen turned and rushed past me and down the steps. As the rest of the people dispersed, I could see past them to the person who seemed to have been the center of attention—a woman, still seated at the table . . . Charlene!

I quickly walked up to her. "Charlene, what's going on? Is anything wrong?"

She tossed her head back in mock exasperation and stood up, flashing her famous smile. I noticed that her hair was perhaps different, but her face was exactly as I remembered: small delicate features, wide mouth, huge blue eyes.

"You wouldn't believe it," she said, pulling me into a friendly hug. "I went to the rest room a few minutes ago and while I was gone, someone stole my briefcase."

"What was in it?"

"Nothing of importance, just some books and magazines I was taking along for the trip. It's crazy. The people at the other tables told me someone just walked in, picked it up, and walked out. They gave the police a description and the officers said they would search the area."

"Maybe I should help them look?"

"No, no. Let's forget about it. I don't have much time and I want to talk with you."

I nodded and Charlene suggested we sit down. A waiter approached so we looked over the menu and gave him our order. Afterward, we spent ten or fifteen minutes chatting in general. I tried to underplay my self–imposed isolation but Charlene picked up on my vagueness. She leaned over and gave me that smile again.

"So what's *really* going on with you?" she asked.

I looked at her eyes, at the intense way she was looking at me. "You want the whole story immediately, don't you?"

"Always," she said.

"Well, the truth is, I'm taking some time for myself right now and staying at the lake. I've been working hard and I'm thinking about changing directions in my life."

"I remember you talking about that lake. I thought you and your sister had to sell it."

"Not yet, but the problem is property taxes. Because the land is so close to the city, the taxes keep increasing."

She nodded. "So what are you going to do next?"

"I don't know yet. Something different."

She gave me an intriguing look. "Sounds as if you're as restless as everyone else."

"I suppose," I said. "Why do you ask?"

"It's in the Manuscript."

There was silence as I returned her gaze.

"Tell me about this Manuscript," I said.

She leaned back in her chair as if to gather her thoughts, then looked me in the eye again. "I mentioned on the phone, I think, that I left the newspaper several years ago and joined a research firm that investigates cultural and demographic changes for the U.N. My last assignment was in Peru.

"While I was there, completing some research at the University of Lima, I kept hearing rumors about an old manuscript that had been discovered— only no one could give me any of the details, not even at the departments of archeology or anthropology. And when I contacted the government about it, they denied any knowledge whatsoever.

"One person told me that the government was actually working to suppress this document for some reason. Although, again, he had no direct knowledge.

"You know me," she continued. "I'm curious. When my assignment was over, I decided to stay around for a couple of days to see what I could find out. At first, every lead I pursued turned out to be another dead end, but then while I was eating lunch in a cafe outside of Lima, I noticed a priest watching me. After a few minutes, he walked over and admitted that he had heard me inquiring about the Manuscript earlier in the day. He wouldn't reveal his name but he agreed to answer all my questions."

She hesitated for a moment, still looking at me intensely. "He said the Manuscript dates back to about 600 B.C. It predicts a massive transformation in human society."

"Beginning when?" I asked.

"In the last decades of the twentieth century."

"Now?!"

"Yes, now."

"What kind of transformation is it supposed to be?" I asked.

She looked embarrassed for a moment, then with force said, "The priest told me it's a kind of renaissance in consciousness, occurring very slowly. It's not religious in nature, but it is spiritual. We're discovering something new about human life on this planet, about what our existence means, and according to the priest, this knowledge will alter human culture dramatically."

She paused again, then added, "The priest told me the Manuscript is divided into segments, or chapters, each devoted to a particular insight into life. The Manuscript predicts that in this time period human beings will begin to grasp these insights sequentially, one insight then another, as we move from where we are now to a completely spiritual culture on Earth."

I shook my head and raised an eyebrow cynically. "Do you really believe all this?"

"Well," she said. "I think. . . "

"Look around," I interrupted, pointing at the crowd sitting in the room below us. "This is the real world. Do you see anything changing out there?"

Just as I said that, an angry remark erupted from a table near the far wall, a remark I couldn't understand, but which was loud enough to hush the entire room. At first I thought the disturbance was another robbery, but then I realized it was only an argument. A woman appearing to be in her thirties was standing up and staring indignantly at a man seated across from her.

"No," she yelled. "The problem is that this relationship is not happening the way I wanted! Do you understand? It's not happening!" She composed herself, tossed her napkin on the table, and walked out.

Charlene and I stared at each other, shocked that the outburst had occurred at the very moment we were discussing the people below us. Finally Charlene nodded toward the table where the man remained alone and said, "It's the real world that's changing."

"How?" I asked, still off balance.

"The transformation is beginning with the First Insight, and according to the priest, this insight always surfaces unconsciously at first, as a profound sense of restlessness."

"Restlessness?"

"Yes."

"What are we looking for?"

"That's just it! At first we aren't sure. According to the Manuscript, we're beginning to glimpse an alternative kind of experience. . . moments in our lives that feel different somehow, more intense and inspiring. But we don't know what this experience is or how to make it last, and when it ends we're left feeling dissatisfied and restless with a life that seems ordinary again."

"You think this restlessness was behind the woman's anger?"

"Yes. She's just like the rest of us. We're all looking for more fulfillment in our lives, and we won't put up with anything that seems to bring us down. This restless searching is what's behind the 'me–first' attitude that has characterized recent decades, and it's affecting everyone, from Wall Street to street gangs."

She looked directly at me. "And when it comes to relationships, we're so demanding that we're making them near impossible."

Her remark brought back the memory of my last two relationships. Both had begun intensely and both within a year had failed. When I focused on Charlene again, she was waiting patiently.

"What exactly are we doing to our romantic relationships?" I asked.

"I talked with the priest a long time about this," she replied. "He said that when both partners in a relationship are overly demanding, when each expects the other to live in his or her world, to always be there to join in his or her chosen activities, an ego battle inevitably develops."

What she said struck home. My last two relationships had indeed degenerated into power struggles. In both situations, we had found ourselves in a conflict of agendas. The pace had been too fast. We had too little time to coordinate our different ideas about what to do, where to go, what interests to pursue. In the end, the issue of who would lead, who would determine the direction for the day, had become an irresolvable difficulty.

"Because of this control battle," Charlene continued, "the Manuscript says we will find it very difficult to stay with the same person for any length of time."

"That doesn't seem very spiritual," I said.

"That's exactly what I told the priest," she replied. "He said to remember that while most of society's recent ills can be traced to this restlessness and searching, this problem is temporary, and will come to an end. We're finally becoming conscious of what we're actually looking for, of what this other, more fulfilling experience really is. When we grasp it fully, we'll have attained the First Insight."

Our dinner arrived so we paused for several minutes as the waiter poured more wine, and to taste each other's food. When she reached across the table to take a bite of salmon from my plate, Charlene wrinkled her nose and giggled. I realized how easy it was to be with her.

"Okay," I said. "What is this experience we're looking for? What is the First Insight?"

She hesitated, as though unsure how to begin.

"This is hard to explain," she said. "But the priest put it this way. He said the First Insight occurs when we become conscious of the *coincidences* in our lives."

She leaned toward me. "Have you ever had a hunch or intuition concerning something you wanted to do? Some course you wanted to take in your life? And wondered how it might happen? And then, after you had half forgotten about it and focused on other things, you suddenly met someone or read something or went somewhere that led to the very opportunity you envisioned?

"Well," she continued, "according to the priest, these coincidences are happening more and more frequently and that, when they do, they strike us as beyond what would be expected by pure chance. They feel destined, as though our lives had been guided by some unexplained force. The experience induces a feeling of mystery and excitement and, as a result, we feel more alive.

"The priest told me that this is the experience that we've glimpsed and that we're now trying to manifest all the time. More people every day are convinced that this mysterious movement is real and that it means something, that something else is going on beneath everyday life. This awareness is the First Insight.

She looked at me expectantly, but I said nothing.

"Don't you see?" she asked. "The First Insight is a reconsideration of the inherent mystery that surrounds our individual lives on this planet. We are experiencing these mysterious coincidences, and even though we don't understand them yet, we know they are real. We are sensing again, as in childhood, that there is another side of life that we have yet to discover, some other process operating behind the scenes."

Charlene was leaning further toward me, gesturing with her hands as she spoke.

"You're really into this, aren't you?" I asked.

"I can remember a time," she said, sternly, "when you talked about these kinds of experiences."

Her comment jolted me. She was right. There had been a period in my life when I had indeed experienced such coincidences and had even tried to understand them psychologically. Somewhere along the way, my view had changed. I had begun to regard such perceptions as immature and unrealistic for some reason, and I had stopped even noticing.

I looked directly at Charlene, then said defensively, "I was probably reading Eastern Philosophy or Christian Mysticism at that time. That's what you remember. Anyway, what you're calling the First Insight has been written about many times, Charlene. What's different now? How is a perception of mysterious occurrences going to lead to a cultural transformation?"

Charlene looked down at the table for an instant and then back at me.

"Don't misunderstand," she said. "Certainly this consciousness has been experienced and described before. In fact, the priest made a point to say that the first insight wasn't new. He said individuals have been aware of these unexplained coincidences throughout history, that this has been the perception behind many great attempts at philosophy and religion. But the difference now lies in the numbers. According to the priest, the transformation is occurring now because of the number of individuals having this awareness all at the same time."

"What did he mean, exactly?" I asked.

"He told me the Manuscript says the number of people who are conscious of such coincidences would begin to grow dramatically in the sixth decade of the twentieth century. He said that this growth would continue until sometime near the beginning of the following century, when we would reach a specific level of such individuals—a level I think of as a critical mass.

"The Manuscript predicts," she went on, "that once we reach this critical mass, the entire culture will begin to take these coincidental experiences seriously. We will wonder, in mass, what mysterious process underlies human life on this planet. And it will be this question, asked at the same time by enough people, that will allow the other insights to also come into consciousness—because according to the Manuscript, when a sufficient number of individuals seriously question what's going on in life, we will begin to find out. The other insights will be revealed. . . one after the other."

She paused to take a bite of food.

"And when we grasp the other insights," I asked, "then the culture will shift?"

"That's what the priest told me," she said.

I looked at her for a moment, contemplating the idea of a critical mass, then said, "You know, all this sounds awfully sophisticated for a Manuscript written in 600 B.C."

"I know," she replied. "I raised the question myself. But the priest assured me that the scholars who first translated the Manuscript were absolutely convinced of its authenticity. Mainly because it was written in Aramaic, the same language in which much of the Old Testament was written."

"Aramaic in South America? How did it get there in 600 B.C?"

"The priest didn't know."

"Does his church support the Manuscript?" I asked.

"No," she said. "He told me that most of the clergy were bitterly trying to suppress the Manuscript. That's why he couldn't tell me his name. Apparently talking about it at all was very dangerous for him."

"Did he say why most church officials were fighting against it?"

"Yes, because it challenges the completeness of their religion."

"How?"

"I don't know exactly. He didn't discuss it much, but apparently the other insights extend some of the church's traditional ideas in a way that alarms the church elders, who think things are fine the way they are."

"I see."

"The priest did say," Charlene went on, "that he doesn't think the Manuscript undermines any of the church's principles. If anything, it clarifies exactly what is meant by these spiritual truths. He felt strongly that the church leaders would see this fact if they would try to see life as a mystery again and then proceed through the other insights."

"Did he tell you how many insights there were?"

"No, but he did mention the Second Insight. He told me it is a more correct interpretation of recent history, one that further clarifies the transformation."

"Did he elaborate on that?"

"No, he didn't have time. He said he had to leave to take care of some business. We agreed to meet back at his house that afternoon, but when I arrived he wasn't there. I waited three hours and he still didn't show up. Finally, I had to leave to catch my flight home."

"You mean you weren't able to talk with him any more?"

"That's right. I never saw him again."

"And you never received any confirmation about the Manuscript from the government?"

"None."

"And how long ago did this take place?"

"About a month and a half."

For several minutes we ate in silence. Finally Charlene looked up and asked, "So what do you think?"

"I don't know," I said. Part of me remained skeptical of the idea that human beings could really change. But another part of me was amazed to think that a Manuscript which spoke in these terms might actually exist.

"Did he show you a copy or anything?" I asked.

"No. All I have are my notes."

Again we were silent.

"You know," she said, "I had thought you would be really excited by these ideas."

I looked at her. "I guess I need some proof that what this Manuscript says is true."

She smiled broadly again.

"What?" I asked.

"That's exactly what I said, too."

"To whom, the priest?"

"Yes."

"What did he say?"

"He said that experience is the evidence."

"What did he mean by that?"

"He meant that our experience validates what the Manuscript says. When we truly reflect on how we feel inside, on how our lives are proceeding at this point in history, we can see that the ideas in the Manuscript make sense, that they ring true." She hesitated. "Does it make sense to you?"

I thought for a moment. Does it make sense? Is everyone as restless as me, and if so, does our restlessness result from the simple insight—the simple awareness built up for thirty years—that there is really more to life than we know, more that we can experience?

"I'm not sure," I finally said, "I guess I need some time to think about it."

I walked out to the garden beside the restaurant and stood behind a cedar bench facing the fountain. To my right I could see the pulsating lights at the airport and hear the roaring engines of a jet ready for take off.

"What beautiful flowers," Charlene said from behind me. I turned to see her walking toward me along the walkway, admiring the rows of petunias and begonias which bordered the sitting area. She stood beside me and I put my arm around her. Memories flooded my mind. Years ago, when we had both lived in Charlottesville, Virginia, we had spent regular evenings together, talking. Most of our discussions were about academic theories and psychological growth. We had both been fascinated by the conversations and by each other. Yet it struck me how platonic our relationship had always been.

"I can't tell you," she said, "how nice it is to see you again."

"I know," I replied. "Seeing you brings back a lot of memories."

"I wonder why we didn't stay in touch?" She asked.

Her question took me back again. I recalled the last time I had seen Charlene. She was telling me good-bye at my car. At the time I felt full of new ideas and was departing for my home town to work with severely abused children. I thought I knew how such children could transcend the intense reactions, the obsessive acting out, that kept them from going on with their lives. But as time had progressed, my approach had failed. I had to admit my ignorance. How humans might liberate themselves from their pasts was still an enigma to me.

Looking back over the previous six years I now felt sure the experience had been worthwhile. Yet I also felt the urge to move on. But to where? To do what? I had thought of Charlene only a few times since she had helped me crystallize my ideas about childhood trauma, and now here she was again, back in my life—and our conversation felt just as exciting as before.

"I guess I got totally absorbed in my work," I said.

"So did I," she replied. "At the paper it was one story after another. I didn't have time to look up. I forgot about everything else."

I squeezed her shoulder. "You know, Charlene, I had forgotten how well we talk together; our conversation seems so easy and spontaneous."

Her eyes and smile confirmed my perception. "I know," she said, "conversations with you give me so much energy."

I was about to make another comment when Charlene stared past me toward the entrance to the restaurant. Her face grew anxious and pale.

"What's wrong?" I asked, turning to look in that direction. Several people were walking toward the parking lot, talking casually, but nothing seemed out of the ordinary. I turned to face Charlene again. She still appeared alarmed and confused.

"What was it?" I repeated.

"Over by the first row of cars—did you see that man in the gray shirt?"

I looked toward the parking lot again. Another group was exiting through the door. "What man?"

"I guess he's not there now," she said, straining to see.

She looked directly into my eyes. "When the people at the other tables described the man who stole my briefcase, they said he had thinning hair and a beard, and wore a gray shirt. I think I just saw him over there by the cars. . . watching us."

A knot of anxiety formed in my stomach. I told Charlene I would be right back and walked to the parking lot to look around, careful not to get too far away. I saw no one who fit the description.

When I returned to the bench, Charlene took a step closer to me and said softly, "Do you suppose this person thinks I have a copy of the manuscript? And that's why he took my briefcase? He's trying to get it back?"

"I don't know," I said. "But we're going to call the police again and tell them what you saw. I think they also ought to check out the passengers on your flight."

We walked inside and called the police, and when they arrived we informed them of what had occurred. They spent twenty minutes checking each car, then explained that they could invest no more time. They did agree to check all the passengers boarding the plane Charlene would be on.

After the police had left, Charlene and I found ourselves standing alone again by the fountain.

"What were we talking about, anyway?" she asked. "Before I saw that man?"

"We were talking about us," I replied. "Charlene, why did you think to contact me about all this?"

She gave me a perplexed look. "When I was in Peru and the priest was telling me about the Manuscript, you kept popping into my mind."

"Oh yeah?"

"I didn't think too much about it then," she continued, "but later, after I returned to Virginia, every time I would think of the Manuscript, I would think of you. I started to call several times but I always got distracted. Then, I received this assignment in Miami that I'm headed to now and discovered, after I had boarded the plane, that I had a layover here. When I landed I looked up your number. Your answering machine said to contact you at the lake only in an emergency, but I decided it would be okay to call."

I looked at her for a moment, unsure of what to think. "Of course," I finally replied. "I'm glad you did."

Charlene glanced at her watch. "It's getting late. I'd better get back to the airport."

"I'll drive you," I said.

We drove to the main terminal and walked toward the embarkation area. I watched carefully for anything unusual. When we arrived, the plane was already boarding and one of the policemen we had met was observing each passenger. When we approached him, he told us that he had observed everyone scheduled to board and no one fit the description of the thief.

We thanked him and after he had left, Charlene turned and smiled at me. "I guess I'd better go," she said, reaching out to hug my neck. "Here are my numbers. Let's keep in touch this time."

"Listen," I said. "I want you to be careful. If you see anything strange, call the police!"

"Don't worry about me," she replied. "I'll be fine."

For an instant we looked deeply into each other's eyes.

"What are you going to do about this Manuscript?" I asked.

"I don't know. Listen for news reports about it, I guess."

"What if it's suppressed?"

She gave me another of her full smiles. "I knew it," she said. "You're hooked. I told you you'd love it. What are *you* going to do?"

I shrugged. "See if I can find out more about it, probably."

"Good. If you do, let me know."

We said good-bye again and she walked away. I watched as she turned once and waved, then disappeared down the boarding corridor. I walked to my truck and drove back to the lake, stopping only for gas.

When I arrived, I walked out to the screened porch and sat in one of the rockers. The evening was loud with crickets and tree frogs and in the distance I could hear a whippoorwill. Across the lake, the moon had sunk lower in the west and sent a rippled line of reflection toward me on the water's surface.

The evening had been interesting, but I was still skeptical about the whole idea of a cultural transformation. Like many people, I had been caught up in the social idealism of the Sixties and Seventies, and even in the spiritual interests of the Eighties. But it was hard to judge what was really happening. What kind of new information could possibly alter the entire human world? It all sounded too idealistic and far-fetched. After all, humans had been alive on this planet for a long time. Why would we suddenly gain insight into existence now, at this late date? I gazed out at the water for a few more minutes, then turned off the lights and went into the bedroom to read.

The next morning I awoke suddenly with a dream still fresh in my mind. For a minute or two I stared at the bedroom ceiling, remembering it fully. I had been making my way through a forest searching for something. The forest was large and exceptionally beautiful.

In my quest I found myself in a number of situations in which I felt totally lost and bewildered, unable to decide how to proceed. Incredibly, at each of these moments, a person would appear out of nowhere as though by design to clarify where I needed to go next. I never became aware of the object of my search but the dream had left me feeling incredibly upbeat and confident.

I sat up and noticed a beam of sunlight coming through the window across the room. It sparkled with suspended dust particles. I walked over and pulled back the curtains. The day was radiant: blue sky, bright sunshine. A stiff breeze gently rocked the trees. The lake would be rippled and glistening this time of day, and the wind chilly against a swimmer's wet skin.

I walked outside and dove in. I surfaced and swam out to the middle of the lake, turning on my back to look at the familiar mountains. The lake rested in a deep valley where three mountain ridges converged, a perfect lake site discovered by my grandfather in his youth.

It had now been a hundred years since he had first walked these ridges, a child explorer, a prodigy growing up in a world that was still wild with cougar and boar and Creek Indians that lived in primitive cabins up the north ridge. He had sworn at the time that one day he would live in this perfect valley with its massive old trees and seven springs, and finally he had— later to build a lake and a cabin and to take countless walks with a young grandson. I never quite understood my grandfather's fascination with this valley, but I had always tried to preserve the land, even when civilization encroached, then surrounded.

From the middle of the lake, I could see a particular rock outcropping near the crest of the north ridge. The day before, in the tradition of my grandfather, I had climbed to that overhang, trying to find some peace in the view and in the smells and in the way the wind whirled in the tree tops. And as I had sat up there, surveying the lake and the dense foliage in the valley below, I had slowly felt better, as if the energy and the perspective were dissolving some block in my mind. A few hours later I had been talking with Charlene and hearing about the Manuscript.

I swam back and pulled myself up on the wooden pier in front of the cabin. I knew all this was too much to believe. I mean, here I was hiding out in these hills, feeling totally disenchanted with my life, when out of the blue,

Charlene shows up and explains the cause of my restlessness—quoting some old manuscript that promises the secret of human existence.

Yet I also knew that Charlene's arrival was exactly the sort of coincidence of which the Manuscript spoke, one that seemed too unlikely to be a mere chance event. Could this ancient document be correct? Have we been slowly building, in spite of our denial and cynicism, a critical mass of people conscious of these coincidences? Were humans now in a position to understand this phenomenon and thus, finally, to understand the purpose behind life itself?

What, I wondered, would this new understanding be? Would the remaining insights in the Manuscript tell us, as the priest had said?

I faced a decision. Because of the Manuscript I felt a new direction open in my life, a new point of interest. The question was what to do now? I could remain here or I could find a way to explore further. The issue of danger entered my mind. Who had stolen Charlene's briefcase? Was it someone working to suppress the Manuscript? How could I know?

I thought about the possible risk for a long time, but finally my mood of optimism prevailed. I decided not to worry. I would be careful and go slowly. I walked inside and called the travel agency with the largest ad in the yellow pages. The agent with whom I spoke said he could indeed arrange a trip to Peru. In fact, by chance, there was a cancellation I could fill—a flight with reservations already confirmed at a hotel in Lima. I could have the whole package at a discount, he said . . . if I could leave in three hours.

Three hours?

THE
LONGER
NOW

After a frenzy of packing and a wild ride on the freeway, I arrived at the airport with just enough time to pick up my ticket and board the flight for Peru. As I walked into the plane's tail section and sat down in a window seat, fatigue swept over me.

I thought about a nap, but when I stretched out and closed my eyes, I found I couldn't relax. I suddenly felt nervous and ambivalent about the trip. Was it crazy to depart with no preparation? Where would I go in Peru? To whom would I talk?

The confidence I had experienced at the lake was quickly fading back into skepticism. Both the First Insight and the idea of a cultural transformation again seemed fanciful and unrealistic. And as I thought about it, the concept of a Second Insight seemed just as unlikely. How could a new historical perspective institute our perception of these coincidences and keep them conscious in the public mind?

I stretched out further and took a deep breath. Maybe it would be a useless trip, I concluded, just a quick run to Peru and back. A waste of money perhaps but no real harm done.

The plane jerked forward and taxied out to the runway. I closed my eyes and felt a mild dizziness as the big jet reached the critical speed and lifted into a thick cloud cover. When we reached cruising altitude, I finally relaxed and drifted into sleep. Thirty or forty minutes later, a stretch of turbulence woke me up and I decided to go to the rest room.

As I made my way through the lounge area I noticed a tall man with round glasses standing near the window talking to a flight attendant. He glanced at me briefly, then continued speaking. He had dark brown hair and appeared to be about forty-five years old. For an instant I thought I recognized him, but after looking at his features closely, I concluded he was no one I knew. As I walked past I could hear part of the conversation.

"Thanks anyway," the man said, "I just thought since you travel to Peru so often that perhaps you had heard something about the Manuscript." He turned away and walked toward the front of the plane.

I was dumbstruck. Was he speaking of the same Manuscript? I walked into the rest room and tried to decide what to do. Part of me wanted to forget about it. Probably he was talking about something else, some other book.

I returned to my seat and closed my eyes again, content to write off the incident, glad I didn't have to ask the man what he meant. But as I sat there, I thought about the excitement I had felt at the lake. What if this man actually had information about the Manuscript? What might happen then? If I didn't inquire, I would never know.

I wavered several more times in my mind, then finally stood up and walked toward the front of the plane, finding him about midway up the aisle. Directly behind him was an empty seat. I walked back and told an attendant I wanted to move, then gathered my things and took the seat. After a few minutes, I tapped him on the shoulder.

"Excuse me," I said. "I heard you mention a manuscript. Were you speaking of the one found in Peru?"

He looked surprised, then cautious. "Yes, I was," he said tentatively.

I introduced myself and explained that a friend had been in Peru recently and had informed me of the Manuscript's existence. He visibly relaxed and introduced himself as Wayne Dobson, an assistant professor of history from New York University.

As we spoke, I noticed a look of irritation coming from the gentleman sitting next to me. He had leaned back in his seat and was attempting to sleep.

"Have you seen the Manuscript?" I asked the professor.

"Parts of it," he said. "Have you?"

"No, but my friend told me about the First Insight." The man beside me changed his position.

Dobson looked his way. "Excuse me, sir. I know we're disturbing you. Would it be too much trouble for you to exchange seats with me?"

"No," the man said. "That would be preferable."

We all stepped into the aisle and then I slid back into the window seat and Dobson sat beside me.

"Tell me what you heard concerning the First Insight," Dobson said.

I paused for a moment, trying to sum up in my mind what I understood. "I guess the First Insight is an awareness of the mysterious occurrences that change one's life, the feeling that some other process is operating."

I felt absurd as I said it.

Dobson picked up on my discomfort. "What do you think of that insight?" He asked.

"I don't know," I said.

"It doesn't quite fit with our modern day common sense, does it? Wouldn't you feel better dismissing the whole idea and getting back to thinking about practical matters?"

I laughed and nodded affirmatively.

"Well, that's everyone's tendency. Even though we occasionally have the clear insight that something more is going on in life, our habitual way of thinking is to consider such ideas unknowable and then to shrug off the awareness altogether. That's why the Second Insight is necessary. Once we see the historical background to our awareness, it seems more valid."

I nodded. "Then as a historian you think the Manuscript's prediction of a global transformation is accurate?"

"Yes."

"As a historian?"

"Yes! But you have to look at history in the correct way." He took a deep breath. "Believe me, I say this as one who has spent a lot of years studying

and teaching history in the wrong way! I used to focus solely on the technological accomplishments of civilization and the great men who brought
about this progress."

"What's wrong with that approach?"

"Nothing, as far as it goes. But what's really important is the world view
of each historical period, what the people were feeling and thinking. It took
me a long time to understand that. History is supposed to provide a knowledge of the longer context within which our lives take place. History is not
just the evolution of technology; it is the evolution of thought. By understanding the reality of the people who came before us, we can see why we
look at the world the way we do, and what our contribution is toward further progress. We can pinpoint where we come in, so to speak, in the longer
development of Civilization, and that gives us a sense of where we are
going."

He paused, then added, "The effect of the Second Insight is to provide
exactly this kind of historical perspective, at least from the point of view of
western thought. It places the Manuscript's predictions in a longer context
that makes them seem not only plausible, but inevitable."

I asked Dobson how many insights he had seen and he told me only the
first two. He had found them, he said, after a rumor about the Manuscript
prompted a short trip to Peru three weeks ago.

"Once I arrived in Peru," he continued, "I met a couple of people who
confirmed the Manuscript's existence yet seemed scared to death to talk
much about it. They said the government had gone a little loco and was
making physical threats against anyone who had copies or dispersed information."

His face turned serious. "That made me nervous. But later a waiter at
my hotel told me about a priest he knew who often spoke of the Manuscript.
The waiter said the priest was trying to fight the government's effort to suppress the artifact. I couldn't resist going to a private dwelling where this
priest supposedly spent most of his time."

I must have looked surprised, because Dobson asked, "What's wrong?"

"My friend," I replied, "the one who told me about the Manuscript, learned what she knew from a priest. He wouldn't give his name, but she talked with him once about the First Insight. She was scheduled to meet with him again but he never showed up."

"It may have been the same man," Dobson said. "Because I couldn't find him either. The house was locked up and looked deserted."

"You never saw him?"

"No, but I decided to look around. There was an old storage building in the back that was open and for some reason I decided to explore inside. Behind some trash, under a loose board in the wall, I found translations of the First and Second Insights."

He looked at me knowingly.

"You just happened to find them?" I asked.

"Yes."

"Did you bring the Insights with you on this trip?

He shook his head. "No. I decided to study them thoroughly and then leave them with some of my colleagues."

"Could you give me a summary of the Second Insight?" I asked.

There was a long pause, then Dobson smiled and nodded. "I guess that's why we're here."

"The Second Insight," he said, "puts our current awareness into a longer historical perspective. After all, when the decade of the nineties is over, we'll be finishing up not only the twentieth century but a thousand year period of history as well. We'll be completing the entire second millennium. Before we in the west can understand where we are, and what is going to occur next, we must understand what has really been happening during this current thousand year period."

"What does the Manuscript say exactly?" I asked.

"It says that at the close of the second millennium—that's now—we will be able to see that entire period of history as a whole, and we will identify a particular preoccupation that developed during the later half of this millennium, in what has been called the Modern Age. Our awareness of the coincidences today represents a kind of awakening from this preoccupation."

"What's the preoccupation?" I asked.

He gave me a mischievous half smile. "Are you ready to relive the millennium?"

"Sure, tell me about it."

"It's not enough for me to tell you about it. Remember what I said before: to understand history, you must grasp how your everyday view of the world developed, how it was created by the reality of the people who lived before you. It took a thousand years to evolve the modern way of looking at things, and to really understand where you are today, you must take yourself back to the year 1000 and then move forward through the entire millennium experientially, as though you actually lived through the whole period yourself in a single lifetime."

"How do I do that?"

"I'll guide you through it."

I hesitated for a moment, glancing out the window at the land formations far below. Time was already beginning to feel different.

"I'll try," I said finally.

"Okay," he replied, "imagine yourself being alive in the year one thousand, in what we have called the Middle Ages. The first thing you must understand is that the reality of this time is being defined by the powerful churchmen of the Christian church. Because of their position, these men hold great influence over the minds of the populace. And the world these churchmen describe as real is, above all, spiritual. They are creating a reality which places their idea about God's plan for mankind at the very center of life.

"Visualize this," he continued. "You find yourself in the class of your father—essentially peasant or aristocrat—and you know that you will always be confined to this class. But regardless of which class you're in, or the particular work that you do, you soon realize that social position is secondary to the spiritual reality of life as defined by the churchmen.

"Life is about passing a spiritual test, you discover. The churchmen explain that God has placed mankind at the center of his universe, surrounded by the entire cosmos, for one solitary purpose: to win or lose salvation. And in this trial you must correctly choose between two opposing forces: the force of God and the lurking temptations of the devil.

"But understand that you don't face this contest alone, "he continued. "In fact, as a mere individual you aren't qualified to determine your status in this regard. This is the province of the churchmen; they are there to interpret the scriptures and to tell you every step of the way whether you are in accordance with God or whether you are being duped by Satan. If you follow their instructions, you are assured that a rewarding afterlife will follow. But if you fail to heed the course they prescribe, then, well . . . there is excommunication and certain damnation."

Dobson looked at me intensely. "The manuscript says that the important thing to understand here is that every aspect of the Medieval world is defined in other-worldly terms. All the phenomena of life—from the chance thunderstorm or earthquake to the success of crops or the death of a loved one—is defined either as the will of God or as the malice of the devil. There is no concept of weather or geological forces or horticulture or disease. All that comes later. For now, you completely believe the churchmen; the world you take for granted operates solely by spiritual means."

He stopped talking and looked at me. "Are you there?"

"Yes, I can see that reality."

"Well, imagine that reality now beginning to break down."

"What do you mean?"

"The Medieval world view, your world view, begins to fall apart in the fourteenth and fifteenth centuries. First, you notice certain improprieties on the part of the churchmen themselves: secretly violating their vows of chastity, for example, or taking gratuities to look the other way when governmental officials violate scriptural laws.

"These improprieties alarm you because these churchmen hold themselves to be the only connection between yourself and God. Remember they are the only interpreters of the scriptures, the sole arbitrators of your salvation.

"Suddenly you are in the midst of an outright rebellion. A group led by Martin Luther is calling for a complete break from papal Christianity. The churchmen are corrupt, they say, demanding an end to the churchmen's reign over the minds of the people. New churches are being formed based on the idea that each person should be able to have access to the scriptures personally and to interpret them as they wish, with no middlemen.

"As you watch in disbelief, the rebellion succeeds. The churchmen begin to lose. For centuries these men defined reality, and now, before your eyes, they are losing their credibility. Consequently, the whole world is being thrown into question. The clear consensus about the nature of the universe and about humankind's purpose here, based as it was on the churchmen's description, is collapsing—leaving you and all the other humans in western culture in a very precarious place.

"After all, you have grown accustomed to having an authority in your life to define reality, and without that external direction you feel confused and lost. If the churchmen's description of reality and the reason for human existence is wrong, you ask, then what is right?"

He paused for a moment. "Do you see the impact of this collapse on the people of that day?"

"I suppose it was somewhat unsettling," I said.

"To say the least," he replied. "There was a tremendous upheaval. The old world view was being challenged everywhere. In fact, by the 1600s, astronomers had proved beyond a doubt that the sun and stars did not revolve around the Earth as maintained by the church. Clearly the Earth was only one small planet orbiting a minor sun in a galaxy that contained billions of such stars."

He leaned toward me. "This is important. Mankind has lost its place at the center of God's universe. See the effect this had? Now, when you watch the weather, or plants growing, or someone suddenly die, what you feel is an anxious bafflement. In the past, you might have said God was responsible, or the devil. But as the medieval world view breaks down, that certainty goes with it. All the things you took for granted now need new definition, especially the nature of God and your relationship to God.

"With that awareness," he went on, "the Modern Age begins. There is a growing democratic spirit and a mass distrust of papal and royal authority. Definitions of the universe based on speculation or scriptural faith are no longer automatically accepted. In spite of the loss of certainty, we didn't want to risk some new group controlling our reality as the churchmen had. If you had been there you would have participated in the creation of a new mandate for science."

"A what?"

He laughed. "You would have looked out on this vast undefined universe and you would have thought, as did the thinkers of that day, that we needed a method of consensus-building, a way to systematically explore this new world of ours. And you would have called this new way of discovering reality the scientific method, which is nothing more than testing an idea about how the universe works, arriving afterward at some conclusion, and then offering this conclusion to others to see if they agree.

"Then," he continued, "you would have prepared explorers to go out into this new universe, each armed with the scientific method, and you would have given them their historic mission: Explore this place and find out how it works and what it means that we find ourselves alive here.

"You knew you had lost your certainty about a God-ruled universe and, because of that, your certainty about the nature of God himself. But you felt you had a method, a consensus-building process through which you could discover the nature of everything around you, including God, and including the true purpose of mankind's existence on the planet. So you sent these explorers out to find the true nature of your situation and to report back."

He paused and looked at me.

"The Manuscript," he said, "says that at this point we began the preoccupation from which we are awakening now. We sent these explorers out to bring back a complete explanation of our existence, but because of the complexity of the universe they weren't able to return right away."

"What was the preoccupation?"

"Put yourself in that time period again," he said. "When the scientific method couldn't bring back a new picture of God and of mankind's purpose on the planet, the lack of certainty and meaning affected Western culture deeply. We needed something else to do until our questions were answered. Eventually we arrived at what seemed to be a very logical solution. We looked at each other and said: 'Well, since our explorers have not yet returned with our true spiritual situation, why not settle into this new world of ours while we are waiting? We are certainly learning enough to manipulate this new world for our own benefit, so why not work in the meantime to raise our standard of living, our sense of security in the world?'"

He looked at me and grinned. "And that's what we did. Four centuries ago! We shook off our feeling of being lost by taking matters into our own hands, by focusing on conquering the Earth and using its resources to better our situation, and only now, as we approach the end of the millennium can we see what happened. Our focus gradually became a preoccupation. We totally lost ourselves in creating a secular security, an economic security, to replace the spiritual one we had lost. The question of why we were alive, of what was actually going on here spiritually, was slowly pushed aside and repressed altogether."

He looked at me intensely, then said, "Working to establish a more comfortable style of survival has grown to feel complete in and of itself as a reason to live, and we've gradually, methodically, forgotten our original question . . . We've forgotten that we still don't know what we're surviving for."

Out the window, far below, I could see a large city. Judging from our flight-path, I suspected it was Orlando, Florida. I was struck by the geometric outline of streets and avenues, the planned and ordered configuration of what humans had built. I looked over at Dobson. His eyes were closed and he appeared to be asleep. For an hour he had told me more about the Second Insight, then our lunch had arrived and we had eaten and I had told him about Charlene and why I had decided to come to Peru. Afterward, I wanted only to gaze out at the cloud formations and consider what he had said.

"So what do you think?" he asked suddenly, looking sleepily over at me. "Have you grasped the Second Insight?"

"I'm not sure."

He nodded toward the other passengers. "Do you feel as if you have a clearer perspective on the human world? Do you see how preoccupied everyone has been? This perspective explains a lot. How many people do you know who are obsessed with their work, who are type A or have stress related diseases and who can't slow down? They can't slow down because they use their routine to distract themselves, to reduce life to only its practical considerations. And they do this to avoid recalling how uncertain they are about why they live.

"The Second Insight extends our consciousness of historical time," he added. "It shows us how to observe culture not just from the perspective of our own lifetimes but from the perspective of a whole millennium. It reveals our preoccupation to us and so lifts us above it. You have just experienced this longer history. You now live in a *longer now*. When you look at the human world now, you should be able to clearly see this obsessiveness, the intense preoccupation with economic progress."

"But what's wrong with that?" I protested. "It's what made western civilization great."

He laughed loudly. "Of course, you're right. No one's saying it was wrong. In fact, the Manuscript says the preoccupation was a necessary development, a stage in human evolution. Now, however, we've spent enough time settling into the world. It's time now to wake up from the preoccupation and reconsider our original question. What's behind life on this planet? Why are we really here?"

I looked at him for a long time, then asked, "Do you think the other insights explain this purpose?"

Dobson cocked his head. "I think it's worth a look. I just hope no one destroys the rest of the Manuscript before we have a chance to find out."

"How could the Peruvian government think they could destroy an important artifact and get away with it?" I asked.

"They would do it covertly," he replied. "The official line is that the Manuscript doesn't exist at all."

"I would think the scientific community would be up in arms."

He looked at me with an expression of resolve. "We are. That's why I'm returning to Peru. I represent ten prominent scientists, all of whom demand that the original manuscript be made public. I sent a letter to the relevant department heads within the Peruvian government telling them that I was coming and that I expected cooperation."

"I see. I wonder how they will respond."

"Probably with denials. But at least it will be an official start."

He turned away, deep in thought, and I stared out the window again. As I looked down, it dawned on me that the airplane on which we were riding contained within its technology four centuries of progress. We had learned much about manipulating the resources we had found on the Earth. How many people, I mused, how many generations did it take to create the products and the understanding that enabled this airplane to come into being? And how many spent their whole lives focused on one tiny aspect, one small step, without ever lifting their heads from that preoccupation?

Suddenly, in that instant, the span of history Dobson and I had been discussing seemed to integrate fully into my consciousness. I could see the millennium clearly, as though it was part of my own life history. A thousand years ago we had lived in a world where God and human spirituality were clearly defined. And then we had lost it, or better, we had decided there was more to the story. Accordingly, we had sent explorers out to discover the real truth and to report back, and when they had taken too long we had become preoccupied with a new, secular purpose, one of settling into the world, of making ourselves more comfortable.

And settle we had. We discovered that metallic ores could be melted down and fashioned into all kinds of gadgets. We invented sources of power, first steam then gas and electricity and fission. We systemized farming and mass production and now commanded huge stores of material goods and vast networks of distribution.

Propelling it all was the call to progress, the desire of the individual to provide his own security, his own purpose while he was waiting for the truth. We had decided to create a more comfortable and pleasurable life for ourselves and our children, and in a mere four hundred years our preoccupation had created a human world where all the comforts of life could now be produced. The problem was that our focused, obsessive drive to conquer nature and make ourselves more comfortable had left the natural systems of the planet polluted and on the verge of collapse. We couldn't go on this way.

Dobson was right. The Second Insight did make our new awareness seem inevitable. We were reaching a climax in our cultural purpose. We were accomplishing what we had collectively decided to do, and as this happened, our preoccupation was breaking down and we were waking up to something else. I could almost see the momentum of the Modern Age slowing as we approached the end of the millennium. A four hundred year old obsession had been completed. We had created the means of material security, and now we seemed to be ready—poised, in fact—to find out why we had done it.

In the faces of the passengers around me I could see evidence of the preoccupation, but also I thought I detected brief glimpses of awareness. How many, I wondered, had already noticed the coincidences?

The plane tilted forward and began its descent as the flight attendant announced that we would soon be landing in Lima.

I gave Dobson the name of my hotel and asked where he was staying. He gave me the name of his hotel and said it was only a couple of miles from mine.

"What is your plan?" I asked.

"I've been thinking about that," he replied. "The first thing, I guess, is to visit the American Embassy and tell them why I'm here, just for the record."

"Good idea."

"After that, I'm going to speak with as many Peruvian scientists as I can. The scientists at the University of Lima have already told me that they have no knowledge of the Manuscript, but there are other scientists who are working at various ruins who may be willing to talk. What about you? What are your plans?"

"I have none," I replied. "Do you mind if I tag along?"

"Not at all. I was going to suggest it."

After the plane landed, we picked up our luggage and agreed to meet later at Dobson's hotel. I walked outside and hailed a taxi in the fading twilight. The air was dry and the wind very brisk.

As my cab drove away, I noticed another taxi pull out quickly behind us, then lag back in the traffic. It stayed with us through several turns and I could make out a lone figure in the back. A rush of nervousness filled my stomach. I asked the driver, who could speak English, not to go directly to the hotel, but to drive around for a while. I told him I was interested in sightseeing. He complied without comment. The taxi followed. What was this all about?

When we arrived at my hotel, I told the driver to stay in the car, then I opened my door and pretended to be paying the fare. The taxi following behind us pulled up to the curb some distance away and the man stepped out and walked slowly toward the hotel entrance.

I jumped back into the vehicle and shut the door, telling the cabbie to drive on. As we sped away, the man walked into the street and watched us until we were out of sight. I could see my driver's face in the rear view mirror. He was watching me closely, his expression tense. "Sorry about this," I said. "I've decided to change accommodations." I struggled to smile, then gave him the name of Dobson's hotel—although part of me wanted to go straight to the airport and take the first plane back to the States.

A half block short of our destination I had the driver pull over. "Wait here," I told him. "I'll be right back."

The streets were filled with people, mostly native Peruvians. But here and there I passed some Americans and Europeans. Something about seeing the tourists made me feel safer. When I was within fifty yards of the hotel, I stopped. Something wasn't right. Suddenly, as I watched, gunshots rang out and screams filled the air. The crowd in front of me flung themselves to the ground, opening up my view down the sidewalk. Dobson was running toward me, wild-eyed, panicked. Figures behind him pursued. One fired his gun into the air and ordered Dobson to halt.

As he ran closer, Dobson strained to focus, then recognized me. "Run!" he yelled. "For godsakes run!" I turned and ran down an alley in terror.

Ahead was a vertical board fence, six feet high, blocking my way. When I reached it, I leaped as high as I could, catching the top of the boards with my hands and flinging my right leg over the top. As I pulled my left leg over and dropped to the other side I looked back down the alley. Dobson was running desperately. More shots were fired. He stumbled and fell.

I continued to run blindly, leaping piles of trash and stacks of cardboard boxes. For a moment I thought I heard footsteps behind me but I didn't dare look back. Ahead, the alley ran into the next street, which was also crowded with people, seemingly unalarmed. As I entered the street, I dared a glance to my rear, my heart pounding. No one was there. I walked hurriedly down the sidewalk to the right trying to fade into the crowd. Why did Dobson run? I asked myself. Was he killed?

"Wait a minute," someone said in a loud whisper from behind my left shoulder. I started to run but he reached out and grabbed my arm. "Please wait a minute," he said again. "I saw what happened. I'm trying to help you."

"Who are you?" I asked, trembling.

"I'm Wilson James," he said. "I'll explain later. Right now we have to get off these streets."

Something about his voice and demeanor calmed my panic, so I decided to follow him. We walked up the street and into a leather goods store. He nodded to a man behind the counter and led me into a musty spare room in the back. He shut the door and closed the curtains.

He was a man in his sixties, although he seemed much younger. A sparkle in his eyes or something. His skin was dark brown and his hair was black. He looked of Peruvian descent, but the English he spoke sounded almost American. He wore a bright blue t-shirt and jeans.

"You'll be safe here for a while," he said. "Why are they chasing you?"

I didn't respond.

"You're here about the Manuscript, aren't you?" he asked.

"How did you know that?"

"I guess the man with you was here for that reason, too?"

"Yes. His name is Dobson. How did you know there were two of us?"

"I have a room over the alley; I was looking out the window as they were chasing you."

"Did they shoot Dobson?" I asked, terrified by what I might hear in reply.

"I don't know," he said. "I couldn't tell. But once I saw you had escaped, I ran down the back steps to head you off. I thought perhaps I could help."

"Why?"

For an instant he looked at me as though he was uncertain how to answer my question. Then his expression changed to one of warmth. "You won't understand this, but I was standing there at the window and thoughts about an old friend came to me. He's dead now. He died because he thought people should know about the Manuscript. When I saw what was happening in the alley, I felt I should help you."

He was right. I didn't understand. But I had the feeling he was being absolutely truthful with me. I was about to ask another question when he spoke again.

"We can talk about this later," he said. "I think we'd better move to a safer place."

"Wait a minute, Wilson," I said. "I just want to find a way back to the States. How can I do this?"

"Call me Wil," he replied. "I don't think you should try the airport, not yet. If they're still looking for you they will be checking there. I have some friends who live out of town. They will hide you. There are several other ways out of the country you can choose. When you're ready they will show you where to go."

He opened the door to the room and checked inside the shop, then walked outside and checked the street. When he returned, he motioned for me to follow. We walked down the street to a blue jeep that Wil pointed out. As we got in, I noticed that the back seat was carefully packed with food-stuffs and tents and satchels, as if for an extended trip.

We rode in silence. I leaned back in the passenger seat and tried to think. My stomach was knotted with fear. I had never expected this. What if I had been arrested and thrown into a Peruvian jail, or killed outright? I had to size up my situation. I had no clothes, but I did have money and one credit card, and for some reason I trusted Wil.

"What had you and—who was it, Dobson?—done to get those people after you?" Wil asked suddenly.

"Nothing that I know of," I replied. "I met Dobson on the plane. He's an historian and he was coming down here to investigate the Manuscript officially. He represents a group of other scientists."

Wil looked surprised. "Did the government know he was coming?"

"Yes, he had written certain government officials that he wanted cooperation. I can't believe they tried to arrest him; he didn't even have his copies with him."

"He has copies of the Manuscript?"

"Only of the first two insights."

"I had no idea there were copies in the United States. Where did he get them?"

"On an earlier trip he was told a certain priest knew of the Manuscript. He couldn't find him but he found the copies hidden behind his house."

Wil looked sad. "Jose."

"Who?" I asked.

"He was the friend I told you about, the one who was killed. He was adamant that as many people as possible hear about the Manuscript."

"What happened to him?"

"He was murdered. We don't know by whom. His body was found in the forest miles from his house. But I have to think it was his enemies."

"The government?"

"Certain people in the government or in the Church."

"His church would go that far?"

"Perhaps. The Church is secretly against the Manuscript. There are a few priests who understand the document and advocate it covertly, but they must be very careful. Jose talked of it openly to anyone who wanted to know. I warned him for months before his death to be more subtle, to stop giving copies to anyone who came along. He told me he was doing what he knew he must."

"When was the Manuscript first discovered?" I asked.

"It was first translated three years ago. But no one knows when it was first discovered. The original floated around for years, we think, among the Indians, until it was found by Jose. He alone managed to get it translated. Of course, once the church found out what the Manuscript said, they tried to suppress it totally. Now all we have are copies. We think they destroyed the original."

Wil had driven east out of town and we were riding on a narrow two-lane road through a heavily irrigated area. We passed several small plank dwellings and then a large pasture with expensive fencing.

"Did Dobson tell you about the first two insights?" Wil asked.

"He told me about the Second Insight," I replied. "I have a friend who told me of the first. She talked to a priest at another time, to Jose, I guess."

"Do you understand these two insights?"

"I think so."

"Do you understand that chance encounters often have a deeper meaning?"

"It seems," I said, "like this whole trip has been one coincidental event after another."

"That begins to happen once you become alert and connected with the energy."

"Connected?"

Wil smiled. "That's something mentioned further in the Manuscript."

"I'd like to hear about it," I said.

"Let's talk about it later," he said, indicating with a nod that he was turning the vehicle onto a gravel driveway. A hundred feet ahead was a modest wood frame house. Wil pulled up beneath a large tree to the right of the house and stopped.

"My friend works for the owner of a large farming estate who owns much of the land in this area," he said, "and provides this house. The man is very powerful and secretly supportive of the Manuscript. You'll be safe here."

A porch light flicked on and a short squat man, who appeared to be a native Peruvian, rushed out, smiling broadly, and saying something enthusi-astically in Spanish. When he reached the jeep, he patted Wil on the back through the open window and glanced pleasantly over at me. Wil asked him to speak in English, then introduced us.

"He needs a little help," Wil said to the man. "He wants to return to the States but he'll have to be very careful. I guess I'm going to leave him with you."

The man was looking closely at Wil. "You're about to go after the Ninth Insight again, aren't you?" he asked.

"Yes," Wil said, getting out of the jeep.

I opened my door and walked around the vehicle. Wil and his friend were strolling toward the house, having a conversation I couldn't hear.

As I walked up the man said, "I will start the preparations," then walked away. Wil turned to me.

"What did he mean," I asked, "when he questioned you about a Ninth Insight?"

"There is part of the Manuscript that has never been found. There were eight insights with the original text, but one more insight, the Ninth, was mentioned there. Many people have been searching for it."

"Do you know where it is?"

"No, not really."

"Then how are you going to find it?"

Wil smiled. "The same way Jose found the original eight. The same way you found the first two, and then ran into me. If one can connect and build up enough energy, then coincidental events begin to happen consistently."

"Tell me how to do that," I said. "Which insight is it?"

Will looked at me as if assessing my level of understanding. "How to connect is not just one insight; it's all of them. Remember in the Second Insight where it describes how explorers would be sent out into the world utilizing the scientific method to discover the meaning of human life on this planet? But they would not return right away?"

"Yes."

"Well, the remainder of the insights represent the answers finally coming back. But they aren't just coming from institutional science. The answers I'm talking about are coming from many different areas of inquiry. The findings of physics, psychology, mysticism, and religion are all coming together into a new synthesis based on a perception of the coincidences.

"We're learning the details of what the coincidences mean, how they work, and as we do we're constructing a whole new view of life, insight by insight."

"Then I want to hear about each insight," I said. "Can you explain them to me before you go?"

"I've found it doesn't work that way. You must discover each one of them in a different way."

"How?"

"It just happens. It wouldn't work for me to just tell you. You might have the information about each of them but you wouldn't have the insights. You have to discover them in the course of your own life."

We stared at each other in silence. Wil smiled. Talking with him made me feel incredibly alive.

"Why are you going after the Ninth Insight now?" I asked.

"It's the right time. I have been a guide here and I know the terrain and I understand all eight insights. When I was at my window over the alley, thinking of Jose, I had already decided to go north one more time. The Ninth Insight is out there. I know it. And I'm not getting any younger. Besides, I've envisioned myself finding it and achieving what it says. I know it is the most important of the insights. It puts all the others into perspective and gives us the true purpose of life."

He paused suddenly, looking serious. "I would have left thirty minutes earlier but I had this nagging feeling that I had forgotten something." He paused again. "That's precisely when *you* showed up."

We looked at each other for a long time.

"You think I'm supposed to go with you?" I asked.

"What do you think?"

"I don't know," I said, unsure of myself. I felt confused. The story of my Peruvian trip was flashing before my mind: Charlene, Dobson, now Wil. I had come to Peru because of a mild curiosity and now I found myself in hiding, an unwitting fugitive who didn't even know who his pursuers were. And the strangest thing of all was that at this moment, instead of being terrified, totally panicked, I found myself in a state of excitement. I should have been summoning all my wits and instincts to find a way home, but what I really wanted to do was to go with Wil—into what would undoubtedly be more danger.

As I considered my options, I realized that in reality I had no choice. The Second Insight had ended any possibility of going back to my old preoccupations. If I was going to stay aware, I had to go forward.

"I plan to spend the night," Wil said. "So you will have until tomorrow morning to decide."

"I've already decided," I told him. "I want to go."

A
MATTER
OF ENERGY

We rose at dawn and drove east all morning in virtual silence. Early on, Wil had mentioned that we would drive straight across the Andes into what he called the High Selva, an area consisting of forest-covered foothills and plateaus, but he had said little else.

I had asked him several questions about his background and about our destination, but he had politely put me off, indicating he wanted to concentrate on driving. Finally I had stopped talking altogether, and had focused instead on the scenery. The views from the mountain peaks were staggering.

About noon, when we had reached the last of the towering ridges, we stopped at an overlook to eat a lunch of sandwiches in the jeep, and to gaze out at the wide, barren valley ahead. On the other side of the valley were smaller foothills, green with plant life. As we ate, Wil said we would spend the night at the Viciente Lodge, an old nineteenth century estate which formerly belonged to the Spanish Catholic Church. Viciente was now owned by a friend of his, he explained, and was operated as a resort specializing in business and scientific conferences.

With only that brief explanation, we departed and rode silently again. An hour later we arrived at Viciente, entering the property through a large iron and stone gate and proceeding northeast up a narrow gravel drive. Once more, I asked a few probing questions concerning Viciente and why we were here, but as he had done earlier, Wil brushed aside my inquiries, only this time he suggested outright that I focus on the landscape.

Immediately the beauty of Viciente touched me. We were surrounded by colorful pastures and orchards, and the grass seemed unusually green and healthy. It grew thickly even under the giant oaks that rose up every hundred feet or so throughout the pastures. Something about these huge trees seemed incredibly attractive, but I couldn't quite grasp what.

After about a mile the road bent east and up a slight rise. At the top of the knoll was the lodge, a large Spanish-style building constructed of hewn timbers and grey stone. The structure appeared to contain at least fifty rooms, and a large screened porch covered the entire south wall. The yard around the lodge was marked by more gigantic oaks and contained beds of exotic plants and walkways trimmed with dazzling flowers and ferns. Groups of people talked idly on the porch and among the trees.

As we got out of the vehicle, Wil lingered a moment and gazed out at the view. Beyond the lodge to the east, the land sloped gradually downward then flattened out into meadows and forests. Another range of foothills appeared bluish purple in the distance.

"I think I'll go in and make sure they have room for us," Wil said. "Why don't you spend some time looking around? You're going to like this place."

"No kidding!" I said.

As he walked away, he turned and looked at me. "Be sure to check out the research gardens. I'll see you at dinner time."

Wil was obviously leaving me alone for some reason, but I didn't care why. I felt great and not the least bit apprehensive. Wil had already told me that because of the substantial tourist dollar Viciente brought into the country, the government had always taken a hands-off approach to the place, even though the Manuscript was often discussed here.

Several large trees and a winding path toward the south attracted me, so I walked that way. Once I reached the trees, I could see that the walkway proceeded through a small iron gate and down several tiers of stone steps to a meadow filled with wild flowers. In the distance was an orchard of some kind and a small creek and more forest land. At the gate I stopped and took several deep breaths, admiring the beauty below.

"It's certainly lovely, isn't it?" a voice from behind asked.

I turned quickly. A woman in her late thirties carrying a hiking pack stood behind me.

"It certainly is," I said. "I've never seen anything quite like it."

For a moment we looked out at the open fields and at the cascading tropical plants in the terraced beds on each side of us, then I asked: "Do you happen to know where the research gardens are?"

"Sure," she said. "I'm heading that way now. I'll show you."

After introducing ourselves, we walked down the steps and onto the well-worn path heading south. Her name was Sarah Lorner and she was sandy-haired and blue-eyed and could have been described as girlish except for her serious demeanor. We walked for several minutes in silence.

"Is this your first visit here?" she asked.

"Yes, it is," I replied." I don't know much about the place."

"Well, I've been here on and off for almost a year now so I can fill you in a bit. About twenty years ago this estate became popular as a sort of international scientific hangout. Various scientific organizations had their meetings here, biologists and physicists mainly. Then a few years ago. . ."

She hesitated for an instant and looked at me. "Have you heard of the Manuscript that was discovered here in Peru?"

"Yes, I have," I said. "I've heard about the first two insights." I wanted to tell her how fascinated I was with the document but I held back, wondering whether to trust her completely.

"I thought maybe that was the case," she said. "It looked as if you were picking up on the energy here."

We were crossing a wooden bridge which traversed the creek. "What energy?" I asked.

She stopped and leaned back against the railing of the bridge. "Do you know anything about the Third Insight?"

"Nothing."

"It describes a new understanding of the physical world. It says we humans will learn to perceive what was formerly an invisible type of energy. The lodge has become a gathering place for those scientists interested in studying and talking about this phenomenon."

"Then scientists think this energy is real?" I asked.

She was turning to walk across the bridge. "Only a few," she said, "and we take some heat for it."

"You're a scientist, then?"

"I teach physics at a small college in Maine."

"So why are some scientists disagreeing with you?"

She was silent for a moment, as if in thought. "You have to understand the history of science," she said, glancing at me as if to ask whether I wanted to get deeper into the subject. I nodded for her to proceed.

"Think about the Second Insight for a moment. After the fall of the medieval world view, we in the west suddenly became aware that we lived in a totally unknown universe. In attempting to understand the nature of this universe we knew we had to somehow separate fact from superstition. In this regard we scientists assumed a particular attitude known as scientific skepticism, which in effect demands solid evidence for any new assertion about how the world works. Before we would believe anything, we wanted evidence that could be seen and grabbed with the hands. Any idea that couldn't be proved in some physical way was systematically rejected."

"God knows," she continued, "this attitude served us well with the more obvious phenomena in nature, with objects such as rocks and bodies and trees, objects everyone can perceive no matter how skeptical they are. We quickly went out and named every part of the physical world, attempting to discover why the universe operated as it did. We finally concluded that everything that occurs in nature does so according to some natural law, that each event has a direct physical and understandable cause." She smiled at me knowingly. "You see, in many ways scientists have not been that different from others in our time period. We decided along with everyone else to master this place in which we found ourselves. The idea was to create an understanding of the universe that made the world seem safe and manageable, and the skeptical attitude kept us focused on concrete problems that would make our existence seem more secure."

We had followed the meandering path from the bridge through a small meadow and into an area more densely covered with trees.

"With this attitude," she went on, "science systematically removed the uncertain and the esoteric from the world. We concluded, following the thinking of Isaac Newton, that the universe always operated in a predictable manner, like an enormous machine, because for a long time that's all it could be proved to be. Events which happened simultaneously to other events yet had no causal relationship were said to occur only by chance.

"Then, two investigations occurred which opened our eyes again to the mystery in the universe. Much has been written over the past several decades about the revolution in physics, but the changes really stem from two major findings, those of quantum mechanics and those of Albert Einstein.

"The whole of Einstein's life's work was to show that what we perceive as hard matter is mostly empty space with a pattern of energy running through it. This includes ourselves. And what quantum physics has shown is that when we look at these patterns of energy at smaller and smaller levels, startling results can be seen. Experiments have revealed that when you break apart small aspects of this energy, what we call elementary particles, and try to observe how they operate, the act of observation itself alters the results—as if these elementary particles are influenced by what the experimenter expects. This is true even if the particles must appear in places they couldn't possibly go, given the laws of the universe as we know them: two places at the same moment, forward or backward in time, that sort of thing."

She stopped to face me again. "In other words, the basic stuff of the universe, at its core, is looking like a kind of pure energy that is malleable to human intention and expectation in a way that defies our old mechanistic model of the universe—as though our expectation itself causes our energy to flow out into the world and affect other energy systems. Which, of course, is exactly what the Third Insight would lead us to believe."

She shook her head. "Unfortunately, most scientists don't take this idea seriously. They would rather remain skeptical, and wait to see if we can prove it."

"Hey Sarah, here we are over here," a voice called faintly from a distance. To the right about fifty yards through the trees, we could see someone waving.

Sarah looked at me. "I need to go talk with those guys for a few minutes. I have a translation of the Third Insight with me, if you would like to pick out a spot and read some of it while I'm gone."

"I sure would," I said.

She pulled a folder from her pack, handed it to me, and walked away.

I took the folder and looked around for a place to sit down. Here the forest floor was dense with small bushes and was slightly soggy, but to the east the land rose toward what looked like another knoll. I decided to walk in that direction in search of dry ground.

At the top of the rise I was awestruck. It was another spot of incredible beauty. The gnarled oaks were spaced about fifty feet apart and their wide limbs grew completely together at the top, creating a canopy overhead. On the forest floor grew broad-leafed tropical plants which stood four or five feet high and had leaves up to ten inches in width. These plants were interspersed with large ferns and bushes lush with white flowers. I picked out a dry place and sat down. I could smell the musty odor of the leaves and the fragrance of the blossoms.

I opened the folder and turned to the beginning of the translation. A brief introduction explained that the Third Insight brings a transformed understanding of the physical universe. Its words clearly echoed Sarah's summary. Sometime near the end of the second millennium, it predicted, humans would discover a new energy which formed the basis of and radiated outward from all things, including ourselves.

I pondered that idea for a moment, then read something that fascinated me: the Manuscript said the human perception of this energy first begins with a heightened sensitivity to beauty. As I thought about this, the sound of someone walking along the path below drew my attention. I saw Sarah at the exact moment she looked toward the knoll and spotted me.

"This place is great," she said when she reached me. "Have you come to the part about the perception of beauty yet?"

"Yes," I said. "But I'm not sure what that means."

"Further in the Manuscript," she said, " it goes into more detail, but I'll explain it briefly. The perception of beauty is a kind of barometer telling each of us how close we are to actually perceiving the energy. This is clear because once you observe this energy, you realize it's on the same continuum as beauty."

"You sound like you see it," I said.

She looked at me without the slightest self-consciousness. "Yes, I do, but the first thing I developed was a deeper appreciation of beauty."

"But how does that work. Isn't beauty relative?"

She shook her head. "The things that we perceive as beautiful may be different, but the actual characteristics we ascribe to beautiful objects are similar. Think about it. When something strikes us as beautiful, it displays more presence and sharpness of shape and vividness of color, doesn't it? It stands out. It shines. It seems almost iridescent compared to the dullness of other objects less attractive."

I nodded.

"Look at this spot," she continued. "I know you are blown away by it because we all are. This place leaps out at you. The colors and shapes seem magnified. Well, the very next level of perception is to see an energy field hovering about everything."

I must have looked bewildered because she laughed, then said very seriously, "Perhaps we should walk on to the gardens. They're about a half mile farther south. I think you'll find them interesting." I thanked her for taking the time to explain the Manuscript to me, a total stranger, and for showing me around Viciente. She shrugged her shoulders.

"You seem like a person friendly to what we're trying to do," she said. "And we all know we're involved in a public relations effort here. For this research to continue, we must get the word out in the United States and elsewhere. The local authorities don't seem to like us much."

Suddenly a voice called out from behind. "Excuse me, please!" We turned to see three men walking quickly up the path toward us. All appeared to be in their late forties and were dressed in stylish clothes.

"Would one of you tell me where the research gardens are?" the taller of the three asked.

"Could you tell me what your business here is?" Sarah asked in return.

"My colleagues and I have permission from the owner of this estate to examine the gardens and to speak with someone about the so-called research being conducted here. We are from the University of Peru."

"Sounds as though you're not in agreement with our findings," Sarah said smiling, obviously trying to lighten the situation.

"Absolutely not," another of the men said. "We think it is preposterous to claim that some mysterious energy can now be seen, when it has never been observed before."

"Have you tried to see it?" Sarah queried.

The man ignored the question and asked again, "Can you direct us to the gardens?"

"Of course," Sarah said. "About a hundred yards ahead you will see a path turning east. Take it and ahead maybe a quarter of a mile you'll run into them."

"Thank you," the tall man said as they hurried on their way.

"You sent them in the wrong direction," I said.

"Not really," she replied. "There are other gardens in that area. And the people there are more prepared to talk with these kinds of skeptics. We get people like this through here occasionally, and not just scientists but curiosity seekers as well, people who can't begin to grasp what we're doing . . . which points out the problem that exists in scientific understanding."

"What do you mean?" I asked.

"As I said before, the old skeptical attitude was great when exploring the more visible and obvious phenomena in the universe, such as trees or sunshine or thunderstorms. But there is another group of observable phenomena, more subtle, that you can't study—in fact, you can't even tell they're there at all—unless you suspend or bracket your skepticism and try every way possible to perceive them. Once you can, then you return to your rigorous study."

"Interesting," I said.

Ahead the woods ended and I could see dozens of cultivated plots, each one growing a different type plant. Most seemed to be food-bearing types: everything from bananas to spinach. At the eastern border of each crop was a wide gravel path which ran north to what appeared to be a public road. Three metal outbuildings were spaced along the path. Four or five people worked near each one.

"I see some friends of mine," Sarah said, and pointed toward the closest building. "Let's go over there. I'd like for you to meet them."

Sarah introduced me to three men and one woman, all of whom were involved in the research. The men spoke with me briefly then excused themselves to continue their work, but the woman, a biologist named Marjorie, seemed free to talk.

I caught Marjorie's eye. "What exactly are you researching here?" I asked.

She appeared to be taken off guard, but smiled and finally answered. "It's hard to know where to start," she said. "Are you familiar with the Manuscript?"

"The first sections of it," I commented. "I've just begun the Third Insight."

"Well, that's what we're all about here. C'mon, I'll show you." She motioned for me to follow her and we walked around the metal building to a plot of beans. I noticed they appeared to be exceptionally healthy, with no noticeable insect damage or dead leaves. The plants were growing in what appeared to be a highly humus, almost fluffy soil, and each plant was carefully spaced, the stems and leaves of one growing near but never touching those of the next.

She pointed to the closest plant. "We've tried to look at these plants as total energy systems, and think of everything they need to flourish—soil, nutrients, moisture, light. What we have found is that the total ecosystem around each plant is really one living system, one organism. And the health of each of the parts impacts on the health of the whole."

She hesitated, then said, "The basic point is that once we started thinking about the energy relationships all around the plant then we started seeing amazing results. The plants in our studies were not particularly larger, but according to nutritional criteria, they were more potent."

"How was that measured?"

"They contained more protein, carbohydrates, vitamins, minerals."

She looked at me expectantly. "But that wasn't the most amazing thing! We found that the plants which had the most direct human attention were even more potent."

"What kind of attention?" I asked.

"You know," she said, "fiddling with the ground around them, checking them every day. That sort of thing. We set up an experiment with a control group: some getting special attention, others not, and the finding was confirmed. What's more," she continued, "we expanded the concept and had a researcher not just give them attention but to mentally ask them to grow stronger. The person would actually sit with them and focus all his attention and concern on their growth."

"Did they grow stronger?"

"By significant amounts, and they also grew faster."

"That's incredible."

"Yes, it is . . ." Her voice trailed off as she watched an older man, appearing to be in his sixties, walk toward us.

"The gentleman approaching is a micro-nutritionist," she said discreetly. "He came down here about a year ago for the first time and immediately took a leave of absence from Washington State University. His name is Professor Hains. He's done some great studies."

As he arrived, I was introduced. He was a strongly built man with black hair, gray streaks at his temples. After some prodding from Marjorie, the professor began to summarize his research. He was most interested, he told me, in the functioning of the body's organs as measured by highly sensitive blood tests, especially as this functioning related to the quality of food eaten.

He told me what interested him most were the results of a particular study which showed that while nutritionally rich plants of the kind grown at Viciente increased the body's efficiency dramatically, the increase was beyond what could be reasonably expected from the nutrients themselves as we understand how they work in human physiology. Something inherent in the structure of these plants created an effect not yet accounted for.

I looked at Marjorie, then asked, "Then the focusing of attention on these plants gave them something that boosts human strength in return when they're eaten? Is this the energy mentioned in the Manuscript?"

Marjorie looked at the Professor. He gave me only a half smile. "I don't know yet," he said.

I asked him about his future research, and he explained that he wanted to duplicate the garden at Washington State and set up some long-term studies, to see if people eating these plants had more energy or were healthier over a longer period of time. As he spoke, I couldn't help glancing periodically at Marjorie. Suddenly she looked incredibly beautiful. Her body appeared long and slender, even under her baggy jeans and t-shirt. Her eyes and hair were dark brown, and her hair fell in tapered curls around her face.

I felt a powerful physical attraction. At the exact moment I became aware of this attraction, she turned her head, stared directly into my eyes, and backed away from me a step.

"I've got to meet someone," she said. "Maybe I'll see you later." She told Hains good-bye, smiled coyly at me, and walked past the metal building and down the path.

After a few more minutes of discussion with the professor, I wished him well and strolled back to where Sarah was standing. She was still talking intensely with one of the other researchers but she followed me with her eyes as I walked.

As I approached, the man she was with smiled, rearranged the notes on his clipboard and walked into the building.

"Find out anything?" Sarah asked.

"Yes," I said, distractedly, "it sounds like these folks are doing some interesting things."

I was looking at the ground when she said, "Where did Marjorie go?"

As I glanced up I could see she had an amused look on her face.

"She said she had to meet someone."

"Did you turn her off?" she asked, smiling now.

I laughed. "I guess I did. But I didn't say a thing."

"You didn't have to," she said. "Marjorie could detect a change in your field. It was pretty obvious. I could see it all the way over here."

"A change in my what?"

"In the energy field around your body. Most of us have learned to see them, at least in certain light. When a person has sexual thoughts the person's energy field sort of swirls about and actually propels out toward the person who's the object of the attraction."

This struck me as totally fantastic, but before I could comment, we were distracted by several people coming out of the metal building.

"Time now for the energy projections," Sarah said. "You'll want to see this."

We followed four young men, apparently students, to a plot of corn. As we walked closer, I realized that the plot was made up of two separate subplots, each about ten feet square. The corn in one was about two feet high. In the other, the plants were less than fifteen inches. The four men walked to the plot containing the taller corn then sat down, each on one corner of the plot facing inward. On cue they all seemed to focus their eyes on the plants. The late afternoon sun shone from behind me, bathing the plot in soft, amber light, yet the woods beyond remained dark in the distance. The plot of corn and the students were silhouetted against the almost black background.

Sarah was standing beside me. "This is perfect," she said. "Look! Can you see that?"

"What?"

"They're projecting their energy onto the plants.

I stared intently at the scene but could detect nothing.

"I can't see anything," I said.

"Squat down lower then," Sarah said, "and focus on the space between the people and the plants."

For a moment I thought I saw a flicker of light, but I concluded it was just an after image, or my eyes playing tricks on me. I tried several more times to see something then gave up.

"I can't do it," I said, standing.

Sarah patted me on the shoulder. "Don't worry about it. The first time is the most difficult. It usually takes some experimenting with the way you focus your eyes."

One of the meditators looked over at us and brought his index finger up to his lips, so we walked back toward the building.

"Are you going to be here at Viciente long?" Sarah asked.

"Probably not," I said. "The person I'm with is looking for the last part of the Manuscript."

She looked surprised. "I thought all of it had been located. Though I guess I wouldn't know. I've been so engrossed in the part that pertains to my work that I haven't read much of the rest."

I instinctively reached for my pants pocket, suddenly uncertain where Sarah's translation was. It was rolled up in my back pocket.

"You know," Sarah said. "We've found two periods of the day most conducive to seeing energy fields. One is sunset. The other is sunrise. If you want, I'll meet you at dawn tomorrow and we'll try again."

She reached out for the folder. "That way," she continued, "I can make you a copy of this translation and you can take it with you."

I pondered this suggestion for a few seconds, then decided it couldn't hurt.

"Why not?" I said. "I'll have to check with my friend, though, and make sure we have enough time." I smiled at her. "What makes you think I can learn to see this stuff?"

"Call it a hunch."

We agreed to meet on the hill at 6:00 A.M., and I started the one mile trek to the Lodge alone. The sun had completely disappeared but its light still bathed the grey clouds along the horizon in hues of orange. The air was chilly but no wind blew.

At the lodge a line was forming in front of the serving bar in the huge dining room. Feeling hungry, I walked toward the head of the line to see what food was being served. Wil and Professor Hains were standing near the front, talking casually.

"Well," Wil said, "how did the afternoon go?"

"Great," I said.

"This is William Hains," Wil added.

"Yes," I said, "we met earlier."

The professor nodded.

I mentioned my early morning rendezvous the next day. Wil saw no problem, as he wanted to find a couple of people he hadn't talked to yet, and didn't anticipate leaving before 9:00 A.M.

The line moved forward then and the people behind us invited me to join my friends. I stepped in beside the professor.

"So what do you make of what we're doing here?" Hains asked.

"I don't know," I said. "I'm trying to let it soak in a little. The whole idea of energy fields is new to me."

"The reality of it is new to everyone," he said, "but the interesting thing is that this energy is what science has always been looking for: some common stuff underlying all matter. Since Einstein particularly, physics has sought a unified field theory. I don't know if this is it or not but at the very least this Manuscript has stimulated some interesting research."

"What would it take for science to accept this idea?" I asked.

"A way to measure it," he said. "The existence of this energy is not that foreign actually. Karate masters have talked about an underlying Chi energy responsible for their seemingly impossible stunts of breaking bricks with their hands and of being able to sit in one place unmoved with four men trying to push them over. And we've all seen athletes make spectacular moves, twisting, turning, hanging in the air in ways that defy gravity. It's all the result of this hidden energy that we have access to.

"Of course, it won't really be accepted until more people can actually see it themselves."

"Have you ever observed it?" I asked.

"I've observed something," he said. "It really depends on what I've eaten."

"How so?"

"Well, the people around here who readily see these energy fields eat mostly vegetables. And they usually eat only these highly potent plants they've grown themselves."

He pointed ahead to the food bar. "This is some of it, though thank goodness they serve some fish and fowl for old guys like me who are addicted to meat. But if I force myself to eat differently, yes, I can see something."

I asked him why he didn't change his diet for longer periods of time.

"I don't know," he said. "Old habits die hard."

The line moved forward and I ordered only vegetables. The three of us joined a larger table of guests and talked casually for an hour. Then Wil and I walked out to the jeep to remove our gear. "Have you seen these energy fields?" I asked.

He smiled and nodded. "My room is on the first floor," he said. "Yours is on the third. Room 306. You can pick your key up at the desk."

The room had no phone, but a lodge attendant I saw in the hallway assured me someone would knock on my door at 5:00 A.M. sharp. I lay down and thought for a few minutes. The afternoon had been long and full, and I understood Wil's silence. He wanted me to experience the Third Insight in my own way.

The next thing I knew someone was banging on the door. I looked at my watch: 5:00 A.M. When the attendant knocked again I said, "Thank you," in a voice loud enough for him to hear, then rose and looked out the small frame window. The only sign of morning was a pale glow of light toward the east.

I walked down the hall and showered, then dressed quickly and went downstairs. The dining room was open and a surprising number of people were moving about. I ate only fruit and hurried outside.

Strands of fog drifted across the grounds and clung to the distant meadows. Songbirds called one another from the trees. As I walked away from the lodge, the very top of the sun breached the horizon toward the east. The color was spectacular. The sky was a deep blue above the bright peach horizon.

I arrived at the knoll fifteen minutes early so I sat down and leaned against the trunk of a large tree, fascinated by the web of gnarled branches growing out above my head. In a few minutes I heard someone walking toward me along the path and I looked that way, expecting to see Sarah. Instead I saw someone I didn't know, a man in his mid-forties. He left the path and walked my way without noticing me. When he was within ten feet he saw me with a start, which made me flinch also.

"Oh, hello," he said in a rich Brooklyn accent. He was dressed in jeans and hiking boots and looked exceptionally fit and athletic. His hair was curly and receding.

I nodded.

"Sorry about walking up on you so suddenly," he said.

"No problem."

He told me his name was Phil Stone and I told him who I was and that I was waiting for a friend.

"You must be doing some research here," I added.

"Not really," he replied. "I work for the University of Southern California. We're doing studies in another province on the rain forest depletion, but whenever I get the chance I drive over here and take a break. I like hanging out where the forests are so different."

He looked around. "Do you realize some of the trees here are close to five hundred years old? This is truly a virgin forest, a rare thing. Everything is in perfect balance: the larger trees filtering the sunlight, allowing a multitude of tropical plant life to thrive underneath. The plant life in a rain forest is old too, but it grows differently. It's basically jungle. This is more like what an old forest looks like in a temperate zone, such as in the United States.

"I've never seen anything like this there," I said.

"I know," he said. "Only a few remain. Most of the ones I know of were sold by the government to lumber interests, as though all they could see in a forest like this is board feet of lumber. Damn shame that anyone would mess with a place like this. Look at the energy."

"You can see the energy here?" I asked.

He looked at me closely, as though deciding whether to elaborate.

"Yes, I can," he said finally.

"Well, I haven't been able to," I said. "I tried yesterday when they were meditating with plants at the garden."

"Oh, I couldn't see fields that large at first either," he said. "I had to start by looking at my fingers."

"How do you mean?"

"Let's move over there," he said, pointing to an area where the trees parted slightly and blue sky showed through overhead. "I'll show you."

When we arrived, he said, "Lean back and touch the tips of your index fingers together. Keep the blue sky in the background. Now separate the tips about an inch and look at the area directly between them. What do you see?"

"Dust on the lens of my eye."

"Ignore that," he said. "Take your eyes out of focus a little and move the tips closer, then further apart."

As he talked I moved my fingers around, unsure what he meant by taking my eyes out of focus. I finally placed my gaze vaguely on the area between my fingers. Both finger-tips went slightly blurry, and as this happened I saw something like strands of smoke stretching between the tips.

"Good grief," I said, and explained what I saw.

"That's it! That's it!" he said. "Now just play with that a while."

I touched all four fingers together, then my palms and forearms. In each case I continued to see streaks of energy between the body parts. I dropped my arms and looked at Phil.

"Oh, you want to see mine?" he asked. He stood up and stepped back a few feet, positioning his head and torso so the sky would be directly behind him. I tried for a few minutes but a noise behind us broke my concentration. I turned and saw Sarah.

Phil stepped forward and grinned broadly. "Is this the person you've been waiting for?"

As Sarah approached, she too was smiling. "Hey, I know you," she said, pointing at Phil.

They embraced warmly, then Sarah looked at me and said, "Sorry I'm late. My mental alarm didn't go off for some reason. But now I guess I know why. It gave you two a chance to talk. What have you been doing?"

"He just learned how to see the fields between his fingers," Phil said.

Sarah looked at me. "Last year Phil and I were up here at this very spot learning to do the same thing." She glanced at Phil. "Let's put our backs together. Maybe he can see the energy between us."

They stood back to back in front of me. I suggested they move closer and they stepped toward me until the space between us was about four feet. They were silhouetted against the sky, which was still a dark blue in that direction. To my surprise, the space between them looked lighter. It was yellow, or a yellowish pink.

"He sees it," Phil said, reading my expression.

Sarah turned and grabbed Phil by the arm and they slowly stepped away from me so that their bodies were perhaps ten feet away. Surrounding their upper torsos was a whitish-pink field of energy.

"Okay," Sarah said seriously. She had walked over and crouched down beside me. "Now look at the scene here, the beauty."

I was immediately awed by the shapes and forms around me. I seemed to be able to focus on each of the massive oaks in a total way, not merely on one part, but on the whole form at once. I was immediately struck by the unique shape and configuration of limbs each displayed. I looked from one to the other, turning all around. Doing this somehow increased the feeling of presence each oak exuded to me, as though I was seeing them for the first time, or at least fully appreciating them for the first time.

Suddenly the tropical foliage underneath the huge trees attracted my attention; I again looked at the unique form each plant exhibited. I also noticed the way each type of plant grew together with others of its own kind in what struck me as little communities. For instance, the tall banana tree-type plants were often encircled by small philodendrons who themselves were poised among even smaller fern-like plants. When I looked at these mini-environments, I was again struck by their uniqueness of outline and presence.

Less then ten feet away, a particular foliage plant caught my eye. I had often owned just this type as a house plant, a particular variegated form of philodendron. Dark green, its foliage branched out to about four feet in diameter. The shape of this plant seemed perfectly healthy and vibrant.

"Yeah, focus on that one, but loosely," Sarah said.

As I did so, I played with the focus of my eyes. At one point I tried to focus on the space six inches to one side of each physical part of the plant. Gradually I began to pick up glimpses of light, then with a single adjustment of my focus, I could see a bubble of white light encircling the plant.

"I'm seeing something now," I said.

"Look around some," Sarah said.

I stepped back in shock. Around each plant within my vision was a field of whitish light, visible, yet totally transparent, so that none of the plant's color or form was obscured. I realized that what I was seeing was an extension of each plant's unique beauty. It was as though first I had seen the plants, then I had seen their uniqueness and presence, and then something had amplified in the pure beauty of their physical expression, at which time I had seen the energy fields.

"See if you can see this," Sarah said. She sat down in front of me and faced the philodendron. A plume of the whitish light encircling her body erupted outward and engulfed the philodendron. The diameter of the plant's energy field, in turn, broadened by several feet.

"Damn!" I exclaimed, which provoked laughter between the two friends. Soon I was laughing myself, conscious of the peculiarity of what was happening, but feeling absolutely no uneasiness at seeing, quite readily, phenomena I had totally doubted minutes earlier. I realized that the perception of the fields, rather than evoking a surrealistic sensation, actually made the things about me seem more solid and real than before.

Yet at the same time, everything around me seemed different. The only reference I had for the experience was perhaps a movie which enhanced the color of a forest in order to make it seem mystical and enchanted. The plants, the leaves, the sky now all stood out with a presence and a slight shimmer that suggested life there, and perhaps consciousness, beyond our ordinary assumption. After seeing this, there would be no way to take a forest for granted again.

I looked at Phil. "Sit down and put your energy on the philodendron," I said. "I'd like to compare."

Phil appeared perplexed. "I can't do it," he said. "I don't know why."

I looked at Sarah.

"Some people can and some can't," she said. "We haven't figured it out. Marjorie has to screen her graduate students to see who can do it. A couple of psychologists are trying to correlate this ability with personality characteristics but so far no one knows."

"Let me try it," I said.

"Okay, go ahead," Sarah replied.

I sat down again and faced the plant. Sarah and Phil stood at right angles to me.

"Okay, how do I begin?"

"Just focus your attention on the plant, as though to inflate it with your energy," Sarah said.

I looked at the plant and imagined energy swelling up inside it, then after a few minutes I looked over at the two.

"Sorry," Sarah said wryly, "you're obviously not one of the chosen few."

I shot a mock frown at Phil.

Angry voices from the path below interrupted our conversation. Through the trees we could see a group of men passing, talking harshly among themselves.

"Who are those people?" Phil asked, looking at Sarah.

"I don't know," she said. "More folks upset with what we're doing, I guess."

I looked back at the forest around us. Everything appeared ordinary again.

"Hey, I can't see the energy fields anymore!"

"Some things bring you right down, don't they?" Sarah remarked.

Phil smiled and patted my shoulder. "You can do it again anytime now. It's just like riding a bicycle. All you have to do is see the beauty and then extend from there."

I suddenly remembered to check the time. The sun was much higher in the sky and a light mid-morning breeze swayed the trees. My watch showed

7:50 A.M.

"I guess I had better head back," I said.

Sarah and Phil joined me. As we walked, I looked back at the wooded hillside. "That's one beautiful place," I said. "Too bad there aren't more places like this in the States."

"Once you see the energy fields in other areas," Phil said, "you'll realize just how dynamic this forest is. Look at these oaks. They are very rare in Peru, but they grow here at Viciente. A cut forest, especially one that's been stripped of hardwoods in order to grow pines for profit, has a very low energy field. And a city, except for the people, has a different kind of energy altogether."

I tried to focus on the plants along the path, but the act of walking disrupted my concentration.

"You're sure I'll see these fields again?" I said.

"Absolutely," Sarah replied. "I've never heard of anyone failing to duplicate the experience once they've seen them initially. We had a research ophthalmologist come through here once and he got all excited after he learned to see the fields. Turned out he had been working with certain sight abnormalities, including forms of color blindness, and concluded that some people have what he called lazy receptors in their eyes. He had taught people how to see colors they'd never experienced before. According to him, seeing energy fields was just a matter of doing the same thing, of waking up other dormant receptors, something that everyone, theoretically, can do."

"I wish I lived near a place like this," I said.

"Don't we all," Phil replied, then looked around me at Sarah. "Is Dr. Hains still here?"

"Yes," Sarah said. "He can't leave."

Phil looked at me. "Now there's a guy whose doing some interesting research on what this energy can do for you."

"Yeah," I said. "I talked with him yesterday."

"The last time I was here," Phil continued, "he was telling me about a study he would like to conduct in which he would look at the physical effects of merely being near certain high energy environments, such as that forest back there. He would use the same measurements of organ efficiency and output to see the effect."

"Well, I already know the effect," Sarah said. "Whenever I drive into this estate, I begin to feel better. Everything is amplified. I seem stronger, I can think more clearly, and quickly. And the insights I have into all this and how it relates to my work in physics is amazing."

"What are you working on?" I asked.

"Do you remember me telling you about the perplexing experiments in particle physics, during which these little bits of atoms appeared wherever the scientists expected them to be?"

"Yes."

"Well, I've tried to expand this idea a bit with some experiments of my own. Not to solve the problems those guys were working on in subatomic particles, but to explore questions I told you about before: To what extent does the physical universe as a whole—since it is made up of the same basic energy—respond to our expectations? To what extent do our expectations create all the things that happen to us?"

"The coincidences, you mean?"

"Yes, think of the events of your life. The old Newtonian idea is that everything happens by chance, that one can make good decisions and be prepared, but that every event has its own line of causation independent of our attitude.

"After the recent discoveries of modern physics, we may legitimately ask if the universe is more dynamic than that. Perhaps the universe runs mechanistically as a basic operation, but then also subtly responds to the mental energy we project out into it. I mean, why not? If we can make plants grow faster, maybe we can make certain events come faster—or slower, depending on how we think."

"Does the Manuscript talk about any of this?"

Sarah smiled at me. "Of course, that's where we're getting these ideas." She began to dig around in her pack as we walked, finally pulling out a folder.

"Here's your copy," she said.

I glanced at it briefly and placed it in my pocket. We were crossing the bridge and I hesitated a moment, observing the colors and forms of the plants around me. I altered my focus and immediately saw the energy fields around everything in my view. Both Sarah and Phil had wide fields which seemed to be tinted yellow green, though Sarah's field occasionally flashed with a pinkish color.

Suddenly they both stopped and looked intently up the trail. Ahead about fifty feet, a man walked quickly toward us. A sensation of anxiety filled my stomach but I was determined to maintain my view of the energy. As he approached I recognized him; he was the taller of the scientists from the University of Peru who had asked for directions the day before. Around him I could detect a layer of red.

When he walked up to us he turned to Sarah and condescendingly said, "You're a scientist, aren't you?"

"That's right," Sarah replied.

"Then how can you tolerate this kind of science? I've seen these gardens and I can't believe the sloppiness. You people haven't controlled for anything. There could be many explanations for certain plants growing larger."

"Controlling for everything is impossible, sir. We're looking for general tendencies."

I could detect an edge growing in Sarah's voice.

"But postulating some newly visible energy that underlies the chemistry of living things—that's absurd. You have no proof."

"Proof is what we're looking for."

"But how can you postulate the existence of anything before you get some proof!"

The voices of both individuals sounded angry now, but I was only vaguely listening. What consumed my attention was the dynamics of their energy fields. When the discussion began, Phil and I had backed up a few feet, and Sarah and the taller man had squared off facing each other with a distance of about four feet between them. Immediately, both their energy fields had seemed to grow more dense and excited somehow, as though from an inner vibration. As the conversation progressed, their fields began to intermingle. When one of them made a point, his field would create a movement which seemed to suck at the other's field with what appeared to be a kind of vacuum maneuver. But then as the other person made his rebuttal the energy would move back in his direction. In terms of the dynamics of energy fields, winning the point seemed to mean capturing part of the opponent's field and pulling it into oneself.

"Besides," Sarah was saying to the man, "we have observed the phenomena we're trying to understand."

The man gave Sarah a disdainful look. "Then you are insane as well as incompetent," he said, and walked away.

"You're a dinosaur," Sarah shouted, which made Phil and me laugh. Sarah, however, was still tense.

"These people can make me angry," Sarah said, as we resumed our walk along the path.

"Forget it," Phil said. "These kinds of people come around sometimes."

"But why so many?" Sarah asked. "And why right now?"

As we walked up to the lodge, I could see Wil at the jeep. The doors of the vehicle were open and gear was spread out on top of the hood. He saw me immediately and motioned for me to come over.

"Well, looks like I'm about to take off," I said.

My comment broke a ten minute silence, which had begun when I had tried to explain what I had seen happen to Sarah's energy during the argument. Evidently, I had not put it very well, because my comments had provoked only blank stares, and had cast us all into a long period of self-absorption.

"It's been nice meeting you," Sarah said, offering her hand.

Phil was looking toward the jeep. "Is that Wil James?" he asked. "Is he the guy you're traveling with?"

"Yes," I said. "Why?"

"I just wondered. I've seen him around. He knows the owner of this place and was one of the early group that first encouraged the research on energy fields here."

"Come on up and meet him," I said.

"No, I have to go," he said. "I'll see you around here later on. I know you won't be able to stay away."

"No doubt," I said.

Sarah interjected that she too needed to go, and that I could contact her through the lodge. I delayed them for a few more minutes, expressing my thanks for the lessons.

Sarah's expression grew serious. "Seeing the energy—grasping this new way of perceiving the physical world—grows through a kind of contagion. We don't understand it, but when a person hangs out with others who see this energy, usually they begin to see it, too. So, go show it to someone else."

I nodded and then hurried up to the jeep. Wil greeted me with a smile.

"Are you about ready?" I asked.

"Almost," he said. "How did the morning go?"

"Interesting," I said. "I've got a lot to talk to you about."

"You'd better save it for now," he said. "We need to get out of here. Things are looking unfriendly."

I walked closer to him. "What's going on?" I asked.

"Nothing too serious," he said. "I'll explain later. Get your stuff."

I walked into the lodge and picked up the few items I had left in my room. Wil had told me earlier there would be no charge, courtesy of the owner, so I walked down to the desk and handed the clerk my key and walked back outside to the jeep.

Wil was under the hood, checking something, and he slammed it closed as I walked up.

"Okay," he said. "Let's go."

We drove out of the parking lot, then down the drive toward the main road. Several cars were leaving at the same time.

"So what's happening?" I asked Wil.

"A group of local officials," he replied, "along with some scientific types, have complained about the people associated with this conference center. They're not alleging that anything illegal is going on. Just that some of the folks hanging around here may be what they call undesirable, not legitimate scientists. These officials could cause a lot of trouble, and that could effectively put the lodge out of business."

I looked at him blankly and he continued: "You see, this lodge normally has several groups booked at any one time. Only a small number have anything to do with research associated with the Manuscript. The others are groups focused on their own disciplines who come down here for the beauty. If the officials get too ugly and create a negative climate, these groups will stop meeting here."

"But I thought you said the local officials wouldn't tamper with the tourist money coming into Viciente?"

"I didn't think they would. Someone has them nervous about the Manuscript. Did anyone at the gardens understand what was occurring?"

"No, not really," I said. "They were just wondering why all of a sudden more angry people were around."

Wil remained silent. We drove out the gate and turned southeast. A mile later we took another road which headed due east toward the mountain range in the distance.

"We'll be going right by the gardens," Wil said after a while.

Ahead I saw the plots and the first metal building. As we came alongside, the door opened and I met eyes with the person coming out. It was Marjorie. She smiled and turned toward me as we passed, our gaze lingering for a long moment.

"Who was that?" Wil asked.

"A woman I met yesterday," I answered.

He nodded, then changed the subject, "Did you get a look at the Third Insight?"

"I was given a copy."

Wil didn't reply, appearing to be lost in thought, so I pulled out the translation and found where I had stopped reading. From there, the Third Insight elaborated on the nature of beauty, describing this perception as the one through which humans would eventually learn to observe energy fields. Once this occurred, it said, then our understanding of the physical universe would quickly transform.

For instance, we would begin to eat more foods which were still alive with this energy, and we would become conscious that certain localities radiate more energy than others, the highest radiation coming from old natural environments, especially forests. I was about to read the final pages when Wil suddenly spoke.

"Tell me what you experienced back at the gardens," he said.

As best as I could, I related in detail the events of the two days, including the people I had met. When I told him of the encounter with Marjorie, he looked at me and smiled.

"How much did you talk to these people about the other insights and how these insights relate to what they're doing in the gardens?" he asked.

"I didn't mention them at all," I replied. "I didn't trust them at first and later I just figured they knew more than me."

"I think you could have given them some important information had you been perfectly honest with them."

"What kind of information?"

He looked at me warmly. "Only you know that."

I was at a loss for words, so I looked out at the landscape. The terrain was growing increasingly hilly and rocky. Large granite outcrops overhung the road.

"What do you make of seeing Marjorie again as we passed the gardens?" Wil asked.

I started to say "just a coincidence" but instead I said, "I don't know. What do you think?"

"I don't think anything happens by coincidence. To me it means you two have unfinished business, something you needed to say to each other that you didn't."

The idea intrigued me, but disturbed me as well. I had been accused all my life of remaining too distant, of asking questions but not expressing opinions or committing to a position. Why, I wondered, was this coming up again now?

I also noticed that I was beginning to feel differently. At Viciente I had felt adventurous and competent and now I was feeling what could only be called a growing depression, mixed with anxiety.

"Now you've made me depressed," I said.

He laughed loudly, then replied, "It wasn't me. It was the effect of leaving the Viciente estate. The energy of that place makes you high as a kite. Why do you think all these scientists began hanging around here years ago? They don't have a clue as to why they like it so much." He turned to look directly at me. "But we do, don't we?"

He checked the road, then looked at me again, his face full of regard. "You have to crank up your own energy when you leave a place like that."

I just looked at him, puzzled, and he gave me a reassuring smile. Afterward we were both silent for perhaps a mile when he said: "Tell me more of what happened at the gardens."

I continued the story. When I described actually seeing energy fields, he looked at me with amazement, but said nothing.

"Can you see these fields?" I asked.

He shot me a glance. "Yes," he said. "Go on."

I related the story without interruption until I came to Sarah's argument with the Peruvian scientist and the dynamics of their energy fields during the confrontation.

"What did Sarah and Phil say about that?" he asked.

"Nothing," I said. "They didn't seem to have a frame of reference for it."

"I didn't think so," Wil said. "They're so fascinated with the Third Insight they haven't yet gone forward. How humans compete for energy is the Fourth Insight."

"Compete for energy?" I asked.

He merely smiled, nodding toward the translation I was holding.

I picked up where I had left off. The text pointed clearly to the Fourth Insight. It said that eventually humans would see the universe as comprised of one dynamic energy, an energy that can sustain us and respond to our expectations. Yet we would also see that we have been disconnected from the larger source of this energy, that we have cut ourselves off and so have felt weak and insecure and lacking.

In the face of this deficit, we humans have always sought to increase our personal energy in the only manner we have known: by seeking to psychologically steal it from others—an unconscious competition that underlies all human conflict in the world.

THE
STRUGGLE
FOR POWER

A pothole in the gravel road jolted the jeep and woke me up. I looked at my watch—3:00 P.M. As I stretched and attempted to fully awaken, I felt a sharp pain in the small of my back.

The drive had been grueling. After leaving Viciente we had traveled the entire day, riding in several different directions as though Wil were looking for something he couldn't find. We had spent the night at a small inn where the beds were hard and lumpy and I had slept little. Now, after traveling hard for the second day in a row, I was ready to complain.

I looked over at Wil. He was focused on the road, and so intent and alert, that I decided not to interrupt him. He seemed to be in the same serious mood he had displayed several hours ago, when he had stopped the jeep and told me we needed to talk.

"Do you remember that I told you the insights had to be discovered one at a time?" he had asked.

"Yes."

"Do you believe that each will indeed present itself?"

"Well, they have so far," I said, half humorously.

Wil looked at me with a serious expression. "Finding the Third Insight was easy. All we had to do was visit Viciente. But from now on, running across the other insights may be much more difficult."

He paused for a moment then said, "I think that we should go south to a small village near Quilabamba, a place called Cula. There is another virgin forest up there that I think you should see. But it is vitally important that you stay alert. Coincidences will occur regularly, but you have to notice them. Do you understand?"

I told him I thought I did and that I would keep what he said in mind. After that, the conversation had lapsed and I had fallen into a deep sleep—a sleep I now regretted because of what it had done to my back. I stretched again and Wil looked over at me.

"Where are we?" I asked.

"In the Andes again," he said.

The hills had turned into high ridges and distant valleys. The vegetation was coarser now, the trees smaller and windblown. Inhaling deeply, I noticed the air was thinner, and cool.

"Better put on this jacket," Wil said, pulling a brown cotton windbreaker from a bag. "It'll be cold up here this afternoon."

Ahead, as the road rounded a bend, we could see a narrow crossroads. On one side, near a white frame store and gas station, a vehicle was parked with the hood open. Tools lay on a cloth covering the fender. As we drove past, a blond man walked out of the store and glanced at us briefly. He was round faced and wore dark-rimmed glasses.

I looked at the man closely, my mind racing back five years.

"I know it wasn't him," I said to Wil. "But that guy looks just like a friend of mine I used to work with. I haven't thought of him in years."

I noticed Wil was scrutinizing me.

"I told you to watch events closely," he said. "Let's go back and see if that fellow needs some help. He didn't look like a local."

We found a place where the shoulders of the road were wide enough and turned around. When we returned to the store, the man was working on the engine. Wil pulled up to the pump and leaned out the window.

"Looks like you have trouble," Wil said.

The man pushed his glasses back up on his nose, a habit my friend also shared.

"Yes," he replied, "I have lost my water pump." The man appeared to be in his early forties and was of a slight build. His English was formal with a French accent.

Wil was quickly out of the vehicle introducing us. The man offered me his hand with a smile that also looked familiar. His name was Chris Reneau.

"You sound French," I said.

"I am," he replied. "But I teach psychology in Brazil. I am here in Peru seeking information about an archaeological artifact that has been found, a manuscript."

I hesitated for a moment, unsure how much I should trust him.

"We're here for the same reason," I finally said.

He looked at me with deep interest. "What can you tell me about it?" he asked. "Have you seen copies?"

Before I could reply, Wil walked out of the building, the screen door slamming behind him. "Great luck," he said to me. "The owner has a place where we can camp, and there's some hot food. We might as well stay for the night." He turned and looked expectantly at Reneau. "If you don't mind sharing your reservations."

"No, no," he said. "I welcome the company. A new pump cannot be delivered here until tomorrow morning."

While he and Wil began a conversation about the mechanics and reliability of Reneau's land cruiser, I leaned back against the jeep, feeling the warmth of the sun, and drifting into a pleasant reverie about the old friend Reneau had brought to mind. My friend had been wide-eyed and curious, very much like Reneau seemed, and a constant reader of books. I could almost recall the theories he liked, but time had obscured my recollection.

"Let's get our stuff down to the campsite," Wil was saying, patting me on the back.

"Okay," I said absently.

He opened the rear door and pulled out the tent and sleeping bags and loaded my arms, then grabbed a duffle bag full of extra clothing. Reneau was locking up his vehicle. We all walked past the store and down a course of steps. The ridge fell away steeply behind the building and we angled to the left along a narrow pathway. After twenty or thirty yards, we could hear water running, and further on we saw a stream cascading down the rocks. The air was cooler and I could smell the strong fragrance of mint.

Directly in front of us, the ground leveled out and the stream formed a pool about twenty-five feet in diameter. Someone had cleared a campsite and built a rock containment for a fire. Wood was stacked against a nearby tree.

"This is fine," Wil said, and began unpacking his large four man tent. Reneau spread his smaller tent to the right of Wil.

"Are you and Wil researchers?" Reneau asked me at one point. Wil had finished with the tent and had walked up to check on dinner.

"Wilson's a guide," I said. "I'm not doing much of anything right now." Reneau gave me a puzzled look.

I smiled and asked, "Have you been able to see any parts of the Manuscript?"

"I have seen the First and Second Insights," he said, stepping closer. "And I'll tell you something. I think it is all happening just as the Manuscript says. We are changing our world view. I can see it in psychology."

"What do you mean?"

He took a breath. "My field is conflict, looking at why humans treat each other so violently. We've always known that this violence comes from the urge humans feel to control and dominate one another, but only recently have we studied this phenomenon from the inside, from the point of view of the individual's consciousness. We have asked what happens inside a human being that makes him want to control someone else. We have found that when an individual walks up to another person and engages in a conversation, which happens billions of times each day in the world, one of two things can happen. That individual can come away feeling strong or feeling weak, depending on what occurs in the interaction."

I gave him a puzzled look and he appeared slightly embarrassed at having rushed into a long lecture on the subject. I asked him to go on.

"For this reason," he added, "we humans always seem to take a manipulative posture. No matter what the particulars of the situation, or the subject matter, we prepare ourselves to say whatever we must in order to prevail in the conversation. Each of us seeks to find some way to control and thus to remain on top in the encounter. If we are successful, if our viewpoint prevails, then rather than feel weak, we receive a psychological boost.

"In other words we humans seek to outwit and control each other not just because of some tangible goal in the outside world that we're trying to achieve, but because of a lift we get psychologically. This is the reason we see so many irrational conflicts in the world both at the individual level and at the level of nations."

"The consensus in my field is that this whole matter is now emerging into public consciousness. We humans are realizing how much we manipulate each other and consequently we're reevaluating our motivations. We're looking for another way to interact. I think this reevaluation will be part of the new world view that the Manuscript speaks of."

Our conversation was interrupted as Wil walked up. "They're ready to serve us," he said.

We hurried up the path and into the basement level of the building, the family's living quarters. We walked through the living room and into the dining area. On the table was a hot meal of stew, vegetables, and salad.

"Sit down. Sit down," the proprietor was saying in English, pulling out chairs and rushing about. Behind him stood an older woman, apparently his wife, and a teenage girl of about fifteen.

While taking his seat, Wil accidently brushed his fork with an arm. It fell noisily to the floor. The man glared at the woman, who in turn spoke harshly to the young girl who had not yet moved to bring a new one. She hurried into the other room and returned holding a fork, then handed it tentatively to Wil. Her back was stooped and her hand shook slightly. My eyes met Reneau's from across the table.

"Enjoy the food," the man said, handing me one of the dishes. For most of the meal Reneau and Wil talked casually about academic life, the challenges of teaching and publishing. The proprietor had left the room but the woman stood just inside the door.

As the woman and her daughter began serving individual dishes of pie the young girl's elbow hit my water glass, spilling the water on the table in front of me. The older woman rushed over in a rage, shouting at the girl in Spanish and pushing her out of the way.

"I am very sorry," the woman said, wiping up the water. "The girl is so clumsy."

The young girl exploded, flinging the remaining pie at the woman, missing, and splattering pie and broken china across the middle of the table—just as the proprietor returned.

The old man shouted and the girl ran from the room.

"I'm sorry," he said, hurrying to the table.

"It's no problem," I replied. "Don't be so hard on the girl."

Wil was on his feet, figuring the bill, and we quickly left. Reneau had been quiet, but as we walked through the door and down the steps, he spoke.

"Did you see that girl?" he asked, looking at me. "She is a classic example of psychological violence. This is what the human need to control others leads to when taken to the extreme. The old man and woman are dominating the girl totally. Did you see how nervous and stooped she was?"

"Yes," I said. "But it appears she's about fed up."

"Exactly! Her parents have never let up. And from her point of view she has no choice but to lash out violently. It is the only way she can gain some control for herself. Unfortunately, when she grows up, because of this early trauma, she will think she has to seize control and dominate others with the same intensity. This characteristic will be deeply ingrained and will make her just as dominating as her parents are now, especially when she is around people who are vulnerable, such as children.

"In fact, this same trauma no doubt happened to her parents before her. They have to dominate now because of the way their parents dominated them. That's the means through which psychological violence is passed down from one generation to another."

Reneau stopped suddenly. "I need to get my sleeping bag out of the truck," he said. "I'll be down is a second."

I nodded and Wil and I continued toward the campsite.

"You and Reneau have been talking a lot," Wil remarked.

"Yes, we have," I said.

He smiled. "Actually Reneau has been doing most of the talking. You listen and answer direct questions but you don't offer much."

"I'm interested in what he has to say," I said, defensively.

Wil ignored my tone. "Did you see the energy moving between the members of that family? The man and woman were sucking the child's energy into themselves until she was almost dead."

"I forgot to watch the energy flow," I said.

"Well, don't you think Reneau would like to see it? What do you make of running into him in the first place?"

"I don't know."

"Don't you think it has some meaning? We were driving down the road and you see someone who reminds you of an old friend and when we meet him he happens to also be looking for the Manuscript. Doesn't that sound beyond coincidence?"

"Yes."

"Perhaps you met so that you could receive some information that will extend your journey here. And doesn't it follow that perhaps you have some information for him as well?"

"Yes, I guess so. What do you think I should tell him?"

Wil again looked at me with his characteristic warmth. "The truth," he said.

Before I could say anything else, Reneau came bounding down the path toward us.

"I brought a flashlight in case we need it later," he said.

For the first time I became aware of the twilight and looked west. The sun had already set but the sky was still a bright orange. The few clouds in that direction carried a darker, reddish color. For an instant I thought I saw a whitish field of light around the plants in the foreground, but the image faded.

"Beautiful sunset," I said, then noticed Wil had disappeared into his tent and Reneau was pulling his sleeping bag from its case.

"Yes, it is," Reneau said distractedly without looking.

I walked over to where he was working.

He looked up and said, "I didn't get to ask you; what insights have you seen?"

"The first two were only described to me," I replied. "But we just spent the last two days at the Viciente Lodge, near Satipo. While we were there, one of the people doing research gave me a copy of the Third Insight. It's pretty amazing."

His eyes lit up. "Do you have it with you?"

"Yes. Do you want to look at it?"

He jumped at the opportunity and took it into his tent to read. I found some matches and old newspaper and started the fire. After it was burning brightly, Wil crawled out of his tent.

"Where's Reneau?" he asked.

"He's reading the translation Sarah gave me," I said.

Wil walked over and sat on a smooth log someone had placed near the fire area. I joined him. Darkness had finally descended and nothing could be seen except for the bare outline of the trees to our left, the dim lights from the station behind us, and a muted glow from Reneau's tent. The woods were alive with night sounds, some of which I had never heard before.

After about thirty minutes, Reneau emerged from his tent, the flashlight in his hand. He walked over and sat at my left. Wil was yawning.

"That insight is amazing," he said. "Could anyone there actually see those energy fields?"

I briefly told him of my experiences, beginning with our arrival and proceeding through the point where I actually saw fields myself.

He was silent for a minute, then he asked: "They were actually doing experiments where they projected their own energy onto plants and affected the plant's growth?"

"It affected their nutritional potency, too," I said.

"But the main insight is broader than that," he commented, almost to himself. "The Third Insight is that the universe on the whole is made up of this energy, and we can affect perhaps not only plants but other things as well, just by what we do with the energy that belongs to us, the part we can control." He paused for a full minute. "I wonder how we affect other people with our energy?"

Wil looked at me and smiled.

"I'll tell you what I saw," I said. "I witnessed an argument between two people, and their energies were doing really strange things."

Reneau pushed up his glasses again. "Tell me about that."

Wil stood up at this point. "I think I need to turn in," he said. "It's been a long day."

We both said good night and Wil entered his tent. Afterward I described as best I could what Sarah and the other scientist had said to each other, emphasizing the action of their energy fields.

"Now wait a minute," Reneau said. "You saw their energies pulling at each other, trying to, say, capture each other as they argued?"

"That's right," I said.

He was thoughtful for a few seconds. "We must analyze this fully. We had two people arguing over who had the correct view of the situation, over who was right—each seeking to win out over the other, even to the point of invalidating the other's confidence and to outright name calling."

Suddenly he looked up. "Yes, this all makes sense!"

"What do you mean?" I said.

"The movement of this energy, if we can systematically observe it, is a way to understand what humans are receiving when we compete and argue and harm each other. When we control another human being we receive their energy. We fill up at the other's expense and the filling up is what motivates us. Look, I must learn how to see these energy fields. Where is this Viciente Lodge? How do I get there?"

I told him the general location but said he would have to ask Wil for specific directions.

"Yes. I'll do that tomorrow," he said with commitment. "For now I should get some sleep. I want to leave as early as possible."

He said good night, then disappeared into his tent, leaving me alone with the crackling fire and the night sounds.

When I awoke, Wil was already out of the tent. I could smell the aroma of hot cereal. I slipped out of my sleeping bag and looked out through the tent flap. Wil was holding a pan over the fire. Reneau was nowhere to be seen, and his tent was gone.

"Where's Reneau?" I asked, climbing out and walking over to the fire.

"He's already packed up," Wil said. "He's up there working on his truck, getting ready so he can leave as soon as his part comes in."

Wil handed me a bowl of oatmeal and we sat on one of the logs to eat.

"Did you two stay up late talking?" Wil asked.

"Not really," I said. "I told him all I knew."

Just then we heard sounds from the path. Reneau was hurriedly walking down to us.

"I am all prepared," he said. "I must say good-bye."

After several minutes of conversation, Reneau walked back up the steps and left. Wil and I took turns bathing and shaving in the station owner's bathroom, then we packed our gear, filled the vehicle with gas, and departed, heading north.

"How far is Cula?" I asked.

"We should be there before nightfall if we're lucky," he said, then added, "So what did you learn from Reneau?"

I looked closely at him. He seemed to be looking for a specific answer. "I don't know," I said.

"What conception did Reneau leave you with?"

"That we humans, although we are unconscious of it, have the tendency to control and dominate others. We want to win the energy that exists between people. It builds us up somehow, makes us feel better."

Wil was looking straight ahead at the road. He looked as if he was suddenly thinking of something else.

"Why do you ask?" I inquired. "Is this the Fourth Insight?"

He looked at me. "Not quite. You have seen the energy flow between people. But I'm not sure you know how it feels when it happens to you."

"Then tell me how it feels!" I said, growing exasperated. "You accuse me of not talking! Getting information out of you is like pulling teeth! I've been trying for days to find out more about your past experiences with the Manuscript, and all you do is put me off."

He laughed, then shot me a smile. "We had a deal, remember? I have a reason for being secretive. One of the insights concerns how to interpret the events of one's past life. It is a process of becoming clear about who you are, what you are here on this planet to do. I want to wait until we reach this insight before we discuss my background, okay?"

I smiled at his adventurous tone. "Yeah, I guess."

For the remainder of the morning we rode in silence. The day was sunny and the sky blue. Occasionally, as we proceeded higher into the mountains, thick clouds would float across our path, covering the windshield with moisture. Around noon, we pulled over at an overlook that afforded a spectacular view of the mountains and valleys to the east.

"Are you hungry?" Wil asked.

I nodded and he pulled two carefully wrapped sandwiches from a bag on the back seat. After he handed me one of them, he asked, "What do you think about this view."

"It's beautiful."

He smiled slightly and stared at me, giving me the impression that he was observing my energy field.

"What are you doing?" I asked.

"Just looking," he said. "Mountain peaks are special places that can build energy in whomever sits on them. You look as though you have an affinity for mountain overlooks."

I told Wil of my grandfather's valley and of the ridge overlooking the lake and how it had made me feel alert and energized the same day Charlene had arrived.

"Perhaps growing up there," he said, "prepared you for something here, now."

I was about to ask him more about the energy that mountains provide when he added, "When a virgin forest is on a mountain, the energy is amplified even more."

"Is the virgin forest we're headed for on a mountain?" I asked.

"Look for yourself," he said. "You can see it."

He pointed toward the east. Miles away, I could see two ridges which ran parallel to each other for what looked like several miles, then they converged, forming a V shape. In the space between the two ridges lay what looked like a small town, and at the vortex, the point where the two ridges met, the mountain rose sharply and butted off into a rocky summit. The summit appeared slightly higher than the ridge we were on and the area around its base seemed much greener, as though covered with lush foliage.

"That area of green?" I asked.

"Yes," Wil said. "It's like Viciente, yet more powerful and special."

"How is it special?"

"It facilitates one of the other insights."

"How?" I asked.

He started the jeep and pulled back onto the road. "I'm betting," he said, "that you will find out."

Neither of us said much more for an hour or so, then I drifted off to sleep. Sometime later Wil was shaking my arm.

"Wake up," he said. "We're coming into Cula."

I sat up in the seat. Ahead of us, in a valley where two roads came together, was a small town. On both sides were the two ridges we had seen. The trees on the ridges seemed as large as those at Viciente and spectacularly green.

"I want to tell you something before we drive in there," he said. "In spite of the energy of this forest, this town is a lot less civilized than other areas of Peru. It's known as a place to get information about the Manuscript, but the last time I was here, it was full of greedy types who didn't feel the energy and didn't understand the insights. They merely wanted the money or recognition they might get by discovering the Ninth."

I looked at the village. It consisted of four or five streets and avenues.

Larger frame buildings lined the two main roads that crossed in the center of town, but the other streets were little more than alleyways lined by small dwellings. Parked at the cross-roads were perhaps a dozen off-the-road vehicles and trucks.

"Why are all these people here?" I asked.

He smiled daringly. "Because it's one of the last places to get gas and supplies before going deeper into the mountains."

He started the jeep and drove slowly into town, then stopped in front of one of the larger buildings. I couldn't read the Spanish signs but from the products in the window I presumed it was a grocery and hardware.

"Wait here for a minute," he said. "I want to go in for a few things."

I nodded and Wil disappeared inside. As I looked around, a truck pulled up across the street and several people got out. One was a dark-haired woman in a fatigue jacket. To my amazement, I realized it was Marjorie. She and a young man in his early twenties crossed the street and walked right in front of me.

I opened my door and got out. "Marjorie," I yelled.

She stopped and looked around, then saw me and smiled. "Hello," she said. As she began to walk toward me, the young man grabbed her arm.

"Robert told us not to talk with anyone," he said very softly, trying not to let me overhear.

"It's okay," she said, "I know this person. Go on in."

He looked at me skeptically, then backed away and went into the store. I tried then, in a stuttering way, to explain what had happened between us at the gardens. She laughed, and told me Sarah had related everything to her. She was about to say something else when Wil walked out with a handful of supplies.

I introduced them, and we all talked for a few minutes as Wil placed the supplies in the back of the jeep.

"I have an idea," Wil said. "Let's get something else to eat across the street."

I looked over at what appeared to be a small cafe. "Sounds good to me," I said.

"I don't know," Marjorie said. "I need to leave soon. My ride."

"Where are you going?" I asked.

"Back to the west a couple of miles. I've come up to visit a group studying the Manuscript."

"We can take you back later, after dinner," Wil commented.

"Well, I guess that will be okay."

Wil looked at me, "I have one more thing to pick up. You two go ahead and order and I'll order something when I get there. I'll only be a few minutes."

We agreed, and Marjorie and I waited as several trucks passed. Wil walked down the street to the south. Suddenly the young man with whom Marjorie had arrived walked out of the store and confronted us again.

"Where are you going?" he said, holding her arm.

"This is a friend of mine," she replied. "We're going to eat and then he can run me back later."

"Look, you can't trust anyone up here. You know Robert wouldn't approve."

"It's okay," she said.

"I want you to come with me, now!"

I took his arm and pulled it off Marjorie. "You heard what she told you," I said. He stepped back and looked at me, suddenly appearing very timid. He turned and walked back into the store.

"Let's go," I said.

We walked across the street and into the small diner. The eating area consisted of one room and just eight tables and was permeated with the smell of grease and smoke. I spotted an unoccupied table on the left. As we walked over, several people glanced up at us for an instant, then returned to what they were doing.

The waitress spoke only Spanish, but Marjorie knew the language well and ordered for us both. Afterward, Marjorie looked at me warmly.

I grinned at her. "Who is that guy you were with?"

"That's Kenny," she said. "I don't know what's wrong with him. Thanks for helping."

She was looking directly into my eyes, and her comment made me feel wonderful. "How did you get connected with that group?" I asked.

"Robert Jensen is an archaeologist. He's formed a group to study the Manuscript and to search for the Ninth Insight. He came by Viciente a few weeks back, then again a couple of days ago. . . I . . ."

"What?" I asked.

"Well, I was in a relationship at Viciente that I wanted to get away from. Then I met Robert and he was so charming and what he was doing seemed so interesting. He convinced me that our research at the gardens would be enhanced by the Ninth Insight, and that he was on his way to find it. He said searching for this insight would be the most exciting thing he has ever done, and when he offered me a place on his team for a few months I decided to accept. . ." She paused again and looked down at the table. She appeared uncomfortable so I changed the subject.

"How many of the insights have you read?"

"Only the one I saw at Viciente. Robert has some others but he believes people have to rid themselves of their traditional beliefs before they can understand them. He says he would rather they learn the key concepts from him."

I must have frowned because she added: "You don't like that much, do you?"

"It sounds suspicious," I said.

She looked at me intensely again. "I wondered about it too. Maybe when you take me back, you can talk with him and tell me what you think."

The waitress arrived and brought our food, and as she was walking away, I saw Wil come in the door. He walked quickly to our table.

"I've got to meet some people about a mile north of here," he said. "I'll be gone about two hours. Take the jeep and take Marjorie back. I'm riding with someone else." He shot me a smile. "We can meet back here."

The thought came to me to tell him about Robert Jensen but I decided against it.

"Okay," I said.

He looked at Marjorie. "Nice to have met you. Wish I had time to stay and talk."

She looked at him with her coy expression. "Maybe some other time."

He nodded, handed me the keys, and walked away.

Marjorie ate for a few minutes, then said: "He seems like a man with a purpose. How did you meet him?"

I told her in detail of my experiences upon first arriving in Peru. As I talked, she listened intently. So intently, in fact, that I found myself telling the story with great ease and expressing the dramatic turns and episodes with insight and true flair. She seemed spell-bound, hanging on every word.

"Goodness," she said at one point, "do you think you're in danger?"

"No, I don't think so," I said. "Not this far from Lima."

She was still looking at me expectantly, so while we finished eating I briefly summarized the events at Viciente up to the point where Sarah and I had arrived at the gardens.

"That's where I met you," I said, "and you ran off."

"Oh, it wasn't like that," she said. "I just didn't know you, and when I saw your feelings, I thought it was best to leave."

"Well, I apologize," I said chuckling, "for letting my energy get out of hand."

She looked at her watch. "I guess I should be getting back. They'll be wondering about me."

I left enough money for the bill and we walked outside to Wil's jeep. The night was chilly and we could see a trace of our breath. As we got in, she said, "Head back north on this road. I'll tell you when to turn."

I nodded, and made a quick u-turn in the street and headed that way.

"Tell me more about this farm we're going to," I said.

"I think Robert rents it. Apparently his group has been using it for a long time while he has studied the insights. Since I've been there everyone has been assembling supplies, and readying the vehicles, things like that. Some of his men seem very rough."

"Why did he invite you along?" I asked.

"He said he wanted a person who could help interpret the last insight, once we found it. At least that's what he said back at Viciente. Here he has only talked about supplies and helping to prepare for the trip."

"Where is he planning to go?"

"I don't know," she replied. "He never answers me when I ask."

After about a mile and a half, she pointed out a turn to the left onto a narrow, rocky road. It meandered up a ridge and down into a flat valley. Ahead was a farmhouse made of rough planking. Behind it were several barns and outbuildings. Three llamas peered at us from a fenced pasture.

As we slowed to a stop, several people walked around a vehicle and stared without smiling. I noticed a gas powered, electric generator humming at the side of the house. Then the door opened and a tall, dark-haired man with strong, lean features walked toward us.

"That's Robert," Marjorie said.

"Good," I said, still feeling strong and confident.

We got out as Jensen walked up to us. He looked at Marjorie.

"I was worried about you," he said. "I understand you ran into a friend."

I introduced myself and he shook my hand firmly.

"I'm Robert Jensen," he said. "Glad you two are all right. Come in."

Inside several people busied themselves with supplies. One carried a tent and camping gear toward the back. Through the dining room, I noticed two Peruvian women in the kitchen, packing food. Jensen sat in one of the chairs in the living room and directed us to two others.

"Why did you say you were glad we were all right?" I asked.

He bent toward me and asked in a sincere tone, "How long have you been in this area?"

"Only since this afternoon."

"Then you couldn't know how dangerous it is here. People are disappearing. Have you heard of the Manuscript, of the missing Ninth Insight?"

"Yes, I have. In fact. . ."

"Then you need to know what's going on," he interrupted. "The search for the last insight is getting ugly. There are dangerous people involved in this."

"Who?" I asked.

"People who don't care about the archaeological value of this discovery at all. People who just want the insight for their own purposes."

A huge man with a beard and paunch interrupted the conversation and showed Jensen a list. They discussed something briefly in Spanish.

Jensen looked at me again. "Are you here to find the missing insight too?" he asked. "Do you have any idea what you're getting into?"

I felt awkward and had difficulty expressing myself. "Well. . .I'm mainly interested in finding out more about the entire Manuscript. I haven't seen that much of it yet."

He straightened in his chair, then said: "Do you realize that the Manuscript is a state artifact and that copies of it have been made illegal except by permit?"

"Yes, but some scientists disagree with that. They feel the government is suppressing new. . ."

"Don't you think the nation of Peru has the right to control its own archaeological treasures? Does the government know that you're in this country?"

I didn't know what to say—the surge of anxiety in my stomach was back.

"Look, don't get me wrong," he said, smiling. "I'm on your side. If you have some sort of academic support from outside the country, then tell me. But I get the feeling you're just floating around."

"Something like that," I said.

I noticed Marjorie's focus had shifted from me to Jensen. "What do you think he should do?" she asked.

Jensen stood up and smiled. "I could perhaps work you into a position with us here. We need more people. Where we are going is relatively safe, I think. And you could find some avenues home along the way if things didn't work out."

He looked at me closely. "But you'll have to be willing to do exactly as I say, every step of the way."

I glanced over at Marjorie. She was still looking at Jensen. I felt confused. Perhaps I should consider Jensen's offer, I thought. If he was in good standing with the government then this might be the only opportunity I had for a legitimate way back to the states. Perhaps I had been fooling myself. Perhaps Jensen was right and I was in way over my head.

"I think you should consider what Robert is saying," Marjorie commented. "It's too frightening out there alone."

Though I knew she might be correct, I still had faith in Wil, in what we were doing. I wanted to express this thought but when I tried to speak, I found I couldn't formulate the words. I could no longer think clearly.

Suddenly the large man walked into the room again and looked out the window. Jensen was quickly up and looking, then he turned to Marjorie and in a casual tone said, "Someone is coming. Go ask Kenny to come up here, please."

She nodded and left. Through the window I could see truck lights approaching. The vehicle parked just outside the fence, fifty feet away.

Jensen opened the door and as he did, I heard my name mentioned outside.

"Who is that?" I asked.

Jensen looked at me sharply. "Be very quiet," he said. He and the large man walked outside and pulled the door closed. Through the window I could see a lone figure silhouetted behind the truck's lights. My first impulse was to stay inside. Jensen's assessment of my situation had filled me with foreboding. But something about the person by the truck seemed familiar. I opened the door and walked outside. As soon as Jensen saw me, he quickly turned and walked my way.

"What are you doing? Go back inside."

Above the generator I thought I heard my name again.

"Go back inside, now!" Jensen said. "It could be a trap." He was standing directly in front of me, blocking my view of the vehicle. "Go back inside now!"

I felt totally confused and panicked, unable to make a decision. Then the figure behind the lights walked closer and I could see his form around Jensen's body. Distinctly I heard: " . . . come here, I need to talk with you!" Then as the figure approached, my head cleared and I realized that it was

Wil. I rushed past Jensen.

"What was wrong with you?" Wil asked quickly. "We need to get out of here."

"But what about Marjorie?" I asked.

"We can't do anything about her right now," Wil said. "We'd better leave."

We started to walk away when Jensen called out. "You'd better stay here. You won't make it."

I glanced back.

Wil stopped and looked at me, giving me a choice to stay or go.

"Let's go," I said.

We passed the truck in which Wil had arrived and I noticed two other men had been waiting in the front seat. When we got to Wil's jeep, he asked me for the keys and we drove away. The truck with Wil's friends followed.

Wil turned and looked at me. "Jensen told me you had decided to stay with his group. What was going on?"

"How do you know his name?" I stammered.

"I just heard all about this guy," Wil replied. "He works for the Peruvian government. He's a real archaeologist, but he's committed to keeping the whole thing secret in return for exclusive rights to study the Manuscript, only he wasn't supposed to go looking for the missing insight. Apparently he's decided to violate that agreement. He is rumored to be leaving soon in pursuit of the Ninth.

"When I learned he was the person Marjorie was with, I thought I'd better get down here. What did he say to you?"

"He told me I was in danger and that I should join up with him and that he'd help me leave the country if that's what I wanted."

Wil shook his head. "He really had you hooked."

"What do you mean?"

"You should have seen your energy field. It was flowing almost totally into his."

"I don't understand."

"Think back to Sarah's argument with the scientist at Viciente. . . . If you had witnessed one of them winning, convincing the other that he was correct, then you would have seen the loser's energy flowing into the winner's, leaving the loser feeling drained and weak and somewhat confused—the way the girl in the Peruvian family appeared and the way," he smiled, "that you look now."

"You saw that happening to me?" I asked.

"Yes," he replied. "And it was extremely difficult for you to stop his control of you and to pull yourself away. I thought for a minute you weren't going to do it."

"Jesus," I said. "That guy must really be evil."

"Not really," he said. "He's probably only half aware of what he's doing. He thinks he's right to control the situation, and no doubt he learned a long time ago that he could control successfully by following a certain strategy. He first pretends to be your friend, then he finds something wrong with what you're doing, in your case that you were in danger. In effect, he subtly undermines your confidence in your own path until you begin to identify with him. As soon as that happens, he has you."

Wil looked directly at me. "This is only one of many strategies people use to con others out of their energy. You'll learn about the remaining ways later, in the Sixth Insight."

I wasn't listening; my thoughts were on Marjorie. I didn't like leaving her there.

"Do you think we should try to get Marjorie?" I asked.

"Not now," he said. "I don't think she's in any danger. We can drive out tomorrow, as we leave, and try to talk to her."

We were silent for a few minutes, then Wil asked: "Do you understand what I said about Jensen not realizing what he was doing? He's no different from most people. He just does what makes him feel the strongest."

"No, I don't think I understand."

Wil looked thoughtful. "All this is still unconscious in most people. All we know is that we feel weak and when we control others we feel better. What we don't realize is that this sense of feeling better costs the other person. It is their energy that we have stolen. Most people go through their lives in a constant hunt for someone else's energy."

He looked at me with a twinkle in his eye. "Although occasionally it works differently. We meet someone who at least for a little while will voluntarily send us their energy."

"What are you getting at?"

"Think back to when you and Marjorie were eating together at the restaurant in town and I walked in."

"Okay."

"I don't know what you two were talking about but obviously her energy was pouring into you. When I walked in, I could see it clearly. Tell me, how did you feel during that time?"

"I felt good," I said. "In fact, the experiences and concepts I was relating seemed crystal clear to me. I could express myself easily. But what does that mean?"

He smiled. "Occasionally, another person will voluntarily want us to define their situation for them, giving us their energy outright, the way Marjorie did with you. It makes us feel empowered, but you'll see that this gift doesn't usually last. Most people—Marjorie included—aren't strong enough to keep giving energy. That's why most relationships eventually turn into power struggles. Humans link up energy and then fight over who is going to control it. And the loser always pays the price."

He stopped abruptly and looked at me. "Do you get the Fourth Insight? Think about what has happened to you. You observed that energy flows between people and wondered what it meant, and then we ran into Reneau, who told you that psychologists were already searching for some reason humans sought to control each other.

"All that was demonstrated with the Peruvian family. You saw clearly that dominating another makes the dominator feel powerful and knowledgeable, but it sucks the vital energy out of those who are being dominated. It makes no difference if we tell ourselves that we are doing it for the person's own good, or that they are our children, and therefore we should be in control all the time. The damage still occurs.

"Next, you ran into Jensen and got a taste of what this actually feels like.

You saw that when someone is dominating you psychically, they actually take your mind away. It was not as if you lost some intellectual debate with Jensen. You didn't have the energy or mental clarity to debate with. All your mental power was going to Jensen. Unfortunately this kind of psychic violence happens all the time throughout human culture, often by otherwise well-meaning people."

I just nodded. Wil had summarized my experience exactly.

"Try to integrate the Fourth Insight fully," Wil continued. "See how it fits together with what you already know. The Third Insight showed you that the physical world is actually a vast system of energy. And now the Fourth points out that for a long time we humans have been unconsciously competing for the only part of this energy we have been open to: the part that flows between people. This is what human conflict has always been about, at every level: from all the petty conflict in families and employment settings to wars between nations. It's the result of feeling insecure and weak and having to steal someone else's energy to feel okay."

"Wait a minute," I protested. "Some wars had to be fought. They were right."

"Of course," Wil replied. "But the only reason that any conflict can't be immediately settled is that one side is holding on to an irrational position, for energy purposes."

Wil appeared to remember something. Reaching into a satchel, he pulled out a bundle of papers clipped together.

"I almost forgot!" he said. "I found a copy of the Fourth Insight."

He handed me the copy and said nothing else, looking straight ahead as he drove.

I picked up the small flashlight Wil kept on the floorboard and for the next twenty minutes read the short document. Understanding the Fourth Insight, it said, is a matter of seeing the human world as a vast competition for energy and thus for power.

Yet, once humans understand their struggle, the insight continued, we would immediately begin to transcend this conflict. We would begin to break free from the competition over mere human energy. . .because we would finally be able to receive our energy from another source.

I looked at Wil. "What's the other source?" I asked.

He smiled, but said nothing.

THE
MESSAGE OF
THE MYSTICS

The next morning I awoke as soon as I heard Wil stirring. We had spent the night at a house belonging to one of his friends, and Wil was sitting up in a cot across the room, dressing quickly. It was still dark outside.

"Let's get packed," he whispered.

We gathered our clothes and made several trips out to the jeep with some extra supplies Wil had bought. The center of town was only a few hundred yards away, but few lights penetrated the darkness. Dawn was but a streak of lighter sky toward the east. Other than a few birds signaling the impending morning, there were no sounds.

When we finished, I stayed with the jeep while Wil spoke briefly with his friend who stood sleepily on the porch while we completed our packing. Suddenly we heard noise at the crossroads. We could see the lights of three trucks as they drove into the center of the town and stopped.

"That could be Jensen," Wil said. "Let's walk over there and see what they're doing, but carefully."

We made our way across several streets and into an alley that entered the main road about a hundred feet from the trucks. Two of the vehicles were being filled with fuel and the other was parked in front of the store. Four or five people stood nearby. I saw Marjorie walk out of the store and place something in the truck there, then walk casually toward us, gazing into the adjacent shops.

"Walk over there and see if you can get her to come with us," Wil whispered. "I'll wait for you here."

I slipped around the corner and as I walked toward her I was horrified. Behind her, in front of the store, I noticed for the first time that several of Jensen's men carried automatic weapons. A few moments later my fright intensified. In the street across from me armed soldiers crouched low and slowly approached Jensen's group.

At the exact time Marjorie saw me, Jensen's men saw the others and scattered. A burst of machine gun fire filled the air. Marjorie looked at me with terror in her eyes. I rushed forward and grabbed her. We ducked into the next alley. More shots were being fired amid angry shouting in Spanish. We tripped over a pile of empty cartons and fell, our faces almost touching.

"Let's go!" I said, jumping to my feet. She struggled up, then pulled me down again, nodding ahead to the end of the alley. Two men with weapons were hiding with their backs to us, looking down the next street. We froze. Finally, the men raced across the street to the wooded area beyond.

I knew we had to get back to the house of Wilson's friend, to the jeep. I was sure Wil would go there. We crept carefully to the next street. Angry shouting and gunfire could be heard toward the right, but we could see no one. I looked left; nothing there either—no sign of Wil. I figured he had run ahead of us.

"Let's run across to the woods," I said to Marjorie, who was now alert and looking determined. "Then," I continued, "we'll stay along the edge of the woods and bear left. The jeep is parked in that direction."

"Okay," she said.

We crossed the street quickly and made our way to within a hundred feet or so of the house. The jeep was still there but we could see no movement anywhere. As we prepared to dash across the last street to the house, a military vehicle turned a corner to our left and proceeded slowly toward the dwelling. Simultaneously, Wil ran across the yard, started the jeep, and sped away in the opposite direction. The vehicle pursued.

"Damn!" I said.

"What'll we do now?" Marjorie asked, panic returning to her face.

More shots were being fired in the streets behind us, closer this time. Ahead, the forest thickened and inclined up the ridge which towered over the town and ran north and south. It was the same ridge that I had seen from the overlook earlier.

"Let's get to the top," I said. "Hurry!"

We climbed several hundred yards up the ridge. At an overlook, we stopped and looked back toward the town. Military vehicles seemed to be pouring into the crossroads and numerous soldiers were conducting what seemed to be a house to house search. Below us, at the base of the ridge, I could hear muffled voices.

We rushed further up the mountain. All we could do now was run.

We followed the ridge north all morning stopping only to crouch down when a vehicle traveled along the ridge parallel to us on our left. Most of the traffic was the same steel-gray military jeep we had seen before, but occasionally a civilian vehicle would pass. Ironically, the road provided a lone landmark and point of security against the wilderness all around us.

Ahead the two ridges grew closer together and more steeply sloped. Jagged outcroppings of rock protected the valley floor between. Suddenly, from the north we saw a jeep like Wil's approach, then turn quickly onto a side road which looped down into the valley.

"That looks like Wil," I said, straining to see.

"Let's get down there," Marjorie said.

"Wait a minute. What if it's a trap? What if they've captured him and are using the jeep to lure us out?"

Her face fell.

"You stay here," I said. "I'll go down there and you watch me. If everything's okay, then I'll motion for you to follow."

Reluctantly she agreed, and I started down the steep mountain toward the spot where the jeep had parked. Through the foliage I could vaguely see someone get out of the vehicle, but couldn't see who it was. Holding onto small bushes and trees, I worked my way between the outcroppings, occasionally sliding down in the thick humus.

Finally, the vehicle was directly across from me on the opposite slope, perhaps a hundred yards away. The driver, leaning against a rear fender, was still obscured. I moved to my right to get a better look. It was Wil. I rushed further to my right and felt myself slide. At the last minute, I reached for a tree trunk and pulled myself back up. My stomach twisted with fright, below me was a sheer drop off of thirty feet or more. I had barely avoided killing myself.

Still holding the tree, I stood up and tried to gain Wil's attention. He was surveying the ridge above my head and then his eyes dropped and he looked right at me. He jerked up and walked toward me in the bushes. I pointed down to the steep gorge.

He surveyed the valley floor, then called to me. "I don't see a way across," he said. "You'll have to move down the valley and cross there."

I nodded and was about to signal Marjorie when I heard a vehicle approaching in the distance. Wil jumped into his jeep and sped back toward the main road. I hurried up the hill. I could see Marjorie through the foliage, walking toward me.

Suddenly from the area behind her came loud shouts in Spanish and the sounds of people running. Marjorie hid below a rock overhang. I changed directions, running as quietly as I could to the left. As I ran, I searched for a view of Marjorie through the trees. Just as I caught sight of her, she screamed loudly as two soldiers grabbed her arms and forced her to stand.

I continued to run up the slope, keeping low, her look of panic frozen in my mind. Once at the top of the ridge, I headed north again, my heart pounding with terror and panic.

After running more than a mile, I stopped and listened. I could hear no movement or talking behind me. Lying flat on my back, I tried to relax and think clearly, but the awful specter of Marjorie's capture was overwhelming. Why did I ask her to remain on the ridge alone? What should I do now?

I sat up and took a deep breath, and gazed over at the road on the other ridge. I had seen no traffic while I was running. Again I listened intently: nothing except the usual forest sounds. Slowly I began to calm down. After all, Marjorie had only been captured. She was guilty of nothing except running from gunfire. Probably she would be detained only until her identity as a legitimate scientist could be established.

Once more I headed north, my back aching slightly. I felt dirty and tired, and pangs of hunger erupted in my stomach. For two hours I walked without thinking and without seeing anyone.

Then, from the slope to my right I heard sounds of running. I froze and listened again but the sounds had stopped. Here the trees were larger, shielding the ground below from the sun, thinning the underbrush. I could see fifty or sixty yards. Nothing moved. I walked past a large boulder on my right and several trees, stepping as softly as possible. Three other massive outcroppings lay along my path and I moved past two of them. Still no movement. I walked around the third boulder. Twigs cracked behind me. I turned around slowly.

There, next to the rock was the bearded man I had seen at Jensen's farm, his eyes wild, panicked, his arms shaking as he pointed an automatic weapon at my stomach. He seemed to be struggling to remember me.

"Wait a minute," I stammered, "I know Jensen."

He looked at me more closely and lowered the weapon. Then from the woods behind us, we heard the sounds of someone moving. The bearded man ran past me toward the north, holding the rifle in one hand. Instinctively I followed. Both of us were running as fast as we could, dodging limbs and rocks and occasionally glancing back.

After several hundred yards, he stumbled and I raced past him. I collapsed between two rocks to rest and to look back, trying to detect movement. I saw a lone soldier, fifty yards away, raise his rifle toward the huge man, who was struggling to his feet. Before I could utter a warning, the soldier fired. The man's chest exploded as bullets tore through from the rear, splattering me with blood. An echo of rifle fire filled the air.

For an instant he stood motionless, his eyes glazed, then his body arched forward and fell. I reacted blindly, running north again away from the soldier, keeping the trees between me and the area from which the bullets had come. The ridge grew constantly more rugged and rocky and began to incline dramatically upwards.

My entire body shook with exhaustion and terror as I struggled up the spaces between the outcroppings. At one point I slipped and dared a glance backward. The soldier was approaching the body. I slithered around a rock just as the soldier looked up, seemingly right at me. I stayed low to the ground and crawled past several other boulders. Then the slope of the ridge leveled off, blocking the soldier's view so I jumped to my feet again, running as fast as I could between the rocks and trees. My mind was numb. Escape was all I could think of. Though I didn't dare look back, I was sure I heard the soldier running behind me.

The ridge inclined ahead and I fought my way up, my strength beginning to wane. At the top of the rise, the ground leveled out and was thick with tall trees and lush undergrowth. Rising behind them was a sheer rock face that I had to scale delicately, searching for hand and footholds as I proceeded. I struggled to the top and my heart fell at the sight before me. A drop-off of a hundred feet or more blocked my way; I could go no further.

I was doomed, finished. Rocks slid along the outcropping behind me, indicating the soldier was closing fast. I sank to my knees. I was exhausted, spent, and with a final sigh I released the last of my fight, accepting my fate. Soon, I knew, the bullets would come. And interestingly, as an end to the terror, death seemed almost a welcome relief. As I waited, my mind flashed to childhood Sundays and to the innocent contemplation of God. What would it be like, death? I tried to open myself to the experience.

After a long period of waiting during which I had no concept of time, I suddenly became aware that nothing had happened! I looked around and noticed for the first time that I was positioned on the highest peak of the mountain. Other ridges and cliffs fell away from this point, leaving me with a panoramic view in all directions.

A movement caught my eye. There, far down the slope toward the south, walking casually away from me, was the soldier, the gun belonging to Jensen's man slung across one arm.

The sight warmed my body and filled me with ripples of silent laughter. I had somehow survived! I turned and sat cross-legged and savored the euphoria. I wanted to stay here forever. The day was brilliant with sunshine and blue sky.

As I sat there, I was struck by the closeness of the purple hills in the distance, or rather, the feeling that they were close. The same perception applied to the few puffs of white cloud drifting overhead. I felt as if I could reach out and touch them with my hand.

As I reached up toward the sky, I noticed something different about the way my body felt. My arm had glided upward with incredible ease and I was holding my back, neck and head perfectly straight with absolutely no effort. From my position—sitting cross-legged—I stood up without using my arms, and stretched. The feeling was one of total lightness.

Looking at the distant mountains, I noticed that a daytime moon had been out and was about to set. It looked to be about a quarter full and hung over the horizon like an inverted bowl. Instantly I understood why it had that shape. The sun, millions of miles directly above me, was shining only on the top of the sinking moon. I could perceive the exact line between the sun and the lunar surface, and this recognition somehow extended my consciousness outward even farther.

I could imagine the moon below the horizon and the exact reflected shape it would present to those who lived further west and could still see it. Then I imagined how it would look if it was directly under me on the other side of the planet. To the people there, it would appear full because the sun over my head would shine past the Earth and strike the moon squarely.

This picture sent a rush of sensation up my spine, and my back seemed to straighten even more as I conceived, no, I experienced, the same amount of space commonly felt over my head as also existing under my feet, on the other side of the globe. For the first time in my life, I knew the earth's roundness not as an intellectual concept but as an actual sensation.

At one level this awareness excited me but at another it seemed perfectly ordinary and natural. All I wanted to do was immerse myself in the feeling of being suspended, floating, amid a space that existed in all directions. Rather than having to push myself away from the Earth with my legs as I stood there, resisting the Earth's gravity, I now felt as though I was held up by some inner buoyancy, as though I was filled like a balloon with just enough helium to hover over the ground and barely touch it with my feet. It was similar to being in perfect athletic condition, as after a year of intense exercise, only far more coordinated and light.

I sat down again on the rock, and, again, everything seemed close: the rugged outcrop on which I was sitting, the tall trees further down the slope and the other mountains on the horizon. And as I watched the limbs of the trees sway gently in the breeze, I experienced not just a visual perception of the event, but a physical sensation as well, as if the limbs moving in the wind were hairs on my body.

I perceived everything to be somehow part of me. As I sat on the peak of the mountain looking out at the landscape falling away from me in all directions, it felt exactly as if what I had always known as my physical body was only the head of a much larger body consisting of everything else I could see. I experienced the entire universe looking out on itself through my eyes.

This perception induced a flash of memory. My mind raced backward in time, past the beginning of my trip to Peru, past my childhood and my birth. The realization was present that my life did not, in fact, begin with my conception and birth on this planet. It began much earlier with the formation of the rest of me, my real body, the universe itself.

The science of evolution had always bored me, but now, as my mind continued to race backward in time, all the things I had read on the subject began to come back to me, including conversations with the friend who resembled Reneau. I recalled that this was the field he was interested in: evolution.

All knowledge seemed to merge with actual memories. Somehow I was recalling what had happened, and the recollection allowed me to look at evolution in a new way.

I watched as the first matter exploded into the universe, and I realized, as the Third Insight had described, that there was nothing truly solid about it. Matter was only energy vibrating at a certain level, and in the beginning matter existed only in its simplest vibratory form: the element we call hydrogen. That's all there was in the universe, just hydrogen.

I observed the hydrogen atoms begin to gravitate together, as if the ruling principal, the urge, of this energy was to begin a movement into a more complex state. And when pockets of this hydrogen reached a sufficient density, it began to heat up and to burn, to become what we call a star, and in this burning the hydrogen fused together and leaped into elements of a higher vibration.

As I continued to watch, these first stars aged and finally blew themselves up and spewed the remaining hydrogen and the newly created elements out into the universe. And the whole process began again. The atoms gravitated together until the temperature became hot enough for new stars to form and that in turn fused the new elements together, creating matter, which vibrated at an even higher level.

And so on . . . each successive generation of stars creating atoms that had not existed before, until the wide spectrum of matter—the basic chemical elements—had been formed and scattered everywhere. Matter had evolved from the element hydrogen, the simplest vibration of energy, to carbon, which vibrated at an extremely high rate. The stage was now set for the next step in evolution.

As our sun formed, pockets of matter fell into orbit around it, and one of them, the Earth, contained all the newly created elements, including carbon. As the Earth cooled, gases once caught in the molten mass, migrated to the surface and merged together forming water vapor, and the great rains came, forming oceans on the then barren crust. Then when water covered much of the Earth's surface, the skies cleared and the sun, burning brightly, bathed the new world with light and heat and radiation.

And in the shallow pools and basins, amid the great lightning storms that periodically swept the planet, matter leaped past the vibratory level of carbon to an even more complex state: to the vibration represented by the amino acids. But for the first time, this new level of vibration was not stable in and of itself. Matter had to continually absorb other matter into itself in order to sustain its vibration. It had to eat. Life, the new thrust of evolution, had emerged.

Still restricted to living only in water, I saw this life split into two distinct forms. One form—the one we call plants—lived on inorganic matter, and turned these elements into food by utilizing carbon dioxide from the early atmosphere. As a by-product, plants released free oxygen into the world for the first time. Plant life spread quickly through the oceans and finally onto the land as well.

The other form—what we call animals—absorbed only organic life to sustain their vibration. As I watched, the animals filled the oceans in the great age of fishes, and, when the plants had released enough oxygen into the atmosphere, began their own trek toward land.

I saw the amphibians—half fish, half something new—leave the water for the first time and use lungs to breathe the new air. Then matter leaped forward again into reptiles and covered the Earth in the great period of the dinosaurs. Then the warm-blooded mammals came and likewise covered the Earth, and I realized that each emerging species represented life—matter—moving into its next higher vibration. Finally, the progression ended. There at the pinnacle stood humankind.

Humankind. The vision ended. I had seen in one flash the entire story of evolution, the story of matter coming into being and then evolving, as if under some guiding plan, toward ever higher vibrations, creating the exact conditions, finally, for humans to emerge. . .for each of us, as individuals, to emerge.

As I sat there on that mountain, I could almost grasp how this evolution was extended even further in the lives of human beings. Further evolution was related somehow to the experience of life coincidences. Something about these events led us forward in our lives and created a higher vibration that pushed evolution ahead as well. Yet, as hard as I tried, I couldn't quite understand.

For a long time I sat on the rock precipice, consumed by peace and completeness. Then, abruptly, I became aware that the sun was beginning to sink in the west. I also noticed that toward the northwest about a mile was a town of some kind. I could make out the shapes of roof tops. The road on the west ridge seemed to meander right to it.

I got up and began the climb down the rocks. I laughed out loud. I was still connected with the landscape so that I felt I was walking alongside my own body, and more, that I was exploring the regions of my own body. The feeling was exhilarating.

I made my way down the bluffs and into the trees. The afternoon sun cast long shadows along the forest floor. Halfway down I came to a particularly thick area of large trees and as I entered, I experienced a perceptible change in my body; I felt even lighter and more coordinated. I stopped and looked closely at the trees and underlying bushes, focusing on their shape and beauty. I could see flickers of white light and what seemed like a pinkish glow around each plant.

I continued to walk, coming to a stream that radiated a pale blue and filled me with an enhanced tranquility and even a drowsiness. Eventually I made my way across the valley floor and up the next ridge until I came to the road. I pulled myself up to the gravel surface and walked casually along the shoulder toward the north.

Up ahead, I caught sight of a man in a priest's robe rounding the next bend. The sight thrilled me. Totally without fear, I jogged ahead to talk with him. I knew I would know exactly what to say and do. I had a feeling of perfect well-being. But to my surprise he had disappeared. To the right, another road angled back down into the valley, but I could see no one in that direction. I ran farther up the main road, but saw no one there either. I thought about going back and taking the road I had passed, but I knew the town was ahead so I continued to walk that way. Still, I thought several more times of the other road.

A hundred yards farther, as I rounded another curve, I heard the roar of vehicles. Through the trees I could see a line of military trucks approaching at a high rate of speed. For a moment I hesitated, thinking I might stand my ground, but then I remembered the terror of the shooting on the ridge.

I had time only to fling myself off the road to the right and lie still. Ten jeeps sped past me. I had landed in a spot which was completely exposed, and all I could do was hope no one looked my way. Each vehicle passed within twenty feet. I could smell the exhaust fumes and see the expression on every face.

Luckily, no one noticed. After they were well past, I crawled behind a large tree. My hands were shaking and my sensation of peace and connection was totally shattered. A now familiar pang of anxiety knotted in my stomach. Finally, I inched up to the road. The sound of more vehicles sent me scurrying down the slope again as two more jeeps raced past. I felt nauseous.

This time I stayed well off the road and retreated the way I had come, moving very cautiously. I came to the road I had passed earlier. After carefully listening for sound and movement, I decided to walk through the woods beside it, angling back into the valley. My body felt heavy again. What had I been doing, I asked myself. Why had I been walking in the road? I must have been crazy, deluded by the shock of the shooting, entranced in some state of euphoria. Get real, I told myself. You have to be careful. There are people here who will kill you if you make the slightest mistake!

I froze. Ahead of me, perhaps a hundred feet, was the priest. He was sitting under a large tree that was surrounded by numerous rock outcroppings. As I stared at him, he opened his eyes and looked right at me. I flinched but he only smiled and motioned for me to walk up.

Cautiously I approached him. He remained motionless, a thin, tall man of about fifty years of age. His hair was cut short and was dark brown in color, matching his eyes.

"You look as though you need some help," he said, in perfect English.

"Who are you?" I asked.

"I am Father Sanchez. And you?"

I explained who I was and where I was from, dizzily sinking to one knee and then to my buttocks.

"You were part of what happened in Cula, weren't you?" he asked.

"What do you know of that?" I asked warily, not knowing whether to trust him.

"I know someone in this government is very angry," he said. "They don't want the Manuscript publicized."

"Why?" I asked.

He stood up and looked down at me. "Why don't you come with me. Our mission is only a half mile away. You'll be safe with us."

I struggled to my feet, realizing I had no choice, and nodded affirmatively. He led me slowly down the road, his manner respectful and deliberate. He weighed each word.

"Are the soldiers still looking for you?" he asked at one point.

"I don't know," I replied.

He said nothing for a few minutes, then asked, "Are you searching for the Manuscript?"

"Not any more," I said. "Right now I just want to survive this and go home."

He nodded reassuringly and I found myself beginning to trust him. Something about his regard and warmth affected me. He reminded me of Wil. Presently we came to the mission, which was a cluster of small houses facing a courtyard and a small church. It was situated in a place of great beauty. As we walked up he told some of the other robed men something in Spanish and they scurried away. I tried to see where they were going but fatigue was engulfing me. The priest led me into one of the houses.

Inside was a small living area and two bedrooms. A fire burned in the fireplace. Soon after we entered, another priest walked in with a tray of bread and soup. Wearily I ate as Sanchez sat politely in a chair beside me. Then, upon his insistence, I stretched out on one of the beds and fell into a deep sleep.

When I walked into the courtyard, I noticed immediately that the grounds were immaculately kept. The gravel walkways were edged with precisely arranged bushes and hedges. Each seemed to be placed so as to accent their full natural shape. None were trimmed.

I stretched and felt the starched shirt I had put on. It was made of coarse cotton and chafed my neck slightly. Still it was clean and freshly ironed. Earlier, I had awakened as two priests poured hot water into a tub and laid out fresh clothes. After I had bathed and dressed I had walked into the other room and found hot muffins and dried fruit on the table. I had eaten ravenously while the priests stood by. After I had finished, the priests had left and I had walked outside to where I now stood.

I walked over and sat on one of the stone benches that faced the courtyard. The sun was just clearing the tops of the trees, warming my face.

"How did you sleep?" a voice asked from behind me. I turned to see Father Sanchez standing very erect, smiling down at me.

"Very well," I replied.

"May I join you?"

"Sure."

Neither of us spoke for several minutes, so long in fact that I felt some discomfort. Several times I looked at him, preparing to say something, but he was looking in the direction of the sun, his face tilted slightly back, his eyes squinting.

Finally he spoke: "This is a nice place you found here." Apparently he meant the bench at this time of the morning.

"Look, I need to ask your advice," I said. "What is the safest way for me to get back to the United States?"

He looked at me seriously. "I don't know. That depends on how dangerous the government thinks you are. Tell me how you happened to be in Cula."

I told him everything from the time I first heard of the Manuscript. My feeling of euphoria on the ridge now seemed fanciful and pretentious, so I only alluded to it briefly. Sanchez, however, immediately questioned me about it.

"What did you do after the soldier failed to notice you and left?" he asked.

"I just sat up there for a few hours," I replied, "feeling relieved, I guess."

"What else did you feel?" he asked.

I squirmed somewhat, then decided to attempt a description. "It's hard to describe," I said. "I felt this euphoric connection with everything, and this total kind of security and confidence. I was no longer tired."

He smiled. "You had a mystical experience. Many people report them in that forest near the peak."

I nodded tentatively.

He turned on the bench to face me more directly. "This is the experience the mystics of every religion have always described. Have you read anything about such experiences?"

"Some, years ago," I said.

"But until yesterday it was only an intellectual concept?"

"Yeah, I suppose."

A young priest walked up and nodded to me, then whispered something to Sanchez. Sanchez nodded and the young priest turned and walked away. The older priest watched every step the young man took. He crossed the courtyard and entered a park-like area about a hundred feet away. I noticed for the first time that this area too was also extremely clean, and full of various plants. The young priest walked to several locations, hesitating at each one as though searching for something, then at one specific location sat down. He appeared to be engaged in an exercise of some kind.

Sanchez smiled and looked pleased, then turned his attention to me.

"I think it is probably unsafe for you to attempt to go back right now," he said. "But I will try to find out what the situation is, and if there is any word about your friends." He stood up and faced me. "I must attend to some chores. Please understand that we will assist you in any way possible. For now I hope you will be comfortable here. Relax and gain your strength."

I nodded.

He reached inside his pocket and pulled out some papers and handed them to me. "This is the Fifth Insight. It speaks about the kind of experience you had. I think you might find it interesting."

I took it reluctantly as he continued speaking. "What was your understanding of the last insight you read?" he asked.

I hesitated. I didn't want to think about manuscripts and insights. Finally I said, "That humans are stuck in a kind of competition for each other's energy. When we can get others to acquiesce to our view, they identify with us and that pulls their energy into us and we feel stronger."

He smiled. "So the problem is that everyone is trying to control and manipulate each other for energy, because we feel short of it?"

"That's right."

"But there is a solution, another source of energy?"

"That's what the last insight implied."

He nodded and walked very deliberately into the church.

For a few moments, I leaned forward and rested my elbows on my knees, not looking at the translation. I continued to feel reluctant. The events of the last two days had dampened my enthusiasm and I preferred instead to think of how I might return to the United States. Then, in the wooded area across the way, I noticed the young priest stand up and walk slowly to another location about twenty feet from where he was. He turned toward me again and sat down.

I was intrigued over what he might be doing. Then it dawned on me that he might be practicing something that was spelled out in the Manuscript. I looked at the first page and began to read.

It described a new understanding of what has long been called mystical consciousness. During the last decades of the twentieth century, it stated, this consciousness would become publicized as a way of being that is actually attainable, a way that has been demonstrated by the more esoteric practitioners of many religions. For most, this consciousness would remain an intellectual concept, to be only talked of and debated. But for a growing number of humans, this consciousness would become experientially real—because these individuals would experience flashes or glimpses of this state of mind during the course of their lives. The manuscript said that this experience was the key to ending human conflict in the world, because during this experience we are receiving energy from another source—a source we will eventually learn to tap at will.

I stopped reading and looked at the young priest again. His eyes were open and he appeared to be looking directly at me. I nodded, even though I couldn't make out the details of his face. To my surprise he nodded back to me and smiled faintly. Then he stood up and walked toward my left, head-ing toward the house in that direction. He avoided my eyes as I watched him cross the courtyard and enter the dwelling.

Behind me I heard footsteps and turned to see Sanchez leaving the church. He smiled as he approached me.

"That didn't take long," he said. "Would you like to see more of the grounds?"

"Yes, I would," I replied. "Tell me about these sitting areas you have." I pointed toward the area where the young priest had been.

"Let's walk up there," he said.

As we strolled across the courtyard, Sanchez told me that the mission was over four hundred years old and was founded by a unique missionary from Spain, who felt the way to convert the local Indians was through their hearts, not through coercion with the sword. The approach had worked, Sanchez went on, and partly because of this success and partly due to the remote location, the priest had been left alone to follow his own course.

"We carry on his tradition of looking inward for the truth," Sanchez said.

The sitting area was landscaped immaculately. About half an acre of dense forest had been cleared and the bushes and flowering plants beneath were interspersed with walkways made of smooth river stone. Like those in the courtyard, the plants here were also spaced perfectly, accentuating their unique shape.

"Where would you like to sit down?" Sanchez asked.

I looked around at my options. In front of us were several arranged areas—nooks which seemed complete unto themselves. All contained open spaces surrounded by beautiful plants and rocks and larger trees of varying shapes. One, to our left, where the young priest had been last sitting, had more outcroppings of stone.

"How about over there?" I said.

He nodded and we walked over and sat down. Sanchez breathed deeply for several minutes, then looked at me.

"Tell me more about your experience on the ridge," he said.

I felt resistant. "I don't know what else I can say about it. It didn't last."

The priest looked at me sternly. "Just because it ended when you became afraid again doesn't negate its importance, does it? Perhaps it is something to be regained."

"Maybe," I said. "But it's hard for me to concentrate on feeling cosmic when people are trying to kill me."

He laughed, then looked at me warmly.

"Are you studying the Manuscript here at the mission?" I asked.

"Yes," he said. "We teach others how to pursue the kind of experience you had on the ridge. You wouldn't mind getting some of that feeling back, would you?"

A voice from the courtyard interrupted: a priest calling for Sanchez. The older man excused himself and walked down to the courtyard and talked with the priest who had summoned him. I sat back and looked at the plants and rocks nearby, taking my eyes slightly out of focus. Around the bush closest to me I could barely make out an area of light but when I tried it on the rocks, I could see nothing.

Then I noticed Sanchez walking back.

"I must leave for a while," he said as he reached me. "I'll be going into town for a meeting so perhaps I can acquire some information concerning your friends, or at least how safe it is for you to travel."

"Good," I said. "Will you be back today?"

"I don't think so," he replied. "More like tomorrow morning."

I must have looked insecure because he walked closer and placed his hand on my shoulder. "Don't worry. You are safe here. Please make yourself at home. Look around. It is fine to talk with any of the priests, but understand that some of them will be more receptive than others depending on their development."

I nodded.

He smiled and walked behind the church and entered an old truck I had not noticed. After several attempts it started and he drove around the back side of the church and onto the road leading back up the ridge.

For several hours I remained in the sitting area, content to gather my thoughts, wondering if Marjorie was all right and if Wil had escaped. Several times the image of Jensen's man being killed flashed across my mind, but I fought off the memory and tried to stay calm.

About noon, I noticed several priests were preparing a long table in the center of the courtyard with dishes of food. When they finished, a dozen or more other priests joined them and began serving their own plates and eating on the benches casually. Most of them smiled pleasantly at each other, but I could hear little talking. One of them looked up at me and pointed to the food.

I nodded and walked down to the courtyard and prepared a plate of corn and beans. Each of the priests seemed very conscious of my presence but no one spoke to me. I made several comments about the food, but my words were met only with smiles and polite gestures. If I attempted direct eye contact, they would lower their eyes.

I sat down on one of the benches alone and ate. The vegetables and beans were unsalted but spiced with herbs. When lunch was over and the priests were stacking their plates on the table, another priest walked out of the church and hastily prepared a plate. When he finished, he looked around for a place to sit and our eyes met. He smiled and I recognized him as the priest who had looked at me from the sitting area earlier. I returned his smile and he walked over and spoke to me in broken English.

"May I sit on bench with you?" he asked.

"Yes, please," I replied.

He sat down and began to eat very slowly, overchewing his food and smiling up at me occasionally. He was short and small with a wiry build and coal black hair. His eyes were a lighter brown.

"You like the food?" he asked.

I was holding my plate in my lap. Several bites of corn remained.

"Oh, yes," I said, and took a bite. I noticed again how slowly and deliberately he chewed and tried to do the same, and then it struck me that all of the priests had been eating that way.

"Are the vegetables grown here at the mission?" I asked. He hesitated before answering, swallowing slowly.

"Yes, food is very important."

"Do you meditate with the plants?" I asked.

He looked at me with obvious surprise. "You have read Manuscript?" he asked.

"Yes, the first four insights."

"Have you grown food?" he asked.

"Oh no. I'm just learning about all this."

"Do you see energy fields?"

"Yes, sometimes."

We sat in silence for a few minutes while he carefully ate several more bites.

"Food is the first way of gaining energy," he said.

I nodded.

"But in order to totally absorb energy in food, the food must be appreciated, eh. . ."

He seemed to be struggling for the right English word. "Savored," he finally said. "Taste is the doorway. You must appreciate taste. This is the reason for prayer before eating. It is not just about being thankful, it is to make eating a holy experience, so the energy from the food can enter your body."

He looked closely at me, as though to see whether I understood.

I nodded without comment. He looked thoughtful.

What he was telling me, I reasoned, was that this kind of deliberate appreciation of food was the real purpose behind the normal religious custom of being thankful, with the result being a higher energy absorption of the food.

"But taking in food is only first step," he said. "After personal energy is increased in this way, you become more sensitive to energy in all things...and then you learn to take this energy into yourself without eating."

I nodded affirmatively.

"Everything around us," he continued, "has energy. But each has its own special kind. That is why some places increase energy more than others. It depends on how your shape fits with the energy there."

"Is that what you were doing up there earlier?" I asked. "Increasing your energy?"

He looked pleased. "Yes."

"How do you do that?" I asked.

"You have to be open, to connect, to use your sense of appreciation, as in seeing fields. But you take this one step further so that you get the sensation of being filled up."

"I'm not sure I follow you."

He frowned at my denseness. "Would you like to walk back to the sitting place? I can show you."

"Okay," I said. "Why not?"

I followed as he led the way across the courtyard and back to the sitting area. As we arrived, he stopped and looked around, as if surveying the area for something.

"Over there," he said, pointing to a spot that bordered the dense forest.

We followed the path as it wound through the trees and bushes. He picked a spot in front of a large tree that grew out of a mound of boulders so that its huge trunk seemed to be perched on the rocks. Its roots wrapped around and through the boulders before finally reaching the soil. Flowering shrubs of some type grew in semicircles in front of the tree and I could detect a strange sweet fragrance from the shrub's yellow blossoms. The dense forest provided a solid sheet of green in the background.

The priest directed me to sit down in a clear spot amid the bushes, facing the gnarled tree. He sat beside me.

"Do you think the tree is beautiful?" he asked.

"Yes."

"Then, uh. . .feel it. . .uh. . ."

He seemed to be struggling again to find the word. He thought for a moment and then asked, "Father Sanchez told me that you had an experience on the ridge; can you remember how you felt?"

"I felt light and secure and connected."

"How connected?"

"That's hard to describe," I said. "Like the whole landscape was part of me."

"But what was the feeling?"

I thought for a minute. What was the feeling? Then it came to me.

"Love," I said. "I guess I felt a love for everything."

"Yes," he said. "That is it. Feel that for the tree."

"But wait a minute," I protested. "Love is something that just happens. I can't make myself love anything."

"You do not make yourself love," he said. "You allow love to enter you. But to do this you must position your mind by remembering what it felt like and try to feel it again."

I looked at the tree and tried to remember the emotion on the ridge. Gradually, I began to admire its shape and presence. My appreciation grew until I actually felt an emotion of love. The feeling was exactly the one I remember as a child for my mother and as a youth for the special little girl that was the object of my "puppy love." Yet even though I had been looking at the tree, this particular love existed as a general background feeling. I was in love with everything.

The priest slid away several feet and looked back at me intensely. "Good," he said. "You are accepting the energy."

I noticed his eyes were slightly out of focus.

"How do you know?" I asked.

"Because I can see your energy field getting larger."

I closed my eyes and tried to reach the intense feelings I had acquired on the ridge top but I couldn't duplicate the experience. What I was feeling was on the same continuum but to a lesser degree than before. The failure made me frustrated.

"What happened?" he asked. "Your energy fell."

"I don't know," I said. "I just couldn't do it as strongly as before."

He just looked at me, amused at first, then with impatience.

"What you experienced on the ridge was a gift, a breakthrough, a look at a new way. Now you must learn to get that experience by yourself, a little at a time."

He slid back a foot farther and looked at me again. "Now try more."

I closed my eyes and tried to feel deeply. Eventually the emotion swept over me again. I stayed with it, attempting to increase the feeling by small increments. I focused my regard on the tree.

"That is very good," he suddenly said. "You are receiving energy and giving it to the tree."

I looked at him squarely. "I'm giving it back to the tree?"

"When you appreciate the beauty and uniqueness of things," he explained, "you receive energy. When you get to a level where you feel love, then you can send the energy back just by willing it so." For a long time I sat there with the tree. The more I focused attention on the tree and admired its shape and color, the more love I seemed to acquire generally, an unusual experience. I imagined my energy flowing over and filling up the tree, but I couldn't see it. Without changing my focus, I noticed the priest get up and begin to walk away.

"What does it look like when I'm giving energy to the tree?" I asked.

He described the perception in detail and I recognized it as the same phenomenon I had witnessed when Sarah projected energy onto the philodendron at Viciente. Though Sarah was successful, she apparently wasn't aware that a state of love was necessary for the projection to take place. She must have been acquiring a love state naturally, without realizing it.

The priest walked down toward the courtyard and out of my range of vision. I remained in the sitting area until dusk.

The two priests nodded politely as I entered the house. A roaring fire fended off the evening chill and several oil lamps illuminated the front room. The air was filled with the smell of vegetable, or perhaps potato, soup. On the table was a ceramic bowl, several spoons, and a plate holding four slices of bread.

One of the priests turned and left without looking at me and the other kept his eyes lowered and nodded at a large cast iron pot sitting on the hearth by the fire. A handle protruded from under its lid. As soon as I saw the pot, the second priest asked, "Is there anything else you need?"

"I think not," I said. "Thank you."

He nodded and left the house as well, leaving me alone. I lifted the lid from the pot—potato soup. It smelled rich and delicious. I poured several ladles full into a bowl and sat down at the table, then pulled the part of the Manuscript Sanchez had given me from my pocket and placed it beside my plate, intending to read. But the soup tasted so good that I focused entirely on eating. After I finished, I placed the dishes in a large pan and stared at the fire, hypnotized, until the flames burned low. Then I turned down the lamps and went to bed.

The next morning, I awakened at dawn feeling totally refreshed. Outside a morning mist rolled through the courtyard. I stoked up the fire and put several pieces of kindling on the coals and fanned it until it caught up. I was about to look through the kitchen for food when I heard Sanchez's truck approaching.

I walked outside as he emerged from behind the church, a backpack in one arm and several packages in the other.

"I have some news," he said, motioning me to follow him back inside the house.

Several other priests appeared with hot corn cakes and grits and more dried fruit. Sanchez greeted the men, then sat with me at the table as the priests scurried away.

"I attended a meeting of some of the priests of the Southern Council," he said. "We were there to talk about the Manuscript. At issue was the government's aggressive actions. This was the first time any group of priests has met publicly in support of this document, and we were just beginning our discussion when a government representative knocked on the door and asked to be admitted."

He paused as he served his plate and took several bites, chewing them thoroughly. "The representative," he continued, "assured us that the government's sole purpose was to protect the Manuscript from outside exploitation. He informed us that all copies being held by Peruvian citizens must be licensed. He said he understood our concern but asked us to comply with this law and turn in our copies. He promised that government duplicates would be issued back to us at once."

"Did you turn them in?" I asked.

"Of course not."

We both ate for a few minutes. I tried to overchew, to appreciate the taste.

"We asked about the violence in Cula," he went on, "and he told us that this was a necessary reaction against a man called Jensen, that several of his men were armed agents from another country. He said they planned to find and steal the undiscovered part of the Manuscript and remove it from Peru, so the government had no choice but to arrest them. There was no mention of you or your friends."

"Did you believe the government man?"

"No, we didn't. After he left we continued the meeting. We agreed that our policy would be one of quiet resistance. We will continue to make copies and distribute them carefully."

"Will your church leaders allow you to do that?" I asked.

"We don't know," Sanchez said. "The church elders have disapproved of the Manuscript but so far have not seriously investigated who is involved with it. Our main concern is a Cardinal who resides farther north, Cardinal Sebastian. He is the most vocal in opposition to the Manuscript and is very influential. If he convinces the leadership to issue strong proclamations, then we will have a very interesting decision to make."

"Why is he so opposed to the Manuscript?"

"He is afraid."

"Why?"

"I haven't spoken with him in a long time, and we always avoid the subject of the Manuscript. But I believe he thinks man's role is to participate in the cosmos ignorant of spiritual knowledge—by faith alone. He thinks the Manuscript will undermine the status quo, the lines of authority in the world."

"How would it do that?"

He smiled and tilted his head back slightly. "The truth shall set you free."

I was looking at him, trying to understand what he meant, eating the last of the bread and fruit on my plate. He ate several more tiny bites and pushed his chair back.

"You seem much stronger," he said. "Did you talk with anyone here?"

"Yes," I replied. "I learned a method of connecting with the energy from one of the priests. I. . .didn't catch his name. He was in the sitting area while we were talking in the courtyard yesterday morning, remember? When I spoke with him later, he showed me how to absorb energy and then to project it back."

"His name is John," Sanchez said, then nodded for me to go on.

"It was an amazing experience," I said. "By remembering the love I felt I was able to open up. I sat up there all day simmering in it. I didn't reach the state I experienced on the ridge but I got close."

Sanchez looked more serious. "The role of love has been misunderstood for a long time. Love is not something we should do to be good or to make the world a better place out of some abstract moral responsibility, or because we should give up our hedonism. Connecting with energy feels like excitement, then euphoria, and then love. Finding enough energy to maintain that state of love certainly helps the world, but it most directly helps us. It is the most hedonistic thing we can do."

I agreed, then noticed he had moved his chair back several more feet and was looking at me intensely, his eyes unfocused.

"So what does my field look like," I asked.

"It is much larger," he said. "I think you feel very good."

"I do."

"Good. That is what we do here."

"Tell me about that," I said.

"We train priests to go farther into the mountains and work with the Indians. It is a lonely job and the priests must have great strength. All of the men here have been screened thoroughly and all have one thing in common: each has had one experience he calls mystical.

"I have been studying this kind of experience for many years," he continued, "even before the Manuscript was found, and I believe that when one has already encountered a mystical experience, getting back into this state and raising one's personal energy level comes much easier. Others can also connect but it takes longer. A strong memory of the experience, as I think you learned, facilitates its re-creation. After that, one slowly builds back."

"What does a person's energy field look like when this is happening?"

"It grows outward and changes color slightly."

"What color?"

"Normally from a dull white toward green and blue. But the most important thing is that it expands. For instance, during your mystical encounter on the ridge top, your energy flashed outward into the whole universe. Essentially you connected and drew energy from the entire cosmos and in turn your energy swelled to encompass everything, everywhere. Can you remember how that felt?"

"Yeah," I said. "I felt as though the entire universe was my body and I was just the head, or perhaps more accurately, the eyes."

"Yes," he said, "and at that moment, your energy field and that of the universe were the same. The universe was your body."

"I had a strange memory during that time," I said. "I seemed to remember how this larger body, this universe of mine, evolved. I was there. I saw the first stars formed from simple hydrogen and then saw more complex matter evolve in successive generations of these suns. Only I didn't see matter. I saw matter as simple vibrations of energy that were evolving systematically into ever more complex higher states. Then. . .life began and evolved to a point where humans appeared. . ."

I stopped suddenly and he noticed my changed mood.

"What's wrong?" he said.

"That's where the memory of evolution stopped," I explained, "with humans. I felt as if the story continued, but I couldn't quite grasp it."

"The story does go on," he said. "Humans are carrying forth the universe's evolution toward higher and higher vibrational complexity."

"How?" I asked.

He smiled but didn't answer. "Let's talk about this later. I really must check on a few things. I'll see you in an hour or so."

I nodded. He picked up an apple and walked out. I wandered outside behind him, then remembered the copy of the Fifth Insight in the bedroom and retrieved it. Earlier I had been thinking of the forest where Sanchez had been sitting when I had first met him. Even in my fatigue and panic I had noticed that the place was extraordinarily beautiful, so I walked down the road toward the west until I came to the exact spot, then sat down there myself.

Leaning back against a tree, I cleared my mind and spent several minutes looking around. The morning was bright and breezy and I watched the wind as it whipped the branches above my head. The air felt refreshing as I took in several deep breaths. During a lull in the wind, I took out the Manuscript and looked for the page where I had stopped reading. Before I could locate it, however, I heard the sound of a truck engine.

I lay flat beside the tree and attempted to determine its direction. The sound was coming from the mission. As it grew closer, I could see it was Sanchez's old truck, with him driving.

"I thought you might be here," he said, as he pulled up to where I was standing. "Get in. We need to leave."

"What's going on?" I asked, sliding into the passenger seat.

He drove on toward the main road. "One of my priests told me of a conversation he overheard in the village. Some government officials are in town and they were asking questions about me and the mission."

"What do you think they want?"

He looked at me reassuringly. "I don't know. Let's just say I'm not as certain as before that they will leave us alone. I thought, as a precaution, that we should drive up into the mountains. One of my priests lives near Machu Picchu. His name is Father Carl. We'll be safe at his house until we can better read the situation." He smiled. "I want you to see Machu Picchu anyway."

I suddenly had a flash of suspicion that he had made a deal and was taking me somewhere to turn me in. I decided to proceed cautiously and to stay alert until I found out for sure.

"Did you finish the translation?" he asked.

"Most of it," I said.

"You had asked about human evolution. Did you finish that part?"

"No."

He turned his eyes from the road and looked at me intensely. I pretended not to notice.

"Is something wrong?" he asked.

"Nothing." I said. "How long will it take to get to Machu Picchu?"

"About four hours."

I wanted to remain silent and let Sanchez talk, hoping he might give himself away, but I couldn't control my curiosity about evolution.

"So how do humans further evolution?" I asked.

He glanced at me. "What do you think?"

"I don't know," I said. "But when I was up on the ridge I thought it might have something to do with the meaningful coincidences that the First Insight talks about."

"That's right," he said. "That would fit with the other insights, wouldn't it?"

I was confused. I almost understood but I couldn't quite grasp it. I remained silent.

"Think of how the Insights fall into sequence," he said. "The First Insight occurs when we take the coincidences seriously. These coincidences make us feel there is something more, something spiritual, operating underneath everything we do.

"The Second Insight institutes our awareness as something real. We can see that we have been preoccupied with material survival, with focusing on controlling our situation in the universe for security, and we know our openness now represents a kind of waking up to what is really going on.

"The Third Insight begins a new view of life. It defines the physical universe as one of pure energy, an energy that somehow responds to how we think.

"And the Fourth exposes the human tendency to steal energy from other humans by controlling them, taking over their minds, a crime in which we engage because we so often feel depleted of energy, and cut off. This shortage of energy can be remedied, of course, when we connect with the higher source. The universe can provide all we need if we can only open up to it. That is the revelation of the Fifth Insight.

"In your case," he continued, "you had a mystical experience that allowed you to briefly see the magnitude of energy one can acquire. But this state is like leaping ahead of everyone else and glimpsing the future. We can't maintain it for very long. Once we try to talk to someone who is operating in normal consciousness, or try to live in a world where conflict is still happening, we get knocked out of this advanced state and fall back to the level of our old selves.

"And then," he continued, "it is a matter of slowly regaining what we glimpsed, a little at a time, and to begin a progression back toward that ultimate consciousness. But to do this, we must learn to consciously fill up with energy because this energy brings on the coincidences, and the coincidences help us actualize the new level on a permanent basis."

I must have looked puzzled because he said, "Think about it: when something occurs beyond chance to lead us forward in our lives, then we become more actualized people. We feel as though we are attaining what destiny is leading us to become. When this occurs, the level of energy that brought on the coincidences in the first place is instituted in us. We can be knocked out of it and lose energy when we are afraid, but this level serves as a new outer limit which can be regained quite easily. We have become a new person. We exist at a level of higher energy, at a level—get this—of higher vibration.

"Can you see the process now? We fill up, grow, fill up and grow again. That is how we as humans continue the evolution of the universe to a higher and higher vibration."

He paused for a moment then seemed to think of something he wanted to add. "This evolution has been going on unconsciously throughout human history. That explains why civilization has progressed and why humans have grown larger, lived longer, and so forth. Now however, we are making the whole process conscious. That is what the Manuscript is telling us. That is what this movement toward worldwide spiritual consciousness is all about."

I was listening intensely, totally fascinated with what Sanchez was telling me. "So all we have to do is fill up with energy, as I learned to do with John, and the coincidences begin to happen more consistently?"

"Well yes, but that's not as easy as you think. Before we can connect with the energy on a permanent basis there is one more hurdle we must pass. The next insight, the Sixth, deals with this issue."

"What is it?"

He looked squarely at me. "We must face up to our particular way of controlling others. Remember, the Fourth Insight reveals that humans have always felt short of energy and have sought to control each other to acquire the energy that flows between people. The Fifth then shows us that an alternative source exists, but we can't really stay connected with this source until we come to grips with the particular method that, we, as individuals, use in our controlling, and stop doing it—because whenever we fall back into this habit, we get disconnected from the source.

"Getting rid of this habit isn't easy because it's always unconscious at first. The key to letting it go is to bring it fully into consciousness, and we do that by seeing that our particular style of controlling others is one we learned in childhood to get attention, to get the energy moving our way, and we're stuck there. This style is something we repeat over and over again. I call it our unconscious *control drama.*

"I call it a drama because it is one familiar scene, like a scene in a movie, for which we write the script as youths. Then we repeat this scene over and over in our daily lives without being aware of it. All we know is that the same kind of events happen to us repeatedly. The problem is if we are repeating one particular scene over and over, then the other scenes of our real life movie, the high adventure marked by coincidences, can't go forward. We stop the movie when we repeat this one drama in order to manipulate for energy."

Sanchez slowed the truck and moved carefully forward through a series of deep ruts in the road. I realized I was frustrated. I couldn't quite grasp how a control drama worked. I almost expressed my feelings to Sanchez but I couldn't. I realized I still felt distant from him and I didn't care to reveal myself.

"Did you understand?" he asked.

"I don't know," I said curtly. "I don't know if I have a control drama."

He looked at me with the warmest regard and chuckled out loud. "Is that so?" he asked. "Then why do you always act so aloof?"

CLEARING
THE PAST

Ahead the road narrowed and bent sharply around the sheer rock face of the mountain. The truck bounced over several large rocks and slowly proceeded through the curve. Below, the Andes rose in massive gray ridges above banks of snow-white clouds.

I looked at Sanchez. He was leaning over the steering wheel, tense. For most of the day we had been scaling steep inclines and edging through passages made more narrow by fallen rock. I had wanted to broach the subject of control dramas again but the time seemed inappropriate. Sanchez appeared to need every ounce of energy for driving, and besides, I wasn't clear on what I wanted to ask. I had read the rest of the Fifth Insight and it had echoed exactly the points Sanchez had related to me. The idea of getting rid of my style of controlling seemed desirable, especially if it would make my evolution accelerate, but I still couldn't grasp how a control drama operated.

"What are you thinking about?" Sanchez asked.

"I finished reading the Fifth Insight," I said. "And I was thinking about these dramas. Considering what you said about me, I assume you think my drama has something to do with being aloof?"

He didn't reply. He was staring up the road. A hundred feet ahead, a large four-wheel drive vehicle blocked the way. A man and a woman stood on a rock precipice fifty feet from the vehicle. They returned our gaze.

Sanchez stopped the truck and looked them over for an instant, then smiled. "I know the woman," he said. "That's Julia. It's all right. Let's talk with them."

Both the man and woman were of dark complexion and appeared Peruvian. The woman was older, appearing to be about fifty, while the man looked approximately thirty. As we got out of the truck, the woman walked toward us.

"Father Sanchez!" she said as she approached.

"How are you Julia?" Sanchez replied. The two embraced, then Sanchez introduced me to Julia. Julia, in turn, introduced her companion, Rolando.

Saying nothing else, Julia and Sanchez turned their backs on us and walked toward the overhang where Julia and Rolando had previously been standing. Rolando looked at me intensely and I instinctively turned and walked in the direction of the other two people. Rolando followed, still looking at me as though he wanted something. Although his hair and features were young, his complexion was ruddy and red. For some reason I felt anxious.

Several times as we walked to the edge of the mountain, he looked as though he was going to speak, but each time I turned my eyes away and increased my pace. He remained silent. When we reached the precipice, I sat on a ledge to prevent him from sitting next to me. Julia and Sanchez were above me about twenty-five feet, sitting together on a large boulder.

Rolando sat as close to me as possible. Although his constant stare bothered me, I was slightly curious about him at the same time.

He caught me looking at him and asked, "Are you here for the Manuscript?"

I took a long time to answer. "I've heard of it."

He looked perplexed. "Have you seen it?"

"Some," I said. "Do you have something to do with it?"

"I am interested," he said, "but I have not seen any copies yet." A period of silence followed.

"Are you from the United States?" he asked.

The question disturbed me, so I decided not to answer.

Instead I asked, "Does the Manuscript have anything to do with the ruins at Machu Picchu?"

"I don't think so," he replied. "Except that it was written about the same time they were built."

I remained silent, looking out at the incredible view of the Andes. Sooner or later, if I remained quiet, he would divulge what he and Julia were doing here and how it concerned the Manuscript. We sat for twenty minutes with no conversation. Finally, Rolando stood and walked up to where the others were talking.

I was perplexed as to what to do. I had avoided sitting with Sanchez and Julia because I had the distinct impression they wanted to talk alone. For perhaps another thirty minutes, I remained there, gazing out at the rocky peaks and straining to overhear the conversation above me. None of them paid me the slightest bit of attention. Finally I decided to join them, but before I could move, the three of them stood and began walking toward Julia's vehicle. I cut across the rocks toward them.

"They have to go," Sanchez remarked as I approached.

"I'm sorry we did not have time to talk," Julia said. "I hope we see you again." She was looking at me with the same warmth Sanchez often displayed. As I nodded, she cocked her head slightly and added, "In fact, I have a feeling we will see you soon."

As we strolled down the rocky path, I felt the need to say something in response but I couldn't think. When we reached her vehicle Julia only nodded slightly and said a quick good-bye. Both she and Rolando got in and Julia drove away toward the north, the way Sanchez and I had come. I felt puzzled by the entire experience.

Once we were in our vehicle, Sanchez asked, "Did Rolando fill you in on Wil?"

"No!" I said. "Had they seen him?"

Sanchez looked confused, "Yes, they saw him at a village forty miles east of here."

"Did Wil say anything about me?"

"Julia said Wil mentioned being separated from you. She said Wil talked mainly with Rolando. Didn't you tell Rolando who you were?"

"No, I didn't know if I could trust him."

Sanchez looked at me in total bewilderment. "I told you it was fine to talk with them. I have known Julia for years. She owns a business in Lima, but since the discovery of the Manuscript she has been looking for the Ninth Insight. Julia would not be traveling with anyone untrustworthy. There was no danger. Now you missed what could have been important information."

Sanchez looked at me with a serious expression. "This is a perfect example of how a control drama interferes," he said. "You were so aloof you didn't allow an important coincidence to take place."

I must have appeared defensive. "It's all right," he said, "everyone plays a drama of one kind or another. At least now you understand how yours works."

"I don't understand!" I said. "What exactly am I doing?"

"Your way of controlling people and situations," he explained, "in order to get energy coming your way, is to create this drama in your mind during which you withdraw and look mysterious and secretive. You tell yourself that you're being cautious but what you're really doing is hoping someone will be pulled into this drama and will try to figure out what's going on with you. When someone does, you remain vague, forcing them to struggle and dig and try to discern your true feelings.

"As they do so, they give you their full attention and that sends their energy to you. The longer you can keep them interested and mystified, the more energy you receive. Unfortunately, when you play aloof, your life tends to evolve very slowly because you're repeating this same scene over and over again. If you had opened up to Rolando, your life movie would have taken off in a new and meaningful direction."

I felt myself becoming depressed. All this was just another example of what Wil had pointed out when he saw me resisting giving information to Reneau. It was true. I did tend to hide what I really thought. I looked out the window as we followed the road higher into the peaks. Sanchez concentrated again on avoiding the fatal drop-offs. When the road straightened, he looked over at me and said, "The first step in the process of getting clear, for each of us, is to bring our particular control drama into full consciousness. Nothing can proceed until we really look at ourselves and discover what we are doing to manipulate for energy. This is what has just happened to you."

"What is the next step?" I asked.

"Each of us must go back into our past, back into our early family life, and see how this habit was formed. Seeing its inception keeps our way of controlling in consciousness. Remember, most of our family members were operating in a drama themselves, trying to pull energy out of us as children. This is why we had to form a control drama in the first place. We had to have a strategy to win energy back. It is always in relation to our family members that we develop our particular dramas. However, once we recognize the energy dynamics in our families, we can go past these control strategies and see what was really happening."

"What do you mean, really happening?"

"Each person must reinterpret his family experience from an evolutionary point of view, from a spiritual point of view, and discover who he really is. Once we do that, our control drama falls away and our real lives take off."

"So how do I begin?"

"By first understanding how your drama was formed. Tell me about your father."

"He is a good man who is fun-loving and capable but. . ." I hesitated, not wanting to sound ungrateful toward my father.

"But what?" Sanchez asked.

"Well," I said, "he was always critical. I could never do anything right."

"How did he criticize you?" Sanchez asked.

A picture of my father, young and strong, appeared in my mind. "He asked questions, then found something wrong with the answers."

"And what happened to your energy?"

"I guess I felt drained so I tried to keep from telling him anything."

"You mean you got vague and distant, trying to say things in a way that would get his attention but not reveal enough to give him something to criticize. He was the interrogator and you dodged around him with your aloofness?"

"Yeah, I guess. But what is an interrogator?"

"An interrogator is another kind of drama. People who use this means of gaining energy, set up a drama of asking questions and probing into another person's world with the specific purpose of finding something wrong. Once they do, then they criticize this aspect of the other's life. If this strategy succeeds then the person being criticized is pulled into the drama. They suddenly find themselves becoming self-conscious around the interrogator and paying attention to what the interrogator is doing and thinking about, so as not to do something wrong that the interrogator would notice. This psychic deference gives the interrogator the energy he desires.

"Think about the times you have been around someone like this. When you get caught up in this drama, don't you tend to act a certain way so that the person won't criticize you? He pulls you off your own path and drains your energy because you judge yourself by what he might be thinking."

I remembered the feeling exactly, and the person that came to mind was Jenson.

"So my father was an interrogator?" I asked.

"That's what it sounds like."

For a moment I was lost in thought about my mother's drama. If my father was an interrogator, what was my mother?

Sanchez asked me what I was thinking.

"I was wondering about my mother's control drama," I said. "How many different kinds are there?"

"Let me explain the classifications spoken of in the Manuscript," Sanchez said. "Everyone manipulates for energy either aggressively, directly forcing people to pay attention to them, or passively, playing on people's sympathy or curiosity to gain attention. For instance, if someone threatens you, either verbally or physically, then you are forced, for fear of something bad happening to you, to pay attention to him and so to give him energy. The person threatening you would be pulling you into the most aggressive kind of drama, what the Sixth Insight calls the intimidator.

"If, on the other hand, someone tells you all the horrible things that are already happening to them, implying perhaps that you are responsible, and that, if you refuse to help, these horrible things are going to continue, then this person is seeking to control at the most passive level, with what the Manuscript calls a poor me drama. Think about this one for a moment. Haven't you ever been around someone who makes you feel guilty when you're in their presence, even though you know there is no reason to feel this way?"

"Yes."

"Well, it's because you have entered the drama world of a poor me. Everything they say and do puts you in a place where you have to defend against the idea that you're not doing enough for this person. That's why you feel guilty just being around them."

I nodded.

"Anyone's drama can be examined," he continued, "according to where it falls on this spectrum from aggressive to passive. If a person is subtle in their aggression, finding fault and slowly undermining your world in order to get your energy, then, as we saw in your father, this person would be an interrogator. Less passive than the poor me would be your aloofness drama. So the order of dramas goes this way: intimidator, interrogator, aloof, and poor me. Does that make sense?"

"I guess. You think everyone falls somewhere among these styles?"

"That's correct. Some people use more than one in different circumstances, but most of us have one dominant control drama that we tend to repeat, depending on which one worked well on the members of our early family."

It suddenly dawned on me. My mother did exactly the same thing to me as my father. I looked at Sanchez. "My mother. I know what she was. She was also an interrogator."

"So you had a double dose," Sanchez said. "No wonder you're so aloof. But at least they weren't intimidating you. At least you never feared for your safety."

"What would have happened in that case?"

"You would have become stuck in a poor me drama. Do you see how this works? If you are a child and someone is draining your energy by threatening you with bodily harm then being aloof doesn't work. You can't get them to give you energy by playing coy. They don't give a damn what's going on inside you. They're coming on too strong. So you're forced to become more passive and to try the poor me approach, appealing to the mercy of the person, guilt tripping them about the harm they are doing.

"If this doesn't work, then, as a child you endure until you are big enough to explode against the violence and fight aggression with aggression." He paused. "Like the child you told me about, the one in the Peruvian family that served you dinner.

"A person goes to whatever extreme necessary to get attention energy in their family. And after that, this strategy becomes their dominant way of controlling to get energy from everyone, the drama they constantly repeat."

"I understand the intimidator," I said, "but how does the interrogator develop?"

"What would you do if you were a child and your family members were either not there or ignored you because they were preoccupied with their careers or something?"

"I don't know."

"Playing aloof would not get their attention; they wouldn't notice. Wouldn't you have to resort to probing and prying and finally finding something wrong in these aloof people in order to force attention and energy? This is what an interrogator does."

I began to get the insight. "Aloof people create interrogators!"

"That's right."

"And interrogators make people aloof! And intimidators create the poor me approach, or if this fails, another intimidator!"

"Exactly. That's how control dramas perpetuate themselves. But remember, there is a tendency to see these dramas in others but to think that we ourselves are free from such devices. Each of us must transcend this illusion before we can go on. Almost all of us tend to be stuck, at least some of the time, in a drama and we have to step back and look at ourselves long enough to discover what it is."

I was silent for a moment. Finally I looked at Sanchez again and asked, "Once we see our drama, what happens next?"

Sanchez slowed the truck in order to look me in the eyes. "We are truly free to become more than the unconscious act we play. As I said before, we can find a higher meaning for our lives, a spiritual reason we were born to our particular families. We can begin to get clear about who we really are."

"We're almost there," Sanchez said. The road was cresting between two peaks. As we passed the huge formation on our right, I saw a small house ahead. It backed up to another majestic pinnacle of rock.

"His truck isn't here," Sanchez said.

We parked and walked to the house. Sanchez opened the door and walked inside while I waited. I took in several breaths. The air was cool and very thin. Overhead, the sky was dark gray and thick with clouds. It looked as though it might rain.

Sanchez walked back to the door, "No one is inside. He must be at the ruins."

"How do we get there?"

He suddenly looked exhausted. "They're up ahead about a half mile," he said, handing me the keys to the truck. "Follow the road past the next ridge and you'll see them down below. Take the truck. I want to stay here and meditate."

"Okay, I will," I said, walking around to get in the vehicle.

I drove forward into a little valley and then up the next ridge, anticipating the view. The sight did not disappoint me. As I crested the ridge I saw the full splendor of the ruins at Machu Picchu: a temple complex of massive, carefully shaped rocks weighing tons sitting atop each other on the mountain. Even in the dull cloudy light, the beauty of the place was overwhelming.

I stopped the truck and soaked up the energy for ten or fifteen minutes. Several groups of people were walking through the ruins. I saw a man wearing a priest's collar leave the remains of a building and walk toward a vehicle parked nearby. Because of the distance, and because the man wore a leather jacket rather than a priest's robe, I couldn't be sure it was Father Carl.

I started the truck and drove closer. As soon as he heard the sound he looked up and smiled, apparently recognizing the vehicle as belonging to Sanchez. When he saw me inside he looked interested and walked over. His build was short and squat, with dull brown hair and pudgy features, with deep blue eyes. He looked to be about thirty. "I'm with Father Sanchez," I said, stepping from the vehicle and introducing myself. "He's up at your house."

He offered his hand. "I'm Father Carl."

I glanced past him to the ruins. The cut stone was even more impressive when in close proximity.

"Is this the first time you've been here?" he asked.

"Yes, it is," I replied. "I've heard about this place for years but I never anticipated this."

"It is one of the highest energy centers in the world," he said.

I looked closely at him. Clearly he spoke about energy in the same sense it was used in the Manuscript. I nodded affirmatively, then said, "I'm at a point where I'm consciously trying to build energy and deal with my control drama." I felt somewhat pretentious at saying that but comfortable enough to be honest.

"You don't seem too aloof," he said.

I was startled. "How did you know that was my drama?" I asked.

"I've developed an instinct for it. That's why I'm here."

"You help people see their way of controlling?"

"Yes, and their true self." His eyes shone with sincerity. He was totally direct, with no hint of embarrassment at revealing himself to a stranger.

I remained silent so he said, "You understand the first five insights?"

"I've read most of them," I said, "and I've talked with several people."

As soon as I made this statement, I realized I was being too vague. "I think I understand the first five," I added. "It's number six that I'm not clear about."

He nodded, then said, "Most of the people I talk with haven't even heard of the Manuscript. They come up here and are entranced by the ener-gy. That alone makes them rethink their lives."

"How do you meet these people?"

He looked at me with a knowing expression. "They seem to find me."

"You said you help them find their true self; how?"

He took a long breath, then said, "There's only one way. Each of us has to go back to our family experience, that childhood time and place, and review what happened. Once we become conscious of our control drama, then we can focus on the higher truth of our family, the silver lining so to speak, that lies beyond the energy conflict. Once we find this truth, it can energize our lives, for this truth tells us who we are, the path we are on, what we are doing."

"That's what Sanchez has told me," I said. "I want to know more about how to find this truth."

He zipped up his coat against the late afternoon chill. "I hope we can talk more about it later," he said. "Right now I would like to greet Father Sanchez."

I looked out at the ruins, and he added, "Feel free to look around as long as you would like. I'll see you back at my house later."

For the next hour and a half, I walked through the ancient site. At cer-tain spots I would linger, feeling more buoyant than at others. I wondered with fascination about the civilization that had built these temples. How did they move these stones up here and place them atop one another in this fashion? It seemed impossible.

As my intense interest in the ruins began to wane, my thoughts turned to my personal situation. Although my circumstances had not changed, I felt less fearful now. Sanchez's confidence had reassured me. I had been stupid to doubt him. And I already liked Father Carl.

As darkness descended I walked back to the truck and returned to Father Carl's house. As I drove up I could see the two men standing close to each other inside. When I entered I heard laughter. Both were busy in the kitchen, preparing dinner. Father Carl greeted me and escorted me to a chair. I sat down lazily in front of a large fire in the fireplace and looked around.

The room was large, and paneled with wide boards which were lightly stained. I could see two other rooms, bedrooms apparently, linked by a narrow hallway. The house was lit with low wattage bulbs and I thought I could detect the faint hum of a generator.

When the preparations were completed, I was summoned to a rough plank table. Sanchez offered a brief prayer, and then we ate, the two men continuing to talk. Afterward we sat together by the fire.

"Father Carl has spoken with Wil," Sanchez said.

"When?" I asked, immediately excited.

"Wil came through here several days ago," Father Carl said. "I had met him a year ago and he came by to bring me some information. He said he thought he knew who was behind the governmental action against the Manuscript."

"Who?" I asked.

"Cardinal Sebastian," Sanchez interjected.

"What is he doing?" I asked.

"Apparently," Sanchez said, "he is using his influence with the government to increase the military pressure against the Manuscript. He has always preferred to work quietly through the government rather than force a division within the church. Now he is intensifying his efforts. Unfortunately, it may be working."

"What do you mean?" I asked.

"Except for the few priests of the Northern Council and a few others like Julia and Wil, no one else seems to have copies any longer."

"What about the scientists at Viciente?" I asked.

Both men were silent for a moment, then Father Carl said, "Wil told me the government has closed it down. All the scientists were arrested and their research data was confiscated."

"Will the scientific community stand for that?" I asked.

"What choice do they have?" Sanchez said. "Besides, that research wasn't accepted by most scientists anyway. The government is apparently selling the idea that these people were breaking the law."

"I can't believe the government could get away with doing that."

"Apparently they have," Father Carl said. "I made some calls to check and I received the same story. Though they're keeping it very quiet, the government is intensifying its crackdown."

"What do you think will happen?" I asked them both.

Father Carl shrugged his shoulders and Father Sanchez said, "I don't know. It may depend on what Wil finds."

"Why?" I asked.

"He appears to be close to finding the missing part of the Manuscript, the Ninth Insight. Perhaps when he does there will be enough interest to create worldwide intervention here."

"Where did he say he was going?" I asked Father Carl.

"He didn't know, exactly, but he said his intuitions were leading him further north, near Guatemala."

"His intuitions were leading him?"

"Yes, you'll understand that after you get clear about who you are and go on to the Seventh Insight."

I looked at both of them, at how incredibly serene they appeared. "How can you remain so calm?" I asked. "What if they come crashing in here and arrest all of us?"

They gazed at me patiently, then Father Sanchez spoke. "Don't confuse calmness with carelessness. Our peaceful countenance is a measure of how well we are connected with the energy. We stay connected because it is the best thing for us to do, regardless of the circumstances. You understand that, don't you?"

"Yes," I said, "of course. I guess I'm having trouble staying connected myself."

Both men smiled.

"Staying connected," Father Carl said, "will be easier once you get clear on who you are."

Father Sanchez stood up then and walked away, announcing that he would be doing the dishes.

I looked at Father Carl. "Okay," I said. "How do I start getting clear about myself?"

"Father Sanchez tells me," he replied, "that you already understand the control dramas of your parents."

"That's right. They were both interrogators and that made me aloof."

"Okay, now you must look past the energy competition that existed in your family and search for the real reason you were there."

I looked at him blankly.

"The process of finding your true spiritual identity involves looking at your whole life as one long story, trying to find a higher meaning. Begin by asking yourself this question: why was I born to this particular family? What might have been the purpose for that?"

"I don't know," I said.

"Your father was an interrogator; what else was he?"

"You mean, what did he stand for?"

"Yes."

I thought for a moment, then said, "My father genuinely believes in enjoying life, in living with integrity but making the most of what life has to offer. You know, living life to the fullest."

"Has he been able to do this?"

"To some extent, but somehow he always seems to have a run of bad luck just when he thinks he's about to enjoy life the most."

Father Carl squinted his eyes in contemplation. "He believes life is for fun and enjoyment but he hasn't quite pulled it off?"

"Yes."

"Have you thought about why?"

"Not really. I always figured he was unlucky."

"Maybe he hasn't found the way to do it yet?"

"Maybe not."

"What about your mother?"

"She's no longer living."

"Can you see what her life represented?"

"Yes, her life was her church. She stood for Christian principles."

"In what way?"

"She believed in community service and in following God's laws."

"Did she follow God's laws?"

"To the letter, at least so far as her church taught."

"Was she able to convince your father to do the same thing?"

I laughed. "Not really. My mother wanted him to go to church every week, and to be involved in community programs. But as I told you, he was more of a free spirit than that."

"So where did that leave you?"

I looked at him. "I've never thought about it."

"Didn't they both want your allegiance? Wasn't that why they were interrogating you, to make sure you weren't siding with the values of the other? Didn't they both want you to think their way was the best?"

"Yes, you're right."

"How did you respond?"

"I just tried to avoid taking a stand, I guess."

"They both monitored you to see if you were measuring up to their particular views, and unable to please both, you became aloof."

"That's about it," I said.

"What happened to your mother?" he asked.

"She developed Parkinson's disease and died after being sick for a long time."

"Did she remain true to her faith?"

"Absolutely," I said. "Throughout it all."

"So what meaning did she leave you with?"

"What?"

"You're looking for the meaning her life has for you, the reason you were born to her, what you were there to learn. Every human being, whether they are conscious of it or not illustrates with their lives how he or she thinks a human being is supposed to live. You must try to discover what she taught you and at the same time what about her life could have been done better. What you would have changed about your mother is part of what you yourself are working on."

"Why only part?"

"Because how you would improve on your father's life is the other part."

I was still confused.

He placed his hand on my shoulder. "We are not merely the physical creation of our parents; we are also the spiritual creation. You were born to these two people and their lives had an irrevocable effect on who you are. To discover your real self, you must admit that the real you began in a position between their truths. That's why you were born there: to take a higher perspective on what they stood for. Your path is about discovering a truth that is a higher synthesis of what these two people believed."

I nodded.

"So how would you express what your parents taught you?"

"I'm not sure," I replied.

"What do you think?"

"My father thought life was about maximizing his aliveness, his enjoyment of who he was, and he tried to pursue that end. My mother believed more in sacrifice and in spending her time in service to others, denying herself. She felt this is what the scriptures command."

"And you, how do you feel about this?"

"I don't know really."

"Which viewpoint would you choose for yourself, that of your mother, or that of your father?"

"Neither. I mean, life is not that simple."

He laughed. "You're being vague."

"I guess I don't know."

"But if you had to choose one or the other?"

I hesitated, trying to think honestly, then the answer came to me.

"They're both correct," I said, "and incorrect."

His eyes beamed. "How?"

"I'm not sure exactly. But I think a correct life must include both views."

"The question for you," Father Carl said, "is how. How does one live a life that is both? From your mother you received the knowledge that life is about spirituality. From your father you learned that life is about self-enhancement, fun, adventure."

"So my life," I interrupted, "is about somehow combining the two approaches?"

"Yes, for you, spirituality is the question. Your whole life will be about finding one that is self-enhancing. This is the problem your parents were unable to reconcile, the one they left for you. This is your evolutionary question, your quest this lifetime."

The idea propelled me into deep thought. Father Carl said something else but I couldn't concentrate on what he was saying. The waning fire was having a calming effect on me. I realized I was tired.

Father Carl sat up straight and said, "I think you're out of energy for tonight. But let me leave you with one thought. You can go to sleep and never think again of what we have discussed. You can go right back into your old drama, or you can wake up tomorrow and hold on to this new idea of who you are. If you do then you can take the next step in the process, which is to look closely at all the other things that have happened to you since birth. If you view your life as one story, from birth to right now, you'll be able to see how you have been working on this question all along. You'll be able to see how you came to be here in Peru and what you should do next."

I nodded and looked at him closely. His eyes were warm and caring and held the same expression I had seen so often on Wil's face, and Sanchez's.

"Good night," Father Carl said, and walked into the bedroom and closed the door. I unrolled my sleeping bag on the floor and fell quickly to sleep.

I woke up with Wil on my mind. I wanted to ask Father Carl what else he knew of Wil's plans. As I lay there thinking, still zipped in the sleeping bag, Father Carl walked into the room quietly and began rebuilding the fire.

I unzipped the bag and he looked over at me, alerted by the sound.

"Good morning," he said. "How did you sleep?"

"Okay," I replied, standing.

He put fresh kindling on the coals and then larger pieces of firewood.

"What did Wil say he was going to do?" I asked.

Father Carl stood and faced me. "He said he was going to a friend's house to wait for some information he expected, apparently information about the Ninth Insight."

"What else did he say?" I asked.

"Wil told me that he thought Father Sebastian intends to find the last insight himself and seems to be close. Wil thinks that the person who controls the last insight will determine whether the Manuscript ever becomes widely distributed and understood."

"Why?"

"I'm not sure really. Wil was one of the first to ever collect and read the insights. He may understand them better than any man alive. He feels, I think, that the last insight will make all the others become more clear and accepted."

"Do you think he is right?" I asked.

"I don't know," he replied. "I don't understand as much as he does. All I understand is what I am supposed to do."

"What is that?"

He paused momentarily, then replied, "As I said before, my truth is to help people discover who they really are. When I read the Manuscript, this mission became clear to me. The Sixth Insight is my special insight. My truth is helping others grasp this insight. And I'm effective because I've gone through the process myself."

"What was your control drama?" I asked.

He looked at me with amusement. "I was an interrogator."

"You controlled people by finding something wrong with the way they lived their lives?"

"That's right. My father was a poor me and my mother was aloof. They completely ignored me. The only way I could get any attention energy was to pry into what they were doing and then point out something wrong with it."

"And when did you work through this drama?"

"About eighteen months ago, when I met Father Sanchez and began to study the Manuscript. After I really looked at my parents, I realized what my experience with them was preparing me to do. You see, my father stood for accomplishment. He was very goal oriented. He planned his time to the minute and judged himself according to how much he got done. My mother was very intuitive and mystical. She believed that each of us received spiritual guidance and that life was about following this direction."

"What did your father think about that?"

"He thought it was crazy."

I smiled but said nothing.

"Can you see where that left me?" Father Carl asked.

I shook my head. I couldn't quite grasp it.

"Because of my father," he said, "I was sensitized to the idea that life was about accomplishment: having something important to do and getting it done. But at the same time my mother was there to tell me life was about inner direction, an intuitive guidance of some sort. I realized that my life was a synthesis of both viewpoints. I was trying to discover how we are guided inwardly toward the mission only we can do, knowing it is of supreme importance to pursue this mission if we are to feel happy and fulfilled."

I nodded.

"And," he continued, "you can see why I was excited about the Sixth Insight. As soon as I read it, I knew that my work was to help people get clear so that they could develop this sense of purpose."

"Do you know how Wil got on the path he is on?"

"Yes, he shared some of this information with me. Wil's drama was to be aloof, like yours. Also, as in your case, each of his parents was an interrogator and each had a strong philosophy they wanted Wil to adopt. Wil's father was a German novelist who argued that the ultimate destiny of the human race was to perfect itself. His father never advocated anything but the purest of humanitarian principles, but the Nazis used his basic idea of perfection to help legitimize their murderous liquidation of what were falsely claimed to be inferior races.

"The corruption of his theme destroyed the old man and led him to move to South America with his wife and Wil. His wife was a Peruvian who grew up in America and was educated there. She was a writer too, but she was basically Eastern in her philosophical beliefs. She held that life was about reaching an inner enlightenment, a higher consciousness marked by peace of mind and detachment from the things of the world. According to her, life was not about perfection; it was about letting go of the need to perfect anything, to go anywhere. . .Can you see where this left Wil?"

I shook my head.

"He was left," Father Carl continued, "in a difficult position. His father championed the Western idea of working for progress and perfection and his mother held the Eastern belief that life was only about reaching inner peace, nothing else.

"These two people had prepared Wil to work on integrating the main philosophical differences between Eastern and Western culture, although he didn't know it at first. He first became an engineer dedicated to progress and then a simple guide who sought peace by bringing people to the beautiful, inwardly moving places in this country.

"But searching out the Manuscript awakened all this in him. The insights speak directly to his main question. They reveal that the thought of both East and West can indeed be integrated into a higher truth. They show us that the West is correct in maintaining that life is about progress, about evolving toward something higher. Yet the East is also correct in emphasizing that we must let go of control with the ego. We can't progress by using logic alone. We have to attain a fuller consciousness, an inner connection with God, because only then can our evolution toward something better be guided by a higher part of ourselves.

"When Wil began to discover the insights, his whole life began to flow. He met Jose, the priest who first found the Manuscript and had it translated. Soon after that, he met the owner of Viciente and helped start the research there. And at about the same time, he met Julia, who was in business, but was also guiding people to the virgin forests.

"It was with Julia that Wil had the most affinity. They hit it off immediately because of the similarity in the questions they pursued. Julia grew up with a father who talked of spiritual ideas but in a capricious and flaky way. Her mother on the other hand was a college speech teacher, a debater, who demanded clear thinking. Naturally, Julia found herself wanting information about spirituality but insisting that it be intelligible and precise.

"Wil wanted a synthesis between East and West that explained human spirituality, and Julia wanted this explanation to be perfectly clear. Something the Manuscript was providing for both."

"Breakfast is ready," Sanchez called from the kitchen.

I turned around, surprised. I didn't realize Sanchez was up. Without pursuing the conversation any further, Father Carl and I got up and joined Sanchez in a meal of fruit and cereal. Afterwards Father Carl asked me to take a walk to the ruins with him. I agreed, wanting very much to go there again. Both of us looked at Father Sanchez and he gracefully declined, explaining that he needed to drive down the mountain and make some phone calls.

Outside, the sky was crystal clear and the sun shone brightly over the peaks. We walked briskly.

"Do you think there is a way to contact Wil?" I asked.

"No," he replied. "He did not tell me who his friends were. The only way would be to drive to Iquitos, a town near the northern border, and I think that might be unsafe right now."

"Why there?" I asked.

"He said he thought his search would take him to this town. There are many ruins near there. Also Cardinal Sebastian has a mission nearby."

"Do you think Wil will find the last insight?"

"I don't know."

We walked in silence for several minutes, then Father Carl asked, "Have you made a decision about what course to take personally?"

"What do you mean?"

"Father Sanchez said you were talking at first about going back immediately to the United States but that lately you seemed to be more interested in exploring the insights. How are you feeling now?"

"Precarious," I said. "But for some reason I also want to continue."

"I understand a man was killed right beside you."

"That's right."

"And still you want to stay?"

"No," I said. "I want to get away, save my life . . . yet here I am."

"Why do you think that is?" he asked.

I scrutinized his expression. "I don't know. Do you?"

"Do you remember where we left our conversation last night?"

I remembered exactly. "We had discovered the question my parents left me with: to find a spirituality that is self-enhancing, that gives one a sense of adventure, and fulfillment. And you said if I looked closely at how my life has evolved, this question would put my life in perspective and clear up what's happening to me now."

He smiled mysteriously. "Yes, according to the Manuscript, it will."

"How does that occur?"

"Each of us must look at the significant turns in our lives and reinterpret them in light of our evolutionary question."

I shook my head, not comprehending.

"Try to perceive the sequence of interests, important friends, coincidences that have occurred in your life. Weren't they leading you somewhere?"

I thought about my life since childhood but could find no pattern.

"How did you spend your time as you grew up?" he asked.

"I don't know. I was a typical child, I guess. I read a lot."

"What did you read?"

"Mystery stuff mostly, science fiction, ghost stories, that kind of thing."

"What happened in your life after that?"

I thought about the effect my grandfather had on me, and told Father Carl about the lake and the mountains.

He nodded his head knowingly. "And after you grew up, what happened?"

"I went away to college. My grandfather died while I was away."

"What did you study at college?"

"Sociology."

"Why?"

"I met a professor I liked. His knowledge of human nature interested me. I decided to study with him."

"What happened then?"

"I graduated and went to work."

"Did you enjoy it?"

"Yes, for a long time."

"Then things changed?"

"I felt that what I was doing wasn't complete. I was working with emotionally disturbed adolescents and I thought I knew how they could transcend their pasts and stop the acting out that was so self-defeating. I thought I could help them go on with their lives. I finally realized something was missing in my approach."

"Then what?"

"I quit."

"And?"

"And then an old friend called and told me of the Manuscript."

"Is that when you decided to come to Peru?"

"Yes."

"What do you think of your experience here?"

"I think I'm crazy," I said. "I think I'm going to get myself killed."

"But what do you think of the way your experience has progressed?"

"I don't understand."

"When Father Sanchez told me what had happened to you since coming to Peru," he said, "I was amazed at the series of coincidences that brought you face to face with the different insights of the Manuscript just when you needed them."

"What do you think that means?" I asked.

He stopped walking and faced me. "It means you were ready. You are like the rest of us here. You came to the point where you needed the Manuscript in order to continue your life evolution.

"Think about how the events of your life fit together. From the beginning you were interested in mysterious topics, and that interest finally led you to study human nature. Why do you think you happened to meet that particular teacher? He crystalized your interests and led you into looking at the greatest mystery: the human situation on this planet, the question of what life is about. Then at some level, you knew that life's meaning was connected to the problem of transcending our past conditioning and moving our lives forward. That's why you were working with those kids.

"But, as you can understand now, it has taken the insights to clear up what was missing in your technique with those youths. In order for emotionally disturbed children to evolve, they have to do what we all have to do: get connected with enough energy to see through their intense control drama, what you call 'acting out,' and go forward in what turns out to be a spiritual process, a process you have been trying to understand all along.

"See the higher perspective on these events. All the interests that led you forward in your past, all these stages of growth, were just preparing you to be here, now, exploring the Insights. You've been working on your evolutionary search for a self-enhancing spirituality throughout your entire life, and the energy you acquired from that natural spot where you grew up, an energy your grandfather was trying to show you, finally gave you the courage to come to Peru. You are here because this is where you need to be to continue the evolution. Your whole life has been a long road leading directly to this moment."

He smiled. "When you fully integrate this view of your life, you will have achieved what the Manuscript calls a clear awareness of your spiritual path. According to the Manuscript we all must spend as much time as necessary going through this process of clearing your past. Most of us have a control drama we have to transcend but once we do, we can comprehend the higher meaning for why we were born to our particular parents, and what all the twists and turns of our lives were preparing us to do. We all have a spiritual purpose, a mission, that we have been pursuing without being fully aware of it, and once we bring it completely into consciousness, our lives can take off.

"In your case, you've discovered this purpose. Now, you must go forward, allowing the coincidences to lead you into a clearer and clearer idea of how to pursue this mission from this point on, what else you must do here. Since you've been in Peru, you've been riding along on Wil's energy and Father Sanchez's. But now it's time to learn to evolve by yourself. . .consciously."

He was about to tell me something more, but we were both distracted by the sight of Sanchez's truck racing up behind us. He pulled along side and rolled down his window.

"What's wrong?" Father Carl asked.

"I must return to the mission as soon as I can get packed," Sanchez said. "Government troops are there. . .and Cardinal Sebastian."

We both jumped into the truck and Sanchez drove back toward Father Carl's house, telling us along the way that the troops were at his mission to confiscate all copies of the Manuscript and possibly to close it down.

We drove up to Father Carl's house and hurriedly walked inside. Father Sanchez immediately began to pack his belongings. I stood there, deliberating on what to do. As I watched, Father Carl approached the other priest and said, "I think I should go with you."

Sanchez turned. "Are you sure?"

"Yes, I believe I should."

"For what purpose?"

"I don't know yet."

Sanchez stared at him for a moment, then returned to packing. "If you think that is best."

I was leaning against the door frame. "What should I do?" I asked.

Both men looked at me.

"That's up to you," Father Carl said.

I just stared.

"You'll have to make the decision," Sanchez interjected.

I couldn't believe they were so detached about my choice. To go with them meant certain capture by the Peruvian troops. Yet how could I stay here, alone?

"Look," I said, "I don't know what to do. You two must help me. Is there anyone else who can hide me?"

Both men looked at one another.

"I don't think so," Father Carl said.

I looked at them, a knot of anxiety growing in my stomach.

Father Carl smiled at me and said, "Stay centered. Remember who you are."

Sanchez walked over to a bag and pulled out a folder. "This is a copy of the Sixth Insight," he said. "Perhaps it will help you decide what to do."

As I took the copy, Sanchez looked at Father Carl and asked, "How long before you can leave?"

"I'll need to contact some people," Father Carl said. "Probably an hour."

Sanchez looked at me. "Read and think for a while, then we will talk."

Both men returned to their preparations, and I walked outside and sat down on a large rock, then opened the Manuscript. It echoed exactly the words of Father Sanchez and Father Carl. Clearing the past was a precise process of becoming aware of our individual ways of controlling learned in childhood. And once we could transcend this habit, it said, we would find our higher selves, our evolutionary identities.

I read the entire text in less than thirty minutes and when I finished I finally understood the basic insight: before we could fully enter the special state of mind that so many people were glimpsing—the experience of ourselves moving onward in life guided by mysterious coincidences—we had to wake up to who we really were.

At that moment Father Carl walked around the house, spotted me, and came to where I was sitting.

"Have you finished?" he asked. His manner was warm and friendly as usual.

"Yes."

"Do you mind if I sit here with you for a moment?"

"I wish you would."

He positioned himself to my right and after a period of silence asked, "Do you understand that you are on your path of discovery here?"

"I guess, but now what?"

"Now you must really believe it."

"How, when I feel this afraid?"

"You must understand what is at stake. The truth you are pursuing is as important as the evolution of the universe itself, for it enables evolution to continue.

"Don't you see? Father Sanchez told me of your vision of evolution on the ridge top. You saw how matter evolved from the simple vibration of hydrogen all the way to humankind. You wondered how humans carried on this evolution. You have now discovered the answer: humans are born into their historical situations and find something to stand for. They form a union with another human being who also has found some purpose.

"The children born to this union then reconcile these two positions by pursuing a higher synthesis, guided by the coincidences. As I'm sure you learned in the Fifth Insight, each time we fill up with energy and a coincidence occurs to lead us forward in our lives, we institute this level of energy in ourselves, and so we can exist at a higher vibration. Our children take our level of vibration and raise it even higher. This is how we, as humans, continue evolution.

"The difference now, with this generation, is that we are ready to do it consciously and to accelerate the process. No matter how afraid you become, you now have no choice. Once you learn what life is about, there is no way to erase the knowledge. If you try to do something else with your life you will always sense that you are missing something."

"But what do I do now?"

"I don't know. Only you know that. But I suggest you first try to gain some energy."

Father Sanchez rounded the corner of the house and joined us, carefully avoiding eye contact or noise as if he desired not to interrupt. I tried to center myself and to focus on the rock peaks that encircled the house. I took a deep breath and realized that I had been totally self-absorbed since coming outside, as if I had had tunnel vision. I had cut myself off from the beauty and majesty of the mountains.

As I gazed out at the surroundings, consciously trying to appreciate what I was seeing, I began to experience that now familiar feeling of closeness. Suddenly everything seemed to exhibit more presence and to glow slightly. I began to feel lighter, my body more buoyant.

I looked at Father Sanchez and then at Father Carl. They were gazing intensely at me and I could tell they were observing my energy field.

"How do I look?" I asked.

"You look as if you feel better," Sanchez said. "Stay here and increase your energy as much as possible. We have about twenty more minutes of packing."

He smiled wryly. "After that," he continued, "you will be ready to begin."

ENGAGING
THE FLOW

The two priests walked back to the house and I spent several more minutes observing the beauty of the mountains in an attempt to gain more energy. Then, I lost my focus and drifted absently into a reverie about Wil. Where was he? Was he close to finding the Ninth Insight?

I imagined him running through the Jungle, the Ninth Insight in his hand, troops everywhere, pursuing. I thought of Sebastian orchestrating the chase. Yet in my daydream, it was clear that Sebastian, even with all his authority, was wrong, that he misunderstood something about the impact the insights would have on people. I felt that someone could persuade him to take a different view, if only we could discover what part of the Manuscript threatened him so.

As I mused over this thought, Marjorie popped into my mind. Where was she? I pictured seeing her again. How might that happen?

The sound of the front door closing brought me back to reality. I felt weak and nervous again. Sanchez walked around the house toward where I was sitting. His pace was quick, purposeful.

He sat down beside me, then asked, "Have you decided what to do?"

I shook my head.

"You don't look very strong," he said.

"I don't feel very strong."

"Perhaps you're not being very systematic in the way you build your energy."

"What do you mean?"

"Let me offer you the way that I personally gain energy. Perhaps my method will help you as you create your own procedure."

I nodded for him to go on.

"The first thing I do," he said, "is to focus on the environment around me, as I think you do also. Then I try to remember how everything looks when I'm being filled with energy. I do this by recalling the presence everything displays, the unique beauty and shape of everything, especially plants, and the way colors seem to glow and appear brighter. Do you follow me?"

"Yes, I try to do the same thing."

"Then," he continued. "I try to experience that feeling of closeness, the feeling that no matter how far away something is, that I can touch it, connect with it. And then I breathe it in."

"Breathe it in?"

"Did Father John not explain this to you?"

"No, he didn't."

Sanchez appeared confused. "Perhaps he intended to come back and tell you about it later. Often he's very dramatic. He walks away and leaves his pupil alone to ponder what he has taught, then he shows up later at just the right time to add something else to the instruction. I suppose he intended to talk with you again but we left too quickly."

"I'd like to hear about it," I said.

"Do you remember the feeling of buoyancy that you experienced on the ridge top?" he asked.

"Yes," I said.

"To regain this buoyancy, I try to breathe in the energy with which I have just connected."

I had been following along as Sanchez spoke. Just hearing his procedure was increasing my connection. Everything around me had increased in presence and beauty. Even the rocks seemed to have a whitish glow and Sanchez's energy field was wide and blue. He was now taking deep, conscious breaths, holding each about five seconds before exhaling. I followed his example.

"When we visualize," he said, "that each breath pulls energy into us and fills us like a balloon, we actually become more energized and feel much lighter and more buoyant."

After several breaths, I began to feel exactly that way.

"After I breath in the energy," Sanchez continued, "I check to see if I have the right emotion. As I've told you before, I consider this the true measure of whether I am really connected."

"You are speaking of love?"

"That's correct. As we discussed at the mission, love is not an intellectual concept or a moral imperative or anything else. It is a background emotion that exists when one is connected to the energy available in the universe, which, of course, is the energy of God."

Father Sanchez was gazing at me, his eyes slightly out of focus. "There," he said, "you've reached it. That's the level of energy you need to have. I'm helping you some, but you are ready to maintain it on your own."

"What do you mean, you're helping me some?"

Father Sanchez shook his head. "Don't worry about that now. You'll learn about it later, in the Eighth Insight."

Father Carl walked around the house then and looked at both of us, as though pleased. As he approached he glanced at me. "Have you decided yet?"

The question irritated me; I fought against the resulting loss of energy.

"Don't fall back into your aloof drama," Father Carl said. "You can't avoid taking a stand here. What are you thinking you need to do?"

"I'm not thinking anything," I said. "That's the problem."

"Are you sure? Thoughts feel different once you get connected with the energy."

I gave him a puzzled look.

"The words you have habitually willed through your head in an attempt to logically control events," he explained, "stop when you give up your control drama. As you fill up with inner energy, other kinds of thoughts enter your mind from a higher part of yourself. These are your intuitions. They feel different. They just appear in the back of your mind, sometimes in a kind of daydream or mini-vision, and they come to direct you, to guide you."

I still didn't understand.

"Tell us what you were thinking about when we left you alone earlier," Father Carl said.

"I'm not sure I remember it all," I said.

"Try."

I tried to concentrate. "I was thinking about Wil, I guess, about whether he was close to finding the Ninth Insight, and about Sebastian's crusade against the Manuscript."

"What else?"

"I was wondering about Marjorie, about what happened to her. But I don't understand how this helps me know what to do."

"Let me explain," Father Sanchez said. "When you have acquired enough energy, you are ready to consciously engage evolution, to start it flowing, to produce the coincidences that will lead you forward. You engage your evolution in a very specific way. First, as I said, you build sufficient energy, then you remember your basic life question—the one your parents gave you—because this question provides the overall context for your evolution. Next you center yourself on your path by discovering the immediate, smaller questions that currently confront you in life. These questions always pertain to your larger question and define where you currently are in your lifelong quest.

"Once you become conscious of the questions active in the moment, you always get some kind of intuitive direction of what to do, of where to go. You get a hunch about the next step. Always. The only time this will not occur is when you have the wrong question in mind. You see, the problem in life isn't in receiving answers. The problem is in identifying your current questions. Once you get the questions right, the answers always come.

"After you get an intuition of what might happen next," he continued, "then the next step is to become very alert and watchful. Sooner or later coincidences will occur to move you in the direction indicated by the intuition. Do you follow me?"

"I think I do."

"So," he continued, "don't you think those thoughts of Wil and Sebastian and Marjorie are important? Think about why these thoughts are coming now, considering the story of your life. You know that you came out of your family wanting to find out how to make the spiritual life an inwardly self- enhancing adventure, right?"

"Yes."

"Then, as you grew up, you became interested in mysterious topics, you studied sociology and worked with people, although you didn't yet know why you were doing these things. Then as you began to wake up, you heard about the Manuscript and came to Peru and found the insights one by one, and each has taught you something about the kind of spirituality you seek. Now that you've become clear, you can become super conscious of this evolution by defining your current questions and then watching the answers come."

I just looked at him.

"What are your current questions?" he asked.

"I guess I want to know about the other insights," I said. "Especially, I want to know if Wil is going to find the Ninth Insight. I want to know what happened to Marjorie. And I want to know about Sebastian."

"And what were your intuitions suggesting about these questions?"

"I don't know. I was thinking of seeing Marjorie again, and of Wil running with troops chasing him. What does it mean?"

"Where was Wil running?"

"In the jungle."

"Perhaps that indicates where you should go. Iquitos is in the jungle. What about Marjorie?"

"I saw myself seeing her again."

"And Sebastian?"

"I fantasized that he was against the Manuscript because he misunderstood, that his mind could be changed if one could find out what he was thinking, what exactly he feared about the Manuscript."

Both men looked at each other in total amazement.

"What does it mean?" I asked.

Father Carl replied with another question, "What do you think?"

For the first time since the ridge top I was beginning to feel fully ener-gized again and confident. I looked at them and said, "I guess it means I should go toward the jungle and try to discover which aspects of the Manuscript the church dislikes."

Father Carl smiled. "Exactly! You can take my truck."

I nodded and we walked around to the front of the house where the vehicles were parked. My things, along with a supply of food and water, were already packed in Father Carl's truck. Father Sanchez's vehicle was also packed.

"I want to tell you this," Sanchez said. "Remember to stop as often as necessary to re-connect your energy. Stay full, stay in a state of love. Remember that once you achieve this state of love, nothing nor anyone can pull more energy from you than you can replace. In fact, the energy flowing out of you creates a current that pulls energy into you at the same rate. You can never run out. But you must stay conscious of this process in order for it to work. This is especially important when you interact with people."

He paused. Simultaneously, as if on cue, Father Carl walked closer and said, "You have read all but two insights: the Seventh and Eighth. Seven deals with the process of consciously evolving yourself, of staying alert to every coincidence, every answer the universe provides for you."

He handed me a small folder. "This is the Seventh. It is very short and general," he continued, "but it talks about the way objects jump out at us, the way certain thoughts come as guidance. As for the Eighth, you will find it yourself when the time is right. It explains how we can aid others as they bring us the answers we seek. And further, it describes a whole new ethic governing the way humans should treat each other in order to facilitate everyone's evolution."

"Why can't you give me the Eighth Insight now?" I asked.

Father Carl smiled and put his hand on my shoulder. "Because we don't feel we should. We must follow our intuitions also. You will get the Eighth Insight as soon as you ask the right question."

I told him I understood. Then both priests hugged me and wished me well. Father Carl stressed that we would soon meet again and that I would indeed find the answers I was here to receive.

We were all about to board our respective vehicles when Sanchez turned suddenly and faced me. "I have an intuition to tell you something. You will learn more about it later. Let your perception of beauty and iridescence lead your way. Places and people who have answers for you will appear more luminous and attractive."

I nodded and climbed into Father Carl's truck, then followed them down the rocky road for several miles until we came to a fork. Sanchez waved out the back window as he and Father Carl headed East. I watched them for a moment then turned the old truck North toward the Amazon basin.

A surge of impatience rose up within me. After making good time for over three hours, I now sat at a crossroads, unable to decide between two particular routes.

To my left was one possibility. Judging from the map, this road bore north along the edge of the mountains for a hundred miles, then turned sharply east toward Iquitos. The other route lead to the right and maintained an eastern angle through the jungle to the same destination.

I took a deep breath and tried to relax, then quickly checked the rear view mirror. No one was in sight. In fact, I hadn't seen anyone—no traffic, no locals walking—in over an hour. I tried to shake off a rush of anxiety. I knew I had to relax and stay connected if I expected to make the right decision.

I focused on the scene. The jungle route to my right progressed between a group of large trees. Several huge outcroppings of rock punctuated the ground around them. Most were encircled by large tropical bushes. The other route through the mountains seemed comparatively bare. One tree grew in that direction, but the remainder of the landscape was rocky, with very little plant life.

I looked to the right again and tried to induce a love state. The trees and bushes were a rich green. I looked to the left and tried the same procedure. Immediately I noticed a patch of flowering grass that bordered the road. The blades of grass were pale and spotty, but the white flowers, viewed together, created a unique pattern into the distance. I wondered why I hadn't noticed the flowers earlier. They now seemed to almost glow. I broadened my focus to include everything in that direction. The small rocks and brown patches of gravel seemed extraordinarily colorful and distinct. Hues of amber and violet and even dark red ran through the entire scene.

I glanced back to the right to the trees and bushes. Although beautiful, they now paled in comparison to the other route. But how could that be, I thought. Initially, the road to the right seemed more attractive. Glancing back to the left, my intuition strengthened. The richness of shape and color amazed me.

I was convinced. I started the truck and headed to the left, sure of the correctness of my decision. The road was bumpy with rocks and ruts. As I bounced along, my body felt lighter. My weight was centered on my buttocks, and my back and neck were straight. My arms were holding the steering wheel but were not resting on it.

For two hours I drove without incident, nibbling from the food basket Father Carl had packed and again seeing no one. The road meandered up and down one small foothill after another. At the top of one hill, I observed two older cars parked to my right. They were pulled far off to the side of the road in a stand of small trees. I could see no occupants and assumed the vehicles were abandoned. Ahead the road turned sharply to the left and circled downward into a wide valley. From the peak I could see for several miles.

I stopped the truck abruptly. Half way across the valley three or four military vehicles sat along both sides of the road. A small group of soldiers stood among the trucks. A chill ran through me. That was a roadblock. I backed off the crest and pulled my vehicle behind two large rocks, then got out and walked back to the overlook to again observe the activity in the valley. One vehicle was driving away in the opposite direction.

Suddenly I heard something behind me. I turned around quickly. It was Phil, the ecologist I had met at Viciente.

He was equally shocked. "What are you doing here?" he asked, as he rushed up to me.

"I'm trying to get to Iquitos," I said.

His face was filled with anxiety. "So are we, but the government's getting crazy over this Manuscript. We're trying to decide whether to risk passing through that roadblock. There are four of us." He nodded to his left. I could see several men through the trees.

"Why are you going to Iquitos?" he asked.

"I'm trying to find Wil. We got separated in Cula. But I heard he might be headed to Iquitos, looking for the rest of the Manuscript."

He looked horrified. "He shouldn't be doing that! The military has prohibited anyone having copies. Didn't you hear what occurred at Viciente?"

"Yeah, some, but what did you hear?"

"I wasn't there but I understand the authorities rushed in and arrested everyone who had copies. All the guests were detained for questioning. Dale and the other scientists were taken away. No one knows what happened to them."

"Do you know why the government is so disturbed about this Manuscript?" I asked.

"No, but when I heard how unsafe it was getting, I decided to return to Iquitos for my research data and then to leave the country myself."

I told him the details of what had happened to Wil and myself after leaving Viciente, especially the shooting on the ridge top.

"Damn," he said. "And you're still fooling around with this thing?"

His statement jarred my confidence, but I said, "Look, if we do nothing, the government is going to suppress the Manuscript completely. The world will be denied its knowledge, and I think the insights are important!"

"Important enough to die for?" he asked.

The sound of vehicles attracted our attention. The trucks were driving across the valley toward us.

"Oh shit!" he said. "Here they come."

Before we could move, we heard the sound of vehicles approaching from the other direction as well.

"They've surrounded us!" Phil shouted. He looked panicked.

I ran to the truck and dumped the basket of food into a small pack. I took the folders containing the Manuscript and placed them in the pack as well, then thought better of it and pushed them under the seat instead.

The sounds were growing louder so I ran across the road to my right in the direction Phil had headed. Down the slope I could see him and the other men huddled behind a group of rocks. I hid with them. My hope was that the military trucks would pass and keep going. My truck was out of sight. Hopefully they would think, as I did, that the other cars were abandoned.

The trucks approaching from the south arrived first and to our horror stopped even with the vehicles.

"Don't move. Police!" a voice shouted. We froze as several soldiers walked up from behind us. All were heavily armed and very cautious. The soldiers searched us thoroughly and took everything, then forced us to walk back to the road. There, dozens of soldiers were searching the vehicles. Phil and his companions were taken and placed in one of the military trucks, which quickly drove away. As he rode past me, I caught sight of him. He looked pale and ghostly.

I was led on foot in the opposite direction and asked to sit near the crest of the hill. Several soldiers stood near me, each carrying an automatic weapon on his shoulder. Finally an officer walked over and tossed the folders containing my copies of the insights on the ground at my feet. On top of them he threw the keys to Father Carl's truck.

"Are these copies yours?" he asked.

I looked at him without answering.

"These keys were found on you," he said. "Inside the vehicle we found these copies. I ask you again, are they yours?"

"I don't think I'll answer until I see a lawyer," I stammered. The remark brought a sarcastic smile to the officer's face. He said something to the other soldiers and walked away. The soldiers directed me to one of the jeeps and into the front seat by the driver. Two other soldiers sat in the back seat, their weapons ready. Behind us, more soldiers climbed aboard a second truck. After a short wait, both vehicles headed north into the valley.

Anxious thoughts filled my mind. Where were they taking me? Why did I put myself into this position? So much for the preparation the priests had given me; I hadn't lasted a day. Back at the crossroads, I had been so certain I had chosen the correct road. This route was the one most attractive; I was sure of it. Where did I make my mistake?

I took a deep breath and attempted to relax, wondering what would happen now. I would plead ignorance, I thought, and present myself as a misguided tourist meaning no harm. I just got mixed up with the wrong people, I would say. Let me go home.

My hands were resting in my lap; they were shaking slightly. One of the soldiers sitting behind me offered a canteen of water and I took it, though I could not drink. The soldier was young and when I handed the canteen back to him, he smiled without a trace of malice on his face. The image of Phil's panicked look flashed across my mind. What would they do with him?

The thought occurred to me that meeting Phil on that hilltop had been a coincidence. What was its meaning? What would we have talked about had we not been interrupted? As it was, all I did was stress the Manuscript's importance, and all he did was warn me about the danger here and counsel me to get out before being captured. Unfortunately, his advice had come too late.

For several hours we rode without anyone speaking. The terrain outside grew progressively more flat. The air warmed. At one point, the young soldier handed me an open can of C rations, something like beef hash, but again I couldn't force anything down. After sunset the light faded quickly.

I rode along without thought, staring straight ahead with the truck's headlights, then I slipped into a restless sleep during which I dreamed of being in flight. I was running desperately from an unknown foe amid hundreds of huge bonfires, certain that somewhere was a secret key that would open the way to knowledge and safety. In the middle of one of the giant fires I saw the key. I darted in to retrieve it!

I jerked awake, sweating profusely. The soldiers glanced at me nervously. I shook my head and leaned against the truck's door. For a long time, I looked out the side window at the dark shapes of the landscape, fighting the urge to panic. I was alone and under guard, heading into blackness, and no one cared about my nightmares.

About midnight we pulled up to a large, dimly lit building constructed of cut stone and two stories high. We walked along a walkway past the front entrance and entered a side door. Steps led down to a narrow hall. The inner walls were also of stone and the ceiling was constructed of large timbers and rough cut planks. Bare bulbs hanging from the ceiling lit our way. We walked through another door and then into an area of cells. One of the soldiers who had disappeared caught up with us and opened one of the cell doors and motioned for me to enter.

Inside were three cots, a wooden table and a vase of flowers. To my surprise, the cell was very clean. As I walked in, a young Peruvian, no more than eighteen or nineteen years old, looked at me meekly from behind the door. The soldier locked the door behind me and walked away. I sat down on one of the cots as the young man reached over and turned up an oil lamp. When the light hit his face I noticed that he was an Indian.

"Do you speak English?" I asked.

"Yes, some," he said.

"Where are we?"

"Near Pullcupa."

"Is this a prison?"

"No, everyone is here for questioning about the Manuscript."

"How long have you been here?" I asked.

He looked up at me with shy, brown eyes. "Two months."

"What have they done to you?"

"They try to make me disbelieve the Manuscript and tell about others who have copies."

"How?"

"By talking to me."

"Just talking, no threats?"

"Just talking," he repeated.

"Have they said when they will let you go?"

"No."

I paused for a moment and he looked at me questioningly. "Were you caught with copies of the Manuscript?" he asked.

"Yes. Were you?"

"Yes. I live near here, in an orphanage. My headmaster was teaching from the Manuscript. He allowed me to teach the children. He was able to escape but I was captured."

"How many insights have you seen?" I asked.

"All that have been found," he said. "You?"

"Eh, I've seen all but the Seventh and Eighth Insights. I had the Seventh but I didn't get a chance to read it before the soldiers showed up."

The young man yawned and asked, "Can we sleep now?"

"Yeah," I said absently. "Sure."

I laid on my cot and shut my eyes, my mind racing. What should I do now? How had I let myself be caught? Could I escape? I concocted several strategies and scenarios before I finally drifted off to sleep.

Again I dreamed vividly. I was searching for the same key but this time I was lost in a deep forest. For a long time I had been walking aimlessly, wishing for some sort of guidance. After a while, a huge thunderstorm came and flooded the landscape. During the deluge, I was washed down a deep ravine and into the river, which was flowing in the wrong direction and threatening to drown me. With all my might I fought against the current, struggling for what seemed like days. Finally, I was able to pull myself from the torrent by clinging to the rocky shoreline. I climbed up the rocks and along the sheer cliffs that bordered the river, ascending higher and higher and into ever more treacherous areas. Although I had summoned all my willpower and expertise to negotiate the cliffs, at one point I found myself clinging perilously to the rock face, unable to proceed any further. I looked down at the terrain below me. In shock, I realized that the river I had been fighting flowed out of the forest and gently up to a beautiful beach and meadow. In the meadow, surrounded by flowers, was the key. Then I slipped and fell screaming down and down until I hit the river and sank.

I sat up quickly in my cot, gasping for air. The young Indian, apparently already awake, walked over to me.

"What is wrong?" he asked.

I caught my breath and looked around, realizing where I was. I also noticed that the room had a window and that it was already light outside.

"Just a bad dream," I said.

He smiled at me as though he was pleased at what I said. "Bad dreams have the most important messages," he commented.

"Messages?" I asked, getting up and putting on my shirt.

He looked embarrassed at having to explain. "The Seventh Insight talks of dreams," he said.

"What does it say about dreams?"

"It tells how to, eh . . ."

"Interpret dreams?"

"Yes."

"What does it say about that?"

"It says to compare the story of the dream to the story of your life."

I thought for a moment, unsure of what that instruction meant. "What do you mean, compare stories?"

The young Indian could barely look me in the eye. "Do you want to interpret your dream?"

I nodded and told him what I had experienced.

He listened intently, then said, "Compare parts of the story with your life."

I looked at him. "Where do I start?"

"At the beginning. What are you doing at the beginning of the dream?"

"I was searching for a key in a forest."

"How did you feel?"

"Lost."

"Compare this situation to your real situation."

"Maybe it does relate," I said "I'm looking for some answers about this Manuscript and I'm damn sure feeling lost."

"And what else is happening to you in real life?" he asked.

"I've been caught," I said. "In spite of everything I tried to do, I've been locked up. All I can hope for now is to talk someone into letting me go home."

"You are struggling against being caught?"

"Of course."

"What happened next in the dream?"

"I fought against the current."

"Why?" he asked.

I began to pick up on where he was headed. "Because at the time I thought it would drown me."

"And if you hadn't fought the water?"

"It would have carried me to the key. What are you saying? That if I don't fight against this situation that I might still get the answers I want?"

He looked embarrassed again. "I'm not saying anything. The dream is saying."

I thought for a moment. Was this interpretation correct?

The young Indian looked up at me, then asked, "If you had to experience the dream again, what would you do different?"

"I wouldn't resist the water, even though it looked as though it might kill me. I would know better."

"What is threatening you now?"

"I guess the soldiers. Being detained."

"So what is the message to you?"

"You think the message of the dream is to look at this capture positively?"

He didn't answer; he only smiled.

I was sitting on my cot leaning back against the wall. The interpretation excited me. If it was accurate, it would mean that I hadn't made a mistake at the crossroads after all, that this was all part of what should be happening.

"What is your name?" I asked.

"Pablo," he said.

I smiled and introduced myself, then briefly told him the story of why I was in Peru and what had happened. Pablo was sitting on his cot, his elbows resting on his knees. He had short, black hair and was very thin.

"Why are you here?" he asked.

"To find out about this Manuscript," I replied.

"Why specifically?" he asked again.

"To find out about the Seventh Insight and to find out about some friends, Wil and Marjorie. . .and I guess to find out why the church is so against the Manuscript."

"There are many Priests here to talk to," he said.

I thought about his statement for a moment then asked, "What else does the Seventh Insight say about dreams?"

Pablo told me that dreams come to tell us something about our lives that we are missing. Then he said something else but instead of listening, I started to think about Marjorie. I could see her face clearly in my mind and I wondered where she might be, then I saw her running up to me smiling.

Suddenly I became aware that Pablo was no longer talking. I looked over at him. "Sorry, my mind was wandering," I said. "What were you saying?"

"That is all right," he replied. "What were you thinking about?"

"Just a friend of mine. It was nothing."

He looked as though he wanted to press the question, but someone was approaching the cell door. Through the bars we could see a soldier sliding back the bolt lock.

"Time for breakfast," Pablo said.

The soldier opened the door and motioned with his head for us to walk into the hall. Pablo led the way down the stone corridor. We proceeded to a stairway and up one flight of stairs to a small dining area. Four or five soldiers stood at the corner of the room while several civilians, two men and a woman, waited in line to be served.

I stopped, not believing my eyes. The woman was Marjorie. Simultaneously, she saw me and covered her mouth with her hand, her eyes opening wide with surprise. I glanced at the soldier behind me. He was walking toward the other military men in the corner, smiling nonchalantly and saying something in Spanish. I followed Pablo as he led us across the room and to the end of the line.

Marjorie was being served. The two other men took their trays to a table, talking. Several times Marjorie gazed over and met my eyes, struggling not to say anything. After the second glance, Pablo guessed that we knew each other and looked at me questioningly. Marjorie carried her food to a table, and after being served, we walked over and sat with her. The soldiers were still talking among themselves, seemingly oblivious to our movements.

"God, I'm glad to see you," she said. "How did you get here?"

"I hid for a while with some priests," I replied. "Then I left to find Wil and was captured yesterday. How long have you been here?"

"Since they found me on the ridge," she said.

I noticed Pablo was looking at us intensely and I introduced him to Marjorie.

"I guessed that this must be Marjorie," he said.

They talked briefly, then I asked Marjorie, "What else has happened?"

"Not much," she said. "I don't even know why I'm being detained. Every day I've been taken to one of the priests or to one of the officers for questioning. They want to know who my contacts were at Viciente, and if I know where any other copies are. Over and over again!"

Marjorie smiled and looked vulnerable and when she did, I felt another strong attraction to her. She looked at me sharply, out of the corner of her eyes. We both laughed quietly. A period of silence followed as we ate our food, and then the door opened and in walked a priest, dressed formally. He was accompanied by a man appearing to be a high ranking military officer.

"That's the head priest," Pablo said.

The officer said something to the soldiers, who had snapped to attention, and then he and the priest walked across the room toward the kitchen. The priest looked directly at me, our eyes meeting for a long second. I looked away and took a bite of food, not wanting to attract attention. Both men continued through the kitchen and out a door there.

"Was that one of the priests you've talked to?" I asked Marjorie.

"No," Marjorie said. "I've never seen him."

"I know that priest," Pablo said. "He arrived yesterday. His name is Cardinal Sebastian."

I sat up straight. "That was Sebastian?"

"It sounds like you've heard of him," Marjorie said.

"I have," I replied. "He's the main person behind the Church's opposition to the Manuscript. I thought he was at Father Sanchez's Mission."

"Who is Father Sanchez?" Marjorie asked.

I was about to tell her when the soldier who had escorted us walked over to the table and motioned for Pablo and me to follow.

"Time for exercise," Pablo said.

Marjorie and I looked at each other. Her eyes revealed an inner anxiety.

"Don't worry," I said, "I'll talk to you at the next meal. Everything will be fine."

As I walked away, I wondered if my optimism was realistic. These people could make any of us disappear without a trace at any time. The soldier guided us into a short hall and through a door that led to an outside stairway. We walked down to a side yard which was surrounded by a tall rock wall. The soldier stood by the entrance. Pablo nodded for me to walk with him around the borders of the yard. As we walked, Pablo bent down several times to pick some of the flowers growing in beds by the wall.

"What else does the Seventh Insight say?" I asked.

He bent down and picked another flower. "It says that not only dreams guide us. Also thoughts or daydreams guide us."

"Yes, Father Carl said that. Tell me how daydreams guide us."

"They show us a scene, a happening, and this is an indication that this event might happen. If we pay attention then we can be ready for this turn in our lives."

I looked at him. "You know, Pablo, an image came to me that I would run into Marjorie. Then I did."

He smiled.

A chill went up my spine. I must indeed be in the right place. I had intuited something that had come true. I had thought several times of finding Marjorie again and now it had happened. The coincidences were taking place. I felt lighter.

"I don't have thoughts like that happen very often," I said.

Pablo looked away, then said, "The Seventh Insight says that we all have many more such thoughts than we realize. To recognize them we must take an observer position. When a thought comes, we must ask why? Why did this particular thought come now? How does it relate to my life questions? Taking this observer position helps us release our need to control everything. It places us in the flow of evolution."

"But what about negative thoughts?" I asked. "Those fear images of something bad happening, such as someone we love getting hurt, or of not achieving something we very much want?"

"Very simple," Pablo said. "The Seventh Insight says that fear images should be halted as soon as they come. Then another image, one with a good outcome, should be willed through the mind. Soon, negative images will almost never happen. Your intuitions will be about positive things. When negative images come after that, the Manuscript says they should be taken very seriously, and not followed. For instance, if the idea comes to you that you're going to have a wreck in a truck and someone comes along and offers you a ride in a truck, then do not accept it."

We had come full circle in our walk around the courtyard and were approaching the guard. Neither of us talked as we passed him. Pablo picked a flower and I took a deep breath. The air was warm and humid, and the plant life outside the wall was dense and tropical. I had noticed several mosquitoes.

"Come!" the soldier suddenly called out.

He prodded us inside and down to our cell. Pablo entered ahead of me, but the soldier put his arm up blocking my way.

"Not you," he said, then nodded for me to walk down the hallway and up the other steps and outside through the same door we had entered the night before. In the parking lot, Father Sebastian was entering the back seat of a large car. A driver shut the door behind him. For an instant Sebastian looked at me again, then he turned and said something to the driver. The car sped away.

The soldier nudged me toward the front of the building. We walked inside and into an office. I was directed to sit in a wooden chair across from a white metal desk. Within minutes a small, sandy-haired priest of about thirty entered and sat at the desk without acknowledging my presence. He looked through a file for a full minute, then looked up at me. His round, gold-rimmed glasses produced an intellectual appearance.

"You've been arrested with illegal state documents," he said matter-of-factly. "I'm here to help determine whether prosecution is in order. I would appreciate your cooperation."

I nodded.

"Where did you get the translations?"

"I don't understand," I said. "Why would copies of an old manuscript be illegal?"

"The government of Peru has its reasons," he said. "Please answer the question."

"Why is the church involved?" I asked.

"Because this Manuscript contradicts the traditions of our religion," he said. "It misrepresents the truth of our spiritual nature. Where . . ."

"Look," I said, interrupting. "I'm just trying to understand this. I'm just a tourist who got interested in this Manuscript. I'm a threat to no one. I only want to know why it is so alarming."

He looked puzzled, as if trying to decide the best strategy for dealing with me. I was consciously pressing for details.

"The church feels the Manuscript is confusing to our people," he said carefully. "It gives the impression that people can decide on their own how to live, without regard to the scriptures."

"Which scriptures?"

"The commandment to honor thy father and mother, for one."

"What do you mean?"

"The Manuscript blames problems on parents, undermining the family."

"I thought it spoke of ending old resentments," I said. "And finding a positive view of our early life."

"No," he said. "It is misleading. There should never have been a negative feeling to begin with."

"Can't parents be wrong?"

"Parents do the best they can. Children must forgive them."

"But isn't that what the Manuscript is clarifying? Doesn't forgiveness take place when we see the positive about our childhoods?"

His voice rose with anger. "But from what authority does this Manuscript speak? How can it be trusted?"

He walked around the desk and stared down at me, still angry. "You don't know what you're talking about," he said. "Are you a religious scholar? I think not. You're direct evidence of the kind of confusion this Manuscript evokes. Don't you understand that there is order in the world only because of law and authority? How can you question the authorities in this matter?"

I said nothing, which seemed to infuriate him even more. "Let me tell you something," he said, "the crime you have committed is punishable by years in prison. Have you ever been in a Peruvian prison? Does your Yankee curiosity yearn to find out what our prisons are like? I can arrange that! Do you understand? I can arrange that!"

He put his hand over his eyes and paused, taking a deep breath, obviously trying to calm down. "I am here to find out who has copies, where they are coming from. I will ask you one more time. Where did you get your translations?"

His outburst had filled me with anxiety. I was making my situation worse with all my questions. What might he do if I failed to cooperate? Still, how could I implicate Father Sanchez and Father Carl?

"I need some time to think before I answer you," I said.

Momentarily he looked as if he might fly into another rage. Then he relaxed and looked very tired.

"I will give you until tomorrow morning," he said, motioning for the soldier standing in the doorway to take me away. I followed the soldier back down the hall and directly to the cell.

Without saying anything I walked over and lay down on my cot, feeling exhausted myself. Pablo was looking out the barred window.

"Did you talk to Father Sebastian?" he asked.

"No, it was another priest. He wanted to know who gave me the copies I had."

"What did you say?"

"Nothing. I asked for time to think and he gave me until tomorrow."

"Did he say anything about the Manuscript?" Pablo asked.

I looked into Pablo's eyes and this time he did not lower his head. "He talked a little about how the Manuscript undermines traditional authority," I said. "Then he started raving and threatening me."

Pablo looked genuinely surprised. "Did he have brown hair and round glasses?"

"Yes."

"His name is Father Costous," Pablo said. "What else did you say?"

"I disagreed with him on whether the Manuscript undermines tradition," I replied. "He threatened me with prison. Do you think he meant that?"

"I don't know," Pablo said. He walked over and sat on his cot across from me. I could tell he had something else on his mind but I was so tired and scared that I closed my eyes. When I awoke Pablo was shaking me.

"Time for lunch," he said.

We followed a guard upstairs and were served a plate of gristly beef and potatoes. The two men who we saw earlier came in after us. Marjorie wasn't with them.

"Where is Marjorie?" I asked them, trying to whisper. The two men looked horrified that I would speak to them and the soldiers stared at me intensely.

"I don't think they speak English," Pablo said.

"I wonder where she is," I said.

Pablo said something in response but again I wasn't listening. I suddenly felt like running away and was picturing myself fleeing down a street of some kind, then ducking through a doorway, to freedom.

"What are you thinking about?" Pablo asked.

"I was fantasizing about an escape," I said. "What were you saying?"

"Wait," Pablo said. "Don't dismiss your thought. It may be important. What kind of escape?"

"I was running down an alley, or a street, then through a doorway. I got the impression I was successfully escaping."

"What do you think of this image?" Pablo asked.

"I don't know," I said. "It didn't seem to be logically connected to what we were talking about."

"Do you remember what we were talking about?"

"Yes. I was asking about Marjorie."

"You don't think there is a connection between Marjorie and your thought?"

"Not an obvious link I can think of."

"What about a hidden link?"

"I can't see a connection. How could escaping be related to Marjorie? Do you think she escaped?"

He looked thoughtful. "Your thought was of you escaping."

"Oh yeah, that's right," I said. "Maybe I'm going to escape without her." I looked at him. "Maybe I'm going to escape *with* her."

"That would be my guess," he said.

"But where is she?"

"I don't know."

We finished eating without talking. I was hungry but the food seemed too heavy. For some reason, I felt tired and sluggish. My hunger left me quickly.

I noticed Pablo wasn't eating either.

"I think we should go back to the cell," Pablo said.

I nodded, and he motioned for the soldier to take us back. When we arrived, I stretched out on my cot and Pablo sat looking at me.

"Your energy seems down," he said.

"It is," I replied. "I'm not sure what is wrong."

"Are you trying to take in energy?" he asked.

"I guess I haven't," I replied. "And that food doesn't help."

"But you don't need much food if you are taking everything in." He swept his arm in front of him to emphasize everything.

"I know. It's hard for me to get the love flowing in a situation like this."

He looked at me quizzically. "But not to do so is to harm yourself."

"What do you mean?"

"Your body is vibrating at a certain level. If you let your energy get too low your body suffers. That is the relationship between stress and disease. Love is the way we keep our vibration up. It keeps us healthy. It is that important."

"Give me a few minutes," I said.

I practiced the method Father Sanchez had taught me. Immediately I felt better. The objects around me stood out with presence. I closed my eyes and concentrated on the feeling.

"That's good," he said.

I opened my eyes and saw him smiling broadly at me. His face and body were still boyish and immature, but his eyes now seemed full of wisdom.

"I can see the energy coming into you," he said.

I could detect a slight field of green around Pablo's body. The new flowers he had placed in the vase on the table seemed radiant.

"To grasp the Seventh Insight and truly enter the movement of evolution," he said, "one must pull all the insights into one way of being."

I didn't say anything.

"Can you sum up how the world has changed for you as a result of the insights?"

I thought for a moment. "I guess I've woken up and seen the world as a mysterious place that provides everything we need, if we get clear and get on the path."

"Then what happens?" he asked.

"Then, we're ready to begin the evolutionary flow."

"And how do we engage this process?"

I thought for a moment. "By keeping our current life questions firmly in mind," I said. "And then watching for direction, either in a dream or in an intuitive thought or in the way the environment illuminates and jumps out at us."

I paused again, trying to pull the whole insight together, then added, "We build our energy and center ourselves in our situations, in the questions we have, then we receive some form of intuitive guidance, an idea of where to go or what to do, and then coincidences occur to allow us to move in that direction."

"Yes! Yes!" Pablo said. "That is the way. And each time that these coincidences lead us into something new, we grow, we become fuller persons, existing at a higher vibration."

He was leaning toward me, and I noticed the incredible energy around him. He was beaming, no longer appearing shy or even young. He seemed full of power.

"Pablo, what has happened to you?" I asked. "Compared to when I first met you, you seem more confident and knowledgeable and full somehow."

He laughed. "When you first came, I had allowed my energy to dissipate. At first, I thought that you might be able to help me with my energy flow, but I realized that you haven't learned to do this yet. That ability is learned in the Eighth Insight."

I was puzzled. "What was it that I didn't do?"

"You must learn that all the answers that mysteriously come to us really come from other people. Think about all that you have learned since you have been in Peru. Haven't all the answers come to you through the actions of other people you mysteriously met?"

I thought about it. He was right. I had met just the right people at just the right time: Charlene, Dobson, Wil, Dale, Marjorie, Phil, Reneau, Father Sanchez and Father Carl, now Pablo.

"Even the Manuscript was written by a person," Pablo added. "But not all the people you meet will have the energy or the clarity to reveal the message they have for you. You must help them by sending them energy." He paused. "You told me of learning to project your energy toward a plant by focusing on its beauty, remember?"

"Yes."

"Well, you do exactly the same thing toward a person. When the energy goes into them, it helps them see their truth. Then they can give this truth to you.

"Father Costous is an example," he continued. "He had an important message for you which you did not help him reveal. You tried to demand answers from him and that created a competition between you and him for energy. When he felt that, his childhood drama, his intimidator, took over the conversation."

"What was I supposed to have said?" I asked.

Pablo didn't answer. Again we heard someone at the cell door.

Father Costous entered.

He nodded at Pablo, a slight smile on his face. Pablo smiled broadly, as if he actually liked the priest. Father Costous shifted his gaze to me, his face becoming stern. Anxiety gripped my stomach.

"Cardinal Sebastian has asked to see you," he said. "You will be transported to Iquitos this afternoon. I would advise you to answer all his questions."

"Why does he want me?" I asked.

"Because the truck you were caught with belongs to one of our priests. We are assuming you received your copies of the Manuscript from him. For one of our own priests to disregard the law is very serious." He looked at me with determination.

I glanced at Pablo, who nodded for me to continue.

"You think that the Manuscript is undermining your religion?" I asked Costous gently.

He looked at me with condescension. "Not just our religion; everyone's religion. Do you think there is no plan for this world? God is in control. He assigns our destiny. Our job is to obey the laws set forth by God. Evolution is a myth. God creates the future the way he wants it. To say humans can make themselves evolve takes the will of God out of the picture. It allows people to be selfish and separate. They think that their evolution is the important thing, not God's plan. They will treat each other even worse than they do now."

I couldn't think of another question. The priest looked at me for a moment, then said, almost kindly, "I hope you will cooperate with Cardinal Sebastian."

He turned and looked at Pablo, obviously proud of the way he had handled my questions. Pablo only smiled at him and nodded again. The priest walked out and a soldier locked the door behind him. Pablo leaned forward on his cot and beamed at me, his demeanor still completely transformed, confidence on his face.

I looked at him for a moment, then smiled.

"What do you think happened just now?" he asked.

I struggled for humor. "I found out I'm in more trouble than I thought?"

He laughed. "What else occurred?"

"I'm not sure what you're getting at."

"What were your questions when you arrived here?"

"I wanted to find Marjorie and Wil?"

"Well, you found one of them. What was your other question?"

"I had a sense that these priests were against the Manuscript not out of malice but because they misunderstood. I wanted to know what they were thinking. For some reason I had the idea they could be talked out of their opposition." After saying this I suddenly understood what Pablo was leading to. I had met Costous, here, now, so that I could find out what bothered him about the Manuscript.

"And what was the message you received?" he asked.

"The message?"

"Yes, the message."

I looked at him. "It's the idea of participating in evolution that bothers them, isn't it?

"Yes," he said.

"That would figure," I added. "The idea of physical evolution is bad enough. But to extend the idea to everyday life, to the individual decisions we make, to history itself. That's unacceptable. They think humans will run amuck with this evolution, that relations between people will degenerate.

No wonder they want to see the Manuscript suppressed."

"Could you convince them otherwise?" Pablo asked.

"No. . .I mean, I don't know enough myself."

"What would it take for someone to be able to convince them?"

"One would have to know the truth. One would have to know how humans would be treating each other if everyone was following the insights and evolving."

Pablo appeared pleased.

"What?" I asked, smiling along with him.

"How humans will act toward each other is in the very next insight, the Eighth. Your question of why the priests were against the Manuscript has been answered, and the answer, in turn, has evolved into another question."

"Yes," I said, deep in thought. "I've got to find the Eighth. I've got to get out of here."

"Don't go too fast," Pablo cautioned. "You must make sure you fully grasp the Seventh before you go further."

"Do you think I grasp it?" I asked. "Am I staying in the flow of evolution?"

"You will," he said, "if you remember to keep your questions always in mind. Even people who are still unaware can stumble into answers and see coincidences in retrospect. The Seventh Insight occurs when we can see these answers as they arrive. It heightens everyday experience.

"We must assume every event has significance and contains a message that somehow pertains to our questions. This especially applies to what we used to call bad things. The Seventh Insight says that the challenge is to find the silver lining in every event, no matter how negative. You first thought that being captured had ruined everything. But now you can see that you were supposed to be here. This is where your answers were."

He was right, but if I was receiving answers here and evolving to a higher level, then Pablo must certainly be doing the same thing.

Suddenly we heard someone coming down the hall. Pablo looked directly at me, a serious look on his face.

"Listen," he said. "Remember what I told you. The Eighth Insight is next for you. It is about an Interpersonal Ethic, a way of treating other people so more messages are shared. But remember not to go too fast. Stay centered in your situation. What are your questions?"

"I want to find out where Wil is," I said. "And I want to find the Eighth Insight. And I want to find Marjorie."

"And what was your guiding intuition concerning Marjorie?"

I thought for a moment. "That I would escape. . .that we would escape."

We could hear someone right outside the door.

"Did I bring you a message?" I asked Pablo hurriedly.

"Of course," he said. "When you arrived I didn't know why I was here. I knew it had something to do with communicating the Seventh Insight, but I doubted my ability. I didn't think that I knew enough. Because of you," he continued, "I now know that I can. That was one of the messages that you brought to me."

"Was there another?"

"Yes, your intuition that the priests can be convinced to accept the Manuscript is a message for me also. It makes me think I'm here to convince Father Costous."

As he finished speaking, a soldier opened the door and motioned for me.

I looked at Pablo.

"I want to tell you one of the concepts the next insight talks about," he said.

The soldier glared at him and took my arm, ushering me out the door and closing it. As I was led away, Pablo stared through the bars.

"The Eighth Insight warns against something," he called out. "It warns against your growth being stopped . . . . It happens when you become addicted to another person."

THE
INTERPERSONAL
ETHIC

I followed the soldier up the steps and out into the bright sunshine. Pablo's warning was echoing in my head. Addiction to another person? What did he mean by that? What kind of addiction?

The soldier led me down the path toward the parking area where two other soldiers stood beside a military jeep. They watched us intensely as we walked their way. When I was close enough to see inside the jeep, I noticed that a passenger was already sitting in the back. Marjorie! She looked pale and anxious. Before I could catch her eye, the soldier behind me grabbed my arm and directed me into the seat beside her. Two other soldiers climbed into the front seats. The one sitting on the driver's side glanced back at us briefly, then he started the vehicle and headed north.

"Do you speak English?" I asked the soldiers.

The soldier in the passenger seat, a beefy man, looked at me blankly and said something in Spanish that I couldn't understand, then turned curtly away.

I turned my attention to Marjorie. "Are you all right?" I asked, in a whisper.

"I. . . uh. . ." Her voice faded, and I noticed tears were flowing down her face.

"It's going to be okay," I said, putting my arm around her. She looked up at me, forcing a smile, then rested her head on my shoulder. A ripple of passion filled my body.

For an hour we bounced along the unpaved road. Outside, the landscape grew continuously more lush and jungle-like. Then, around one bend, the dense vegetation opened up into what appeared to be a small town. Wood frame buildings lined both sides of the road.

A hundred yards ahead, a large truck blocked the way. Several soldiers motioned for us to stop. Beyond them were other vehicles, some with flashing yellow lights. I became more alert. As we pulled to a stop, one of the soldiers outside walked up and said something I couldn't understand. The only word I recognized was "gasoline." Our escorts left the jeep and stood outside talking with the other soldiers. They glanced at us occasionally, weapons at their side.

I noticed a small street which angled to the left. As I looked at the shops and doorways, something changed in my perception. The shapes and colors of the buildings suddenly stood out and became more distinct.

I whispered Marjorie's name and felt her look up, but before she could say anything, an enormous explosion rocked the jeep. A blast of fire and light shot up from the area in front of us, and the soldiers were blown to the ground. Immediately, our vision was obscured by smoke and falling ash.

"Come on!" I yelled, pulling Marjorie from the vehicle. Amid the confusion, we ran down the street in the direction I had been looking. Behind us I could hear distant shouts and moans. Still engulfed with smoke, we ran perhaps fifty yards. Suddenly, I noticed a doorway to the left.

"In here!" I shouted. The door was open and we both ran inside. I fell against the door, closing it securely. When I turned around, I saw a middle-aged woman staring at us. We had dashed into someone's home.

As I looked at her, attempting a smile, I noticed that the woman's expression was not one of horror, nor anger, at having had two strangers rush into her house after an explosion. Instead, what she displayed was an amused half smile that looked more like resignation, as though she half expected us and now had to *do* something. On a chair nearby was a small child about four years old.

"Hurry!" she said in English. "They will be looking for you!" She ushered us to the back of the sparsely furnished living room, through a hall, and down some wooden steps to a long cellar. The child walked at her side. We moved quickly through the cellar and up some other steps to an outside door leading to an alley.

The woman unlocked a small compact car which was parked there and hurried us inside. She directed us to lie down in the back seat, threw a blanket over us, and pulled away in what seemed to be a northerly direction. Through it all, I remained speechless, carried along by the woman's initiative. A rush of energy filled my body as I fully realized what had happened. My intuition of escape had occurred.

Marjorie lay beside me, her eyes tightly closed.

"Are you all right?" I whispered.

She looked up at me with tearful eyes and nodded.

After about fifteen minutes, the woman said, "I think you can sit up now."

I pushed away the blanket and looked around. We seemed to be on the same road as before the explosion, only farther north.

"Who are you?" I asked.

She turned and looked at me with her half smile. She was a shapely woman of about forty with shoulder length dark hair.

"I'm Karla Deez," she said. "This is my daughter, Mareta."

The child was smiling and looking over the passenger seat at us with large, inquisitive eyes. Her hair was jet black and also long.

I told them who we were, then asked, "How did you know to help us?"

Karla's smile grew wider. "You are running from the soldiers because of the Manuscript, aren't you?"

"Yes, but how did you know?"

"I know the Manuscript, too."

"Where are you taking us?" I asked.

"I don't know that," she said. "You will have to help me."

I glanced at Marjorie. She was watching me closely as I spoke. "Right now I don't know where to go," I said. "Before I was captured, I was trying to get to Iquitos."

"Why did you want to go there?" she asked.

"I'm trying to find a friend. He's looking for the Ninth Insight."

"That is a dangerous thing."

"I know."

"We will take you there, won't we, Mareta?"

The little girl giggled and said with a sophistication beyond her years, "Of course."

"What kind of explosion was that back there?" I asked.

"I think it was a gas truck," she answered. "Earlier, an accident had occurred, a leak."

I was still amazed at how quickly Karla had decided to help us so I decided to press the question. "How did you know we were running from the soldiers?"

She took a deep breath. "Yesterday, many military trucks were passing through the village going north. This is unusual and it made me think of the time two months ago when my friends were taken away. My friends and I studied the Manuscript together. We were the only ones in this village who had all eight insights. Then the soldiers came and took my friends. I have not heard from them.

"As I watched the trucks yesterday," she continued, "I knew the soldiers were continuing to hunt copies of the Manuscript and that others, like my friends, would need help. I envisioned myself helping those people if I could. Of course, I suspected that it was meaningful that I was having that particular thought at that particular time. So, when you came into my house, I was not surprised."

She paused, then asked, "Have you ever experienced this?"

"Yes," I said.

Karla slowed the car. Ahead was a crossroads.

"I think we should turn to the right here," she said. "It will take longer but it will be safer."

As Karla turned the car to the right, Mareta slid to the left and had to hold onto the seat to keep from falling over. She giggled. Marjorie was staring appreciatively at the little girl.

"How old is Mareta?" Marjorie asked Karla.

Karla looked disturbed, then said gently, "Please don't talk about her as if she wasn't here. If she was an adult you would have addressed the question to her."

"Oh, I'm sorry," Marjorie said.

"I'm five," Mareta said proudly.

"Have you studied the Eighth Insight?" Karla asked.

"No," Marjorie said, "I have only seen the Third Insight."

"I'm at the Eighth," I said. "Do you have any copies?"

"No," Karla said. "All the copies were taken away by the soldiers."

"Does the Eighth talk about how to relate to children?"

"Yes, it is about how humans will eventually learn to relate to each other, and talks of many things, such as how to project energy to others and how to avoid addictions to people."

There was that warning again. I was about to ask Karla what it meant when Marjorie spoke.

"Tell us about the Eighth Insight," she said.

"The Eighth Insight," Karla explained, "is about using energy in a new way when relating to people in general, but it begins at the beginning, with children."

"How should we view children?" I asked.

"We should view them as they really are, as end points in evolution that lead us forward. But in order to learn to evolve they need our energy on a constant basis, unconditionally. The worst thing that can be done to children is to drain their energy while correcting them. This is what creates control dramas in them, as you already know. But these learned manipulations on the child's part can be avoided if the adults give them all the energy they need no matter what the situation. That is why they should always be included in conversations, especially conversations about them. And you should never take responsibility for more children than you can give attention to."

"The Manuscript says all this?" I asked.

"Yes," she said, "and the point about the number of children is highly stressed."

I felt confused. "Why is the number of children one has important?"

She glanced at me for an instant as she drove. "Because any one adult can only focus on and give attention to one child at a time. If there are too many children for the number of adults, then the adults become overwhelmed and unable to give enough energy. The children begin to compete with each other for the adult's time."

"Sibling rivalry," I said.

"Yes, but the Manuscript says that this problem is more important than people think. Adults often glamorize the idea of large families and children growing up together. But children should learn the world from adults, not from other children. In too many cultures, children are running in gangs. The Manuscript says humans will slowly understand that they should not bring children into the world unless there is at least one adult committed to focus full attention, all of the time, on each child."

"But wait a minute," I said. "In many situations both parents must work to survive. This denies them the right to have children."

"Not necessarily," she replied. "The Manuscript says humans will learn to extend their families beyond blood ties. So that someone else is able to provide one on one attention. All the energy does not have to come from the parents alone. In fact, it is better if it does not. But whoever cares for the children must provide this one on one attention."

"Well," I said, "you've done something right. Mareta certainly seems mature."

Karla frowned and said, "Don't tell me, tell her."

"Oh, right." I looked at the child. "You act very grown-up, Mareta."

She looked away shyly for a moment, then said, "Thank you." Karla hugged her warmly.

Karla looked at me proudly. "For the last two years I have been trying to relate to Mareta according to the Manuscript's guidelines, haven't I, Mareta?"

The child smiled and nodded.

"I have tried to give her energy and to always tell her the truth of every situation in language she can understand. When she asked the questions a young child asks, I treated them very seriously, avoiding the temptation of giving her a fanciful answer which is plainly for the entertainment of adults."

I smiled. "Do you mean untruths like, 'storks bring babies,' that sort of thing?"

"Yes, but these cultural expressions aren't so bad. Children figure these out quickly because they stay the same. Worse are the distortions created on the spot by adults just because they want to have a little fun, and because they believe the truth is too complicated for a child to comprehend. But this is not right; the truth can always be expressed at a child's level of understanding. It just takes some thought."

"What does the Manuscript say about this issue?"

"It says we should always find a way to tell a child the truth."

Part of me resisted this idea. I was one who enjoyed kidding around with children.

"Don't kids usually understand that adults are just playing?" I said. "All this seems to make them grow up too fast and take some of the fun out of childhood."

She looked at me sternly. "Mareta is full of fun. We chase and tumble and play all the childhood fantasy games. The difference is that when we are fantasizing, she knows it."

I nodded. She was right, of course.

"Mareta seems confident," Karla continued, "because I was there for her. I gave her one on one attention when she needed it. And if I wasn't there, my sister, who lives next door, was there. She always had an adult to answer her questions, and because she has had this sincere attention, she has never felt she had to act out or show off. She has always had enough energy and that makes her assume she will continue to have enough, which makes the transition from receiving energy from adults to getting it from the universe—which we already talk about—much easier for her to grasp."

I noticed the terrain outside. We were traveling through deep jungle now and though I couldn't see it, I knew the sun was low in the afternoon sky.

"Can we get to Iquitos tonight?" I asked.

"No," Karla said. "But we can stay at a house I know."

"Near here?" I asked.

"Yes, it is the house of a friend. He works for the wildlife service."

"He works for the government?"

"Some of the Amazon is a protected area. He is the local agent, but influential. His name is Juan Hinton. Do not worry. He believes in the Manuscript and they have never bothered him."

By the time we arrived, the sky was completely dark. Around us the jungle was alive with night sounds, the air muggy. A large well-lit, wood frame house stood at the end of a clearing in the dense foliage. Nearby were two large buildings and several jeeps. Another vehicle was up on blocks and two men worked around lights underneath.

A thin Peruvian, dressed in expensive clothing, answered Karla's knock and smiled at her until he noticed Marjorie, Mareta and myself waiting on the steps. His face turned nervous and displeased as he talked to her in Spanish. She said something pleadingly in return, but his mannerism and inflection indicated that he did not want us to stay.

Then, through the crack in the door, I noticed a lone female figure standing in the foyer. I moved a little to bring her face into view. It was Julia. As I looked, she turned her head and saw me, then quickly walked forward with a surprised look on her face. She touched the shoulder of the man at the door and said something quietly into his ear. The man nodded, then opened the door with a look of resignation. We all introduced ourselves as Hinton led the way into the den area. Julia looked at me and said, "We meet again." She wore khaki pants with pockets on the legs and a bright red t-shirt.

"Yes we do," I said.

A Peruvian servant stopped Hinton, and after talking for a minute, the two walked into another part of the house. Julia sat in a chair by a coffee table and motioned for the rest of us to sit on a couch across from her. Marjorie appeared panicked. She looked at me intensely. Karla also seemed to be aware of Marjorie's distress. She walked over and took her by the hand. "Let's get some hot tea," she suggested.

As they walked away, Marjorie glanced back at me. I smiled and watched them until they turned the corner into the kitchen, then I turned to face Julia.

"So what do you think it means?" she asked.

"What does what mean?" I replied, still distracted.

"That we have run into each other again."

"Oh. . .I don't know."

"How did you wind up with Karla and where are you going?"

"She saved us. Marjorie and I had been detained by Peruvian troops. When we escaped, she happened to be there to help us."

Julia looked intense. "Tell me what occurred."

I leaned back and told her the whole story, beginning at the point in which I had taken Father Carl's truck and then all about the capture and our eventual escape.

"And Karla agreed to take you to Iquitos?" Julia asked.

"Yes."

"Why do you want to go there?"

"That's where Wil told Father Carl he was going. Wil apparently has a lead about the Ninth Insight. Also, Sebastian is there for some reason."

Julia nodded. "Yes, Sebastian has a mission near there. It's where he made his reputation, converting the Indians."

"What about you?" I asked. "What are you doing here?"

Julia told me that she too wanted to find the Ninth Insight, but that she had no leads. She had come to this house after thinking repeatedly of her old friend, Hinton.

I was hardly listening. Marjorie and Karla had walked out of the kitchen and were standing in the hall talking, cups of tea in their hands. Marjorie caught my eye but said nothing.

"Has she read much of the Manuscript?" Julia asked, nodding toward Marjorie.

"Just the Third Insight," I said.

"We can probably get her out of Peru if that's what she wants."

I turned and looked at her. "How?"

"Rolando is leaving tomorrow for Brazil. We have some friends at the American Embassy there. They can get her back to the United States. We have helped other Americans this way."

I looked at her and nodded tentatively. I realized I was having mixed feelings about what she had said. Part of me knew that leaving would be best for Marjorie. But another part wanted her to stay, to remain with me. I felt changed, energized, when she was around.

"I think I need to talk with her," I finally said.

"Of course," Julia replied. "We can talk later."

I got up and walked toward her. Karla was heading back toward the kitchen. Marjorie stepped around the corner of the hall out of sight. When I walked up, she was leaning back against the wall.

I pulled Marjorie into my arms. My body pulsated.

"Feel that energy?" I asked, whispering into her ear.

"It's incredible," she said. "What does it mean?"

"I don't know. We have some kind of connection."

I glanced around. No one could see us. We kissed passionately.

When I pulled back to look at her face, she looked different, stronger somehow, and I thought back to the day we had met at Viciente and to the conversation in the restaurant at Cula. I couldn't believe the amount of energy I felt in her presence and when she touched me.

She held me tightly. "Since that day at Viciente," she said, "I've wanted to be with you. I didn't know what to think about it then, but the energy is wonderful. I've never experienced anything like this."

Out of the corner of my eye I noticed Karla walking up, smiling. She told us that dinner was ready so we made our way into the dining room and found a huge buffet of fresh fruits and vegetables and breads. Everyone served their plates and sat around a large table. After Mareta sang a blessing song we spent an hour and a half eating and talking casually. Hinton had lost his nervousness and he set a light-hearted mood which helped to ease the tension of our escape. Marjorie was talking freely and laughing. Sitting beside her filled me with warm love.

After dinner, Hinton took us back into the den where a custard dessert was served with a sweet liqueur. Marjorie and I sat on the couch and fell into a long conversation about our pasts and significant life experiences. We seemed to grow closer and closer. The only difficulty we discovered was that she lived on the west coast and I resided in the south. Later Marjorie dismissed the problem and laughed heartily.

"I can't wait until we get back to the United States," she said. "We'll have so much fun traveling back and forth."

I sat back and gave her a serious look. "Julia said she could arrange a way for you to go home now."

"You mean both of us, don't you?" she replied.

"No, I. . .I can't go."

"Why?" she asked, "I can't leave without you. But I can't stand to stay here any longer either. I'll go crazy."

"You'll have to go on ahead. I'll be able to leave soon."

"No!" she said loudly. "I can't stand that!"

Karla, who was walking back into the den from putting Mareta in bed, glanced toward us, then looked quickly away. Hinton and Julia were still talking, seemingly oblivious to Marjorie's outburst.

"Please," Marjorie said. "Let's just go home."

I looked away.

"Okay, fine!" she said. "Stay!" She stood and walked briskly toward the bedroom area.

My gut wrenched as I watched Marjorie walk away. The energy I had gained with her collapsed, and I suddenly felt weak and confused. I tried to shake it off. After all, I told myself, I hadn't known her that long. On the other hand, I thought, maybe she was correct. Maybe I should just go home. What difference could I make here anyway? Back at home I could perhaps marshal some support for the Manuscript, and stay alive, as well. I stood up and started to follow her down the hall, but for some reason I sat back down. I couldn't decide what to do.

"May I join you for a minute?" Karla was suddenly asking. I hadn't noticed that she was standing beside the sofa.

"Sure," I said.

She sat down and looked at me with regard. "I couldn't help overhearing what is going on," she said. "And I thought that before you made your decision, you might want to hear what the Eighth Insight says about addictions to people."

"Yes, please, I want to know what that means."

"When one first learns to be clear and to engage one's evolution, any of us can be stopped, suddenly, by an addiction to another person."

"You're speaking of Marjorie and me, aren't you?"

"Let me explain the process," she said. "And you judge for yourself."

"Okay."

"First, let me say that I had a very hard time with this part of the insight. I don't think I would have ever understood if I had not met Professor Reneau."

"Reneau?!" I exclaimed. "I know him. We met when I was learning the Fourth Insight."

"Well," she said, "we met when we both had reached the Eighth Insight. He stayed at my house for several days."

I nodded in amazement.

"He said that the idea of an addiction, as used in the Manuscript, explains why power struggles arise in romantic relationships. We've always wondered what causes the bliss and euphoria of love to end, to suddenly turn into conflict, and now we know. It is a result of the flow of energy between the individuals involved.

"When love first happens, the two individuals are giving each other energy unconsciously and both people feel buoyant and elated. That's the incredible high we all call being "in love." Unfortunately, once they expect this feeling to come from the other person, they cut themselves off from the energy in the universe and begin to rely even more on the energy from each other—only now there doesn't seem to be enough and so they stop giving each other energy and fall back into their dramas in an attempt to control each other and force the other's energy their way. At this point the relationship degenerates into the usual power struggle."

She hesitated for a moment, as if checking whether I understood, then added, "Reneau told me that our susceptibility to this kind of addiction can be described psychologically, if that will help you understand?"

I nodded again for her to continue. "Reneau said the problem starts in our early family. Because of the energy competition there, none of us were able to complete an important psychological process. We weren't able to integrate our opposite sexual side."

"Our what?"

"In my case," she continued. "I wasn't able to integrate my male side. In your case you weren't able to integrate your female side. The reason we can become addicted to someone of the opposite sex is that we've yet to access this opposite sex energy ourselves. You see, the mystical energy that we can tap as an inner source is both male and female. We can eventually open up to it, but when we first begin to evolve, we have to be careful. The integration process takes some time. If we connect prematurely with a human source for our female or male energy, we block the universal supply."

I told her I didn't understand.

"Think of how this integration is supposed to work in an ideal family," she explained, "and then perhaps you can see what I mean. In any family, the child must first receive energy from the adults in his life. Usually, identifying with and integrating the energy of the same-sexed parent is accomplished easily, but receiving energy from the other parent can be more difficult because of the differences in the sexes.

"Let's use a female child as an example. All the little girl knows as she first attempts to integrate her male side is that she is extremely attracted to her father. She wants him around and close to her all the time. The Manuscript explains that what she really wants is male energy—because this male energy complements her female side. From this male energy she receives a sense of completion and euphoria. But she mistakenly thinks that the only way to have this energy is by sexually possessing her father and keeping him close physically.

"Interestingly, because she intuits that this energy is really supposed to be her own and that she should be able to command this energy at will, she wants to direct the father as if he were that part of herself. She thinks he is magical and perfect and able to supply her every whim. In a less than ideal family, this sets up a power conflict between the little girl and her dad. Dramas are formed as she learns to posture herself in order to manipulate him into giving her the energy she desires.

"But in an ideal family, the father would remain uncompetitive. He would continue to relate honestly and have enough energy so as to supply her unconditionally even though he can't do everything she asks. The important thing to know here, in our ideal example, is that the father would remain open and communicative. She thinks he is ideal and magical but if he honestly explains who he is and what he is doing and why, then the little girl can integrate his particular style and abilities and proceed past an unrealistic view of her father. In the end she will see him as just a particular human being, a human being with his own talents and faults. Once this true emulation takes place, then the child makes an easy transition from receiving her opposite-sex energy from her father to receiving it as part of the overall energy existing in the universe at large.

"The problem," she went on, "is that most parents, up to now, have been competing with their own children for energy, and that has affected all of us. Because this competition was taking place, none of us have quite resolved this opposite-sex issue. We're all stuck at the stage where we are still looking for our opposite-sex energy outside of ourselves, in the person of a male or female we can think of as ideal and magical and can possess sexually. See the problem?"

"Yes," I said. "I think I do."

"In terms of our ability to evolve consciously," she continued, "we are faced with a critical situation. As I said before, according to the Eighth Insight, when we first begin to evolve, we automatically begin to receive our opposite-sex energy. It comes in naturally from the energy in the universe. But we must be careful, because if another person comes along who offers this energy directly we can cut ourselves off from the true source. . . and regress." She chuckled to herself.

"What are you laughing at?" I asked.

"Reneau once made this analogy," she said. "He said that until we learn how to avoid this situation, we are walking around like a circle half complete. You know, we look like the letter C. We are very susceptible to a person of the opposite sex, some other circle half complete, coming up and joining with us—completing the circle that way—and giving us a burst of euphoria and energy that feels like the wholeness that a full connection with the universe produces. In reality, we have only joined up with another person who is looking for their other half on the outside too.

"Reneau said that this is a classical co-dependent relationship and that it has built-in problems that begin to arise immediately."

She hesitated, as though she expected me to say something. But I only nodded.

"You see, the problem with this completed person, this O, that both people think they have reached, is that it has taken two people to make this one whole person, one supplying the female energy and one supplying the male. This one whole person consequently has two heads, or egos. Both people want to run this whole person they have created and so, just as in childhood, both people want to command the other, as if the other were themselves. This kind of illusion of completeness always breaks down into a power struggle. In the end, each person must take the other for granted and even invalidate them so that they can lead this whole self in the direction they want to go. But of course that doesn't work, at least not any more. Perhaps in the past, one of the partners was willing to submit themselves to the other—usually the woman, sometimes the man. But we are waking up now. No one wants to be subservient to anyone else any longer."

I thought of what the First Insight had conveyed about power struggles within intimate relationships, and of the woman's outburst at the restaurant with Charlene. "So much for romance," I said.

"Oh, we can still have romance." Karla replied. "But first we have to complete the circle on our own. We have to stabilize our channel with the universe. That takes time, but afterward we are never susceptible to this problem again and we can have what the Manuscript calls a higher-relationship. When we connect romantically with another whole person after that, we create a super-person. . .but it never pulls us from the path of our individual evolution."

"Which is what you think Marjorie and I are doing to each other now, isn't it? Pulling ourselves off our paths?"

"Yes."

"So how do we avoid these encounters?" I asked.

"By resisting the 'love at first sight' feeling for a while, by learning to have platonic relationships with members of the opposite sex. But remember the process. You must have these relationships only with people who will reveal themselves totally, telling you how and why they are doing what they are doing—just as this would have happened with the opposite-sexed parent during an ideal childhood. By understanding who these opposite-sexed friends really are on the inside, one breaks past one's own fantasy projection about that gender, and that releases us to connect again with the universe.

"Remember, also," she continued, "that this is not easy, especially if one has to break away from a current co-dependent relationship. It is a real pulling apart of energy. It hurts. But it must be done. Co-dependence is not some new malady some of us have. We're all co-dependent, and we're all growing out of it now.

"The idea is to begin to experience that sense of well-being and euphoria experienced in the first moment of a co-dependent relationship when you are alone. You get to have him or her on the inside. After that, you evolve forward and can find that special romantic relationship that really fits you."

She paused. "And who knows, if both you and Marjorie evolve further, perhaps you will find that you truly belong with each other. But understand: your relationship with her has no way of working now."

Our conversation was interrupted as Hinton walked over and explained that he was retiring for the night, and that our rooms had been prepared. We both expressed our appreciation for his hospitality, and as he walked away, Karla said, "I think I'm going to bed also. We'll talk later."

I nodded and watched her as she left. Then I felt a hand on my shoulder. It was Julia.

"I'm going to my room," she said. "Do you know where yours is? I can show you."

"Please," I said, then asked, "Where is Marjorie's room?"

She smiled as we walked down the hall and stopped in front of a particular door. "Nowhere near yours," she said. "Mr. Hinton is a very conservative man."

I smiled back and bid her good night, then entered my room and held my stomach until I went to sleep.

I awoke to the smell of rich coffee. The aroma permeated the entire house. After I dressed, I walked into the den. An older male houseworker offered me a glass of fresh grape juice which I accepted.

"Good morning," Julia said from behind me.

I turned around. "Good morning."

She looked at me intensely, then asked, "Have you discovered yet why we've run into each other again?"

"No," I said. "I haven't been able to think about it. I've been trying to understand addictions."

"Yes," she replied. "I saw."

"What do you mean?"

"I could tell what was happening by the way your energy field looked."

"How did it look?" I asked.

"Your energy was connected to Marjorie's. When you were sitting here and she was in the other room, your field stretched all the way in there and attached to hers."

I shook my head.

She smiled and put her hand on my shoulder. "You had lost your connection with the universe. You had become addicted to Marjorie's energy as a substitute. It is the same way with all addictions—one goes through someone or something else to connect with the universe. The way to deal with this is to get your energy up and then center yourself again in what you are really doing here."

I nodded and walked outside. She waited in the den. For about ten minutes I practiced the method of building energy that Sanchez had taught me. Gradually the beauty returned and I felt much lighter. I returned to the house. "You look better," Julia said.

"I feel better," I replied.

"So what are your questions at this point?"

I thought for a minute. I had found Marjorie. That question had been answered. But I still wanted to find out where Wil was. And I still wanted to understand how people would be acting toward each other if they follow this Manuscript. If the Manuscript's effect was positive, why would Sebastian and the other priests be worried?

I looked at Julia. "I need to grasp the rest of the Eighth Insight and I still want to find Wil. Maybe he has the Ninth."

"I'm going to Iquitos tomorrow," she said. "Would you like to go?"

I hesitated.

"I think Wil is there," she added.

"How do you know?"

"Because of the thoughts I had about him last night."

I said nothing.

"I had thoughts of you, too," Julia continued. "Of both of us going to Iquitos. You're involved in this somehow."

"Involved in what?" I asked.

She grinned. "In finding this last insight before Sebastian does."

As she spoke, the image came to my mind of Julia and me arriving at Iquitos, but then deciding to go in separate directions for some reason. I felt I had a purpose but it was unclear.

I focused again on Julia. She was smiling.

"Where were you?" she asked.

"Sorry," I said. "I was thinking about something."

"Was it important?"

"I don't know. I was thinking that once we get to Iquitos. . .that we would go in two different directions."

Rolando came into the room.

"I brought the supplies you wanted," he said to Julia. He recognized me and nodded politely.

"Good, thank you," Julia replied. "Did you see many soldiers?"

"No, I did not see any," he said.

Marjorie walked into the room then and distracted me but I could hear Julia explaining to Rolando that she thought Marjorie wanted to go with him to Brazil, where she would arrange passage back to the States.

I went over to Marjorie. "How did you sleep?" I asked.

She looked at me as though deciding whether to remain angry. "Not very well," she said.

I nodded toward Rolando. "He is Julia's friend. He is leaving this morning for Brazil. From there he will help you get back to the States."

She appeared frightened.

"Look, you're going to be okay," I said. "They've helped other Americans. They know people at the American Embassy in Brazil. In no time you will be home."

She nodded. "I'm worried about you."

"I'll be fine. Don't worry. As soon as I get back to the U.S., I'll call you."

From behind me, Hinton announced that breakfast was being served. We walked into the dining room and ate. Afterward, Julia and Rolando seemed to be in a hurry. Julia explained that it was important for Rolando and Marjorie to get across the border before dark and the journey would take all day.

Marjorie packed some clothes that Hinton had given her, and later, while Julia and Rolando were talking by the door, I pulled Marjorie to the side.

"Don't worry about anything," I said. "Just keep your eyes open and perhaps you'll see the other insights."

She smiled but said nothing. I watched with Julia as Rolando helped her load her things into his small car. Her eyes met mine briefly as they drove away.

"Do you think they will get through all right?" I asked Julia.

She looked at me and winked. "Of course. And now, we had better go, as well. I have some clothes for you." She handed me a satchel of clothes and we loaded these and several boxes of foodstuff into the pick-up truck. We then said good-bye to Hinton and Karla and Mareta, and drove northeast toward Iquitos.

As we traveled, the landscape grew even more jungle-like and we saw very few signs of people. I began thinking of the Eighth Insight. Clearly it was a new understanding of how to treat others, but I didn't understand it completely. Karla had told me of the way one should treat children and the dangers of an addiction to a person. But both Pablo and Karla had alluded to a way to consciously project energy onto others. What was this about?

I caught Julia's eye and said, "I haven't quite grasped the Eighth Insight."

"How we approach other people determines how quickly we evolve, how quickly our life questions are answered," she said.

"How does that work?" I asked.

"Think about your own situation," she said. "How have your questions been answered?"

"By people who came along, I guess."

"Were you completely open to their messages?"

"Not really. I was mainly aloof."

"Were the people who brought messages to you pulled back also?"

"No, they were very open and helpful. They . . ." I hesitated, unable to think of the correct way to express my idea.

"Did they help you by opening you up?" she asked. "Did they fill you with warmth and energy somehow?"

Her remark uncapped an eruption of memories. I recalled Wil's soothing attitude when I was on the verge of panic in Lima, and Sanchez's fatherly hospitality, and Father Carl's and Pablo's and Karla's concerned counsel. And now Julia's. They all had the same look in their eyes.

"Yes," I said. "All of you have done that."

"That's right," she said. "We have, and we were doing it consciously, following the Eighth Insight. By lifting you up and helping you to get clear, we could search for the truth, the message, that you had for us. Do you understand that? Energizing you was the best thing we could do for ourselves."

"What does the Manuscript say about all this, exactly?"

"It says that whenever people cross our paths, there is always a message for us. Chance encounters do not exist. But how we respond to these encounters determines whether we're able to receive the message. If we have a conversation with someone who crosses our path and we do not see a message pertaining to our current questions, it does not mean there was no message. It only means we missed it for some reason."

She thought for a moment, then continued. "Have you ever run into an old friend or acquaintance, talked for a minute and left, then run into him or her again the same day or the same week?"

"Yes, I have," I replied.

"And what do you usually say? Something like 'Well, fancy seeing you again,' and laugh and go on your way."

"Something like that."

"The Manuscript says that what we should do instead in that situation is to stop what we are doing, no matter what, and find out the message we have for that person, and that the person has for us. The Manuscript predicts that once humans grasp this reality, our interaction will slow down and become more purposeful and deliberate."

"But isn't that hard to do, especially with someone who wouldn't know what you were talking about?"

"Yes, but the Manuscript outlines the procedures."

"You mean, the exact way we're supposed to treat each other?"

"That's right."

"What does it say?"

"Do you remember the Third Insight, that humans are unique in a world of energy in that they can project their energy consciously?"

"Yes."

"Do you remember how this is done?"

I recalled John's lessons. "Yes, it is done by appreciating the beauty of an object until enough energy comes into us to feel love. At that point we can send energy back."

"That's right. And the same principle holds true with people. When we appreciate the shape and demeanor of a person, really focus on them until their shape and features begin to stand out and to have more presence, we can then send them energy, lifting them up.

"Of course, the first step is to keep our own energy high, then we can start the flow of energy coming into us, through us, and into the other person. The more we appreciate their wholeness, their inner beauty, the more the energy flows into them, and naturally, the more that flows into us."

She laughed. "It's really a rather hedonistic thing to do," she said. "The more we can love and appreciate others, the more energy flows into us. That's why loving and energizing others is the best possible thing we can do for ourselves."

"I've heard that before," I said. "Father Sanchez says it often."

I looked at Julia closely. I had the feeling I was seeing her deeper personality for the first time. She returned my gaze for an instant, then focused again on the road. "The effect on the individual of this projection of energy is immense," she said. "Right now, for instance, you're filling me with energy. I can feel it. What I feel is a greater sense of lightness and clarity as I'm formulating my thoughts to speak.

"Because you are giving me more energy than I would have otherwise, I can see what my truth is and more readily give it to you. When I do that, you have a sense of revelation about what I'm saying. This leads you to see my higher self even more fully and so appreciate and focus on it at an even deeper level, which gives me even more energy and greater insight into my truth and the cycle begins over again. Two or more people doing this together can reach incredible highs as they build one another up and have it immediately returned. You must understand, though, that this connection is completely different from a co-dependent relationship. A co-dependent relationship begins this way but soon becomes controlling because the addiction cuts them off from their source and the energy runs out. Real projection of energy has no attachment or intention. Both people are just waiting for the messages."

As she spoke I thought of a question. Pablo had said that I didn't get Father Costous' message at first because I set off his childhood drama.

"What do we do," I asked Julia, "if the person we are speaking with is already operating in a control drama and trying to pull us into it? How do we cut through that?"

Julia answered quickly. "The Manuscript says if we do not assume the matching drama, then the person's own drama will fall apart."

"I'm not sure I understand," I said.

Julia was looking at the road ahead. I could tell she was in thought. "Somewhere right through here is a house where we can buy some gasoline."

I looked down at the gas gauge. It indicated the truck's tank was half full.

"We still have plenty of gas," I said.

"Yes, I know," she replied. "But I had a thought about stopping and filling it up, so I think we should."

"Oh, okay."

"There's the road," she said, pointing to the right.

We made the turn and drove almost a mile into the jungle before arriving at what looked like a supply house for fishermen and hunters. The dwelling was built at the edge of a river and several fishing boats were tied to the dock. We pulled up to a rusty pump and Julia went inside to find the owner.

I climbed out and stretched then walked around the building to the water's edge. The air was extremely humid. Although the thick canopy of trees blocked the sun, I could tell it was almost directly overhead. Soon the temperature would be scorching.

Suddenly a man behind me was speaking angrily in Spanish. I turned to see a short stocky Peruvian. He looked at me menacingly and repeated the statement.

"I don't understand what you're saying."

He switched to English. "Who are you? What are you doing here?"

I tried to ignore him. "We're just here for gas. We'll be gone in a few minutes." I turned around and faced the water again, hoping he would go away.

He walked to the side of me. "I think you better tell me who you are, Yankee."

I looked at him again. He appeared to be serious.

"I'm an American," I said. "I'm not sure where I'm going. I'm riding with a friend."

"A lost American," he said hostilely.

"That's right," I said.

"What are you after here, American?"

"I'm not after anything," I said, trying to walk back to the car. "and I've done nothing to you. Leave me alone."

I noticed suddenly that Julia was standing at the vehicle. When I looked, the Peruvian turned and looked too.

"It's time to leave," Julia said. "They're not in business any longer."

"Who are you?" the Peruvian asked her in his hostile tone.

"Why are you so angry?" Julia asked in response.

The man's demeanor changed. "Because it is my job to look after this place."

"I'm sure you do a good job. But it's hard for people to talk if you're frightening them."

The man stared, trying to figure Julia out.

"We're on our way to Iquitos," Julia said. "We're working with Father Sanchez and Father Carl. Do you know them?"

He shook his head, but the mention of the two priests settled him down even more. He finally nodded and walked away.

"Let's go," Julia said.

We got in the truck and drove away. I realized how anxious and nervous I had been. I tried to shake it off.

"Did anything happen inside?" I asked.

Julia looked at me. "What do you mean?"

"I mean did anything happen inside to explain why you had the thought to stop?"

She laughed, then said, "No, all the action was outside."

I looked at her.

"Have you figured it out?" she asked.

"No," I replied.

"What were you thinking about just before we arrived?"

"That I wanted to stretch my legs."

"No, before that. What were you asking about when we were talking?"

I tried to think. We were talking about childhood dramas. Then I remembered. "You had said something that had confused me," I said. "You had said that a person cannot play a control drama with us unless we play the matching drama. I didn't understand that."

"Do you understand now?"

"Not really. What are you getting at?"

"The scene outside clearly demonstrated what happens if you *do* play the matching drama."

"How?"

She glanced at me briefly. "What drama was the man playing with you?"

"He was obviously the Intimidator."

"Right, and what drama did you play?"

"I was just trying to get him off my back."

"I know, but what drama were you playing?"

"Well, I started off in my aloofness drama, but he kept coming after me."

"Then?"

The conversation was irritating me but I tried to get centered and stay with it. I looked at Julia and said, "I guess I was playing a Poor Me."

She smiled. "That's right."

"I noticed you handled him with no problem," I said.

"Only because I didn't play the drama he expected. Remember that each person's control drama was formed in childhood in relation to another drama. Therefore each drama needs a matching drama to be fully played out. What the intimidator needs in order to get energy is either a poor me, or another intimidator.

"How did you handle it?" I asked, still confused.

"My drama response would have been to play the Intimidator myself, trying to out intimidate him. Of course, this would probably have resulted in violence. But instead I did what the Manuscript instructs. I named the drama he was playing. All dramas are covert strategies to get energy. He was trying to intimidate you out of your energy. When he tried that on me, I named what he was doing."

"That's why you asked why he was so angry?"

"Yes. The Manuscript says that covert manipulations for energy can't exist if you bring them into consciousness by pointing them out. They cease to be covert. It is a very simple method. The best truth about what's going on in a conversation always prevails. After that the person has to be more real and honest."

"That makes sense," I said. "I guess I've even named dramas myself before, though I didn't know what I was doing."

"I'm sure. That's something all of us have done. We're just learning more about what is at stake. And the key to making it work is to simultaneously look beyond the drama at the real person in front of you, and send as much energy their way as possible. If they can feel energy coming in anyway, then it's easier for them to give up their way of manipulating for it."

"What could you appreciate in that guy?" I said.

"I could appreciate him as a little insecure boy needing energy desperately. Besides, he brought you a very timely message, right?"

I looked at her. She appeared to be on the verge of laughter.

"You think we stopped there just so I could grasp how to deal with someone playing a drama?"

"That was the question you asked, wasn't it?"

I smiled, my good feeling beginning to return. "Yes, I guess it was."

A mosquito buzzing around my face forced me awake. I looked over at Julia. She was smiling as though recalling something humorous. For several hours after leaving the river camp we had ridden in silence, munching on the food Julia had prepared for the trip.

"You're awake," Julia said.

"Yes," I replied. "How far is Iquitos?"

"The town is about thirty miles, but the Stewart Inn is only a few minutes ahead. It's a small Inn and hunting camp. The owner is English and supports the Manuscript." She smiled again. "We have had many good times together. Unless something has happened, he should be there. I hope we can get a lead on where Wil is."

She pulled the truck to the side of the road and looked at me. "We'd better get centered in where we are," she said. "Before I ran into you again, I had been floundering around wanting to help find the Ninth Insight but not knowing where to go. At one point I realized I had been thinking repeatedly of Hinton. I get to his house and who should show up but you. And you tell me that you're looking for Wil and that he's rumored to be in Iquitos. I have the intuition that we'll both be involved in finding the Ninth Insight, and then you have the intuition that at some point we separate and go in different directions. Is that pretty much it?"

"Yes," I said.

"Well, I want you to know that after that, I got to thinking about Willie Stewart and the inn. Something is going to happen there."

I nodded.

She drove the vehicle back on the road and around a curve. "There's the inn," Julia said.

Ahead about two hundred yards, where the road took another sharp bend to the right, was a two-story, Victorian style home.

We pulled into a gravel parking area and stopped. Several men were talking on the porch. I opened the door of the vehicle and was about to get out when Julia touched my shoulder.

"Remember," she said, "no one is here by accident. Stay alert for the messages."

I followed her as we walked up on the porch. The men, well-dressed Peruvians, nodded distractedly as we walked by them and into the house.

Once in the large foyer, Julia pointed to a dining room and asked me to pick a table and wait there while she looked for the owner.

I surveyed the room. It contained a dozen or so tables lined in two rows. I picked a table about halfway down and sat with my back against the wall. Three more men, all Peruvians, came in behind me and sat down across from my table. Another man came in soon after and took a table about twenty feet to my right. He sat at an angle where his back was slightly toward me. I noticed he was a foreigner, perhaps European.

Julia entered the room, spotted me, and then walked over and sat down facing me.

"The owner isn't here," she said, "and his clerk knew nothing of Wil."

"Now what?" I asked.

She looked at me and shrugged. "I don't know. We'll have to assume that someone here has a message for us."

"Who do you think it is?"

"I don't know."

"How do you know it will happen?" I asked, suddenly feeling skeptical. Even after all the mysterious coincidences that had happened to me since I had been in Peru, I still had trouble believing one would occur now just because we wanted it to.

"Don't forget the Third Insight," Julia replied. "The universe is energy, energy that responds to our expectations. People are part of that energy universe too, so when we have a question, the people show up who have the answer."

She cut her eyes to the other people in the room. "I don't know who these people are, but if we could talk with them long enough, we would find a truth each had for us, some part of the answer to our questions."

I looked at her askance. She leaned toward me across the table. "Get it into your head. Everyone who crosses our path has a message for us. Otherwise they would have taken another path, or left earlier or later. The fact that these people are here means that they are here for some reason."

I looked at her, still not sure whether I believed it was that simple.

"The hard part," she said, "is figuring out who to take time to talk with when talking with everyone is impossible."

"How do you decide?" I asked.

"The Manuscript says there are signs."

I was listening intently to Julia but for some reason I glanced around and looked at the man to my right. He turned around at exactly the same time and looked back at me. As I caught his eye, he shifted his gaze back to his food. I also looked away.

"What signs?" I asked.

"Signs like that," she said.

"Like what?"

"Like what you just did." She nodded toward the man to my right.

"What do you mean?"

Julia leaned toward me again. "The Manuscript says we will learn that sudden, spontaneous eye contact is a sign that two people should talk."

"But doesn't that happen all the time?" I asked.

"Yes, it does," she said. "And after it happens, most people just forget about it and go on with what they are doing."

I nodded. "What other signs does the Manuscript mention?" I asked.

"A sense of recognition," she replied. "Seeing someone who looks familiar, even though you know you've never seen the person before."

When she said that, I thought of Dobson and Reneau, of how familiar they looked when I had first seen them.

"Does the Manuscript say anything about why some people look familiar?" I asked.

"Not much. It just says we are members of the same thought group with certain other people. Thought groups are usually evolving along the same lines of interest. They think the same and that creates the same expression and outward experience. We intuitively recognize members of our thought group and very often they provide messages for us."

I looked at the man to my right one more time. He did look vaguely familiar. Incredibly, as I gazed at him, he turned and glanced at me again. I quickly looked back at Julia.

"You *must* talk with this man," Julia said.

I didn't respond. I felt uncomfortable with the idea of just walking up to him. I wanted to leave, to go on to Iquitos. I was about to make that suggestion when Julia spoke again, "This is where we need to be," she said, "not Iquitos. We have to play this out. The trouble with you is that you're resisting the idea of walking up to him and starting a conversation."

"How did you do that?" I asked.

"Do what?" she replied.

"Know what I was thinking."

"There is nothing mysterious about it. It is a matter of looking closely at your expressions."

"What do you mean?"

"When you are appreciating someone at a deeper level, you can see their most honest self beyond any facades they may put up. When you really focus at this level, you can perceive what someone is thinking as a subtle expression on their face. This is perfectly natural."

"It sounds telepathic to me," I said.

She grinned. "Telepathy is perfectly natural."

I glanced over at the man again. He did not look.

"You had better get your energy together and talk with him," Julia said, "before you lose the opportunity."

I focused on increasing my energy until I felt stronger, then asked, "What am I going to say to this guy?"

"The truth," she said. "Put the truth in a form you think he would recognize."

"Okay, I will."

I slid back my chair and walked over to where the man was sitting. He looked shy and nervous, the way I remembered Pablo looking the night I met him. I tried to look beyond the man's nervousness to a deeper level. When I did I seemed to perceive a new look on his face, one with more energy.

"Hello," I said. "You appear not to be a native Peruvian. I'm hoping you can help me. I'm looking for a friend of mine, Wil James."

"Please sit down," he said in a Scandinavian accent. "I'm Professor

Edmond Connor."

He offered me his hand and said, "I'm sorry. I do not know your friend, Wil."

I introduced myself and then explained—just on a hunch that it would mean something to him—that Wil was searching for the Ninth Insight.

"I'm familiar with the Manuscript," he said. "I'm here to study its authenticity."

"Alone?"

"I was to meet a Professor Dobson here. But so far he has not come. I don't understand the delay. He assured me that he would be here when I arrived."

"You know Dobson?!"

"Yes. He is the one who is organizing an inspection of the Manuscript."

"And he's all right? He's coming here?"

The Professor looked at me questioningly. "Those were the plans we made. Has something been wrong?"

My energy fell. I realized that Dobson's meeting with Connor had been set up before Dobson's arrest. "I met him on the airplane," I explained, "when I came to Peru. He was arrested in Lima. I have no idea what happened to him."

"Arrested! My God!"

"When did you last speak with him?" I asked

"Several weeks ago, but our meeting time here was firm. He said he would call me if anything changed."

"Do you remember why he wanted you to meet him here instead of in Lima?" I asked.

"He said there were some ruins around here and that he would be up in this area speaking with another scientist."

"Did he mention where he would be talking to this scientist?"

"Yes, he said he had to go to, uh, San Luis, I believe. Why?"

"I don't know. . .I was just wondering."

As I said this, two things happened simultaneously. First, I began thinking of Dobson, of seeing him again. We were meeting along a road with large trees. And then, at the same time, I looked out the window and saw, to my amazement, Father Sanchez walking up the porch steps. He looked tired and his clothes were dirty. In the parking lot another priest waited in an old car.

"Who is that?" Professor Connor asked.

"It's Father Sanchez!" I replied, barely able to contain my excitement.

I turned around and looked for Julia but she was no longer sitting at our table. I got up just as Sanchez walked into the room. When he saw me, he stopped abruptly, a look of total surprise on his face, then he walked over and embraced me.

"Are you all right?" he asked.

"Yes, fine," I said. "What are you doing here?"

Through his fatigue, he chuckled lightly. "I didn't know where else to go. And I almost didn't make it here. Hundreds of troops are headed this way."

"Why are the troops coming?" Connor asked from behind me, walking up to where Sanchez and I were standing.

"I'm sorry," Sanchez replied. "I do not know what the troops have in mind. I just know there are many."

I introduced the two men and told Father Sanchez of Connor's situation. Connor appeared panicked.

"I must leave," he said, "but I have no driver."

"Father Paul is waiting outside," Sanchez said. "He is going back to Lima immediately. You may ride with him if you wish."

"Indeed I do," Connor said.

"Wait, what if they run into those troops?" I asked.

"I don't think they would stop Father Paul," Sanchez said. "He is not well-known."

At that moment Julia came back into the room and saw Sanchez. The two hugged warmly and, again, I introduced Connor. As I spoke, Connor seemed to grow even more fearful and after only a few minutes, Sanchez told him that it was time for Father Paul to start back. Connor left to get his belongings from his room and quickly returned. Both Sanchez and Julia escorted him outside, but I told him good-bye there and waited at the table. I wanted to think. I knew meeting Connor was significant somehow, and that Sanchez finding us here was important, but I couldn't quite figure it out.

Before long, Julia came back into the room and sat down beside me. "I told you something was going to happen here," she said. "If we hadn't stopped we wouldn't have seen Sanchez, or Connor for that matter. By the way, what did you learn from Connor?"

"I'm not sure yet," I said. "Where is Father Sanchez?"

"He checked into a room to rest for a while. He hasn't slept in two days."

I looked away. I knew that Sanchez was tired, but hearing that he was unavailable disappointed me. I wanted very much to talk with him, to see if he could add some perspective to what was happening, especially concerning the soldiers. I felt uneasy and part of me wanted to flee with Connor.

Julia picked up on my impatience. "Take it easy," she said. "Slow down and tell me what you think of the Eighth Insight so far."

I looked at her and tried to center myself. "I'm not sure where to start."

"What do you think the Eighth Insight is saying?"

I thought back. "It's about a way of relating to other people, to children and to adults. It's about naming control dramas and breaking through them and focusing on other people in a way that sends them energy."

"And?" she asked.

I focused on her face and immediately saw what she was getting at. "And if we are observant about who to talk with, then we get the answers we desire as a result."

Julia smiled broadly.

"Have I grasped the Insight?" I asked.

"Almost," she said. "But there's one more thing. You understand how one person can uplift another. Now you're about to see what happens in a group when all of the participants know how to interact this way."

I walked out to the porch and sat in one of the wrought-iron chairs. After a few minutes Julia came through the door and joined me. We had eaten a leisurely dinner without much talking and afterward had decided to sit outside in the night air. Three hours had gone by since Sanchez had gone to his room and I was beginning to feel impatient again. When Sanchez suddenly walked outside and sat down with us I was relieved.

"Have you heard anything about Wil?" I asked him.

When I spoke, he slid his chair around to face Julia and me. I noticed that he was carefully adjusting the position of his chair so that he was an equal distance from each of us.

"Yes," he said finally. "I have."

He paused again and appeared to be in thought, so I asked, "What did you hear?"

"Let me tell you everything that happened," he said. "When Father Carl and I left to go back to my mission, we expected to find Father Sebastian there, along with the military. We expected an inquisition. When we arrived we found that Father Sebastian and the soldiers had left abruptly several hours earlier, after receiving a message.

"For a whole day we didn't know what was going on, then yesterday we were visited by a Father Costous, whom I understand you have met. He told us that he was directed to my mission by Wil James. Apparently Wil remembered the name of my mission from his conversation earlier with Father Carl, and intuitively knew that we would need the information Father Costous was bringing. Father Costous has decided to support the Manuscript."

"Why did Sebastian leave so suddenly?" I asked.

"Because," Sanchez said, "he wanted to speed up the implementation of his plans. The message he received told him that Father Costous was about to expose his intention to destroy the Ninth Insight."

"Sebastian found it?"

"Not yet, but he expects to. They found another document that indicated where the Ninth is."

"Where is it supposed to be?" Julia asked.

"At the Celestine ruins," Sanchez replied.

"Where is that?" I inquired.

Julia looked at me. "About sixty miles from here. It's a dig the Peruvian scientists have excavated exclusively and with quite a lot of secrecy. It consists of several layers of ancient temples, first Mayan, then Inca. Apparently both cultures believed there was something special about that location."

I suddenly realized that Sanchez was concentrating on the conversation with unusual intensity. When I talked, he would focus totally on me, without breaking his gaze at all. When Julia spoke, Father Sanchez shifted his position to focus completely on her. He seemed to be acting very deliberately. I wondered what he was doing, and at that precise moment there occurred a lull in the conversation. They both looked at me expectantly.

"What?" I asked.

Sanchez smiled. "It's your time to speak."

"Are we taking turns?" I asked.

"No," Julia said, "we are having a conscious conversation. Each person speaks when the energy moves to him. We could tell it had moved to you."

I didn't know what to say.

Sanchez looked at me warmly. "Part of the Eighth Insight is learning to interact consciously when in a group. But don't get self-conscious. Just understand the process. As the members of a group talk, only one will have the most powerful idea at any one point in time. If they are alert, the others in the group can feel who is about to speak, and then they can consciously focus their energy on this person, helping to bring out his idea with the greatest clarity.

"Then, as the conversation proceeds, someone else will have the most powerful idea, then someone else and so forth. If you concentrate on what is being said, you can feel when it is your turn. The idea will come up into your mind."

Sanchez shifted his eyes to Julia, who asked, "What idea were you having that you didn't express?"

I tried to think. "I was wondering," I said finally, "why Father Sanchez was looking intensely at whomever was speaking. I guess I was wondering what it meant."

"The key to this process," Sanchez said, "is to speak up when it is your moment and to project energy when it is someone else's time."

"Many things can go wrong," Julia interjected. "Some people get inflated when in a group. They feel the power of an idea and express it, then because that burst of energy feels so good, they keep on talking, long after the energy should have shifted to someone else. They try to monopolize the group.

"Others are pulled back and even when they feel the power of an idea, they won't risk saying it. When this happens, the group fragments and the members don't get the benefit of all the messages. The same thing happens when some members of the group are not accepted by some of the others. The rejected individuals are prevented from receiving the energy and so the group misses the benefit of their ideas."

Julia paused and we both looked at Sanchez who was taking a breath to speak. "How people are excluded is important," he said. "When we dislike someone, or feel threatened by someone, the natural tendency is to focus on something we dislike about the person, something that irritates us. Unfortunately, when we do this—instead of seeing the deeper beauty of the person and giving them energy—we take energy away and actually do them harm. All they know is that they suddenly feel less beautiful and less confident, and it is because we sapped their energy."

"That is why," Julia said, "this process is so important. Humans are aging each other at a tremendous rate out there with their violent competitions."

"But remember," Sanchez added, "in a truly functional group, the idea is to do the opposite of this, the idea is for every member's energy and vibration to increase because of the energy sent by all of the others. When this occurs, everyone's individual energy field merges with everyone else's and makes one pool of energy. It is as if the group is just one body, but one with many heads. Sometimes one head speaks for the body. Sometimes another talks. But in a group functioning this way, each individual knows when to speak and what to say because he truly sees life more clearly. This is the Higher Person the Eighth insight talked about in connection with a romantic relationship between a man and a women. But other groups can form one as well."

Father Sanchez's words made me think of Father Costous suddenly, and of Pablo. Had this young Indian finally changed Father Costous' mind, leading him to now want to preserve the Manuscript? Was Pablo able to do this because of the power of the Eighth Insight?

"Where is Father Costous now?" I asked.

Both individuals looked mildly surprised at my question, but Father Sanchez quickly replied, "He and Father Carl decided to go to Lima to speak with our church leaders about what Cardinal Sebastian seems to have planned."

"I guess that's why he was so adamant about going to your mission with you. He knew there was something else he was supposed to do."

"Exactly," Sanchez said.

A lull developed in the conversation and we looked at one another, each of us waiting for the next idea.

"The question now," Father Sanchez finally said, "is what are *we* supposed to do?"

Julia spoke first. "I've had thoughts all along about being involved with the Ninth Insight somehow, of getting hold of it long enough to do something. . . but I can't quite see it clearly."

Sanchez and I gazed at her intensely.

"I see this happening at a particular place. . ." she continued. "Wait a minute. The place I've been thinking about is at the ruins, at the Celestine ruins. There is a particular spot there between the temples. I'd almost forgotten." She looked back at us. "That's where I need to go; I need to go to the Celestine ruins."

As Julia finished, both she and Sanchez shifted their gaze to me.

"I don't know," I said. "I've been interested in why Sebastian and his people are so against the Manuscript. I found out it's because they fear the idea of our inner evolution . . . but now I don't know where to go . . . those soldiers are coming . . . it appears that Sebastian is going to find the Ninth Insight first . . . I don't know; I've been thinking I'm involved somehow in convincing him not to destroy it."

I stopped speaking. My thoughts went to Dobson again and then abruptly to the Ninth Insight. I suddenly realized that the Ninth Insight was going to reveal where we humans were going with this evolution. I had wondered how humans would be acting toward each other as a result of the Manuscript, and that question had been answered with the Eighth Insight, and now the logical next question was: where is it all going to lead, how will human society change? That had to be what the Ninth was about.

I knew somehow that this knowledge could also be used to ease Sebastian's fears about conscious evolution. . .If he would listen.

"I still think Cardinal Sebastian can be convinced to support the Manuscript!" I said with conviction.

"You see yourself convincing him?" Sanchez asked me.

"No . . . no, not really. I'm with someone else who can reach him, someone who knows him and can speak at his level."

As I said that, Julia and I both spontaneously looked at Father Sanchez.

He struggled to smile and spoke with resignation. "Cardinal Sebastian and I have avoided a confrontation over the Manuscript for a long time. He has always been my superior. He considered me his protégé and I must admit that I looked up to him. But I guess I always knew that it would come to this. The first time you mentioned it, I knew that the task of convincing him was mine. My whole life has set me up for it."

He looked intensely at Julia and me, then continued, "My mother was a Christian reformer. She hated the use of guilt and coercion when evangelizing. She felt that people should come to religion because of love, not out of fear. My father, on the other hand, was a disciplinarian who later became a priest, and like Sebastian, believed adamantly in tradition and authority. That left me wanting to work within church authority, but always seeking ways it should be amended so that higher religious experience is emphasized.

"Dealing with Sebastian is the next step for me. I've been resisting it, but I know I have to go to Sebastian's mission at Iquitos."

"I'll ride with you," I said.

THE
EMERGING
CULTURE

The road north wound through dense jungle and across several large streams—tributaries, Father Sanchez told me—of the Amazon. We had risen early and said a quick good-bye to Julia, then left in a vehicle Father Sanchez had borrowed, a truck with raised, oversized tires and four-wheel drive. As we traveled, the terrain rose slightly and the trees became more widely spaced and larger.

"This looks like the land around Viciente," I told Sanchez.

He smiled at me and said, "We've entered a fifty mile stretch of land about twenty miles wide that is different, more energized. It runs all the way to the Celestine ruins. On all sides of this area is pure jungle."

Far to the right, at the edge of the jungle, I noticed a patch of cleared land. "What is that?" I asked, pointing.

"That," he said, "is the government's idea of agricultural development."

A wide stretch of trees had been bulldozed and pushed into piles, some partially burned. A herd of cattle grazed aimlessly amid the wild grasses and eroded topsoil. As we passed, several looked our way, distracted by the sound. I noticed another patch of freshly bull-dozed land and realized the development was moving toward the larger trees we were traveling through.

"That looks awful," I said.

"It is," Sanchez replied. "Even Cardinal Sebastian is against it."

I thought of Phil. Maybe this was the place he was trying to protect. What had happened to him? Suddenly, I thought of Dobson again. Connor had said Dobson intended to come to the inn. Why had Connor been there to tell me that? Where was Dobson now? Deported? Imprisoned? It did not escape my notice that I had spontaneously perceived an image of Dobson in connection with Phil.

"How far away is Sebastian's mission?" I asked.

"About an hour," Sanchez replied. "How are you feeling?"

"What do you mean?"

"I mean, how is your energy level?"

"I think it's high," I said. "Lots of beauty here."

"What did you think of the talk we three had last night?" he asked.

"I thought it was amazing."

"Did you understand what was happening?"

"You mean, the way ideas were bubbling up in each of us at different times?"

"Yes, but the greater meaning of that."

"I don't know."

"Well, I've been thinking about it. This way of consciously relating, in which everyone attempts to bring out the best in others rather than to have power over them, is a posture the entire human race will eventually adopt. Think of how everyone's energy level and pace of evolution will increase at that point!"

"Right," I said, "I've been wondering how human culture will change as the overall energy level rises."

He looked at me as if I had hit on the exact question. "That's what I want to know, too," he said.

We looked at each other for an instant and I knew we were both waiting to see who would have the next idea. Finally he said, "The answer to that question must be in the Ninth Insight. It must explain what will happen as the culture evolves forward."

"That's what I think," I said.

Sanchez slowed the truck. We were approaching a crossroads and he seemed undecided about which route to take.

"Do we go anywhere near San Luis?" I asked.

He looked directly into my eyes. "Only if we turn left at this intersection. Why?"

"Connor told me Dobson had been planning to come through San Luis on his way to the inn. I think it was a message."

We continued to look at each other.

"You were already slowing down at this cross-roads." I said. "Why?"

He shrugged. "I don't know; the most direct route to Iquitos is straight ahead. I just felt hesitant for some reason."

A chill shot through my body.

Sanchez raised one eyebrow and grinned. "I guess we had better go through San Luis, huh?"

I nodded and felt a rush of energy. I knew that stopping at the inn and making contact with Connor was taking on more meaning. As Sanchez turned left and proceeded toward San Luis, I watched the roadside expectantly. Thirty or forty minutes passed and nothing happened. We rode through San Luis and still nothing of note occurred. Then, suddenly, a horn blew and we turned to see a silver jeep roaring up behind us. The driver was frantically waving. He looked familiar.

"That's Phil!" I said.

We pulled to the side of the road and Phil jumped out and ran to my side of the truck, grabbing my hand and nodding at Sanchez.

"I don't know what you're doing here," he said, "but the road ahead is full of soldiers. You'd better come back and wait with us."

"How did you know we were coming?" I asked.

"I didn't," he said. "I just looked up and saw you pass by. We're about a half mile back." He looked around for a second, then added, "We'd better get off this road!"

"We'll follow you," Father Sanchez said.

We followed as Phil turned his jeep around and headed back the way we'd come. He turned east onto another road and quickly parked. From behind a group of trees, another man walked out to greet the vehicle. I couldn't believe my sight. It was Dobson!

I climbed out of the truck and walked toward him. He was equally surprised and hugged me warmly.

"It's great to see you!" he said.

"Same here," I replied. "I thought you were shot!"

Dobson patted my back and said, "No, I guess I panicked; they simply detained me. Later, some officials sympathetic to the Manuscript let me go. I've been running ever since."

He paused, smiling at me. "I'm glad you're all right. When Phil told me he had met you at Viciente and then was arrested with you later, I didn't know what to think. But I should have known we would run into each other again. Where are you headed?"

"To see Cardinal Sebastian. We think he intends to destroy the last Insight."

Dobson nodded and was about to say something, but Father Sanchez walked up.

I quickly introduced them.

"I think I heard your name mentioned in Lima," Dobson said to Sanchez, "in connection with a couple of priests that were being detained."

"Father Carl and Father Costous?" I asked.

"I think those were their names, yes."

Sanchez only shook his head slightly. I watched him for a moment, then Dobson and I spent several minutes describing our experiences since being separated. He told me he had studied all eight insights and seemed anxious to say something else, but I interrupted to tell him that we had met Connor and that he had returned to Lima.

"He'll probably be detained himself," Dobson said. "I regret I couldn't get to the inn in time, but I wanted to come to San Luis first to see another scientist. As it turned out I couldn't find him, but I did run into Phil and . . ."

"What is it?" Sanchez asked.

"Maybe we ought to sit down," Dobson said. "You won't believe this. Phil found a copy of part of the Ninth Insight!"

No one moved.

"He found a translated copy?" Father Sanchez asked.

"Yes."

Phil had been doing something inside his vehicle and was now walking toward us.

"You found part of the Ninth?" I asked him.

"I didn't find it, really," he said. "It was given to me. After you and I were captured, I was taken to another town. I don't know where. After a while, Cardinal Sebastian showed up. He kept probing me about the work at Viciente and my efforts to save the forests. I didn't know why until a guard brought me a partial copy of the Ninth Insight. The guard had stolen it from some of Sebastian's people, who had apparently just translated it. It talks about the energy of old forests."

"What did it say?" I asked Phil.

He paused, thinking, so Dobson asked again that we sit down. He led us to a spot where a tarpaulin was laid out in the center of a partial clearing. The place was beautiful. A dozen large trees formed a circle about thirty feet in diameter. Within the circle were highly fragrant tropical bushes and long-stemmed ferns of the brightest green I had ever seen. We sat facing each other.

Phil looked at Dobson. Then Dobson looked at Sanchez and me and said, "The Ninth Insight explains how human culture will change in the next millennium as a result of conscious evolution. It describes a significantly different way of life. For instance, the Manuscript predicts that we humans will voluntarily decrease our population so that we all may live in the most powerful and beautiful places on the Earth. But remarkably, many more of these areas will exist in the future, because we will intentionally let the forests go uncut so that they can mature and build energy.

"According to the Ninth Insight, by the middle of the next millennium," he continued, "humans will typically live among five hundred year old trees and carefully tended gardens, yet within easy travel distance of an urban area of incredible technological wizardry. By then, the means of survival—foodstuffs and clothing and transportation—will all be totally automated and at everyone's disposal. Our needs will be completely met without the exchange of any currency, yet also without any overindulgence or laziness.

"Guided by their intuitions, everyone will know precisely what to do and when to do it, and this will fit harmoniously with the actions of others. No one will consume excessively because we will have let go of the need to possess and to control for security. In the next millennium, life will have become about something else.

"According to the Manuscript," he went on, "our sense of purpose will be satisfied by the thrill of our own evolution—by the elation of receiving intuitions and then watching closely as our destinies unfold. The Ninth depicts a human world where everyone has slowed down and become more alert, ever vigilant for the next meaningful encounter that comes along. We will know that it could occur anywhere: on a path that winds through a forest, for instance, or on a bridge that traverses some canyon.

"Can you visualize human encounters that have this much meaning and significance? Think how it would be for two people meeting for the first time. Each will first observe the other's energy field, exposing any manipulations. Once clear, they will consciously share life stories until, elatedly, messages are discovered. Afterward, each will go forward again on their individual journey, but they will be significantly altered. They will vibrate at a new level and will thereafter touch others in a way not possible before their meeting."

As we gave him energy, Dobson became ever more eloquent and inspired with his description of the new human culture. And what he said rang true. I personally had no doubt that he was describing an achievable future. Yet I also knew that throughout history many visionaries had glimpsed such a world, Marx for example, yet no way had been found to create such a utopia. Communism had become a tragedy.

Even with the knowledge imparted in the first eight insights, I couldn't imagine how the human race could get to the place described by the Ninth, considering human behavior generally. When Dobson paused, I voiced my concern.

"The Manuscript says our natural pursuit of the truth will lead us there," Dobson explained, smiling directly at me. "But to grasp how this movement will occur, perhaps it is necessary to visualize the next millennium in the same manner you studied the current one with me on the airplane, remember? As though you were living through it in one lifetime?"

Dobson briefly informed the other men of the process and then continued, "Think about what has occurred already in this millennium. During the Middle Ages we lived in a simple world of good and evil, defined by the churchmen. But during the Renaissance we broke free. We knew there had to be more to man's situation in the universe than the churchmen knew, and we wanted the full story.

"We then sent science out to discover our true situation, but when this effort didn't provide the answers we needed right away, we decided to settle in, and turned our modern work ethic into a preoccupation that secularized reality and squeezed the mystery out of the world. But now, we can see the truth of that preoccupation. We can see that the real reason we spent five centuries creating material supports for human life was to set the stage for something else, a way of life that returns the mystery to existence.

"That is what the information now returning from the scientific method indicates: mankind is on this planet to consciously evolve. And as we learn to evolve and pursue our particular path, truth by truth, the Ninth Insight says the overall culture will transform in a very predictable way."

He paused, but no one said anything. Obviously we wanted to hear more.

"Once we reach the critical mass," he continued, "and the insights begin to come in on a global scale, the human race will first experience a period of intense introspection. We'll grasp how beautiful and spiritual the natural world really is. We'll see trees and rivers and mountains as temples of great power to be held in reverence and awe. We'll demand an end to any economic activity that threatens this treasure. And those closest to this situation will find alternative solutions to this pollution problem because someone will intuit these alternatives as they seek their own evolution.

"This will be part of the first great shift that will occur," he continued, "which will be a dramatic movement of individuals from one occupation to another—because when people begin to receive clear intuitions of who they really are and what they're supposed to be doing, they very often discover they're in the wrong job and they have to jump to another type work in order to continue to grow. The Manuscript says that during this period people will sometimes change careers several times during their lifetimes.

"The next cultural shift will be an automation of the production of goods. To the people who are doing the automating, the technicians, this will feel like a need to make the economy run more efficiently. But as their intuitions become clearer, they will see that what automation is actually doing is freeing up everyone's time, so that we can pursue other endeavors.

"The rest of us, meanwhile, will be following our own intuitions within our chosen occupations and wishing we had even more of this free time. We will realize that the truth we have to tell and the things we have to do are too unique to fit within a usual job setting. So we will find ways to cut our employment hours to pursue our own truth. Two or three people will hold what used to be one full-time job. This trend will make it easier for those displaced by the automation to find at least part-time jobs."

"But what about money?" I asked. "I can't believe people will voluntarily reduce their incomes."

"Oh, we won't have to," Dobson said. "The Manuscript says our incomes will remain stable because of the people who are giving us money for the insights we provide."

I almost laughed. "What?"

He smiled and looked directly at me. "The Manuscript says that as we discover more about the energy dynamics of the universe, we will see what really happens when we give someone something. Right now the only spiritual idea about giving is the narrow concept of religious tithing."

He moved his gaze to Father Sanchez. "As you know, the scriptural notion of tithing is interpreted most commonly as an injunction to give ten percent of one's income to a church. The idea behind this is that whatever we give will be returned many times. But the Ninth Insight explains that giving is really a universal principle of support, not just for churches, but for everyone. When we give, we receive in return because of the way energy interacts in the universe. Remember, when we project energy into someone this creates a void in ourselves which, if we are connected, fills up again. Money works exactly the same way. The Ninth Insight says that once we begin to give constantly, we will always have more coming in than we could possibly give away.

"And our gifts," he went on, "should go to the persons who have given us spiritual truth. When people come into our lives at just the right time to give us the answers we need, we should give them money. This is how we will begin to supplement our incomes and ease out of the occupations which limit us. As more people engage in this spiritual economy we will begin a real shift into the culture of the next millennium. We will have moved through the stage of evolving into our right occupation and will be entering the stage of getting paid for evolving freely and offering our unique truth to others."

I looked at Sanchez; he was listening intensely and appeared radiant.

"Yes," he said to Dobson. "I see that clearly. If everyone were participating then we would be giving and receiving constantly and this interaction with others, this exchange of information, would become everyone's new work, our new economic orientation. We'd be paid by the people we touched. This situation would then allow the material supports of life to become fully automated, because we would be too busy to own those systems, or to operate them. We would want material production automated and run like a utility. We'd own stock in it, perhaps, but the situation would free us up to expand what is already the information age.

"But the important thing for us right now is that we can now understand where we are going. We could not save the environment and democratize the planet and feed the poor before because for so long we could not release our fear of scarcity and our need to control, so that we could give to others. We couldn't release it because we had no view of life that served as an alternative. Now we do!"

He looked at Phil. "But wouldn't we need a cheap source of energy?"

"Fusion, superconductivity, artificial intelligence," Phil said. "The technology to automate is probably not that far away, now that we have the knowledge of why to do it."

"That's right," Dobson said. "The most important thing is that we see the truth of this way of life. We're here on this planet not to build personal empires of control, but to evolve. Paying others for their insights will begin the transformation and then as more and more parts of the economy are automated, currency will disappear altogether. We won't need it. If we are correctly following our intuitive guidance then we will take only what we need."

"And we'll understand," Phil interjected, "that the natural areas of the Earth have to be nurtured and protected for the sources of incredible power that they are."

As Phil spoke, our full attention went to him. He seemed surprised by the lift it provided.

"I haven't studied all of the insights," he said, looking at me. "In fact, after the guard helped me escape, I might not have kept this part of the Ninth at all if I hadn't run into you earlier. I remembered what you said about this Manuscript being important. But even though I haven't read the other insights, I do understand the importance of keeping the automation in harmony with the energy dynamics of the Earth.

"My interest has been forests and the part they play in the ecosphere," he continued. "I know now that it always has been, ever since I was a child. The Ninth Insight says that as the human race evolves spiritually, we will voluntarily decrease the population to a point sustainable by the Earth. We will be committed to living within the natural energy systems of the planet. Farming will be automated except for the plants one wants to energize personally and then consume. The trees necessary for construction will be grown in special, designated areas. This will free the remainder of the Earth's trees to grow and age and finally mature into powerful forests.

"Eventually, these forests will be the rule rather than the exception, and all human beings will live in close proximity to this kind of power. Think what an energy-filled world we will live in."

"That ought to raise everyone's energy level," I said.

"Yes, it would," Sanchez said distractedly, as though he were thinking ahead about what the increase in energy would mean.

Everyone waited.

"It would accelerate," he said finally, "the pace of our evolution. The more readily we have energy flowing into us, the more mysteriously the universe responds by bringing people into our lives to answer our questions." He looked thoughtful again. "And every time we follow an intuition and some mysterious encounter leads us forward, our personal vibration increases.

"Onward and upward," he continued, half to himself. "If history continues, then . . ."

"We'll continue to achieve higher and higher levels of energy and vibration," Dobson said, finishing his sentence.

"Yes," Sanchez said. "That's it. Excuse me for a minute." He got up and walked several yards into the forest and sat down alone.

"What else does the Ninth Insight say?" I asked Dobson.

"We don't know," he said. "That's where the part we have ends. Would you like to see it?"

I told him I would, so he walked to his truck and came back with a manila folder. Inside were twenty typed pages. I read the manuscript, impressed with how thoroughly Dobson and Phil had captured its basic points. When I came to the last page I understood why they said it was only a part of the Ninth Insight. It ended abruptly, in the middle of a concept. Having just introduced the idea that the transformation of the planet would create a totally spiritual culture and would raise human beings to higher and higher vibrations, it suggested that this rise would lead to the occurrence of something else, but it didn't say what.

After an hour, Sanchez stood up and walked over to me. I had been content to sit with the plants, observing their incredible energy fields. Dobson and Phil were standing behind their jeep talking. "I think we should go on to Iquitos," he said.

"What about those soldiers?" I asked.

"I think we should risk it. I've had a clear thought that we can make it through if we leave right now."

I agreed to go with his intuition and we walked over and told Dobson and Phil our plans.

Both men supported the idea, then Dobson said, "We've also been discussing what to do. We're going directly to the Celestine ruins, I think. Maybe we can help save the rest of the Ninth Insight."

We bade them good-bye and drove north again.

"What are you thinking about?" I asked after a period of silence.

Father Sanchez slowed the truck and looked at me. "I'm thinking about Cardinal Sebastian, about what you have said: that he would stop fighting the Manuscript if only he could be made to understand."

As Father Sanchez made this statement, my mind wandered into a daydream of actually confronting Sebastian. He was standing in a courtly room looking down at us. At that moment he had the power to destroy the Ninth Insight and we were fighting to make him understand before it was too late.

When I finished the thought, I noticed Sanchez was smiling at me.

"What were you seeing?" he asked.

"I was just thinking of Sebastian."

"What was happening?"

"The image of confronting Sebastian was clearer. He was about to destroy the last insight. We were trying to talk him out of it."

Sanchez took a deep breath, "It looks like whether the rest of the Ninth Insight becomes known will depend on us."

My stomach drew into a knot at the idea. "What should we say to him?"

"I don't know. But we must persuade him to see the positive, to understand that the Manuscript as a whole doesn't negate but clarifies the truth of the Church. I'm sure the rest of the Ninth Insight does just that."

We rode in silence for an hour, seeing no other traffic of any kind. My thoughts raced through the events which had transpired since I'd come to Peru. I knew the Manuscript's insights had finally merged in my mind into one consciousness. I was alert to the mysterious way my life evolved, as revealed by the First Insight. I knew that the whole culture was sensing this mystery again as well, and we were in the process of constructing a new world view, as pointed out by the Second. The Third and Fourth had showed me that the universe was in reality a vast system of energy and that human conflict was a shortage of and a manipulation for this energy.

The Fifth Insight revealed that we could end this conflict by receiving an inpouring of this energy from a higher source. For me, this ability had almost become habit. The Sixth, that we could clear our old repeated dramas, and find our true selves, was also permanently etched in my mind. And the Seventh had set in motion the evolution of these true selves: through question, intuition of what to do, and answer. Staying in this magic flow was truly the secret of happiness.

And the Eighth, knowing how to relate in a new way to others, bringing out in them the very best, was the key to keeping the mystery operating and the answers coming.

All the Insights had integrated into a consciousness that felt like a heightened sense of alertness and expectation. What was left, I knew, was the Ninth, which revealed where our evolution was taking us. We had discovered some of it. What about the rest?

Father Sanchez pulled the truck to the side of the road.

"We're within four miles of Cardinal Sebastian's mission," he said. "I think we should talk."

"Okay."

"I don't know what to expect but I presume all we can do is drive right in."

"How large a place is this?"

"Large. He has developed this mission for twenty years. He selected this location to serve the rural Indians whom he felt had been neglected. But now students come from all over Peru. He has administrative duties with the church organization in Lima, but this is his special project. He is totally devoted to this mission."

He looked directly into my eyes. "Please stay alert. There may come a time when we need to help each other."

After saying this, Sanchez drove ahead. For several miles we saw nothing, then we passed two military jeeps parked at the right side of the road. The soldiers inside looked at us intensely as we drove by.

"Well," Father Sanchez said, "they know we are here."

A mile further we came to the entrance to the mission. Large iron gates protected the paved drive. Although the gates were open, a jeep and four soldiers blocked our way and signaled us to stop. One of the military men talked into a short-wave radio.

Sanchez smiled as a soldier walked up. "I'm Father Sanchez, here to see Cardinal Sebastian."

The soldier scrutinized Sanchez, then me. He turned and walked back to the soldier with the radio. They talked without taking their eyes off us. After several minutes the soldier came back and said we should follow them.

The jeep led us up the tree-lined drive for several hundred yards until we came to the mission grounds. The church was built of cut stone and was massive, capable of seating, I guessed, over a thousand people. On both sides of the church were two other buildings which looked like classrooms. Both were four stories high.

"This place is impressive," I said.

"Yes, but where are the people?" he asked.

I noticed the paths and walkways were empty.

"Sebastian runs a famous school here," he said. "Why are there no students?"

The soldiers led us to the entrance of the church and asked us politely but firmly to get out and follow them inside. As we walked up the cement steps, I could see several trucks parked behind an adjacent building. Thirty or forty soldiers stood at attention nearby. Once inside we were led through the sanctuary and asked to enter a small room. There we were searched thoroughly and told to wait. The soldiers left and the door was locked.

"Where is Sebastian's office?" I asked.

"Further back toward the rear of the church," he said.

The door suddenly opened. Flanked by several soldiers stood Sebastian. His posture was tall and erect.

"What are you doing here?" Sebastian asked Sanchez.

"I want to talk with you," Sanchez said.

"About what?"

"The Ninth Insight of the Manuscript."

"There's nothing to discuss. It will never be found."

"We know you've already found it."

Sebastian's eyes widened. "I will not allow this insight to be disseminated," he said. "It is not the truth."

"How do you know it's not the truth?" Sanchez asked. "You could be wrong. Let me read it."

Sebastian's face softened as he looked at Sanchez. "You used to think I would make the correct decision in a matter of this kind."

"I know," Sanchez said. "You were my mentor. My inspiration. I patterned my mission after yours."

"You respected me until this Manuscript was discovered," Sebastian said. "Don't you see how divisive it is? I tried to let you go your own way. I even let you alone after I knew you were teaching the insights. But I will not let this document destroy everything our church has built."

Another soldier walked up behind Sebastian and asked to see him. Sebastian glanced at Sanchez, then walked back into the hall. We could still see but could no longer hear the conversation. The message obviously alarmed Sebastian. As he turned to walk away, he signaled for all the soldiers to follow him except for one, whom he apparently told to wait with us.

The soldier walked into the room and leaned against the wall, a disturbed look on his face. He was only about twenty years old.

"What is wrong?" Sanchez asked him.

The soldier only shook his head.

"Is it about the Manuscript, the Ninth Insight?"

The soldier's face displayed surprise. "What do you know of the Ninth Insight?" he asked timidly.

"We're here to save it," Sanchez said.

"I too want it saved," the soldier replied.

"Have you read it?" I asked.

"No," he said. "But I have heard the talk. It brings our religion alive."

Suddenly, from outside the church came the sound of gunfire.

"What's going on?!" Sanchez asked.

The soldier stood motionless.

Sanchez gently touched his arm, "Help us."

The young soldier walked to the door and checked the hall, then said. "Someone has broken into the church and stolen a copy of the Ninth Insight. They seem to still be here on the grounds somewhere."

More gunfire broke out.

"We must try to help them," Sanchez told the young man.

He looked horrified.

"We must do what's right," Sanchez stressed. "This is for the whole world."

The soldier nodded and said we should move to another area of the church where there would be less activity, that perhaps he could find a way to help. He led us down the hall and up two flights of stairs to a larger corridor which spanned the full width of the church.

"Sebastian's office is right below us, two stories down," the young man said.

Suddenly we could hear a group of people running down an adjacent corridor, heading our way. Sanchez and the soldier were ahead of me and ducked into a room to the right. I knew I couldn't reach that room so I ran into the one next to it and closed the door.

I was in a classroom. Desks, podium, closet. I ran to the closet, found it unlocked, and squeezed in amid boxes and several musty smelling jackets. I attempted to conceal myself as best I could, but I knew if anyone checked in the closet, I would be discovered. I tried not to move, not even to breathe. The door to the classroom squeaked open and I could hear several people enter and walk about the room. One seemed to be coming toward the closet, then stopped and headed in the other direction. They were talking loudly in Spanish. Then silence. No movement.

I waited ten minutes before I slowly cracked the closet door and looked out. The room was empty. I walked to the door. There was no indication of anyone outside. I quickly walked to the room where Sanchez and the soldier had hidden. To my surprise, I found it was not a room at all but a hallway. I listened but could hear nothing. I leaned against the wall, feeling anxiety in the pit of my stomach. I quietly called out Sanchez's name. No response. I was alone. I could feel a slight dizziness from the anxiety.

I took a deep breath and tried to talk to myself; I had to keep my wits about me and increase my energy. For several minutes, I struggled until the colors and shapes in the hallway had more presence. I tried to project love. Finally I felt better, and thought of Sebastian again. If he was in his office, Sanchez would go there.

Ahead, the hallway ended at another stairway, so I walked two flights down to the first level. Through the window of the stairway door, I looked down the corridor. No one was in view. I opened the door and walked ahead, not sure where I wanted to go.

Then I heard Sanchez's voice coming from a room in front of me. The door was cracked. Sebastian's voice boomed back at him. As I approached the door, a soldier inside opened it suddenly and pointed a rifle at my heart, forcing me inside and against the wall. Sanchez acknowledged me with a glance and put his hand on his solar plexus. Sebastian shook his head in disgust. The young soldier who had helped us was nowhere to be seen.

I knew that Sanchez's gesture to his stomach meant something. All I could think of was that he needed energy. As he spoke, I focused on his face, trying to see his higher self. His energy field widened.

"You can't stop the truth," Sanchez said. "People have a right to know."

Sebastian looked condescendingly at Sanchez. "These insights violate the scriptures. They could not be true."

"But do they really violate the scriptures, or do they just show us what the scriptures mean?"

"We know what they mean," Sebastian said. "We've known for centuries. Have you forgotten your training, your years of study?"

"No, I haven't," Sanchez said. "But I also know that the insights expand our spirituality. They . . ."

"According to whom?" Sebastian shouted. "Who wrote this Manuscript anyway? Some pagan Mayan who learned somewhere how to speak

Aramaic? What did these people know? They believed in magic places and mysterious energy. They were primitives. The ruins where the Ninth was found is called the Celestine Temples, the *Heavenly* Temples. What could this culture possibly know about heaven?

"Did their culture endure?" he continued. "No. No one knows what happened to the Mayans. They just disappeared without a trace. And you want us to believe this Manuscript? This document makes it sound as though humans are in control, as though we are in charge of change in the world. We are not. God is. The only issue humans face is whether to accept the scriptural teachings and thereby win our own salvation."

"But think about that," Sanchez replied, "What does accepting the teachings and winning salvation really mean? What is the process through which this happens? Doesn't the Manuscript show us the exact process of becoming more spiritual, connected, saved—the way it actually feels? And doesn't the Eighth and Ninth show us what would happen if everyone were acting this way?"

Sebastian shook his head and walked away, then turned and looked at Sanchez piercingly. "You haven't even seen the Ninth Insight."

"Yes I have. Part of it."

"How?"

"Part of it was described to me before we arrived here. I read another section a few minutes ago."

"What?! How?"

Sanchez walked closer to the older priest. "Cardinal Sebastian, people everywhere want this last insight revealed. It places the other insights into perspective. It shows us our destiny. What spiritual consciousness really is!

"We know what spirituality is, Father Sanchez."

"Do we? I think not. We've spent centuries talking about it, visualizing it, professing our belief in it. But we've always characterized this connection as something abstract, something we believe in intellectually. And we've always cast this connection as something an individual must do to avoid something bad happening, rather than to acquire something good and tremendous. The Manuscript describes the inspiration that comes when we are truly loving others and evolving our lives forward."

"Evolve! Evolve! Listen to yourself, Father, you have always fought against the influence of evolution. What has happened to you?"

Sanchez collected himself. "Yes, I fought against the idea of evolution as a replacement for God, as a way to explain the universe without reference to God. But now I see that the truth is a synthesis of the scientific and religious world views. The truth is that evolution is the way God created, and is still creating."

"But there is no evolution," Sebastian protested. "God created this world and that's it."

Sanchez glanced at me but I had no ideas to express.

"Cardinal Sebastian," he continued, "the Manuscript describes the progress of succeeding generations as an evolution of understanding, an evolution toward a higher spirituality and vibration. Each generation incorporates more energy and accumulates more truth and then passes that status on to the people of the next generation, who extend it further."

"That's nonsense," Sebastian said. "There is only one way to become more spiritual and that's by following the examples in the scriptures."

"Exactly!" Sanchez said. "But again, what are the examples? Isn't the story of the scriptures a story of people learning to receive God's energy and will within? Isn't that what the early prophets led the people to do in the Old Testament? And isn't that receptivity to God's energy within what culminated in the life of a carpenter's son, to the extent that we say God, himself, descended to Earth?

"Isn't the story of the New Testament," he continued, "the story of a group of people being filled with some kind of energy that transformed them? Didn't Jesus, himself, say that what he did, we could do also, and more? We've never really taken that idea seriously, not until now. We're only now grasping what Jesus was talking about, where he was leading us. The Manuscript clarifies what he meant! How to do it!"

Sebastian looked away, his face red with anger. During the pause in the conversation, a high ranking officer burst into the room and told Sebastian that the intruders had been seen.

"Look!" the officer said, pointing out the window. "There they are!"

Three or four hundred yards away we could see two figures running through an open field headed toward the forest. A number of soldiers at the edge of the clearing seemed ready to open fire.

The officer turned from the window and looked at Sebastian, his radio raised.

"If they get to the wooded area," he said, "they will be hard to find. Do I have your permission to open fire?"

As I watched the two running, I suddenly recognized who they were.

"That's Wil and Julia!" I shouted.

Sanchez walked even closer to Sebastian. "In the name of God, you cannot commit murder over this!"

The officer persisted. "Cardinal Sebastian, if you want this Manuscript contained, I must give the order now."

I was frozen.

"Father, trust me," Sanchez was saying. "The Manuscript will not erode all you have built, all you have stood for. You cannot kill these people."

Sebastian shook his head. "Trust you . . ?" Then he sat down on his desk and looked at the officer. "We will shoot no one. Tell your troops to capture them alive."

The officer nodded and walked out of the room. Sanchez said, "Thank you, you made the right choice."

"Not to kill, yes," Sebastian said. "But I will not change my mind. This Manuscript is a curse. It would undermine our basic structure of spiritual authority. It would entice people to think they are in control of their spiritual destiny. It would undermine the discipline needed to bring everyone on the planet into the church, and people would be caught wanting when the rapture comes." He looked hard at Sanchez. "At this moment, thousands of troops are arriving. It doesn't matter what you or anyone else does. The Ninth Insight will never leave Peru. Now get out of my mission."

As we sped away, we could hear dozens of trucks approaching in the distance.

"Why did he let us go?" I asked.

"I suppose because he thinks it makes no difference," Sanchez replied, "that there's nothing we can do. I really don't know what to think." His eyes met mine. "We didn't convince him, you know."

I too, was confused. What did it mean? Perhaps we hadn't been there to convince Sebastian after all. Perhaps we were just supposed to delay him.

I glanced back at Sanchez. He was concentrating on driving and searching the roadside for any sign of Wil and Julia. We had decided that we would double back in the direction they had been running, but so far we had seen nothing. As we rode, my mind wandered to the Celestine ruins. I imagined what the site looked like: the tiered excavations, the scientist's tents, the looming pyramidal structures in the background.

"They don't seem to be in these woods," Sanchez said. "They must have had a vehicle. We must decide what to do."

"I think we should go to the ruins," I said.

He looked at me. "We might as well. There's no where else to go."

Sanchez made a turn to the west.

"What do you know of these ruins?" I asked.

"They were built by two different cultures, as Julia said. The first, the Mayans, had a thriving civilization there, though most of their temples were further north in the Yucatan. Mysteriously, all signs of their civilization suddenly vanished about 600 B.C. without apparent cause. The Incas developed another civilization afterward at the same location."

"What do you think happened to the Mayans?"

Sanchez glanced at me. "I don't know."

We rode for several minutes in silence, then I suddenly remembered that Father Sanchez had told Sebastian he had read more of the Ninth Insight.

"How did you see more of the Ninth Insight?" I asked.

"The young soldier who helped us knew where another part was being hidden. After you and I were separated, he took me to another room and showed it to me. It added only a few more concepts to what Phil and

Dobson told us, but it gave me the points I used with Sebastian."

"What did it say specifically?"

"That the Manuscript would clarify many religions. And would help them fulfill their promise. All religion, it says, is about humankind finding relationship to one higher source. And all religions speak of a perception of God within, a perception that fills us, makes us more than we were. Religions become corrupted when leaders are assigned to explain God's will to the people instead of showing them how to find this direction within themselves.

"The Manuscript says that sometime in history one individual would grasp the exact way of connecting with God's source of energy and direction and would thus become a lasting example that this connection is possible." Sanchez looked at me. "Isn't that what Jesus really did? Didn't he increase his energy and vibration until he was light enough to . . .?" Sanchez ended his sentence without finishing it and seemed to be deep in thought.

"What are you thinking?" I asked.

Sanchez looked perplexed. "I don't know. The soldier's copy ended right there. It said that this individual would blaze a path that the whole human race was destined to follow. But it didn't say where this path led."

For fifteen minutes we rode in silence. I attempted to receive some indication of what would happen next, but I could think of nothing. I seemed to be trying too hard.

"There are the ruins," Sanchez said.

Ahead, through the forest to the left of the road, I could make out three large pyramidal shaped structures. After we parked and walked closer, I could tell the pyramids were constructed of cut stone and were spaced an equal distance apart, about a hundred feet. Between them was an area paved with a smoother stone. Several excavation sites were dug into the base of the pyramids.

"Look, there!" Sanchez said, pointing toward the more distant pyramid.

A lone figure was sitting in front of the structure. As we walked that way, I noticed an increase in my energy level. By the time we reached the center of the paved area I felt incredibly energized. I looked at Sanchez and he raised an eyebrow. When we got closer I recognized the person by the pyramid to be Julia. She sat cross-legged and held several papers in her lap.

"Julia," Sanchez called.

Julia turned and stood up. Her face seemed iridescent.

"Where is Wil?" I asked.

Julia pointed to her right. There, perhaps a hundred yards away was Wil. He seemed to be glowing in the fading twilight.

"What is he doing?" I asked.

"The Ninth," Julia replied, holding the papers toward us. Sanchez told Julia that we had seen some of the insight, the part which foretold of a human world transformed by conscious evolution.

"But where does this evolution take us?" Sanchez asked.

Julia didn't answer. She just held up the papers in her hand, as though she expected us to read her mind.

"What?" I asked.

Sanchez reached over and touched my forearm. His look reminded me to stay alert and to wait.

"The Ninth reveals our ultimate destiny," Julia said. "It makes it all crystal clear. It reiterates that as humans, we are the culmination of the whole of evolution. It talks about matter beginning in a weak form and increasing in complexity, element by element, then species by species, always evolving into a higher state of vibration.

"When primitive humans came along, we continued this evolution unconsciously by conquering others and gaining energy and moving forward a little bit, and then being conquered ourselves by someone else and losing our energy. This physical conflict continued until we invented democracy, a system that didn't end the conflict but shifted it from a physical to a mental level.

"Now," Julia went on, "we're bringing this whole process into consciousness. We can see that all of human history has prepared us to achieve conscious evolution. Now, we can increase our energy and experience the coincidences consciously. This carries evolution onward at a faster pace, lifting our vibrations even higher."

She hesitated for a moment, looking at each of us, then repeated what she had said, "Our destiny is to continue to increase our energy level. And as our energy level increases, the level of vibration in the atoms of our bodies increases."

She hesitated again.

"What does that mean?" I asked.

"It means," Julia said, "that we are getting lighter, more purely spiritual."

I looked at Sanchez. He was focused intensely on Julia.

"The Ninth Insight," Julia continued, "says that as we humans continue to increase our vibration, an amazing thing will begin to happen. Whole groups of people, once they reach a certain level, will suddenly become invisible to those who are still vibrating at a lower level. It will appear to the people on this lower level that the others just disappeared, but the group themselves will feel as though they are still right here—only they will feel lighter."

As Julia talked I noticed her face and body changing somewhat. Her body was taking on the characteristics of her energy field. Her features were still clear and distinct but it was no longer muscles and skin at which I was looking. She looked as though she were made of pure light, glowing from within.

I looked at Sanchez. He appeared the same way. To my amazement, everything appeared this way: the pyramids, the stone under our feet, the surrounding forest, my hands. The beauty I was able to perceive had increased beyond anything I had experienced before, even when on the ridge top.

"When humans begin to raise their vibrations to a level where others cannot see them," Julia continued, "it will signal that we are crossing the barrier between this life and the other world from which we came and to which we go after death. This conscious crossing over is the path shown by the Christ. He opened up to the energy until he was so light he could walk on water. He transcended death right here on Earth, and was the first to cross over, to expand the physical world into the spiritual. His life demonstrated how to do this, and if we connect with the same source we can head the same way, step by step. At some point everyone will vibrate highly enough so that we can walk into heaven, in our same form."

I noticed Wil was walking slowly toward us. His movements seemed unusually graceful, as though he was gliding.

"The Insight says," Julia went on, "that most individuals will reach this level of vibration during the third millennium, and in groups consisting of the people with whom they are most connected. But some cultures in history have already achieved the vibration. According to the Ninth Insight, the Mayans crossed over together."

Julia abruptly stopped talking. From behind us, we heard muffled voices in Spanish. Dozens of soldiers were entering the ruins, coming right for us. To my surprise I was unafraid. The soldiers continued to walk in our general direction but strangely not directly toward us.

"They can't see us!" Sanchez said. "We're vibrating too highly!"

I looked again at the soldiers. He was right. They were walking twenty or thirty feet to our left, completely ignoring us.

Suddenly we heard loud shouts in Spanish by the pyramid to our left. The soldiers closest to us stopped and ran in that direction.

I strained to see what was happening. Another group of soldiers were emerging from the forest holding the arms of two other men. Dobson and Phil. The sight of their capture jolted me, and I could feel my energy level plummet. I looked at Sanchez and Julia. Both were staring intently toward the soldiers and appearing equally disturbed.

"Wait!" Wil seemed to shout from the opposite direction. "Don't lose your energy!" I felt the words as well as heard them. They were slightly garbled.

We turned to see Wil walking quickly toward us. As we watched he seemed to say something else, but this time the words were completely unintelligible. I realized I was having trouble focusing. His image was becoming hazy, distorted. Gradually, as I stared in disbelief, he disappeared altogether.

Julia turned to face Sanchez and me. Her energy level seemed lower but she was completely undaunted, as though whatever just happened clarified something.

"We weren't able to maintain the vibration," she said. "Fear lowers one's vibration tremendously." She looked toward the spot where Wil had faded from view. "The Ninth Insight says that while some individuals may cross over sporadically, a general rapture will not occur until we have abolished fear, until we can maintain a sufficient vibration in all situations."

Julia's excitement grew. "Don't you see? We can't do it yet but the role of the Ninth Insight is to help create that confidence. The Ninth Insight is the insight of knowing where we are headed. All the other insights create a picture of the world as one of incredible beauty and energy, and of ourselves as increasing our connection with and thus seeing this beauty.

"The more beauty we can see, the more we evolve. The more we evolve, the higher we vibrate. The Ninth Insight shows us that ultimately, our increased perception and vibration will open us up to a Heaven that is already before us. We just can't see it yet.

"Whenever we doubt our own path, or lose sight of the process, we must remember what we are evolving toward, what the process of living is all about. Reaching heaven on Earth is why we are here. And now we know how it can be done . . . how it will be done."

She paused momentarily, "The Ninth mentions that a Tenth Insight exists. I think it must reveal . . ."

Before she could finish, a burst of machine-gun fire ripped up the stone tiles by our feet. We all dived to the ground, our hands raised. No one spoke as the soldiers came and confiscated the papers and took each of us in a different direction.

The first weeks after my capture were spent in constant terror. My energy level fell dramatically as one military officer after another questioned me threateningly about the Manuscript.

I played the dumb tourist and claimed ignorance. After all, it was true that I had no idea who among the other priests had copies, or how widespread public acceptance of the document had become. Gradually, my tactic worked. Over time the soldiers seemed to grow tired of me and passed me on to a group of civilian authorities, who took a different approach.

These officials sought to convince me that my trip to Peru had been crazy from the beginning, crazy because according to them the Manuscript never really existed. They argued that the insights had in fact been invented by a small group of priests with the intent to foster rebellion. I had been duped, these officials told me, and I let them talk.

After a while, the conversations became almost cordial. Everyone began to treat me as a guiltless victim of this plot, as a gullible Yankee who had read too many adventure tales and found himself lost in a foreign country.

And because my energy was so low, I possibly would have become vulnerable to this brainwashing, had something else not occurred. I was suddenly transferred from the military base where I was being held to a governmental compound near the airport in Lima—a compound in which Father Carl was also being detained. The coincidence brought back some of my lost confidence.

I was walking in the open courtyard when I first saw him sitting on a bench, reading. I strolled over, restraining my exuberance and hoping I wouldn't attract attention from the officials inside the building. When I sat down, he looked up at me and grinned.

"I've been expecting you," he said.

"You have?"

He put down his book, and I could see the delight in his eyes.

"After Father Costous and I came to Lima," he explained, "we were immediately detained and separated, and I've been here in custody ever since. I couldn't understand why, nothing seemed to be happening. Then I began to think repeatedly of you." He gave me a knowing look. "So, I figured you would show up."

"I'm grateful you're here," I said. "Did anyone tell you what happened at the Celestine ruins?"

"Yes," Father Carl replied. "I spoke briefly with Father Sanchez. He was held here for a day before being taken away."

"Is he all right? Did he know what happened to the others? And what about him? Were they going to imprison him?"

"He had no information about the others, and as for Father Sanchez, I don't know. The government's strategy is to methodically search out and destroy all copies of the Manuscript. Then to treat the whole affair as a grand hoax. We'll all be thoroughly discredited, I imagine, but who knows what they will ultimately do with us."

"What about Dobson's copies," I said, "the First and Second Insights he left in the States?"

"They already have them," Father Carl replied. "Father Sanchez told me that agents of the government found out where they were hidden and stole them. Apparently Peruvian agents have been everywhere. They knew about Dobson from the beginning, and about your friend, Charlene."

"And you think when the government is through, no copies will remain?"

"I think it will be a miracle if any survive."

I turned away, feeling my new-found energy diminish.

"You know what this means, don't you?" Father Carl asked.

I looked at him but said nothing.

"This means," he continued, "that each of us must remember exactly what the Manuscript said. You and Sanchez didn't convince Cardinal Sebastian to release the Manuscript, but you delayed him long enough for the Ninth Insight to be understood. Now it has to be communicated. You have to be involved in communicating it."

His statement made me feel pressured and my Aloof drama activated inside me. I leaned against the back of the bench and looked away, which made Father Carl laugh. Then, at just that moment, we both realized several embassy officials were watching us from an office window.

"Listen," Father Carl said quickly. "From now on the insights will have to be shared between people. Each person, once they hear the message and realize that the insights are real, must pass on the message to everyone who is ready for it. Connecting with energy is something humans have to be open to and talking about and expecting, otherwise the whole human race can go back to pretending that life is about having power over others and exploiting the planet. If we go back to doing this, then we won't survive. Each of us must do what we can to get this message out."

I noticed that the two officials were out of the building walking toward us.

"One more thing," Father Carl said, speaking lowly.

"What?" I asked.

"Father Sanchez told me Julia had spoken of a Tenth Insight. It hasn't yet been found and no one knows where it might be."

The officials were almost on us.

"I've been thinking," Father Carl continued, "that they're going to release you. You may be the only one that can look for it."

The men suddenly interrupted our conversation and escorted me toward the building. Father Carl smiled and waved and said something else but I could only half pay attention. As soon as Father Carl had mentioned a Tenth Insight, I had been consumed by a thought of Charlene. Why was I thinking of her? How was she connected to a Tenth Insight?

The two men insisted that I pack the few things I had left and follow them to the front of the Embassy and into a state vehicle. From there I was taken directly to the airport and up to a boarding concourse, where one of them smiled faintly and looked at me from behind thick glasses.

His smile faded as he handed me a passport and a ticket for a flight to the United States . . . then told me in a heavy Peruvian accent to never, never return.

THE
TENTH
INSIGHT

Holding the Vision

Further Adventures of *The Celestine Prophecy*

For my wife and inspiration
Salle Merrill Redfield

ACKNOWLEDGMENTS

My heartfelt thanks to everyone who had a part in this book, particularly Joann Davis at Warner Books for her ongoing guidance and Albert Gaulden for his sage counsel. And certainly, my friends in the Blue Ridge Mountains, who keep the fires of a safe haven burning.

AUTHOR'S NOTE

Like *The Celestine Prophecy*, this sequel is an adventure parable, an attempt to illustrate the ongoing spiritual transformation that is occurring in our time. My hope with both books has been to communicate what I would call a *consensus picture*, a lived portrait, of the new perceptions, feelings, and phenomena that are coming to define life as we enter the third millennium.

Our greatest mistake, in my opinion, is to think that human spirituality is somehow already understood and established. If history tells us anything, it is that human culture and knowledge are constantly evolving. Only individual opinions are fixed and dogmatic. Truth is more dynamic than that, and the great joy of life is in letting go, in finding our own special truth that is ours to tell, and then watching the synchronistic way this truth evolves and takes a clearer form, just when it's needed to impact someone's life.

Together we are going somewhere, each generation building upon the accomplishments of the previous one, destined for an end we can only dimly remember. We're all in the process of awakening and opening up to who we really are, and what we came here to do, which is often a very difficult task. Yet I firmly believe that if we always integrate the best of the traditions we find before us and keep the process in mind, each challenge along the way, each interpersonal irritation can be overcome with a sense of destiny and miracle.

I don't mean to minimize the formidable problems still facing humanity, only to suggest that each of us in our own way is involved in the solution. If we stay aware and acknowledge the great mystery that is this life, we will see that we have been perfectly placed, in exactly the right position . . . to make all the difference in the world.

JR
Spring, 1996

. . . I looked, and behold,
a door was opened in heaven:
and the first voice which I heard was as . . . a trumpet
talking with me; which said, Come up hither, and I will show you
things which must be hereafter. And immediately
I was in the spirit: and, behold, a throne was set in heaven. . . .
and there was a rainbow round about the throne,
in sight like unto an emerald. And round about the throne
were four and twenty seats: and upon the seats I saw four
and twenty elders sitting, clothed in white raiment. . . .
And I saw a new heaven and a new earth: for the first
heaven and the first earth were passed away. . . .

REVELATION

CONTENTS

IMAGING
THE
PATH

I walked out to the edge of the granite overhang and looked northward at the scene below. Stretching across my view was a large Appalachian valley of striking beauty, perhaps six or seven miles long and five miles wide. Along the length of the valley ran a winding stream that coursed through stretches of open meadowland and thick, colorful forests—old forests, with trees standing hundreds of feet high.

I glanced down at the crude map in my hand. Everything in the valley coincided with the drawing exactly: the steep ridge on which I was standing, the road leading down, the description of the landscape and the stream, the rolling foothills beyond. This had to be the place Charlene had sketched on the note found in her office. Why had she done that? And why had she disappeared?

Over a month had now passed since Charlene had last contacted her associates at the research firm where she worked, and

1

by the time Frank Sims, her officemate, had thought to call *me*, he had become clearly alarmed.

"She often goes off on her own tangents," he had said. "But she's never disappeared for this long before, and never when she had meetings already set with long-term clients. Something's not right."

"How did you know to call me?" I asked.

He responded by describing part of a letter, found in Charlene's office, that I had written to her months earlier chronicling my experiences in Peru. With it, he told me, was a scribbled note that contained my name and telephone number.

"I'm calling everyone I know who is associated with her," he added. "So far, no one seems to know a thing. Judging from the letter, you're a friend of Charlene's. I was hoping you had heard from her."

"Sorry," I told him. "I haven't talked to her in four months."

Even as I had said the words, I couldn't believe it had been that long. Soon after receiving my letter, Charlene had telephoned and left a long message on my answering machine, voicing her excitement about the Insights and commenting on the speed with which knowledge of them seemed to be spreading. I remembered listening to Charlene's message several times, but I had put off calling her back—telling myself that I would call later, maybe tomorrow or the day after, when I felt ready to talk. I knew at the time that speaking with her would put me in the position of having to recall and explain the details of the Manuscript, and I told myself I needed more time to think, to digest what had occurred.

The truth, of course, was that parts of the prophecy still eluded me. Certainly I had retained the ability to connect with a spiritual energy within, a great comfort to me considering that everything had fallen through with Marjorie, and I was now spending large amounts of time alone. And I was more aware than ever of intuitive thoughts and dreams and the luminosity of a room or landscape. Yet, at the same time, the sporadic nature of the coincidences had become a problem.

I would fill up with energy, for instance, discerning the question foremost in my life, and would usually perceive a clear hunch about what to do or where to go to pursue the answer—yet, after acting accordingly, too often nothing of importance would occur. I would find no message, no coincidence.

This was especially true when the intuition was to seek out someone I already knew to some extent, an old acquaintance perhaps, or someone with whom I worked routinely. Occasionally this person and I would find some new point of interest, but just as frequently, my initiative, in spite of my best efforts to send energy, would be completely rebuked, or worse, would begin with excitement only to warp out of control and finally die in a flurry of unexpected irritations and emotions.

Such failure had not soured me on the process, but I had realized something was missing when it came to living the Insights long-term. In Peru, I had been proceeding on momentum, often acting spontaneously with a kind of faith born out of desperation. When I arrived back home, though, dealing again with my normal environment, often surrounded by outright skeptics, I seemed to lose the keen expectation, or firm belief, that my hunches were really going to lead somewhere. Apparently there was some vital part of the knowledge I had forgotten . . . or perhaps not yet discovered.

"I'm just not sure what to do next," Charlene's associate had pressed. "She has a sister, I think, somewhere in New York. You don't know how to contact her, do you? Or anyone else who might know where she is?"

"I'm sorry," I said, "I don't. Charlene and I are actually rekindling an old friendship. I don't remember any relatives and I don't know who her friends are now."

"Well, I think I'm going to file a police report, unless you have a better idea."

"No, I think that would be wise. Are there any other leads?"

"Only a drawing of some kind; could be the description of a place. It's hard to tell."

Later he had faxed me the entire note he had found in Charlene's office, including the crude sketch of intersecting lines and numbers with vague marks in the margins. And as I had sat in my study, comparing the drawing to the road numbers in an *Atlas of the South,* I had found what I suspected to be the actual location. Afterward I had experienced a vivid image of Charlene in my mind, the same image I had perceived in Peru when told of the existence of a Tenth Insight. Was her disappearance somehow connected to the Manuscript?

A wisp of wind touched my face and I again studied the view below. Far to the left, at the western edge of the valley, I could make out a row of rooftops. *That* had to be the town Charlene had indicated on the map. Stuffing the paper into my vest pocket, I made my way back to the road and climbed into the Pathfinder.

The town itself was small—population two thousand, according to the sign beside the first and only stoplight. Most of the commercial buildings lined just one street running along the edge of the stream. I drove through the light, spotted a motel near the entrance to the National Forest, and pulled into a parking space facing an adjacent restaurant and pub. Several people were entering the restaurant, including a tall man with a dark complexion and jet-black hair, carrying a large pack. He glanced back at me and we momentarily made eye contact.

I got out and locked the car, then decided, on a hunch, to walk through the restaurant before checking into the motel. Inside, the tables were near empty—just a few hikers at the bar and some of the people who had entered ahead of me. Most were oblivious to my gaze, but as I continued to survey the room, I again met eyes with the tall man I had seen before; he was walking toward the rear of the room. He smiled faintly, held the eye contact another second, then walked out a back exit.

I followed him through the exit. He was standing twenty feet away, bending over his pack. He was dressed in jeans, a western shirt and boots, and appeared to be about fifty years old. Behind him, the late afternoon sun cast long shadows among the tall trees and grass, and, fifty yards away, the stream flowed by, beginning its journey into the valley.

He smiled halfheartedly and looked up at me. "Another pilgrim?" he asked.

"I'm looking for a friend," I said. "I had a hunch that you could help me."

He nodded, studying the outlines of my body very carefully. Walking closer, he introduced himself as David Lone Eagle, explaining, as though it was something I might need to know, that he was a direct descendant of the Native Americans who originally inhabited this valley. I noticed for the first time a thin scar on his face that ran from the edge of his left eyebrow all the way to his chin, just missing his eye.

"You want some coffee?" he asked. "They're good at Perrier

in the saloon there, but lousy at coffee." He nodded toward an area near the stream where a small tent stood among three large poplars. Dozens of people were walking in the area, some of them along a path that crossed a bridge and led into the National Forest. Everything appeared safe.

"Sure," I replied. "That would be good."

At the campsite he lit a small butane camp stove, then filled a boiler with water and set it on the burner.

"What's your friend's name?" he finally asked.

"Charlene Billings."

He paused and looked at me, and as we gazed at each other, I saw a clear image in my mind's eye of him in another time. He was younger and dressed in buckskins, sitting in front of a large fire. Streaks of war paint adorned his face. Around him was a circle of people, mostly Native Americans, but including two whites, a woman and a very large man. The discussion was heated. Some in the group wanted war; others desired reconciliation. He broke in, ridiculing the ones considering peace. How could they be so naive, he told them, after so much treachery?

The white woman seemed to understand but pleaded with him to hear her out. War could be avoided, she maintained, and the valley protected fairly, if the spiritual medicine was great enough. He rebuked her argument totally, then, chiding the group, he mounted his horse and rode away. Most of the others followed.

"Your instincts are good," David said, snapping me from my vision. He was spreading a homespun blanket between us, offering me a seat. "I know of her." He looked at me questioningly.

"I'm concerned," I said. "No one has heard from her and I just want to make sure she's okay. And we need to talk."

"About the Tenth Insight?" he asked, smiling.

"How did you know that?"

"Just a guess. Many of the people coming to this valley aren't just here because of the beauty of the National Forest. They're here to talk about the Insights. They think the Tenth is somewhere out there. A few even claim to know what it says."

He turned away and put a tea ball filled with coffee into the steaming water. Something about his tone of voice made me think he was testing me, trying to check out whether I was who I claimed.

"Where is Charlene?" I asked.

He pointed a finger toward the east. "In the Forest. I've never met your friend, but I overheard her being introduced in the restaurant one night, and I've seen her a few times since. Several days ago I saw her again; she was hiking into the valley alone, and judging from the way she was packed, I'd say she's probably still out there."

I looked in that direction. From this perspective, the valley looked enormous, stretching forever into the distance.

"Where do you think she was going?" I asked.

He stared at me for a moment. "Probably toward the Sipsey Canyon. That's where one of the *openings* is found." He was studying my reaction.

"The openings?"

He smiled cryptically. "That's right, the dimensional openings."

I leaned over toward him, remembering my experience at the Celestine Ruins. "Who knows about all this?"

"Very few people. So far it's all rumor, bits and pieces of information, intuition. Not a soul has seen a manuscript. Most of the people who come here looking for the Tenth feel they're being synchronistically led, and they're genuinely trying to live the

Nine Insights, even though they complain that the coincidences guide them along for a while and then just *stop*." He chuckled lightly. "But that's where we all are, right? The Tenth Insight is about understanding this whole awareness—the perception of mysterious coincidences, the growing spiritual consciousness on Earth, the Ninth Insight disappearances—all from the higher perspective of the other dimension, so that we can understand why this transformation is happening and participate more fully."

"How do you know that?" I asked.

He looked at me with piercing eyes, suddenly angry. "I know!"

For another moment his face remained serious, then his expression warmed again. He reached over and poured the coffee into two cups and handed one to me.

"My ancestors have lived near this valley for thousands of years," he continued. "They believed this forest was a sacred site midway between the upper world and the middle world here on Earth. My people would fast and enter the valley on their vision quests, looking for their specific gifts, their medicine, the path they should walk in this life.

"My grandfather told me about a shaman who came from a faraway tribe and taught our people to search for what he called a state of purification. The shaman taught them to leave from this very spot, bearing only a knife, and to walk until the animals provided a sign, and then to follow until they reached what they called the sacred opening into the upper world. If they were worthy, if they had cleared the lower emotions, he told them, they might even be allowed to enter the opening, and to meet directly with the ancestors, where they could remember not just their own vision but the vision of the whole world.

"Of course, all that ended when the white man came. My

grandfather couldn't remember how to do it, and neither can I. We're having to figure it out, like everyone else."

"You're here looking for the Tenth, aren't you?" I asked.

"Of course . . . of course! But all I seem to be doing is this penance of forgiveness." His voice became sharp again, and he suddenly seemed to be talking more to himself than to me. "Every time I try to move forward, a part of me can't get past the resentment, the rage, at what happened to my people. And it's not getting any better. How could it happen that our land was stolen, our way of life overrun, destroyed? Why would that be allowed?"

"I wish it hadn't happened," I said.

He looked at the ground and chuckled lowly again. "I believe that. But still, there is a rage that comes when I think of this valley being misused.

"You see this scar," he added, pointing to his face. "I could have avoided the fight where this happened. Texas cowboys with too much to drink. I could have walked away but for this anger burning within me."

"Isn't most of this valley now protected in the National Forest?" I asked.

"Only about half of it, north of the stream, but the politicians always threaten to sell it or allow development."

"What about the other half? Who owns that?"

"For a long time, this area was owned mostly by individuals, but now there's a foreign-registered corporation trying to buy it up. We don't know who is behind it, but some of the owners have been offered huge amounts to sell."

He looked away momentarily, then said, "My problem is that I want the past three centuries to have happened differently. I resent the fact that Europeans began to settle on this continent with no regard for the people who were already here. It was criminal. I want it to have happened differently, as though I could somehow change the past. Our way of life was important. We were learning the value of *remembering*. This was the great message the Europeans could have received from my people if they had stopped to listen."

As he talked, my mind drifted into another daydream. Two people—another Native American and the same white woman—were talking on the banks of a small stream. Behind them was a thick forest. After a while, other Native Americans crowded around to hear their conversation.

"We can heal this!" the woman was saying.

"I'm afraid we don't know enough yet," the Native American replied, his face expressing great regard for the woman. "Most of the other chiefs have already left."

"Why not? Think of the discussions we've had. You yourself said if there was enough faith, we could heal this."

"Yes," he replied. "But faith is a certainty that comes from knowing how things should be. The ancestors know, but not enough of us here have reached that knowing."

"But maybe we can reach this knowledge now," the woman pleaded. "We have to try!"

My thoughts were interrupted by the sight of several young Forest Service officers, who were approaching an older man on the bridge. He had neatly cut gray hair and wore dress slacks and a starched shirt. As he moved, he seemed to limp slightly.

"Do you see the man with the officers?" David asked.

"Yeah," I replied. "What about him?"

"I've seen him around here for the past two weeks. His first name is Feyman, I think. I don't know his last name." David leaned toward me, sounding for the first time as if he trusted me completely. "Listen, something very strange is going on. For several weeks the Forest Service seems to have been counting the hikers who go into the forest. They've never done that before, and yesterday someone told me they have completely closed off the far eastern end of the wilderness. There are places in that area that are ten miles from the nearest highway. Do you know how few people ever venture out that far? Some of us have begun to hear strange noises in that direction."

"What kind of noises?"

"A dissonance of some kind. Most people can't hear it."

Suddenly he was up on his feet, quickly taking down his tent.

"What are you doing?" I asked.

"I can't stay here," he replied. "I've got to get into the valley."

After a moment he interrupted his work and looked at me again. "Listen," he said. "There's something you have to know. That man Feyman. I saw your friend with him several times."

"What were they doing?"

"Just talking, but I'm telling you there's something wrong here." He began packing again.

I watched him in silence for a moment. I had no idea what to think about this situation, but I sensed that he was right about Charlene being somewhere out in the valley. "Let me get my equipment," I said. "I'd like to go with you."

"No," he said quickly. "Each person must experience the valley alone. I can't help you now. It's my own vision I must find." His face looked pained.

"Can you tell me exactly where this canyon is?"

"Just follow the stream for about two miles. You'll come to another small creek that enters the stream from the north. Follow this creek for another mile. It will lead you right through the mouth of the Sipsey Canyon."

I nodded and turned to walk away, but he grabbed my arm.

"Look," he said. "You can find your friend if you raise your energy to another level. There are specific locations in the valley that can help you."

"The dimensional openings?" I asked.

"Yes. There you can discover the perspective of the Tenth Insight, but to find these places you must understand the true nature of your intuitions, and how to *maintain* these mental images. Also watch the animals and you'll begin to remember what you are doing here in this valley . . . why we're all here together. But be very careful. Don't let them see you enter the forest." He thought for a moment. "There's someone else out there, a friend of mine, Curtis Webber. If you see Curtis, tell him that you've talked to me and that I will find him."

He smiled faintly and returned to folding his tent.

I wanted to ask what he meant about intuition and watching the animals, but he avoided eye contact and stayed focused on his work.

"Thanks," I said.

He waved slightly with one hand.

I quietly shut the motel door and eased out into the moonlight. The cool air and the tension sent a shiver through my body. Why, I thought, was I doing this? There was no proof that Charlene was still out in this valley or that David's suspicions were correct. Yet my gut told me that indeed something was wrong. For several hours I had mulled over calling the local sheriff. But what would I have said? That my friend was missing and she had been seen entering the forest of her own free will, but was perhaps in trouble, all based on a vague note found hundreds of miles away?

Searching this wilderness would take hundreds of people, and I knew they would never mount such an effort without something more substantial.

I paused and looked at the three-quarters moon rising above the trees. My plan was to cross the stream well east of the rangers' station and then to proceed along the main path into the valley. I was counting on the moon to light my way, but not to be this bright. Visibility was at least a hundred yards.

I made my way past the edge of the pub to the area where David had camped. The site was completely clean. He had even spread leaves and pine straw to remove any sign of his presence. To cross where I had planned, I would have to walk about forty yards in plain sight of the rangers' station, which I could now see clearly. Through the station's side window, two officers were busy in conversation. One rose from his seat and picked up a telephone.

Crouching low, I pulled my pack up on my shoulders and walked out onto the sandy flood wash that bordered the stream, and finally into the water itself, sloshing through mounds of smooth river stone and stepping over several decayed logs. A symphony of tree frogs and crickets erupted around me. I glanced at the rangers again: both were still talking, oblivious to my stealth. At its deepest point, the moderately swift water reached my upper thigh, but in seconds I had moved across the thirty feet of current and into a stand of small pines.

I carefully moved forward until I found the hiking path leading into the valley. Toward the east, the path disappeared into the darkness, and as I stared in that direction, more doubts entered my mind. What was this mysterious noise that so worried David? What might I stumble upon in the darkness out there?

I shook off the fear. I knew I had to go on, but as a compromise, I walked only a half mile into the forest before making my way well off the path into a heavily wooded area to raise the tent and spend the rest of the night, glad to take off my wet boots and let them dry. It would be smarter to proceed in the daylight.

The next morning I awoke at dawn thinking about David's cryptic remark about *maintaining* my intuitions, and as I lay in my sleeping bag, I reviewed my own understanding of the Seventh Insight, particularly the awareness that the experience of synchronicity follows a certain structure. According to this Insight, each of us, once we work to clear our past dramas, can identify certain questions that define our particular life situation, questions related to our careers, relationships, where we should live, how we should proceed on our path. Then, if we remain aware, gut feelings, hunches, and intuitions will provide impressions of where to go, what to do, with whom we should speak, in order to pursue an answer.

After that, of course, a coincidence was supposed to occur, revealing the reason we were urged to follow such a course and providing new information that pertained in some way to our question, leading us forward in our lives. How would maintaining the intuition help?

Easing out of my sleeping bag, I pulled the tent flaps apart and checked outside. Sensing nothing unusual, I climbed out into the crisp fall air and walked back to the stream, where I washed my face in the cool water. Afterward I packed up and headed east again, nibbling on a granola bar and keeping myself hidden as much as possible in the tall trees that bordered the stream. After traveling perhaps three miles, a perceptible wave of fear and nervousness passed through my body and I immediately felt fatigued, so I sat down and leaned against a tree, attempting to focus on my surroundings and gain inner energy. The sky was cloudless and the morning sun danced through the trees and along the ground around me. I noticed a small green plant with yellow blossoms about ten feet away and focused on its beauty. Already draped in full sunlight, it seemed brighter suddenly, its leaves a richer green. A rush of fragrance reached my awareness, along with the musty smell of leaves and black soil.

Simultaneously, from the trees far toward the north, I heard the call of several crows. The richness of the sound amazed me, but surprisingly I couldn't distinguish their exact location. As I concentrated on listening, I became fully aware of dozens of individual sounds that made up the morning chorus: songbirds in the trees above me, a bumblebee among the wild daisies at the edge of the stream, the water gurgling around the rocks and fallen branches . . . and then something else, barely perceptible, a low, dissonant *hum*. I stood up and looked around. What was this noise?

I picked up my pack and proceeded east. Because of the crunching sound created by my footsteps on the fallen leaves, I had to stop and listen very intensely to still hear the hum. But it was there. Ahead the woods ended, and I entered a large meadow, colorful with wildflowers and thick, two-foot-tall sage grass that seemed to go on for half a mile. The breeze brushed the tops of the sage in currents. When I had almost reached the edge of the meadow, I noticed a patch of blackberry brambles growing beside a fallen tree. The bushes struck me as exceedingly beautiful, and I walked over to look at them more closely, imagining that they were full of berries.

As I did this, I experienced an acute feeling of déjà vu. The surroundings suddenly seemed very familiar, as though I had been here in this valley before, eaten berries before. How was that possible? I sat down on the trunk of the fallen tree. Presently, in the back of my mind rose a picture of a crystal-clear pool of water and several tiers of waterfalls in the background, a location that, as I imaged it, seemed equally familiar. Again I felt anxious.

Without warning, an animal of some kind ran noisily from the berry patch, startling me, and headed north for about twenty feet and then abruptly stopped. The creature was hidden in the tall sage, and I had no idea what it was, but I could follow its wake in the grass. After a few minutes it darted back a few feet to the south, remained motionless again for several seconds, then darted ten or twenty feet back again toward the north, only to stop again. I guessed it was a rabbit, although its movements seemed especially peculiar.

For five or six minutes I watched the area where the animal had last moved, then slowly walked that way. As I closed to about five feet, it suddenly sped away again toward the north. At one point, before it disappeared into the distance, I glimpsed the white tail and hind legs of a large rabbit.

I smiled and proceeded east again along the trail, coming finally to the end of the meadow, where I entered an area of thick woods. There I spotted a small creek, perhaps four feet wide, that entered the stream from the left. I knew this must be the landmark David had mentioned. I was to turn northward. Unfortunately there was no trail in that direction, and worse, the woods along the creek were a snarl of thick saplings and prickly briers. I couldn't get through; I would have to backtrack into the meadow behind me until I could find a way around.

I made my way back into the grass and walked along the edge of the woods looking for a break in the dense undergrowth. To my surprise, I ran into the trail the rabbit had made in the sage and followed its path until I caught sight of the small creek again. Here the dense undergrowth receded partially, allowing me to push my way through into an area of larger, old-growth trees, where I could follow the creek due north.

After proceeding for what I judged to be about another mile, I could see a range of foothills rising in the distance on both sides of the creek. Walking farther, I realized that these hills were forming steep canyon walls and that up ahead was what looked to be the only entrance.

When I arrived, I sat down beside a large hickory and surveyed the scene. A hundred yards on both sides of the creek, the hills butted off in fifty-foot-high limestone bluffs, then bent outward into the distance, forming a huge bowl-like canyon perhaps two miles wide and at least four long. The first half mile was thinly wooded and covered with more sage. I thought about the hum and listened carefully for five or ten minutes, but it seemed to have ceased.

Finally I reached into my pack and pulled out a small butane stove and lit the burner, then filled a small pan with water from my canteen, emptied the contents of a package of freeze-dried vegetable stew into the water, and set the pan on the flame. For a few moments I watched as strands of steam twisted upward and disappeared into the breeze. In my reverie I again saw the pool and the waterfall in my mind's eye, only this time I seemed to be there, walking up, as if to greet someone. I shook the picture from my head. What was happening? These images were growing more vivid. First David in another time; now these falls.

Movement in the canyon caught my eye. I glanced at the creek and then beyond to a lone tree two hundred yards away which had already lost most of its leaves. It was now covered with what looked like large crows; several flew down to the ground. It came to me that these were the same crows I had heard earlier. As I watched, they suddenly all flew and dramatically circled above the tree. At the same moment, I could hear their cawing again, although, as before, the loudness of their cries didn't match the distance; they sounded much closer.

Splashing water and hissing steam pulled my attention back to the camp stove. Boiling stew was overflowing onto the flame. I grabbed the pan with a towel, turning off the gas with the other hand. When the boiling subsided, I returned the pan to the burner and looked back at the tree in the distance. The crows were gone.

I hurriedly ate the stew, cleaned up, and packed the gear, then headed into the canyon. As soon as I passed the bluffs, I noticed the colors had amplified. The sage seemed amazingly golden, and I noticed, for the first time, that it was peppered with hundreds of wildflowers—white and yellow and orange. From the cliffs to the east, the breeze carried the scent of cedar and pine.

Although I continued to follow the creek running north, I kept my eye on the tall tree to my left where the crows had circled. When it was directly west of me, I noticed the creek was suddenly widening. I made my way through some willows and cattails and realized I had come to a small pool that fed not only the creek I was following but a second creek angling off farther to the southeast. At first I thought this pool was the one I had seen in my mind, but there were no waterfalls.

Ahead was another surprise: to the north of the pool, the creek had completely disappeared. Where was the water coming from? Then it dawned on me that the pool and the creek I had been following were all fed from an enormous underground spring surfacing at this location.

To my left, fifty feet away, I noticed a mild rise on which grew three sycamore trees, each more than two feet in diameter—a perfect place to think for a moment. I walked over and snuggled in among them, sitting down and leaning against the trunk of one of the trees. From this perspective, the two remaining trees were six or seven feet to my front, and I could look both to the left to see the crow tree and to the right to observe the spring. The question now was where to go from here. I could wander for days without seeing any sign of Charlene. And what about these images?

I closed my eyes and attempted to bring back the earlier picture of the pool and waterfalls, but as much as I struggled, I couldn't remember the exact details. Finally I gave up and gazed out again at the grass and wildflowers and then at the two sycamores right in front of me. Their trunks were a scaly collage of dark gray and white bark, streaked with brushstrokes of tan and multiple shades of amber. As I focused on the beauty of the scene, these colors seemed to intensify and grow more iridescent. I took another deep breath and looked out again at the meadow and flowers. The crow tree seemed particularly illuminated.

I picked up my pack and walked toward the tree. Immediately the image of the pool and waterfalls flashed across my mind. This time I tried to remember the entire picture. The pool I saw was large, almost an acre, and the water flowing into it came in from the rear, cascading down a series of steep terraces. Two smaller falls dropped only about fifteen feet, but the last dropped over a long, thirty-foot bluff into the water below. Again, in the image that came to mind, I seemed to be walking up to the scene, meeting someone.

The sound of a vehicle to my left stopped me firmly in my tracks. I kneeled down behind several small bushes. From the forest on the left a gray Jeep moved across the meadow heading southeast. I knew that Forest Service policy prohibited private vehicles this far into the wilderness, so I expected to see a Forest Service insignia on the Jeep's door. To my surprise it was unmarked. When it was directly in front of me, fifty yards away, the vehicle stopped. Through the foliage I could make out a lone figure inside; he was surveying the area with field glasses, so I lay flat and hid myself completely. Who was he?

The vehicle started up again and quickly vanished out of sight in the trees. I turned and sat down, listening again for the hum. Still nothing. I thought about returning to town, of finding another way to search for Charlene. But deep inside I knew there was no alternative. I shut my eyes, and thought again of David's instruction to maintain my intuitions, and finally retrieved the full image of the pool and falls in my mind's eye. As I got to my feet and headed again toward the crow tree, I tried to keep the details of the scene in the back of my mind.

Suddenly I heard the shrill cry of another bird, this time a hawk. To my left, far past the tree, I could barely make out her shape; she was streaking hard toward the north. I increased my pace, trying to keep the bird in sight for as long as possible.

The bird's appearance seemed to increase my energy, and even after she had disappeared over the horizon, I kept moving in the direction she had been flying, walking for another mile and a half over a series of rocky foothills. At the top of the third hill, I froze again, hearing another sound in the distance, a sound much like water running. No, it was water *falling*.

Carefully I walked down the slope and through a deep gorge that evoked another experience of déjà vu. I climbed the next hill and there, beyond the crest, were the pool and falls, exactly as I had pictured them—except that the area was much larger and more beautiful than I had pictured. The pool itself was almost two acres, nestled in a cradle of enormous boulders and outcroppings, its crystal-clear water a sparkling blue under the afternoon sky. To the left and right of the pool were several large oak trees, themselves surrounded by a multicolored array of smaller maples and sweet gums and willows.

The far edge of the pool was an explosion of white spray and mist, the foam accentuated by the churning action of the two smaller falls higher up the ridge. I realized there was no runoff from the pool. The water went underground from here, traveling silently to emerge as the source of the large spring near the crow tree.

As I surveyed the beauty of this sight, the sense of déjà vu increased. The sounds, the colors, the scene from the hill—it all looked extremely familiar. I had been at this location too. But when?

I moved down to the pool and then walked around the entire area, to the edge to taste the water, up the cascades to feel the spray from each of the falls, over atop the large boulders, where I could touch the trees. I wanted to immerse myself in the place. Finally I stretched out on one of the flatter rocks twenty feet above the pool and looked toward the afternoon sun with my eyes closed, feeling its rays against my face. In that moment another familiar sensation swept across my body—a particular warmth and regard I hadn't sensed in months. In fact, until this instant, I had forgotten its exact feeling and character, although it was perfectly recognizable now. I opened my eyes and turned around quickly, certain of whom I was about to see.

REVIEWING
THE
JOURNEY

On a rock above my head, half obscured by an overhanging ledge, stood Wil, his hands on his hips, smiling broadly. He appeared slightly out of focus, so I blinked hard and concentrated, and his face cleared somewhat.

"I knew you would be here," he said, nimbly climbing off the ledge and jumping to the rock beside me. "I've been waiting."

I looked at him in awe, and he pulled me into an embrace; his face and hands looked slightly luminescent but otherwise seemed normal.

"I can't believe you're here," I stammered. "What happened when you disappeared in Peru? Where have you been?"

He gestured for me to sit facing him on a nearby shelf.

"I'll tell you everything," he said, "but first I have to know about you. What circumstances brought you to this valley?"

In detail I told him about Charlene's disappearance, the map of the valley, and meeting David. Wil wanted to know more of what David had said, so I told him everything I could remember about the conversation.

Wil leaned toward me. "He told you the Tenth was about understanding the spiritual renaissance on Earth in light of the other dimension? And learning the true nature of your intuitions?"

"Yes," I said. "Is that right?"

He seemed to think for a moment, then asked, "What has been your experience since entering the valley?"

"I immediately started to see images," I said. "Some were of other historical times, but then I began to see repeated visions of this pool. I saw everything: the rocks, the falls, even that someone was waiting here, although I didn't know it was you."

"Where were you in the scene?"

"It was as if I was walking up and seeing it."

"So it was a scene of a *potential future* for you."

I squinted at him. "I'm not sure I follow."

"The first part of the Tenth, as David said, is about understanding our intuitions more fully. In the first nine Insights, one experiences intuitions as fleeting gut feelings or vague hunches. But as we gain familiarity with this phenomenon, we can now grasp the nature of these intuitions more clearly. Think back to Peru. Didn't intuitions come to you as pictures of what was going to happen, images of yourself and others at a specific location, doing certain things, leading you to go there? Wasn't that how you knew when to go to the Celestine Ruins?

"Here in the valley the same thing has been happening. You received a mental image of a potential event—finding the falls and meeting someone—and you were able to live it out, bringing on the coincidence of actually discovering the location and encountering me. If you had shrugged off the image, or lost faith in looking for the falls, you would have missed the synchronicity, and your life would have stayed flat. But you took the image seriously; you *kept* it in your mind."

"David said something about learning to 'maintain' the intuition," I said.

Wil nodded.

"What about the other images," I asked, "the scenes of an earlier time? And what about these animals? Does the Tenth Insight talk about all this? Have you seen the Manuscript?"

With a gesture of his hand, Wil waved off my questions. "First, let me tell you about my experience in the other dimension, what I call the *Afterlife* dimension. When I was able to maintain my energy level in Peru, even when the rest of you grew fearful and lost your vibration, I found myself in an incredible world of beauty and clear form. I was right there in the same place, but everything was different. The world was luminous and awing in a way I still can't describe. For a long time I just walked around in this incredible world, vibrating even higher, and then I discovered something quite amazing. I could will myself anywhere on the planet, just by imaging a destination in my mind. I traveled everywhere I could think of, looking for you and Julia and the others, but I couldn't find any of you.

"Finally I began to detect another ability. By imaging just a blank field in my mind, I could travel off the planet, into a place of pure ideas. There I could create anything I wanted just by imaging it. I made oceans and mountains and scenic vistas, images of people who behaved just as I wanted, all kinds of things. And every bit of it seemed just as real as anything on Earth.

"Yet in the end, I realized that such a constructed world was not a fulfilling place. Just creating arbitrarily gave me no inner satisfaction. After a while, I went home and thought about what I wanted to do. At that time I could still become dense enough so that I could talk with most people of a higher awareness. I could eat and sleep, although I didn't have to. Finally I realized that I had forgotten about the thrill of evolving and experiencing coincidences. Because I was already so buoyant, I had mistakenly thought that I was maintaining my inner connection, but in fact, I had become too controlling and had lost my path. It is very easy to lose one's way at this level of vibration, because it is so easy and instantaneous to create with one's will."

"What happened then?" I asked.

"I focused within, looking for a higher connection with divine energy, just the way we've always done it. That's all it took; my vibration rose even higher and I began to receive intuitions again. I saw an image of you."

"What was I doing?"

"I couldn't tell; the image was hazy. But when I thought about the intuition and maintained it in my mind, I began to move into a new area of the Afterlife where I could actually see other souls, groups of souls really, and while I couldn't exactly speak to them, I could vaguely pick up on their thoughts and knowledge."

"Were they able to show you the Tenth Insight?" I asked.

He swallowed hard and looked at me as though he was about to land a bombshell. "No, the Tenth Insight has never been written down."

"What? It's not part of the original Manuscript?"

"No."

"Does it even exist?"

"Oh yes, it exists. But not in the Earthly dimension. This Insight hasn't made it to the physical plane yet. This knowledge exists only in the Afterlife. Only when enough people on Earth sense this information, intuitively, can it become real enough in everyone's consciousness for someone to write it down. That's what happened with the first nine Insights. In fact, that's what has happened with all spiritual texts, even our most sacred scriptures. Always it is information that first exists in the Afterlife, and is finally picked up clearly enough in the physical dimension to be manifested by someone who is supposed to write it down. That's why these writings are called divinely inspired."

"So why has it taken so long for someone to grasp the Tenth?"

Wil looked perplexed. "I don't know. The soul group I was communicating with seemed to know, but I couldn't quite understand. My energy level was not high enough. It has something to do with the Fear that arises in a culture that is moving from a material reality to a transformed, spiritual worldview."

"Then you think the Tenth is ready to come in?"

"Yes, the soul groups saw the Tenth coming in now, bit by bit, all over the world, as we gain a higher perspective that comes from a knowledge of the Afterlife. But it has to be grasped in sufficient numbers, just as with the first nine, in order to overcome the Fear."

"Do you know what the rest of the Tenth is about?"

"Yes, apparently just knowing the first nine isn't enough. We have to understand how we will implement this destiny. Such knowledge comes from grasping the special relationship between the physical dimension and the Afterlife. We have to understand the birth process, where we come from, the larger picture of what human history is trying to accomplish."

A thought suddenly came to me. "Wait a minute. Weren't you able to see a copy of the *Ninth* Insight? What did it say about the Tenth?"

Wil leaned toward me. "It said that the first nine Insights

have described the reality of spiritual evolution, both personally and collectively, but actually implementing these Insights, living them, and fulfilling this destiny requires a fuller understanding of the process, a Tenth Insight. This Insight would show us the reality of Earth's spiritual transformation not just from the perspective of the Earthly dimension but from the perspective of the Afterlife dimension as well. It said we would understand more fully why we were uniting the dimensions, why humans must fulfill this historical purpose, and it would be this understanding, once integrated into culture, that would ensure this eventual outcome. It also mentioned the Fear, saying that at the same time a new spiritual awareness was emerging, a reactive polarization would also rise up in fearful opposition, seeking to willfully control the future with various new technologies—technologies even more dangerous than the nuclear menace—that are already being discovered. The Tenth Insight resolves this polarization."

He stopped abruptly and nodded toward the east. "Do you hear that?"

I listened but could hear only the falls.

"What?" I asked.

"That hum."

"I heard it earlier. What is it?"

"I'm not sure, exactly. But it can be heard in the other dimension as well. The souls I saw seemed very disturbed about it."

As Wil spoke, I clearly saw Charlene's face in the back of my mind.

"Do you think the hum is related to this new technology?" I asked, partially distracted.

Wil didn't answer. I noticed he had an absent look on his face.

"The friend that you're looking for," he asked, "does she have blond hair? And large eyes . . . very inquisitive-looking?"

"Yes."

"I just saw an image of her face."

I stared at him. "So did I."

He turned and looked at the falls for a moment, and I followed his gaze. The white foam and spray formed a majestic background to our conversation. I could feel the energy increasing in my body.

"You don't have enough energy yet," he said. "But because this place is so powerful, I think that if I help, and we both focus on your friend's face, we can move fully into the spiritual dimension and maybe find out where she is and what's happening in this valley."

"Are you sure I can do that?" I said. "Maybe you can go and I can wait here for you." His face was fading out of focus.

Wil touched my lower back, giving me energy, smiling again. "Don't you see how purposeful it is that we are here? Human culture is beginning to understand the Afterlife and grasp the Tenth. I think we have the opportunity to explore the other dimension together. You know this feels destined."

At that moment I noticed the noise of the hum in the background, even over the sound of the falls. In fact, I could feel it in my solar plexus.

"The hum's getting louder," Wil said. "We have to go now. Charlene could be in trouble!"

"What do we do?" I asked.

Wil moved slightly closer, still touching my back. "We have to re-create the image we received of your friend."

"Maintain it?"

"Yes. As I said, we are learning to recognize and believe in our intuitions at a higher level. We all want the coincidences to come more consistently, but for most of us, this awareness is new and we're surrounded by a culture that still operates too much in the old skepticism, so we lose the expectation, the faith. Yet what we're beginning to realize is that when we fully pay attention, inspecting the details of the potential future we're shown, purposely keeping the image in the back of our minds, intentionally believing—when we do this—then whatever we are imaging tends to happen more readily."

"Then we 'will' it to happen?"

"No. Remember my experience in the Afterlife. There you can make anything happen just by wishing it so, but such creation isn't fulfilling. The same is true of this dimension, only everything moves at a slower rate. On Earth, we can will and create almost anything we wish, but real fulfillment comes only when we first tune into our inner direction and divine guidance. Only then do we use our will to move toward the potential futures we received. In this sense, we become cocreators with the divine source. Do you see how this knowledge begins the Tenth Insight? We are learning to use our visualization in the same way it is used in the Afterlife, and when we do, we fall into alignment with that dimension, and that helps unite Heaven and Earth."

I nodded, understanding completely. After taking several deep breaths, Wil exerted more pressure on my back and instructed me to re-create the details of Charlene's face. For a moment nothing happened, and then suddenly I felt a rush of energy, twisting me forward and pushing me into a wild acceleration.

I was streaking at fantastic speeds though a multicolored tunnel of some kind. Fully conscious, I wondered why I had no fear, for what I really felt was a sense of recognition and contentment and peace, as though I had been here before. When the movement stopped, I found myself in an environment of warm, white light. I looked for Wil and realized he was standing to my left and slightly behind me.

"There you are," he said, smiling. His lips weren't moving, but I could clearly hear his voice. I then noticed the appearance of his body. He looked exactly the same, except he seemed to be completely illuminated from within.

I reached over to touch his hand and noticed that my body appeared the same way. When I touched him, what I felt was a field several inches outside the arm I could see. Pushing harder, I realized I couldn't penetrate this energy; I only moved his body away from me.

Wil was near bursting with mirth. In fact, his expression was so humorous that I laughed myself.

"Amazing, isn't it?" he asked.

"This is a higher vibration than at the Celestine Ruins," I replied. "Do you know where we are?"

Wil was silent, gazing out at our surroundings. We seemed to be in an environment that was spatial, and we had a sense of up and down, but we were suspended motionless in midair and there were no horizons. The white light was a constant hue in all directions.

Finally Wil said, "This is an observation point; I came here briefly, when I first imaged your face. More souls were here."

"What were they doing?"

"Observing the people who had come over after death."

"What? You mean this is where people come right after they have died?" •

"Yes."

"Why are we here? Has something happened to Charlene?"

He turned more directly toward me. "No, I don't think so. Remember what happened to me when I began to image you. I moved to many locations before we finally met at the falls. There's probably something we need to see here before we can find Charlene. Let's wait and see what happens with these souls." He nodded to our left, where several humanlike entities were materializing directly in front of us, at a distance of what appeared to be about thirty feet.

My first reaction was to be cautious. "Wil, how do we know their intentions are friendly? What if they try to possess us or something?"

He gave me a serious expression. "How do you know if someone on Earth is trying to control you?"

"I would pick up on it. I could tell that the person was being manipulative."

"What else?"

"I guess they would be taking energy away from me. I would feel a decrease in my sense of wisdom, self-direction."

"Exactly. They wouldn't be following the Insights. All these principles work the same way in both dimensions."

As the entities formed completely, I remained cautious. But eventually I felt a loving and supportive energy emanating from their bodies, which seemed to be comprised of a whitish-amber light that danced and shimmered in and out of focus. Their faces had human characteristics but could not be looked at directly. I couldn't even tell how many souls were there. At one moment, three or four seemed to be facing us, then I would blink and there would be six, then three again, all dancing in and out of view. Overall, they looked like a flickering, animated cloud of amber, against the background color of white.

After several minutes, another form began to materialize beside the others, only this figure was more clearly in focus and appeared in a luminous body similar to Wil and myself. We could see that it was a middle-aged man; he looked around wildly, then saw the group of souls and began to relax.

To my surprise, when I focused closely on him, I could pick up on what he was feeling and thinking. I glanced at Wil, who nodded that he was also sensing the person's reaction.

I focused again and observed that, in spite of a certain detachment and sense of love and support, he was in a state of shock at having discovered he had died. Only minutes before, he had been routinely jogging, and while attempting to run up a long hill, had suffered a massive heart attack. The pain had lasted only a few seconds, and then he was hovering outside his body, watching a stream of bystanders rush up to help him. Soon a team of paramedics arrived and worked feverishly to bring him back.

As he sat beside his body in the ambulance, he had listened in horror as the team leader had pronounced him dead. Frantically he had attempted to communicate, but no one could hear. At the hospital a doctor confirmed to the crew that his heart had literally exploded; that no one could have done anything to save his life.

Part of him tried to accept the fact; another resisted. How could he be dead? He had called out for help and had instantly found himself in a tunnel of colors that had brought him to where he now stood. As we watched, he seemed to become more aware of the souls and moved toward them, shifting out of focus to us, appearing more like them.

Then abruptly he pulled back toward us and was quickly surrounded by an office of some kind, filled with computers and wall charts and people working. Everything looked perfectly real, except the walls were semitransparent, so that we could see what was happening inside, and the sky above the office was not blue, but a strange olive color.

"He's deluding himself," Wil said. "He's re-creating the office where he worked on Earth, trying to pretend he hasn't died."

The souls moved closer and others came until there were dozens of them, all flickering in and out of focus in the amber light. They seemed to be sending the man love and some kind of information I couldn't understand. Gradually the constructed office began to fade and eventually disappeared completely.

The man was left with an expression of resignation on his face, and he again moved into focus with the souls.

"Let's go with them," I heard Wil say. At the same moment, I felt his arm, or rather, the energy of his arm, pushing against my back.

As soon as I inwardly agreed, there was the slight sensation of movement, and the souls and the man all came into clearer focus. The souls now had glowing faces much as Wil and I did, but their hands and feet, instead of being clearly formed, were mere radiations of light. I could now focus on the entities for as long as four or five seconds before losing them and having to blink to find them again.

I became aware that the group of souls, as well as the deceased individual, was watching an intense point of bright light moving toward us. It eventually swelled into a massive beam that covered everything. Unable to look directly at the light, I turned so I could just see the silhouette of the man, who was staring fully at the beam without apparent difficulty.

Again I could pick up on his thoughts and emotions. The light was filling him with an unimaginable sense of love and calm perspective. As this sensation swept over him, his viewpoint and knowledge expanded until he could clearly see the life he had just lived from a broad and amazingly detailed perspective.

Immediately he could see the circumstances of his birth and early family life. He was born John Donald Williams to a father who was slow intellectually and to a mother who was extremely detached and absent because of her involvement in various social events. He himself had grown up angry and defiant, an interrogator eager to prove to the world that he was a brilliant achiever who could master science and mathematics. He earned a doctorate in physics at MIT at age twenty-three and taught at four prestigious universities before moving on to the Defense Department and then later to a private energy corporation.

Clearly he had thrown himself into this latter position with total abandon and disregard for his health. After years of fast food and no exercise he was diagnosed with a chronic heart condition. An exercise routine pursued too aggressively had proved fatal. He had died in his prime at age fifty-eight.

At this point Williams' awareness shifted and he began to have profound regrets and severe emotional pain concerning the way he had led his life. He realized that his childhood and early family had been set up perfectly to expose what was already his soul's tendency to use defiance and elitism to feel more important. His main tool had been ridicule, putting down others by criticizing their abilities and work ethic and personality. Yet now he could see that all the teachers had been in place to help him overcome this insecurity. All of them had arrived at just the right time to show him another way, but he had ignored them completely.

Instead he had just pursued his tunnel vision to the end. All the signs had been there to choose his work more carefully, to slow down. There were a multitude of implications and dangers inherent in his research of new technologies that he had failed to consider. He had allowed his employers to feed him new theories, and even unfamiliar physical principles, without even questioning their origin. These procedures worked, and that was all he cared about, because they led to success, gratitude, recognition. He had succumbed to his need for *recognition* . . . again. My God, he thought, I've failed just as I did before.

His mind abruptly shifted to a new scene, an earlier existence. He was in the southern Appalachians, nineteenth century, a military outpost. In a large tent several men leaned over a map. Lanterns flickered their light against the walls. A consensus had been reached among all the field officers present: there was no hope for peace now. War was inevitable, and sound military principles dictated an attack, quickly.

As one of the commanding general's top two aides, Williams had been forced to concur with the others. No other choice existed, he had concluded; disagreement would have ended his career. Besides, he couldn't have dissuaded the others even if he had wanted to. The offensive would have to be carried out, likely the last major battle in the eastern war against the Natives.

A sentry interrupted with a communication for the general. A settler wanted to see the commander immediately. Looking through the open tent flap, Williams had seen the frail white woman, perhaps thirty, desperation in her eyes. He found out later that she was the daughter of a missionary, bringing word of a possible new Native American initiative for peace, an appeal that she personally had negotiated at great risk.

But the general had refused to see her, remaining in the tent as she shouted at him, finally ordering her from his camp at gunpoint, not knowing the content of her message, not wanting to know. Again Williams kept quiet. He knew his commander was under great pressure, having already promised that the region would be opened up for economic expansion. A war was necessary if the vision of the power brokers and their political allies was to be actualized. It was not enough to let the settlers and the Indians create their own frontier culture. No, in their view, the future had to be shaped and manipulated and controlled for the best interests of those who made the world secure and abundant. It would be far too frightening and altogether irresponsible to let the little people decide.

Williams knew that a war would greatly please the railroad and coal tycoons and the newly emerging oil interests, and would, of course, ensure his own future as well. All he had to do was keep his mouth shut and play along. And he would, under silent protest—unlike the general's other primary aide. He remembered looking across the room at his colleague, a small man who limped slightly. No one knew why he limped. Nothing was wrong with his leg. Here was the ultimate yes-man. He knew what the secret cartels were up to and he loved it, admired it, wanted to become a part of it. And there was something more.

This man, like the general and the other controllers, feared the Native Americans and wanted them removed not just because of the Natives' alienation from the expanding industrial economy that was poised to overrun their lands. They feared these people because of something deeper, some terrifying and transformative idea, known in its entirety only by a few of the elders, but which bubbled up throughout their culture and called out for the controllers to change, to remember another vision of the future.

Williams had found out that the missionary's daughter had arranged for the great medicine chiefs to come together in one last attempt to agree on this knowledge, to find the words to share it—one last bid to explain themselves, to establish their value to a world quickly turning against them. Williams had known, deep within, that the woman should have been heard, but in the end he had remained silent, and with one quick nod the general had pushed away the possibility of reconciliation and had ordered the battle to begin.

As we watched, Williams' recollection shifted to a gorge in the deep woods, site of the coming battle. Cavalry poured over a ridge in a surprise offensive. The Native Americans rose to the defense, attacking the cavalry from the bluffs on either side. A short distance away, a large man and a woman huddled among the rocks. The man was a young academic, a congressional aide, there only to observe, terrified he was this close to the battle. It was wrong, all wrong. His interest was economics; he knew nothing of violence. He had come there convinced that the white man and the Indian need not be in conflict, that the growing economic surge through the region might be adapted, evolved, integrated to include both cultures.

Beside him in the rocks was the young woman seen at the military tent earlier. At this moment she felt abandoned, betrayed. Her effort could have worked, she knew, if those with the power had listened to what was possible. But she would not give up, she had told herself, not until the violence stopped. She kept saying, "It can be healed! It can be healed."

Suddenly on the downslope behind them, two cavalrymen rode hard toward a single Native. I strained to see who it was, finally recognizing the man as the angry chief I had seen in my mind when talking to David, the chief who had been so vocal against the white woman's ideas. As I watched, he turned quickly and shot an arrow into the chest of one of his pursuers. The other soldier leaped from his horse and fell upon the Native American. Both struggled furiously, the soldier's knife finally plunging deep into the throat of the darker man. Blood gushed across the torn ground.

Watching the events, the panicked economist pleaded with the woman to flee with him, but she motioned for him to stay, to be calm. For the first time Williams could see an old medicine man beside a tree next to them, his form flickering in and out of focus. At that instant another troop of cavalry crested the rise and was on top of them, firing indiscriminately. Bullets tore through both the man and the woman. With a smile the Indian defiantly stood and was likewise destroyed.

At this point Williams' focus drifted to a hill that overlooked the entire scene. Another individual was looking down on the battle. He was dressed in buckskins and led a pack mule, a mountain man. He turned from the battle and walked down the hill in the opposite direction, past the pool and falls, and then out of sight. I was astounded: the battle had taken place right here in the valley, just south of the falls.

When my attention returned to Williams, he was reliving the horror of the bloodshed and the hatred. He knew his failure to act during the Native American wars had set up the conditions and hopes of his most recent life, but just as before, he had failed to awaken. He had been together again with the congressional aide who had been killed with the woman, and still he had failed to remember their mission. Williams intended to meet the younger man on a hilltop, among a circle of large trees, and there his friend was supposed to awaken and go on to find six others in the valley, forming a group of seven. Together the group was to help resolve the Fear.

The idea seemed to thrust him into a deeper recollection. Fear had been the great enemy throughout humanity's long and tortuous history, and he seemed to know that present human culture was polarizing, giving the controllers in this historical time one last opportunity to seize power, to exploit the new technologies for their own purpose.

He seemed to cringe in agony. He knew that it was tremendously important for the group of seven to come together. History was poised for such groups, and only if enough of them formed, and only if enough of them *understood* the Fear, could the polarization be dispelled and the experiments in the valley ended.

Very slowly I became aware that I was again in the place of soft, white light. Williams' visions had ended, and both he and the other entities had quickly vanished. Afterward I had experienced a quick movement backward that had left me dizzy and distracted.

I noticed Wil beside me to the right.

"What happened?" I asked. "Where did he go?"

"I'm not sure," he replied.

"What was happening to him?"

"He was experiencing a *Life Review.*"

I nodded.

"Are you aware of what that is?" he asked.

"Yeah," I said. "I know that people who have had near-death experiences often report that their whole lives flash before them. Is that what you mean?"

Wil looked thoughtful. "Yes, but the increased awareness of this review process is having great impact on human culture. It's another part of the higher perspective provided by a knowledge of the Afterlife. Thousands of people have had near-death experiences, and as their stories are shared and talked about, the reality of the Life Review is becoming part of our everyday understanding. We know that after death, we have to look at our lives again; and we're going to agonize over every missed opportunity, over every case in which we failed to act. This knowledge is contributing to our determination to pursue every intuitive image that comes to mind, and keep it firmly in awareness. We're living life in a more deliberate way. We don't want to miss a single important event. We don't want the pain of looking back later and realizing that we blew it, that we failed to make the right decisions."

Suddenly Wil paused, cocking his head as though hearing something. Immediately I felt another jolt in my solar plexus and heard the dissonant hum again. Moments later the sound faded.

Wil was looking around. The solid white environment was shimmering with intermittent streaks of dull gray.

"Whatever is going on is affecting this dimension too!" he said. "I don't know if we can maintain our vibration."

As we waited, the dull streaks gradually diminished and the solid white background returned.

"Remember the warning about new technology in the Ninth Insight," Wil added, "and Williams' comment about those in Fear trying to control this technology."

"What about this *group of seven* coming back?" I asked. "And those visions that Williams was having of this valley in the nineteenth century? Wil, I've seen them too. What do you think the visions mean?"

Wil's expression grew more serious. "I think all this is what we're supposed to be seeing. And I think *you* are part of this group."

Suddenly the hum began to increase again.

"Williams said we first had to understand this Fear," Wil

stressed, "in order to help resolve it. That's what we have to do next; we have to find a way to understand this Fear."

Wil had barely finished his thought when an ear-shattering sound tore through my body, pushing me backward. Wil reached out for me, his face distorted and out of focus. I tried to grab his arm, but he was suddenly gone, and I was falling downward, out of control, amid a panorama of colors.

OVERCOMING
THE
FEAR

Shaking off the vertigo, I became aware that I was back at the falls. Across from me, under a rocky overhang, was my pack, lying exactly where I had placed it earlier. I looked around: no sign of Wil. What had happened? Where did he go?

According to my watch, less than an hour had passed since Wil and I had entered the other dimension, and as I thought about the experience, I was struck with how much love and calm I had felt, and how little anxiety—until now. Now everything around me seemed dull and muted.

Wearily I walked over and picked up my pack, fear welling up in my stomach. Sensing too much exposure in the openness of the rocks, I decided to walk back into the hills to the south until I could decide what to do. When I had crested the first hill and started down the slope, I spotted a small man, perhaps fifty years old, walking up to my left. He had red hair and a thin goatee and wore hiking clothes. Before I could hide, he spotted me and headed straight my way.

When he reached me, he smiled cautiously and said, "I'm afraid I'm turned around a bit. Could you direct me back to town?"

I gave him directions south to the spring and then on to the main stream, which he could follow west to the rangers' station.

He appeared relieved. "I ran into someone east of here, earlier, who told me how to get back, but I must have made a wrong turn. Are you also heading toward town?"

Looking closely at the expression on his face, I seemed to pick up a sadness and anger in his personality.

"I don't think so," I said. "I'm looking for a friend who is out here somewhere. What did the person you met look like?"

"It was a woman with blond hair and bright eyes," he replied. "She talked rapidly. I didn't catch her name. Who are you looking for?"

"Charlene Billings. Is there anything else about the woman you saw that you can remember?"

"She said something about the National Forest that made me think she might be one of those *searcher* types that hang out around here. But I couldn't tell. She warned me to leave the valley. She told me she had to get her gear and then she was leaving also. She seemed to think something was wrong out here, that everyone was in danger. She was actually very secretive. Frankly I didn't know what she was talking about." His tone suggested he was accustomed to speaking with directness.

As friendly as possible I said, "It sounds as if the person you met could have been my friend. Where did you see her exactly?"

He pointed toward the south, and told me he had run into her about half a mile back. She had been walking alone and had headed southeast from there.

"I'll walk with you as far as the spring," I said.

I picked up my pack, and as we walked down the hill, he asked, "If that was your friend, where do you think she was going?"

"I don't know."

"Into some mystical space, perhaps? Looking for utopia." He was smiling cynically.

I realized he was baiting me. "Maybe," I said. "Don't you believe in the possibility of utopia?"

"No, of course not. It's neolithic thinking. Naive."

I glanced at him, fatigue beginning to overwhelm me, trying to end the conversation. "Just a difference of opinion, I guess."

He laughed. "No, it's fact. There's no utopia coming. Everything is getting worse out there, not better. Economically things are swinging out of control, and eventually it will explode."

"Why do you say that?"

"It's simple demographics. For most of this century there has been a large middle class in the Western countries, a class who have promoted order and reason and carried a general faith that the economic system could work for everyone.

"But this faith is beginning to collapse now. You can see it everywhere. Fewer people every day now believe in the system, or play by the rules. And it's all because the middle class is shrinking. Technological development is making labor valueless and splitting human culture into two groups: the haves and the have-nots, those who have investments and ownership in the world economy and those who are restricted to menial, service jobs. Couple this with the failure of education and you can see the scope of the problem."

"That sounds awfully cynical," I said.

"It's realistic. It's the truth. For most people it takes more and more effort just to survive out there. Have you seen the surveys on stress? Tension is off the scale. Nobody feels secure, and the worst hasn't even begun yet. Population is exploding, and as technology expands even more, the distance will grow between the educated and the uneducated, and the haves will control more and more of the global economy, while drugs and crime will continue to soar with the have-nots.

"And what do you think," he continued, "will happen in the underdeveloped countries? Already much of the Middle East and Africa is in the hands of religious fundamentalists whose aim is to destroy organized civilization, which they think is a satanic empire, and replace it with some kind of perverted theocracy, where religious leaders are in charge of everything and they have the sanctioned power to condemn to death those they consider heretics, anywhere in the world.

"What kind of people would agree with this kind of butchery in the name of spirituality? Yet they are increasing every day. China still practices female infanticide, for example. Do you believe that?

"I'm telling you: law and order and respect for human life are on their way out. The world is degenerating into a mob mentality, ruled by envy and revenge and led by shrewd charlatans, and it's probably too late to stop it. But do you know what? Nobody really cares. Nobody! The politicians won't do anything. All they care about is their personal fiefdoms, and how to retain them. The world is changing too fast. No one can catch up, and that makes us just look out for number one and get whatever we can as fast as we can, before it's too late. This sentiment permeates the whole of civilization and every occupational group."

He took a breath and looked at me. I had stopped on the crest of one of the hills to view the impending sunset, and our eyes met. He seemed to realize he had gotten carried away with his tirade, and in that moment he began to look deeply familiar to me. I told him my name and he responded with his, Joel Lipscomb. We looked at each other for another long moment, but he offered no indication that he knew me. Why had we met in this valley?

As soon as I had formulated that last question in my mind, I knew the answer. He was voicing the vision of Fear that Williams had mentioned. A chill ran through me. This was supposed to happen.

I looked at him with a new seriousness. "Do you really think things are that bad?"

"Yes, absolutely," he replied. "I'm a journalist, and you can see this attitude playing out in our profession. In the past we at least attempted to do our job with certain standards of integrity. But no longer. It's all hype and sensationalism. No one's looking for the truth anymore or trying to present it in the most accurate way. Journalists are looking for the scoop, the most outrageous perspective—every bit of dirt they can dig up.

"Even if particular accusations have a logical explanation, they are reported anyway, for their impact on ratings and circulation. In a world where the people are numbed and distracted, the only thing that sells is the unbelievable. And the pity is that this kind of journalism is self-perpetuating. A young journalist looks at this situation and thinks that to survive in the business he has to play the game. If he doesn't, he thinks he'll be left behind, ruined, which is what leads to so-called investigative reports being intentionally faked. It happens all the time."

We had proceeded south and were making our way down the rocky terrain.

"Other occupational groups suffer from the same condition," Joel went on. "God, look at attorneys. Perhaps there was a time when being an officer of the court meant something, when the participants in the process shared a common respect for the truth, for justice. But no longer. Think about the recent celebrity trials covered by television. Lawyers now do everything they can to subvert justice, intentionally, trying to convince jurors to believe the hypothetical when there is no evidence—hypotheticals that the attorneys know are lies—just to get someone off. And other attorneys comment on the proceedings as though these tactics are common practice and absolutely justified under our system of law, which is not true.

"Under our system, everyone is entitled to a fair trial. But the lawyers are beholden to ensure fairness and correctness, not to distort the truth and undermine justice simply to get their client off at all costs. Because of television, at least we've been able to see these corrupt practices for what they represent: simple expediency on the part of trial lawyers to enhance their reputations in order to command higher fees. The reason they're so blatant is that they think no one cares, and obviously no one does. Everyone else is doing the same thing.

"We're cutting corners, maximizing short-term profits instead of planning long-term, because inside, consciously or unconsciously, we don't think our success can last. And we're doing this even if we have to break the spirit of trust we have with others and advance our own interests at the expense of someone else.

"Pretty soon all the subtle assumptions and agreements that hold civilization together will be totally subverted. Think what will happen once unemployment gets to a certain level in the inner cities. Crime is out of control now. Police officers aren't going to keep risking their lives for a public that doesn't notice anyway. Why find yourself on the stand twice a week getting grilled by some attorney who's not interested in the truth anyway, or worse, writhing in pain while your lifeblood runs out on the ground in some dark alley somewhere, when no one cares? Better to look the other way and do your twenty years as quietly as possible, maybe even take a few bribes on the side. And it goes on and on. What's going to stop it?"

He paused and I glanced back at him as we walked.

"I guess you think some spiritual renaissance is going to change all this?" he asked.

"I sure hope so."

He struggled over a fallen tree to catch up with me. "Listen," he continued, "I bought into this spirituality stuff for a while, this idea of purpose and destiny and Insights. I could even see some interesting coincidences happening in my own life. But I decided it was all crazy. The human mind can imagine all sorts of silly things; we don't even realize we're doing it. When you get right down to it, all this talk of spirituality is just weird rhetoric."

I started to counter his argument but changed my mind. My intuition was to hear him out first.

"Yeah," I said. "I guess it sometimes sounds that way."

"Take for instance the talk I've heard about this valley," he went on. "That's the kind of nonsense I used to listen to. This is just a valley full of trees and bushes like a thousand others." He put his hand on a large tree as we passed. "You think this National Forest is going to survive? Forget it. With the way humans are polluting the oceans, and saturating the ecosystem with man-made carcinogenics, and consuming paper and other wood products, this place will become a garbage bin, like everywhere else. In fact, no one cares about trees now. How do you think the government gets away with building roads in here at taxpayer expense and then selling the timber at below-market value? Or swapping the best, most beautiful areas for ruined land some-where else, just to make the developers happy?

"You probably think something mystical is happening here in this valley. And why not? Everyone would love for there to be something mystical going on, especially considering the dimin-ishing quality of life. But the fact is, there's nothing esoteric hap-pening. We're just animals, creatures smart enough and unlucky enough to have figured out we're alive, and we're going to die without ever knowing any purpose. We can pretend all we want and we can wish all we want, but that basic existential fact re-mains—we can't know."

I looked back at him again. "Don't you believe in any kind of spirituality?"

He laughed. "If a God exists, he must be an exceedingly cruel monster of a God. There couldn't be a spiritual reality operating here! How could there be? Look at the world. What kind of God would design such a devastating place where children die horri-bly by earthquakes and senseless crimes and *starvation,* when res-taurants toss out tons of food every day?

"Although," he added, "perhaps that's the way it's supposed to be. Perhaps that's God's plan. Maybe the 'end times' scholars are correct. They think life and history are all just a test of faith to see who will win salvation and who won't, a divine plan to destroy civilization in order to separate the believers from the wicked." He attempted a smile, but it quickly faded as he drifted into his own thoughts.

Finally he quickened his pace to walk up even with me. We were entering the sage meadow again, and I could see the crow tree a quarter of a mile away.

"Do you know what these end-times people really believe is

happening?" he asked. "I did a study of them several years ago; they're fascinating."

"Not really," I said, nodding for him to go on.

"They study the prophecies hidden in the Bible, especially in the book of Revelation. They believe that we live in what they call the *last days,* the time when all the prophecies will come true. Essentially what they think is this: History is now set up for the return of the Christ and the creation of the heavenly kingdom on Earth. But before this can occur the Earth has to suffer a series of wars, natural disasters, and other apocalyptic events predicted in the Scriptures. And they know every one of these predictions, so they spend their time watching world events very closely, waiting for the next event on the timetable."

"What's the next event?" I asked.

"A peace treaty in the Middle East that will allow the rebuilding of the Temple in Jerusalem. Sometime after that, according to them, a massive rapture will begin among true believers, whoever they are, and they will be snatched off the face of the Earth and lifted into Heaven."

I stopped and looked at him. "They think these people will begin to disappear?"

"Yeah, that's in the Bible. Then comes the tribulation, which is a seven-year period when all hell breaks loose for whoever is left on Earth. Apparently everything is expected to fall apart: giant earthquakes destroy the economy; ocean levels destroy many cities; plus rioting and crime and the rest of it. And then a politician emerges, probably in Europe, who offers a plan to pull things back together, if, of course, he's set up with supreme power. This includes a centralized electronic economy which co-ordinates commerce in most parts of the world. To participate in this economy, however, and take advantage of the automation, one has to swear allegiance to this leader and have a chip implanted in one's hand, through which all economic interactions are documented.

"This Antichrist at first protects Israel and facilitates a peace treaty, then attacks later, starting a world war that ultimately involves the Islamic nations, Russia, and finally China. According to the prophecies, just as Israel is about to fall, the angels of God swoop down and win the war, installing a spiritual utopia that lasts a thousand years."

He cleared his throat and looked at me. "Walk through a religious bookstore sometime and look around; there are commentaries and novels about these prophecies everywhere, and more coming out all the time."

"Do you think these end-times scholars are correct?"

He shook his head. "I don't think so. The only prophecy that's being played out in this world is man's greed and corruption. Some dictator might rise up and take over, but it will be because he saw a way to take advantage of the chaos."

"Do you think this will happen?"

"I don't know, but I'll tell you one thing. If the collapse of the middle class continues, and the poor get poorer and the inner cities get more crime-infested and spread into the suburbs, and then on top of that we experience, say, a series of big natural disasters and the whole economy crashes for a while, we'll have bands of hungry marauders preying on the masses and total panic everywhere. In the face of this kind of violence, if someone comes along and proposes a way to save us, to straighten things out, asking only that we surrender some civil liberties, I have no doubt that we'll do it."

We stopped and drank some water from my canteen. Fifty yards ahead was the crow tree.

I perked up; far in the background I could detect the faint dissonance of the hum.

Joel's eyes squinted in concentration, watching me closely. "What are you hearing?"

I turned around and faced him. "It's a strange noise, a hum we've been perceiving. I think it may be some kind of experiment going on in the valley."

"What kind of experiment? Who's conducting it? Why can't I hear it?"

I was about to tell him more when we were interrupted by another sound. We listened carefully.

"That's a vehicle," I said.

Two more gray Jeeps were approaching from the west and heading toward us. We ran behind a patch of tall briers and hid, and they passed within a hundred yards without stopping, heading southeast along the same path the earlier Jeep had followed.

"I don't like this," Joel said. "Who was that?"

"Well, it's not the Forest Service, and no one else is supposed to be driving in here. I think it must be the people involved with the experiment."

He looked horrified.

"If you want," I said, "you can take a more direct route back to town. Just head southwest toward that ridge in the distance. You'll run into the stream after about three-quarters of a mile and you can follow it west into town from there. I think you can arrive before it gets too dark."

"You're not coming?"

"Not now. I'm going directly south to the stream and wait awhile for my friend."

He tensed his forehead. "These people couldn't be conducting an experiment without someone in the Forest Service knowing about it."

"I know."

"You don't think you can do anything about this, do you? This is something big."

I didn't respond; a pang of anxiety rushed through me.

He listened for a moment and then moved past me into the valley, walking quickly. He looked back once and shook his head.

I watched him until he crossed the meadow and disappeared into the forest on the other side, then I hurriedly walked toward the south, thinking again of Charlene. What had she been doing out here? Where was she going? I had no answers.

Pushing hard, I reached the stream in about thirty minutes. The sun was now completely hidden by the band of clouds at the western horizon, and the twilight cast the woods in ominous gray tones. I was tired and dirty, and I knew that listening to Joel and seeing the Jeeps had affected my mood severely. Perhaps I had enough evidence now to go to the authorities; perhaps that was the way I could help Charlene most. Several options danced through my head, all rationalizing my return to town.

Because the woods on both sides of the stream were thin, I decided to wade across and make my way into the thicker forest on the other side, although I knew that area was private property.

Once across, I stopped abruptly, hearing another Jeep, then broke into a run. Fifty feet ahead the land rose quickly into a knob of boulders and outcroppings, twenty feet high. Climbing quickly, I reached the top and accelerated my pace, then leaped upon a pile of large rocks, intending to jump them quickly to the other side. When my foot hit the topmost rock, the huge stone rolled forward, throwing my feet out from under me and starting the whole pile moving. I bounced once on my hip and landed in a small gully, the pile still tumbling my way. Several of the rocks, each two or three feet in diameter, were careening down, coming squarely for my chest. I had time to roll onto my left side and raise my arms, but I knew I couldn't get out of the way.

Then, out of the corner of my eye, I saw a wispy white form moving in front of my body. Simultaneously an unusual knowing came over me that the huge rocks would somehow miss. I closed my eyes and heard them crash on both sides. Slowly I opened my eyes and peered out through the dust, wiping the dirt and rock chips from my face. The rocks were lying neatly beside me. How had that happened? What was that white form?

For a moment I looked around the scene, and then behind one of the rocks I saw a slight movement. A small bobcat cub eased around and looked directly into my eyes. I knew it was big enough to have run away, but it was lingering, looking at me.

The rising sound of the approaching vehicle finally sent the bobcat scampering into the woods. I jumped to my feet and ran several more steps before landing awkwardly on another rock. A bolt of throbbing pain raced through my whole leg as my left foot gave way. I fell to the ground and crawled the last two yards into the trees. I rolled around behind a huge oak as the vehicle pulled up to the stream, slowed for a few minutes, then raced away, again toward the southeast.

My heart pounding, I sat up and pulled off my boot to inspect the ankle. It was already beginning to swell. Why this? I thought. As I slid around to stretch out my leg, I observed a woman staring at me from about thirty feet away. I froze as she walked toward me.

"Are you all right?" she asked, her voice concerned but wary. She was a tall black woman, perhaps forty, dressed in loose-fitting sweat clothes and tennis shoes. Strands of dark hair had pulled out of her ponytail and dangled in the breeze above her temples. In her hand was a small green knapsack.

"I was sitting over there and saw you fall," she said. "I'm a doctor. Do you want me to take a look?"

"I'd appreciate that," I said dizzily, not believing the coincidence.

She knelt down beside me and moved the foot gently, at the same time surveying the area toward the creek. "Are you out here alone?"

I told her briefly about looking for Charlene, but left out everything else. She said she had seen no one of that description. As she talked, finally introducing herself as Maya Ponder, I became convinced that she was completely trustworthy. I told her my name and where I lived.

When I finished, she said, "I'm from Asheville, although I have a health center, with a partner, a few miles south of here. It's new. We also own forty acres of the valley right here that joins the National Forest." She pointed to the area where we were sitting. "And another forty acres up the ridge to the south."

I unzipped a pocket on my hiking pack and pulled out my canteen.

"Would you like some water?" I asked.

"No thanks, I have some." She reached inside her own pack, retrieved a canteen, and opened the top. But instead of drinking, she soaked a small towel and wrapped my foot, an action that made me grimace in pain.

Turning and looking into my eyes, she said, "You've definitely sprained this ankle."

"How badly?" I asked.

She hesitated. "What do you think?"

"I don't know. Let me try to walk on it."

I attempted to stand, but she stopped me. "Wait a minute," she said. "Before you try to walk, analyze your attitude. How badly do you think you're hurt?"

"What do you mean?"

"I mean that very often your recuperation time depends on what *you* think, not me."

I looked down at the ankle. "I think it could be pretty bad. If it is, I'll have to get back to town somehow."

"What then?"

"I don't know. If I can't walk, I may have to go find someone else to look for Charlene."

"Do you have any idea why this accident happened now?"

"Not really. Why does that matter?"

"Because, again, very often your attitude about why an accident or illness has happened has an effect on your recuperation."

I looked at her closely, well aware that I was resisting. Part of me felt as though I didn't have time for this discussion right now. It seemed too self-involved for the situation. Although the hum had ceased, I had to assume that the experiment was continuing. Everything felt too dangerous and it was almost dark . . . and Charlene could be in terrible trouble for all I knew.

I was also aware of a deep sense of guilt toward Maya. Why would I feel guilty? I tried to shake off the emotion.

"What kind of doctor are you?" I asked, sipping some water.

She smiled, and for the first time I saw her energy lift. She had decided to trust me too.

"Permit me to tell you about the kind of medicine I practice," she said. "Medicine is changing, and changing rapidly. We don't think of the body as a machine anymore, with parts that eventually wear out and have to be fixed or replaced. We're beginning to understand that the health of the body is determined to a great degree by our mental processes: what we think of life and especially of ourselves, at both the conscious and the unconscious levels.

"This represents a fundamental shift. Under the old method the doctor was the expert and healer, and the patient the passive recipient, hoping the doctor would have all the answers. But we know now that the inner attitude of the patient is crucial. A key factor is fear and stress and the way we handle it. Sometimes the fear is conscious, but very often we repress it entirely.

"This is the brave, macho attitude: deny the problem, push it away, conjure up our heroic agenda. If we take this attitude, then the fear continues to eat at us unconsciously. Adopting a positive outlook is very important in staying healthy, but we have to engage in this attitude in full awareness, using love, not macho, for this attitude to be completely effective. What I believe is that our unspoken fears create blocks or crimps in the body's energy flow, and it's these blocks that ultimately result in problems. The fears keep manifesting in ever-greater degrees until we deal with them. Physical problems are the last step. Ideally these blocks would be dealt with early, in a preventive way, before illness develops."

"So you think all illness can ultimately be prevented or cured?"

"Yes, I'm sure we will have longer or shorter life spans; that's probably up to the Creator, but we don't have to be sick, and we don't have to be the victim of so many accidents."

"So you think this applies to an accident, like my sprain, as well as to illnesses?"

She smiled. "Yes, in many cases."

I was confused. "Look, I don't have time for this right now. I'm really worried about my friend. I've got to do something!"

"I know, but I have a hunch this conversation won't take

long. If you rush by and disregard what I'm saying, you may miss the meaning of what is obviously quite a coincidence here." She looked at me to see whether I had picked up on her reference to the Manuscript.

"You're aware of the Insights?" I asked.

She nodded.

"What exactly do you suggest I do?"

"Well, the technique I've had great success with is this: first, we try to remember the nature of your thoughts just prior to the health problem—in your case, the sprain. What were you thinking? What is the fear this problem is revealing to you?"

I thought for a moment, then said, "I felt afraid, ambivalent. The situation here in this valley seemed much more sinister than I thought. I didn't feel as though I could handle it. On the other hand, I knew Charlene might need help. I was confused and torn over what to do."

"So you sprained your ankle?"

I leaned toward her. "Are you saying that I sabotaged myself so I wouldn't have to take action? Isn't that too simple?"

"That's for you to say, not me. But very often it is simple. Besides, the most important thing is not to spend time defending or proving. Just play with it. Try to remember everything you can about where the health problem came from. Explore for yourself."

"How do I do that?"

"You have to calm your mind and receive this information."

"Intuitively?"

"Intuitively, prayerfully, however you conceive the process."

I resisted again, not sure whether I could relax and clear my mind. Finally I closed my eyes, and for a moment my thoughts ceased, but then a succession of memories of Wil and the day's events intruded. I let them go by and cleared my mind again. Immediately I saw a scene of myself at age ten, limping away from a touch football game, well aware that I was faking the injury. That's right! I thought. I used to fake sprains to avoid having to perform under pressure. I had forgotten all about this! I realized that later I began to actually hurt the ankle frequently, in all kinds of situations. As I pondered the memory, another flash of recollection entered my mind, a cloudy scene of myself in another time, feeling cocky, confident, impulsive, then as I worked in a dark, candlelit room, the door crashed in and I was dragged away in terror.

I opened my eyes and looked at Maya. "Maybe I have something."

I shared the content of my childhood memory, but the other vision felt too vague to be described, so I didn't mention it.

Afterward, Maya asked, "What do you think?"

"I don't know; the sprain seemed the result of pure chance. It's hard to imagine that the accident came from this need to avoid the situation. Besides, I've been in worse situations than this many times and I didn't sprain an ankle. Why did it happen now?"

She looked thoughtful. "Who knows? Perhaps now is the time to see through the habit. Accidents, illness, healing, they're all more mysterious than any of us ever imagined. I believe that we have an undiscovered ability to influence what happens to us in the future, including whether we are healthy—although, again, the power has to remain with the individual patient.

"There was a reason that I didn't offer an opinion concerning how badly you were hurt. We in the medical establishment have learned that medical opinions have to be offered very carefully. Over the years the public has developed almost a worship of doctors, and when a physician says something, patients have tended to take these opinions totally to heart. The country doctors of a hundred years ago knew this, and would use this principle to actually paint an overly optimistic picture of any health situation. If the doctor said that the patient would get better, very often the patient would internalize this idea in his or her mind and actually defy all odds to recover. In later years, however, ethical considerations have prevented such distortions, and the establishment has felt that the patient is entitled to a cold scientific assessment of his or her situation.

"Unfortunately when this was given, sometimes patients dropped dead right before our eyes, just because they were told their condition was terminal. We know now that we have to be very careful with these assessments, because of the power of our minds. We want to focus this power in a positive direction. The body is capable of miraculous regeneration. Body parts thought of in the past as solid forms are actually energy systems that can transform overnight. Have you read the latest research on prayer? The simple fact that this kind of spiritual visualization is being scientifically proven to work totally undermines our old physical model of healing. We're having to work out a new model."

She paused and poured more water on the towel around my ankle, then continued, "I believe the first step in the process is to identify the fear with which the medical problem seems to be connected; this opens up the energy block in your body to conscious healing. The next step is to pull in as much energy as possible and focus it at the exact location of the block."

I was about to ask how this was done, but she stopped me. "Go ahead and raise your energy level as much as you can."

Accepting her guidance, I began to observe the beauty around me and to concentrate on a spiritual connection within, evoking a heightened sensation of love. Gradually the colors became more vivid and everything in my awareness increased in presence. I could tell that she was raising her own energy at the same time.

When I felt as though my vibration had increased as much as possible, I looked at her.

She smiled back at me. "Okay, now you can focus the energy on the block."

"How do I do that?" I asked.

"You use the pain. That's why it's there, to help you focus."

"What? Isn't the idea to get rid of pain?"

"Unfortunately that's what we've always thought, but pain is really a beacon."

"A beacon?"

"Yes," she said, pressing several locations on my foot. "How badly does it hurt right now?"

"It's a throbbing ache, but not too bad."

She unwrapped the towel. "Focus your attention on the pain and try to feel it as much as possible. Determine its exact location."

"I know where it is. It's in the ankle."

"Yes, but the ankle is a large area. Where exactly?"

I studied the throbbing. She was correct. I had been generalizing the pain to the whole ankle. But as my leg was stretched out with the toes of my foot pointed upward, the pain was more precisely centered in the top left portion of this joint and about an inch inward.

"Okay," I said. "I've got that."

"Now place all your attention on that specific area. Be there with all of your being."

For a few minutes I said nothing. With total concentration I felt this location in my ankle completely. I noticed that all the other perceptions of my body—breathing, the location of my hands and arms, sticky sweat on the back of my neck—faded far into the background.

"Feel the pain totally," she reminded.

"Okay," I said. "I'm there."

"What's happening with the pain?" she asked.

"I still feel it, but it has changed in character or something. It's becoming warmer, less bothersome, more like a tingling." As I talked, the pain began to take on its normal sensation again.

"What happened?" I asked.

"I believe that pain serves another function beyond just telling us that something is wrong. Perhaps it also points out exactly where the difficulty is, so that we can follow it into our bodies like a beacon and place our attention and energy in exactly the right spot. It's almost as if both the pain and our concentrated attention can't occupy the same space. Of course, in cases of severe pain, where concentration is impossible, we can use anesthetics to ease the intensity, although I think it's best to leave some pain so that the beacon effect can be utilized."

She paused and looked at me.

"What's next?" I asked.

"Next," she replied, "is to consciously send higher divine energy into the exact spot identified by the pain, intending that the love will transform the cells there into a state of perfect functioning."

I just stared.

"Go ahead," she said. "Get completely connected again. I'll guide you through it."

I nodded when I was ready.

"Feel the pain with all your being," she began, "and now

image your love energy going right into the heart of the pain, lifting that exact point of your body, the atoms themselves, into a higher vibration. See the particles take a quantum jump into the pure energy pattern that is their optimum state. Literally feel a tingling sensation in that spot as the vibration accelerates."

After pausing for a full minute, she continued. "Now, without changing your focus on the point of the pain, begin to feel your energy, the tingle, moving up both legs . . . through your hips . . . into your abdomen and chest . . . and finally into your neck and head. Feel your whole body tingling with the higher vibration. See every organ operating at optimal efficiency."

I followed her instructions exactly, and after a few moments my whole body felt lighter, more energized. I held that state for about ten minutes, then opened my eyes and looked at Maya.

Using a flashlight in the darkness, Maya was putting up my tent on a flat area between two pines. Glancing over at me, she said, "Feel better?"

I nodded.

"Do you understand the process so far?"

"I think so. I sent energy into the pain."

"Yes, but what we did earlier was just as important. You begin by looking at the meaning of the injury or illness, what its occurrence is pointing out about some fear in your life that is holding you back, manifesting in your body. This is what opens the fear block so that the visualization can penetrate.

"After the block is open, then you can use pain as a beacon, raising the vibration in that area and then in your entire body. But finding the origin of the fear is vitally important. When the origin of the illness or accident is very deep, it often requires hypnosis or intensive counseling."

I told her about the medieval image I had seen of the door being kicked in and of myself being dragged away.

She looked thoughtful. "Sometimes the root of the block goes back a very long way. But as you explore it further, and begin to work through the fear that is holding you back, you will usually discover a fuller understanding of who you are, of what your current life on Earth is all about. And this sets the stage for the last—and, I firmly believe, the most important—step in the healing process. Most important of all is to look deeply enough to *remember* what you want to do with your life. Real healing takes place when we can envision a new kind of future for ourselves that excites us. *Inspiration* is what keeps us well. People aren't healed to watch more TV."

I looked at her for a moment, then said, "You mentioned that prayer works. How is the best way to pray for someone who is not well?"

"We're still trying to figure that out. It has something to do with the Eighth Insight process of sending the energy and love that flow through us from the divine source to the person, and at the same time visualizing that the individual will remember what they really want to do with their life. Of course, sometimes what the person remembers is that it's time to make a transition into the other dimension. When that's the case, we have to accept it."

Maya was finishing with the tent and added, "Also keep in mind that the procedures I've recommended should be done in conjunction with the very best in traditional medicine. If we were near my clinic, I would take you in for a full examination, but in this case, unless you disagree, I suggest you stay here tonight. It's better if you don't move much."

As I watched, she set up my stove, turned it on, and placed a boiler containing freeze-dried soup on the flame. "I'm going back into town. I need to get a splint for your ankle and some other supplies, just in case we need them, then I'll hike back out and check on you. I'll bring a radio too, in case we have to send for help."

I nodded.

She poured her canteen's water into mine and looked over at me. Behind her, the last streak of light was vanishing toward the west.

"Did you say your clinic was near here?" I asked.

"Actually it's only about four miles to the south," she said, "over the ridge, but there's no way to come into the valley from that direction. The only pass is the main road that comes in south of town."

"How did you happen to be here?"

She smiled and looked slightly embarrassed. "It's funny. I had a dream last night about hiking into the valley again, and this morning I decided I would do just that. I've been working hard and I guess I needed some time to reflect on what I'm doing at the clinic. My partner and I have a great deal of experience with alternative approaches, Chinese medicine, herbs, yet at the same time, we have the resources of the world's best in traditional medicine at our fingertips through computer. I'd dreamed about this kind of clinic for years."

She paused for a moment, then said, "Before you showed up I was sitting right over there, and my energy just shot through the roof. It seemed as though I could see the whole story of my life, every experience I've had, from my early childhood all the way up until this moment, stretched out before me in plain view. It was the clearest Sixth Insight experience I've ever had.

"All those events were a preparation," she continued. "I grew up in a family where my mother struggled with chronic disease all her life, but would never participate in her own healing. At the time, the doctors knew no better, but throughout my childhood, her refusal to explore her own fears irritated me, and I noticed every bit of new information about diet, vitamins, stress levels, meditation, and their role in health, trying to convince her to become involved. During my adolescence I was torn between joining the clergy and becoming a doctor. I don't know; it was as if I was driven to figure out how we use insight, faith, to change the future, to heal.

"And my father," she continued. "He was something else. He worked in the biological sciences, but he never would explain any of his results except in his academic papers. 'Pure research,' he called it. His associates treated him like a god. He was unapproachable, the ultimate authority. I was grown, and he had died of cancer, before I understood his real interest—the immune system, and specifically how commitment and excitement with life enhance the immune system.

"He was the first one to see this relationship, and that's what all the current research shows now. Yet I never got to talk with him about it. At first I wondered why I would be born to a father who behaved like that. But I finally accepted the fact that my parents had the exact combination of traits and interests to inspire my own evolution. That's why I wanted to be with them in my early life. Looking at my mother, I knew that each of us must take responsibility for our own healing. We can't just turn it over to others. Healing in its essence is about breaking through the fears associated with life—fears that we don't want to face—and finding our own special inspiration, a vision of the future, that we know we're here to help create.

"From my father, I saw clearly that medicine must be more

responsive, must acknowledge the intuition and vision of the people we treat. We have to come down from our ivory tower. The combination of the two set me up to look for a new paradigm in medicine: one based on the patient's ability to take control of his or her life and to get back on the right path. That's my message, I guess, the idea that inwardly we know how to participate in our own healing, physically and emotionally. We can become inspired to shape a higher, more ideal future, and when we do, *miracles happen*."

Standing up, she glanced at my ankle, then at me. "I'm leaving now," she said. "Try not to put any weight on your foot. What you need is complete rest. I'll be back in the morning."

I think I must have looked anxious, because she knelt down again and put both hands on the ankle. "Don't worry," she said. "With enough energy there's nothing that can't be healed—hatred . . . war. It's just a matter of coming together with the right vision." She patted my foot gently. "We can heal this! We can heal this!"

She smiled once, then turned and walked away.

I suddenly wanted to call out and tell her everything I had experienced in the other dimension and what I knew about the Fear and about the group coming back, but instead I remained quiet, fatigue overwhelming me, content to watch her disappear into the trees. Tomorrow would be soon enough, I thought . . . because I knew exactly who she was.

REMEMBERING

The next morning I jerked awake, the shrill cry of a hawk, high overhead, pulling me into awareness. For a few moments I listened carefully, imagining her lofty rolls. She cried one more time then stopped. I sat up quickly and looked through the tent flap; the day was cloudy but warm, and a light breeze swayed the treetops.

Taking an Ace bandage from my pack, I carefully wrapped the ankle, working the joint carefully and feeling very little pain, then crawled out of the tent and stood up. After a few moments I put weight on my foot and took a tentative step. The ankle felt weak, but if I limped slightly, it seemed to support me. I wondered: had Maya's procedure helped, or had the ankle not been hurt that badly? There was no way to know.

Digging into my pack again, I retrieved a change of clothes, then grabbed the dirty dishes from the night before. Cautiously, alert for any odd sound or movement, I made my way back to the stream. When I located a place where I was shielded from view, I slipped off my clothes and entered the water, finding it cold and refreshing. I lay there without thinking, trying to forget the anxiety rising in my gut, gazing out at the colors of the leaves above my head.

Suddenly I began to recall a dream from the night before. I was sitting on a rock . . . something was happening . . . Wil was there . . . and others. I vaguely remembered a field of blue and amber. I struggled a moment longer but could recall nothing more.

As I opened a bottle of soap, I noticed that the trees and bushes around me were amplified in appearance. Somehow the act of remembering my dream had increased my energy. Feeling lighter, I hastily bathed and washed off the dishes, noticing as I finished that a large rock to my right looked very similar to the one on which I was sitting in my dream. I stopped and inspected the boulder more closely. Flat and about ten feet in diameter, its shape and color matched exactly.

In a few minutes I had taken down the tent, packed, and hidden my gear under some fallen limbs. Then, returning to the rock, I sat down and tried to recall the blue field and the exact position Wil had occupied in the dream. He had been to my left and slightly behind me. At that moment a clear image of his face came to my mind, as in a close-up photo. Struggling to maintain the exact detail, I re-created his image and surrounded it with the blue field.

Seconds later I felt a pulling sensation in my solar plexus, and then I was again streaking through the colors. When I stopped, the environment was pale blue and luminous, and Wil was beside me.

"Thank God you're back!" he said, moving in closer. "You became so dense I couldn't find you."

"What happened before?" I asked. "Why did the hum get so loud?"

"I don't know."

"Where are we now?"

"It's a particular level where dreams seem to take place."

I looked out into the blue. Nothing was moving. "You've been here?"

"Yes, I came here before I found you at the falls, although at the time I didn't know why."

For a moment we both surveyed the environment again, then Wil asked, "What happened to you when you went back?"

With excitement I began to describe everything that had occurred, focusing first on Joel's forecast of environmental and civil collapse. Wil listened intently, digesting every aspect of Joel's outlook.

"He was voicing the Fear," Wil commented.

I nodded. "That's what I think. Do you suppose all of what he said is really occurring?" I asked.

"I think the danger is that a lot of people are beginning to believe it's happening. Remember what the Ninth Insight said: as the spiritual renaissance progresses, it must overcome a polarization of Fear."

I caught Wil's eye. "I met someone else, a woman."

Wil listened as I described my experience with Maya, particularly the injury to my ankle and her healing procedures.

When I finished, he gazed into the distance, thinking.

"I think Maya is the woman in Williams' vision," I added. "The woman who was trying to stop the war with the Native Americans."

"Perhaps her idea of healing holds the key to dealing with the Fear," Wil replied.

I nodded for him to continue.

"This all makes sense," he said. "Look at what has already occurred. You came here searching for Charlene and met David, who said the Tenth was a greater understanding of the spiritual renaissance happening on this planet, an understanding attained by grasping our relationship to the Afterlife dimension. He said the Insight has something to do with clarifying the nature of intuitions, of maintaining them in our minds, of seeing our synchronistic path in a fuller way.

"Later, you figured out how to maintain your intuitions in this way and found me at the falls, and I confirmed that maintaining the intuitions, the mental images of ourselves, was the operative mode in the Afterlife as well, and that humans are moving into alignment with this other dimension. Soon after, we found ourselves watching Williams' Life Review, watching him agonize over not remembering something he had wanted to do, which was to come together with a group of people to help deal with this Fear that threatens our spiritual awakening.

"He says we have to understand this Fear in order to do something about it, and then we get separated and you run into a journalist, Joel, who takes a long time to enunciate what? A fearful vision of the future. In fact, a fear of the complete destruction of civilization.

"Then, of course, you next run into a woman whose life is all about healing, and the way she facilitates healing is to help people work through fear blocks by prodding their memory, helping them to discern why they're on the planet. This *remembering* has to be the key."

A sudden movement drew our attention. Another group of souls seemed to be forming about a hundred feet away.

"They are probably here to help someone with their dreaming," Wil said.

I looked hard at him. "They help us dream?"

"Yes, in a way. Some other souls were here when you dreamed last night."

"How did you know about my dream?"

"When you were jolted back into the physical, I tried to find you but I couldn't. Then, when I waited, I began to see your face, and moved here. The last time I came to this place, I couldn't quite grasp what was occurring, but now I think I understand what happens when we dream."

I shook my head, not comprehending.

He gestured out toward the souls. "It apparently all happens synchronistically. These beings you see probably found themselves here just as I did earlier, by coincidence, and now they're probably waiting to see who comes by in their dream body."

The background hum grew louder and I couldn't respond. I felt confused, dizzy. Wil came closer to me, touching my back again. "Stay with me!" he said. "There's some reason we need to see this."

I struggled to clear my head, then noticed another form manifesting in the space beside the souls. At first I thought other souls were appearing, but then I realized the formation was much larger than anything I'd seen before: a whole scene was being projected in front of us, like a hologram, complete with characters, setting, and dialogue. A single individual seemed to be at the center of the action, a man vaguely familiar. After a moment of concentration I realized that the person before us was Joel.

As we watched, the scene began to unfold, like the plot of a movie. I strained to follow along, but my head was still foggy; I couldn't quite understand what was happening. As the episode progressed and the dialogue became more intense, both the souls and the journalist moved closer together. After several minutes the drama seemed to end, and everyone disappeared.

"What was happening?" I asked.

"The individual in the center of the scene was dreaming," Wil said.

"That was Joel, the man I told you about," I replied.

Wil turned to me in astonishment. "Are you sure?"

"Yes."

"Did you understand the dream he just had?"

"No, I couldn't quite get it. What happened?"

"The dream was about a war of some kind. He was fleeing a bomb-ravaged city with shells exploding all around him, running for his life, thinking of nothing but safety and survival. When he successfully evaded the horror and climbed a mountain to look back at the city, he remembered that his orders had been to meet another group of soldiers and supply a secret part to a new device that would make the enemy weapons inactive. To his horror he now realized that because he had failed to show up, the soldiers and the city were being systematically destroyed before his eyes."

"A nightmare," I commented.

"Yes, but it has meaning. When we dream, we unconsciously travel back to this sleep level, and other souls come and help us. Don't forget what dreams do: they clarify how to handle current situations in our lives. The Seventh Insight says to interpret dreams by superimposing the plot of the dream against the real situation facing us in life."

I turned and looked at Wil. "But what role do the souls play?"

As soon as I had asked that question, we began to move again. Wil kept his hand against my back. When we stopped, the light was shifting to a rich green, but I could observe beautiful waves of amber circulating around us. When I focused intently, the amber streaks became individual souls.

I glanced at Wil, who was smiling broadly. This location seemed to carry an increased mood of celebration and joy. As I watched the souls, several moved directly in front of us and closed together into a group. Their faces were broad and smiling, although still hard to focus on for any length of time.

"They're so full of love," I said.

"See if you can pick up on their knowledge," Wil advised.

When I focused on them with this intent, I realized that these souls were associated with Maya. In fact, they were ecstatic about her recent self-revelations, especially her understanding of the life preparation her mother and father had provided. They seemed to know that Maya had experienced a full Sixth Insight review and was on the verge of remembering why she had been born.

I turned to face Wil, who acknowledged that he, too, was seeing the images.

At this moment I could hear the hum again; my stomach tensed. Wil held my shoulders and back tightly. When the sound had ceased, my vibration fell dramatically, and I looked out at the group of souls, attempting to open up and connect with their energy in an attempt to boost my own. To my amazement they suddenly shifted out of focus and moved away from me to a new position twice as far away.

"What happened?" I asked.

"You tried to connect with them to increase your energy," Wil replied, "instead of going within and connecting directly to God's energy inside. I did this myself once. These souls won't allow you to mistake them for the divine source. They know such an identification would not help your growth."

I concentrated within and my energy returned. "How do we get them back?" I asked.

As soon as I spoke, they returned to their original position.

Wil and I glanced at each other, then he began to stare intensely at the group, a look of surprise on his face.

"What are you seeing?" I asked.

He nodded toward them without breaking his gaze, and I focused on the soul group as well, trying to pick up on their knowledge again. After several moments I began to see Maya. She was immersed in the green environment. Her features seemed slightly different and were glowing brightly, but I was absolutely certain it was her. As I focused on her face, a holographic image appeared in front of us—an image of Maya again in the time of the nineteenth-century war, standing in a log cabin with several other people, excited about stopping the conflict.

She seemed to sense that accomplishing such a feat was just a matter of remembering how to attain the energy. It could be done only if the right people came together with a common intention, she thought. Most attentive was a young man who was richly dressed. I recognized him to be the large man who was later killed with her. Racing forward, the vision moved to her failed attempt to speak with the army leaders and then to the wilderness, where she and the young man were killed.

As we watched, she awakened after her death in the Afterlife and reviewed her lifetime, appalled at how single-mindedly, even naively, she had pursued her goal of stopping the war. She knew many of the others had been correct: the time wasn't right. We had not remembered enough of the Afterlife knowledge to accomplish such a feat. Not yet.

After the review, we saw her move into the green environment, surrounded by the same group of souls that was in front of us now. Amazingly there seemed to be a common core expression in the faces throughout the group. At a certain level, beneath their features, the souls all resembled Maya.

I glanced questioningly at Wil.

"This is Maya's *soul group*," he said.

"What do you mean?" I asked.

"It's a group of souls with whom she resonates closely," he said with excitement. "This makes perfect sense. One of the journeys I took, before I found you, was to another group who, in a way, looked like *you*. I think it was *your* soul group."

Before I could say anything, there was movement in the soul group in front of us. Again, an image of Maya was emerging. Still surrounded by her group in the green environment, she seemed to be standing quietly in front of an intense white light, similar to the one we had seen at Williams' Life Review. She was aware that something very profound was happening. Her ability to move around in the Afterlife had diminished, and her attention was shifting toward Earth again. She could see her prospective mother, newly married, sitting on a porch, wondering if her health would hold up well enough to have a child.

Maya was beginning to realize the great progress that could be achieved if she were to be born to this mother. The woman had deep fears about her own health and so would generate an awareness of health issues very quickly in the mind of a child. It would be the perfect place to develop an interest in medicine and healing, and it wouldn't be a knowledge contemplated on merely intellectual terms, where the ego comes up with some fancy theory and never tests it against the challenges of real life, not if she was growing up with the psychology of this woman. Maya knew that she herself had the tendency to be unrealistic and fanciful, and she had already paid dearly for such brashness. That wouldn't happen again, not with the unconscious memory of what had occurred in the nineteenth century reminding her to be very cautious. No, she would go slow, be more isolated, and the environment established by this woman would be perfect.

Wil caught my eye. "We're seeing what occurred when she began to contemplate her current life," he said.

Maya now envisioned how her relationship with her mother could unfold. She would grow up exposed to her mother's negativity, her fears, her tendency to blame the doctors, which would inspire her interest in the mind/body connection and the patient's responsibility in healing, and she would bring this information back to her mother, who could then become involved in her own recovery. Her mother would become her first patient, and then a key supporter, a prime example of the benefits of the new medicine.

Maya's focus moved to the prospective father, sitting next to the woman on the swing. Occasionally the woman would ask a question and he would utter a one-line answer. Mainly he wanted just to sit and contemplate, not to talk. His mind was virtually exploding with research possibilities and exotic biological questions he knew had never been posed before—most particularly the relationship between inspiration and the immune system. Maya saw the advantages of this aloofness. With him, she would be able to work through her own tendency to delude herself; she would have to think for herself and become realistic, right from the beginning. Eventually she and her father would be able to communicate on a scientific basis, and he would open up and provide her with a rich technical background with which to ground her new methods.

She saw clearly that her birth to these parents could be equally advantageous for them. At the same time her parents were stimulating an early interest in healing, she would be stretching them in a destined direction as well: the mother toward an acceptance of her personal role in avoiding illness, the father toward overcoming his tendency to hide from others and to live only in his head.

As we watched, her vision proceeded past her anticipated birth and into what might happen in childhood. She saw a multitude of specific people arriving in her life at just the right moment to stimulate learning and experience. In medical school, just the right patients and doctors would cross her path to stimulate an alternative orientation in her practice.

Her vision moved to the meeting of her clinic partner and the establishment of a new model of healing. And then her vision revealed something else: she would be involved in a more global awakening. Before us, we saw her discovery of the Insights and then her reunion with a particular group, one of many independent groups that would begin to gravitate together all over the world. These groups would remember who they were at a higher level and be instrumental in overcoming the polarization of Fear.

She suddenly saw herself engaged in important conversations with one particular man. He was large, athletic, capable, and dressed in army fatigues. To my amazement I realized that she knew he was the man with whom she had been killed during the nineteenth century. I focused on him intently and received another shock. This was the same man I had seen in Williams' Life Review, the work colleague he had failed to help awaken.

With this, her vision seemed to amplify to a level beyond my ability to comprehend, her body uniting with the blinding light behind it. All I could receive was that her personal vision of what she might accomplish with this birth was being enveloped within a larger vision that encompassed the whole history and future of humankind. She seemed to see her possible lifetime in ultimate perspective, situated clearly within the full expanse of where humanity had been and where it was going. I could sense all this but could not quite see the images themselves.

Finally Maya's vision seemed to be over, and we could see her again in the green environment, still surrounded by her group. Now they were watching a scene on Earth. Apparently her prospective parents had indeed decided to conceive a child and were coming together in the very act of love that would ensure her conception.

Maya's soul group had intensified in energy and now appeared as a large whitish swirl of moving amber, drawing its intensity from the bright light in the background. I could sense the energy myself as a deeply felt, almost orgasmic level of love and vibration. Down below, the couple embraced, and at the moment of orgasm, a whitish-green energy seemed to flow from the light, passing through Maya and her soul group, and enter into the couple. With an orgasmic rush, the energy came through their bodies toward each other, pushing the sperm and egg toward their fated union.

As we watched, we could see the moment of conception and the miraculous joining of the two cells into one. Slowly at first, and then more rapidly, the cells began to divide and differentiate, finally forming the shape of a human being. When I looked at Maya, I realized that with every cell division, she became more hazy and out of focus. Finally, as the fetus matured, she disappeared from view completely. Her soul group remained.

More knowledge seemed to be available on what we had just witnessed, but I lost concentration and missed it. Then suddenly the soul group itself was gone and Wil and I were left staring at each other. He seemed terribly excited.

"What were we watching?" I asked.

"It was the whole process of Maya's birth into her current lifetime," Wil replied, "held in the memory of her soul group. We got to see it all: her awareness of prospective parents, what she felt might be accomplished, and then the actual way she was drawn into the physical dimension at conception."

I nodded for Wil to continue.

"The act of lovemaking itself opens up a portal from the Afterlife into the Earthly dimension. The soul groups seem to exist in a state of extreme love even beyond what you and I can experience, extreme to the point that it feels orgasmic in nature. Sexual culmination creates an opening into the Afterlife, and what we experience as orgasm is just a glimpse of the Afterlife level of love and vibration as the portal is opened and the energy rushes through, potentially bringing in a new soul. We watched that happen. Sexual union is a holy moment in which a part of Heaven flows into the Earth."

I nodded, thinking about the implications of what we had seen, then said, "Maya seemed to know how her life could turn out if she was born to these particular parents."

"Yes, apparently, before we are born, each of us experiences a vision of what our life can be, complete with reflections on our parents and on our tendencies to engage in particular control dramas, even how we might work through these dramas with these parents and go on to be prepared for what we want to accomplish."

"I saw most of that," I said, "but it seemed strange. Based on what she told me about her real life, her pre-life vision was more ideal than what really happened—for instance, her relationship to her family. It didn't exactly turn out the way she wanted. Her mother never understood Maya, or faced her own illness, and her father was so aloof she never knew what he was researching until after his death."

"But that makes sense," Wil said. "The vision apparently is an ideal guide for what our highest self intends to happen in life, the best-case scenario, so to speak, if all of us were following our intuitions perfectly. What actually occurs is an approximation of this vision, the best everyone can do under the actual circumstances. But all this is more Tenth Insight information about the Afterlife that clarifies our spiritual experience on Earth, particularly the perception of coincidences, and how synchronicity really operates.

"When we have an intuition or a dream to pursue a particular course in our lives and we follow this guidance, certain events transpire that feel like magic coincidences. We feel more alive and excited. The events seem *destined,* as though they were supposed to happen.

"What we just saw puts all this into a higher perspective. When we have an intuition, a mental image of a possible future, we're actually getting flashes of memory of our Birth Vision, what we wanted to be doing with our lives at that particular point on our journey. It may not be exact, because people have free will, but when something happens that is close to our original vision, we feel inspired because we recognize that we are on a path of destiny that we intended all along."

"But how does our soul group fit in?"

"We're connected with them. They know us. They share our Birth Visions, follow us through life, and afterward stay with us while we review what happened. They act as a reservoir for our memories, maintaining the knowledge of who we are as we evolve."

He paused momentarily, looking straight into my eyes. "And

apparently, when we're in the Afterlife, and one of them is born into the physical dimension, we act in the same capacity toward them. We become part of the soul group that supports them."

"So while we are on Earth," I commented, "our soul groups give us our intuition and direction?"

"No, not at all. Judging from what I could pick up from the soul groups I've seen, the intuitions and dreams are our own, coming from a higher connection with the divine. The soul groups just send us extra energy and uplift us in a particular manner—a manner that I haven't been able to pinpoint. By uplifting us in this way, they help us to more readily remember what we already knew."

I was fascinated. "So that explains what was happening with my dream and Joel's."

"Yes. When we dream, we reunite with our soul group, and that jogs our memory of what we really wanted to do in our current life situation. We get glimpses of our original intention. Then when we return to the physical, we retain that memory, although it is sometimes expressed in archetypal symbols. In the case of your dream, because you are more open to spiritual meaning, you could remember the dream information in very literal terms. You recalled that in your original intention, you saw us finding each other again when you imaged my face, and so you dreamed almost exactly that.

"Joel, on the other hand, was less open; his dream came through in a more garbled, symbolic fashion. His memory was fuzzy, and his conscious mind fashioned the message in the symbolism of a war, conveying to him only the general message that in his Birth Vision he intended to stay and help with the current problem in the valley, making it clear that if he ran away, he would regret it."

"So the soul groups are always sending us energy," I said, "and hoping we will remember our Birth Visions?"

"That's right."

"And that's why Maya's group was so happy?"

Wil's expression grew more serious. "They were happy because she was remembering why she was born to her particular parents, and how her life experiences had prepared her for a career in healing. But . . . this was only the first part of her Birth Vision. She still has more to remember."

"I saw the part when she was meeting again in this life with the man with whom she was killed in the nineteenth century. But there were other parts that I couldn't understand. How much of that did you get?"

"Not all of it. There was more about the rising Fear. It confirmed that she's part of the group of seven that Williams saw coming back. And she saw the group able to remember some kind of larger vision that's behind our individual intentions, a remembrance that is necessary if we are to dispel the Fear."

Wil and I gazed at each other for a long time, then I felt another vibration in my body from the experiment. In that moment an image of the large man with whom Maya had seen herself reuniting came into my mind. Who was he?

I was about to mention the image to Wil, when my breath left me, forced out by a cramping pain that seized my stomach. Simultaneously, another high-pitched screech rocked me backward. As before, I reached out for Wil and saw his face fading out of focus. I struggled to look one more time, then completely lost my equilibrium, slipping again into free fall.

OPENING
TO THE
KNOWLEDGE

Damn, I thought—lying flat on the rock, the coarse surface of the stone edging into my back—I was back at the stream again. For a long moment I stared up at the gray sky, now threatening rain, listening to the water flow past me. I raised up on one elbow and looked around, noticing immediately that my body felt heavy and fatigued, just as it had the last time I left the other dimension.

Clumsily I got to my feet, a slight pain throbbing in my ankle, and limped back into the forest. I uncovered my pack and prepared some food, moving very slowly without thinking. Even as I ate, my mind remained surprisingly blank, like after a long meditation. Then slowly I began to increase my energy, taking several deep breaths and holding them. Suddenly I could hear the hum again. As I listened, another image came to mind. I was walking east in the direction of the sound, in search of its cause.

The thought terrified me and I felt the old urge to flee. Instantly the hum vanished, and I heard a rustling of leaves to my rear. I jerked around and saw Maya.

"Do you always show up at the right time?" I stammered.

"Show up! Are you crazy? I've been looking for you everywhere around here. Where did you come from?"

"I was down by the stream."

"No, you weren't; I've been looking down there." She stared at me for a moment, then glanced at my foot. "How's that ankle?"

I managed a smile. "It's fine. Listen, I've got to talk to you about something."

"I have to speak with you too. There's something very strange happening. One of the Forest Service agents saw me walking into town last night, and I told him about your situation. He seemed to want to keep it quiet, and he insisted on sending a truck to get you this morning. I told him your general location, and he made me promise to ride out here with him this morning. Something about the way he was talking felt so odd, I decided to hike up ahead of him instead, but he'll probably be here any minute."

"Then we need to go," I said, scrambling to pack.

"Wait a minute! Tell me what is happening." She looked panicked.

I stopped and faced her. "Someone—I don't know who it is—is doing some kind of experiment or something like that here in the valley. I think my friend Charlene is involved somehow, or may be in danger. Someone in the Forest Service must have secretly approved this."

She stared, trying to take it all in.

I picked up my pack and took her hand. "Walk with me for a while. Please. There's more I need to tell you."

She nodded and grabbed her pack, and as we walked east

along the edge of the stream, I told her the whole story, from meeting David and Wil to seeing Williams' Life Review and listening to Joel. When I came to the part about her Birth Vision, I moved over to some rocks and sat down. She leaned against a tree to my right.

"You're involved in this too," I said. "Obviously you already know that your life is supposed to be about introducing alternative techniques of healing, but there's more that you intended to do. You're supposed to be part of this group that Williams saw coming together."

"How do you know all that?"

"Wil and I saw your Birth Vision."

She shook her head and closed her eyes.

"Maya, each of us comes here with a vision of how our lives can be, what we want to do. The intuitions we have, the dreams and coincidences, they're all designed to keep us on the right path, to bring back our memory of how we wanted our lives to unfold."

"And what else did I want to do?"

"I don't know exactly; I couldn't get it. But it had something to do with this collective Fear that is rising in human consciousness. The experiment is a result of this Fear . . . Maya, you intended to use what you've learned about physical healing to help resolve what's happening in this valley. You must remember!"

She stood and looked away. "Oh no, you can't put that kind of responsibility on me! I don't remember any of this. I'm doing exactly what I'm supposed to be doing as a doctor. I hate this kind of intrigue! Understand? I hate it! I finally have the clinic set up just as I want. You can't expect me to get involved in all this. You've got the wrong person!"

I looked at her, trying to think of something else to say. During the silence, I heard the hum again.

"Can you hear that sound, Maya, a dissonance in the air, a hum? That's the experiment. It's happening right now. Try to hear it!"

She listened for a moment, then said, "I don't hear anything."

I grabbed her arm. "Try to raise your energy!"

She pulled away. "I don't hear a hum!"

I took a breath. "Okay, I'm sorry. I don't know, maybe I'm wrong. Maybe it's not supposed to happen this way."

She looked at me for a moment. "I know someone with the Sheriff's Department. I'll try to get in touch with him for you. That's all I can do."

"I don't know if that will help," I said. "Apparently not everyone can hear this sound."

"Do you want me to call him?"

"Yes, but tell him to investigate independently. I'm not sure he can trust everyone in the Forest Service." I picked up my pack again.

"I hope you understand," she said. "I just can't be involved in this. I feel as though something horrible would happen."

"But that's just because of what happened when you tried this before, in the nineteenth century, here in this valley. Can you remember any of that?"

She closed her eyes again, not wanting to listen.

I suddenly saw a clear image of myself in buckskins, running up a hill, pulling a packhorse. It was the same image I had seen before. The mountain man was me! As the vision continued, I made my way to the top of the hill and then paused to glance back to my rear. From there I could see the falls and the gorge on the other side. There was Maya and the Indian and the young congressional aide. As before, the battle was just beginning. Anxiety swept over me, and I pulled at the horse and walked on, unable to help them avoid their fate.

I shook off the images. "It's okay," I said, giving up. "I know how you feel."

Maya walked closer. "Here's some extra water and food I brought. What are you planning to do?"

"I'm going to head toward the east . . . for at least a while. I know Charlene was going in that direction."

She looked at my foot. "Are you sure your ankle will hold up?"

I moved closer and said, "I haven't really thanked you for what you did. My ankle will be fine, I think, just a little sore. I guess I'll never know how bad it might have been."

"When it happens this way, no one ever does."

I nodded, then picked up my pack and headed east, glancing back once at Maya. She looked guilty for an instant, than an expression of relief swept across her face.

I walked toward the sound of the hum, keeping the stream in sight to my left, pausing only to rest my foot. About noon the sound ceased, so I stopped to eat lunch and assess the situation. My ankle was swelling slightly and I rested for an hour and a half before resuming my journey. After covering only another mile, fatigue overwhelmed me, and I rested again. By midafternoon I was looking for a place to camp.

I had been walking through thick woods that grew right to the edge of the stream, but ahead the landscape opened up in a series of gently rolling foothills covered with old-growth forest—three- and four-hundred-year-old trees. Through a break in the limbs, I could see a large ridge rising toward the southeast, perhaps another mile away.

I spotted a small grassy knoll near the top of the first hill, which looked like a perfect place to spend the night. As I approached, movement in the trees caught my eye. I slipped behind a large outcropping and looked. What was that? A deer? A person? I waited for several minutes, then carefully moved away toward the north. As I inched along, I saw a large man a hundred yards to the south of the knoll I had seen before, apparently setting up a camp himself. Staying very low to the ground and moving with skill, he deftly raised a small tent and camouflaged it with branches. For an instant I thought it might be David, but his movements were different, and he was too big. Then I lost sight of him.

After waiting for several more minutes I decided to move farther to the north until I was completely out of sight. I'd been moving no more than five minutes when the man suddenly stepped out in front of me.

"Who are you?" he asked. I told him my name and decided to be open. "I'm trying to find a friend."

"It's dangerous out here," he said. "I would recommend that you go back. This is all private property."

"Why are *you* out here?" I asked.

He was silent, staring.

Then I remembered what David had told me. "Are you Curtis Webber?" I inquired.

He looked at me for a moment longer, then abruptly smiled. "You know David Lone Eagle!"

"I only talked to him briefly, but he told me you were out here, and to tell you he was coming into the valley and that he would find you."

Curtis nodded and looked toward his camp. "It's getting late, and we need to get out of sight. Let's go up to my tent. You can spend the night up there."

I followed him down a slope and up into the deep cover of the larger trees. While I pitched my tent, he fired up his camp stove for coffee and opened a can of tuna. I contributed a package of bread Maya had given me.

"You mentioned that you were looking for someone," Curtis said. "Who?"

Briefly I told him about Charlene's disappearance and that David had seen her hiking into the valley; also that I thought she had been seen coming in this direction. I didn't talk about what had occurred in the other dimension, but I did mention hearing the hum and seeing the vehicles.

"The hum," he responded, "comes from an energy-generating device; someone's experimenting with it here for some reason. I can confirm that much. But I don't know whether the experiment is being conducted by some secret government agency or a private group. Most of the Forest Service agents seem to be unaware that it's happening; but I don't know about the administrators."

"Have you gone to the media," I asked, "or to the local authorities about this?"

"Not yet. The fact that not everyone hears the hum is a real problem." He looked out at the valley. "If I just knew where they were. Counting the private land and the National Forest, there are tens of thousands of acres where they might be. I think they want to conduct the experiment and get out before anyone knows what happened. That is, if they can avoid a tragedy."

"What do you mean?"

"They could totally ruin this place, make it into a twilight zone, another Bermuda Triangle where the laws of physics are in unpredictable flux." He looked directly at me. "The things they know how to do are incredible. Most people have no idea of the complexity of electromagnetic phenomena. In the latest superstring theories, for instance, one has to assume this radiation emanates across nine dimensions just to make the math work. This device has the potential to disrupt these dimensions. It could trigger massive earthquakes or even complete physical disintegration of certain areas."

"How do you know all this?" I asked.

His face fell. "Because in the decade of the eighties I helped develop some of this technology. I was employed with a multinational corporation I thought was named Deltech, although later, after I was fired, I found out that Deltech was a fictitious name. You've heard of Nikola Tesla? Well, we expanded many of his theories and tied some of his discoveries to other technologies that the company supplied. The funny thing is that this technology is composed of several dissimilar parts, but basically it works this way. Imagine that the electromagnetic field of the Earth is a giant battery that can provide plenty of electrical energy if you can tie into it in the correct way. For that you combine a room temperature, superconductive generator system with a very complicated electronic feedback inhibitor, which mathematically enhances certain static output resonances. Then you tie several of these in a series, amplifying and generating the charge, and when you get the calibrations exact, presto, you have virtually free energy right out of the immediate space. You need a small amount of power to start, perhaps a single photocell or a battery, but then it's self-perpetuating. A device the size of a heat pump could power several houses, even a small factory.

"However, there are two problems. First, calibrating these minigenerators is unbelievably complicated. We had access to some of the largest computers in existence and couldn't do it. Second, we discovered that when we tried to increase the total output beyond this relatively small size by enlarging the mass displacement, the space around the generator became very unstable and began to warp. We didn't know it then, but we were tapping into the energy of another dimension, and strange things began to happen. Once, we made the whole generator disappear, exactly like what happened in the Philadelphia Experiment."

"Do you think they really made a ship disappear and show up again in a new location, in 1943?"

"Of course they did! There's a lot of secret technology around, and they're smart. In our case, they were able to shut our team down in less than a month and fire all of us without a breach of security because each team was working on an isolated part of the technology. Not that I wondered much about it then. I mostly bought the idea that the obstacles were just too great to proceed, so I thought it was dead-end research—although I did hear that several of the old employees were hired again by another company."

He looked thoughtful for a moment, then continued. "I knew I wanted to do something else anyway. I'm a consultant now, working with small technology firms, providing advice for improving their research efficiency and use of resources and disposal of wastes, that sort of thing. And the more I work with them, the more I'm convinced the Insights are having an effect on the economy. The way we do business is shifting. But I figured we had to work with traditional power sources for a long time. I hadn't thought about the energy experiments in years until I moved into this area. You can imagine how shocked I was to walk into this valley and hear the same sound—this characteristic hum—that I heard every day for years when we were working on the project.

"Someone has continued the research, and judging from the resonances, they're much further along than we were. Afterward I tried to contact the two people who could verify the sound and maybe go to the EPA or a congressional committee with me, but I found out one had been deceased for ten years and the other, my best friend when I was at the corporation, was also dead. He had a heart attack just yesterday." His voice trailed off.

"Since then," he went on, "I've been out here listening, trying to figure out why they're in this valley. Ordinarily one would expect this kind of experiment to be done in a laboratory some-where. I mean, why not? Its energy source is space itself, and that's everywhere. But then it dawned on me. They must think they are very close to perfecting the calibrations, which means they're working on the amplification problem. I think they're try-ing to tie into the energy vortexes in this valley in an attempt to stabilize the process."

A wave of anger crossed his face. "Which is crazy and totally unnecessary. If they really can find the calibrations, then there's no reason not to utilize the technology in small units. In fact, that's the perfect way of using it. What they're trying now is in-sane. I know enough to see the dangers. I'm telling you, they could totally wreck this valley, or worse. If they focus this thing on the interdimensional pathways, who knows what might happen?"

He stopped suddenly. "Do you know what I'm talking about? Have you heard of the Insights?"

I stared for a moment, then said, "Curtis, I have to tell you what I've been experiencing in this valley. You may find it unbe-lievable."

He nodded and then listened patiently as I described meeting Wil and exploring parts of the other dimension. When I came to the Life Review, I asked, "This friend of yours who recently died? Was he named Williams?"

"That's right. Dr. Williams. How did you know that?"

"We saw him reach the other dimension after his death. We watched as he experienced a Life Review."

He appeared shaken. "That's hard for me to believe. I know the Insights, at least intellectually, and I believe in the probable existence of other dimensions, but as a scientist, the Ninth Insight stuff is much harder to take literally, the idea of being able to communicate with people after death . . . You're saying that Dr. Williams is still alive in the sense that his personality is intact?"

"Yes, and he was thinking about you."

He looked at me intently as I continued to tell him about Williams' realization that Curtis and he were supposed to be involved in resolving the Fear . . . and stopping this experiment.

"I don't understand," he said. "What did he mean when he talked about a growing *Fear*?"

"I don't know exactly. It has to do with a certain percentage of the population refusing to believe that a new spiritual awareness is emerging. Instead, they think human civilization is degenerating. This is creating a polarization of opinion and belief. Human culture can't continue to evolve until the polarization is ended. I was hoping that you might remember something about it."

He looked at me blankly. "I don't know anything about a polarization, but I *am* going to stop this experiment." His face grew angry again and he looked away.

"Williams seemed to understand the process for stopping it," I said.

"Well, we'll never know now, will we?"

As he said that, I fleetingly saw again the image of Curtis and Williams talking on the grassy hilltop, surrounded by several large trees.

Curtis served our food, still appearing upset, and we finished eating in silence. Later as I stretched out and leaned against a small hickory, I glanced up the hill at the grassy knoll above us. Four or five huge oaks made almost a perfect semicircle on its crest.

"Why didn't you camp up on the hill?" I asked Curtis, pointing.

"I don't know," he said. "The idea came to me, but I guess I thought it was too exposed, or maybe too powerful. It's called Codder's Knoll. Do you want to walk up there?"

I nodded and rose to my feet. A gray twilight was descending across the forest. Commenting on the beauty of the trees and shrubs as we walked, Curtis led the way up the slope. At the top, in spite of the fading light, we could see almost a quarter of a mile toward the north and east. In the latter direction a near full moon was rising above the tree line.

"Better sit down," Curtis advised. "We don't want to be seen."

For a long while we sat in silence, admiring the view and feeling the energy. Curtis took a flashlight out of his pocket and laid it on the ground beside him. I was mesmerized by the colors of the fall foliage.

Presently Curtis looked over at me and asked, "Do you smell something, smoke?"

I immediately looked out at the woods, suspecting a forest fire, and sniffed the air. "No, I don't think so." Something about Curtis' demeanor was shifting the mood, introducing a feeling of sadness or nostalgia. "What kind of smoke do you mean?"

"Cigar smoke."

In the growing moonlight I could tell he was smiling reflectively, thinking about something. Then suddenly I began to smell the smoke.

"What is that?" I asked, looking around again.

He caught my eye. "Dr. Williams smoked cigars that smelled just like that. I can't believe he's gone."

As we talked, the smell subsided and I dismissed the whole experience, content to stare out at the sage and the large oaks beside us. In that moment I realized that this was the very spot where Williams saw himself meeting with Curtis. It was to take place right here!

Seconds later I observed a figure forming just beyond the trees.

"Do you see anything out there?" I quietly asked Curtis, pointing in that direction.

As soon as I spoke, the form disappeared.

Curtis was straining to see. "What? I don't see anything."

I didn't respond. Somehow I had begun to intuitively receive knowledge, exactly as I had received it from the soul groups, except the connection was more distant and garbled. I could sense something about the energy experiment, a confirmation of Curtis' suspicions; the experimenters were indeed attempting to focus in on the dimensional vortexes.

"I just remembered," Curtis said abruptly. "One of the devices Dr. Williams was working on years ago was a remote focus, a dish projection system. I bet that's what they're using to focus on the openings. But how do they know where the openings *are*?"

Immediately I perceived an answer. Someone of a higher awareness pointed them out until they learned the spatial variances as they showed up on the remote focus computer. I had no idea what that meant.

"There's only one way," Curtis said. "They would have to find someone to point them out—someone who could sense these higher energy locations. Then they could map out an energy profile of the site and focus precisely by scanning with a focus beam. Probably the individual wouldn't even know what they were doing." He shook his head. "These people are vicious. There's no doubt about it. How could they do this?"

As if in response, I sensed other knowledge that was too vague to understand completely, but seemed to maintain that there was, in fact, a reason. But we had to first understand the Fear and how to overcome it.

When I looked at Curtis, he seemed to be deep in thought.

Finally he looked at me and said, "I wish I knew why this Fear is coming up now."

"During a transition in culture," I said, "old certainties and views begin to break down and evolve into new traditions, causing anxiety in the short run. At the same time that some people are waking up and sustaining an inner connection of love that sustains them and allows them to evolve more rapidly, others feel as though everything is changing too fast and that we're losing our way. They become more fearful and more controlling to try to raise their energy. This polarization of fear can be very dangerous because fearful people can rationalize extreme measures."

As I was saying all of this, I felt as though I was expanding on what I had earlier heard Wil say, and Williams, but I also had the distinct sensation that it was something I knew all along but didn't realize I knew until this very moment.

"I understand that," Curtis said with certainty. "That's why these people are so willing to waste this valley. They rationalize that civilization will fall apart in the future, and they won't be safe unless they seize more control. Well, I'm not going to allow it to happen. I'll blow the whole thing sky-high."

I looked hard at him. "What do you mean?"

"Just that. I used to be a demolitions expert. I know how."

I must have looked alarmed because he said, "Don't worry, I'll figure out a way to do it where no one gets hurt. I wouldn't want that on my conscience."

A wave of knowledge filled me. "Any kind of violence," I said, "just makes it worse, don't you see?"

"What other way is there?"

Out of the corner of my eye I glimpsed the form again for an instant, and then it disappeared. "I don't know exactly," I said, "But if we fight them with anger, hate, they just see an enemy. It makes them more entrenched. They become more fearful. Somehow this group that Williams was talking about is supposed to do something else. We're supposed to fully remember our Birth Visions . . . and then we can remember something more, a *World Vision.*"

Somehow I knew the term, but I couldn't remember where I had heard it before.

"A World Vision . . ." Curtis pondered, deep in thought again. "I think David Lone Eagle mentioned that."

"Yes," I said. "That's right."

"What do you think a World Vision is?"

I was about to say I didn't know when a thought came to me. "It's an understanding—no, a memory—of how we will fulfill human purpose. It brings in another level of love, an energy, that can bridge the polarization, end this experiment."

"I don't see how that's possible," Curtis said.

"It involves the energy level around people who are in Fear,"

I said, somehow knowing. "They would be touched, awakened from their preoccupation. They would choose to stop."

For several moments we were silent, then Curtis said, "Maybe, but how do we bring in this energy?"

Nothing more came to mind.

"I wish I knew how far they're prepared to go with this experiment," he added.

"What causes the hum?" I asked.

"The hum is a linking dissonance between the small generators. It means that they're still trying to calibrate the device. The more grating and disharmonious it is, the more it's out of phase." He thought for another moment. "I just wonder which energy vortex they're going to focus on."

I suddenly sensed a particular nervousness, not within myself, but outwardly, as if I was around someone else who was anxious. I looked at Curtis, who seemed relatively calm. Beyond the trees I again saw the vague outlines of a form. It moved as if agitated or frightened.

"I would imagine," Curtis said absently, "that if one were close to the target location, one would hear the hum and then feel a kind of static electricity in the air."

We looked at each other, and in the silence I could hear a faint sound, merely a vibration.

"Do you hear that?" Curtis asked, now alarmed.

As I looked at him, I felt the hair rise on the back of my neck and forearms. "What is this?"

For an instant Curtis observed his own arms, then looked at me in horror.

"We've got to get out of here!" he screamed, grabbing his flashlight, leaping to his feet, and half dragging me off the crest of the slope.

Suddenly the same ear-shattering roar I had heard with Wil descended again and carried with it a shock wave that knocked both of us to the ground. Simultaneously the earth beneath us shook violently and a massive fissure opened twenty feet away, creating an explosion of dust and debris.

Behind us one of the towering oaks, undermined by the shifting earth, leaned and then fell to the ground in a thunderous roar, adding to the noise. Seconds later another, larger fissure tore open right beside us and the ground tilted. Curtis, unable to hold on, slid toward the widening abyss. I held onto a small bush and reached out for Curtis' hand. For a moment we held tight, then our grip slipped, and I watched helplessly as he slid over the edge. The fissure moved and widened, spewed another plume of dust and rock, shook once more, and then was still. A limb under the fallen tree cracked loudly, and then the night was again silent.

As the dust cleared, I let go of the bush and crawled toward the edge of the massive hole. When I could see, I realized that Curtis was lying prone at the edge, even though I was sure I had seen him fall in. He rolled toward me and jumped to his feet.

"Let's go!" he yelled. "It could start again!"

Without speaking we ran down the hill toward the campsite, Curtis ahead, me limping behind. When Curtis reached the site, he seized both tents and ripped them from the ground, stakes dangling, and stuffed them into the packs. I pushed in the other gear, and we continued toward the southwest until the ground flattened into thick underbrush. After another half mile, exhaustion and my weakening ankle forced me to stop.

Curtis surveyed the terrain. "Maybe we'll be safe here," he said, "but let's move deeper into the thicket." I followed as he led us fifty feet farther into the dense woods.

"This will do right here," he commented. "Let's put up the tents."

Within a couple of minutes both tents were up and covered with limbs and we were looking at each other breathlessly, sitting on his tent's large entrance flap.

"What do you think happened?" I asked.

Curtis' face looked gaunt as he dug into his pack for water. "They're doing exactly what we thought," he said. "They're trying to focus the generator on a remote space." He took a long drink from his canteen. "They're going to ruin this valley; these people have to be stopped."

"What about the smoke we smelled?"

"I don't know what to think," Curtis said. "It was as though Dr. Williams was there. I could almost hear his inflection, his tone of voice, what he would have said in that situation."

I caught Curtis' eye. "I think he *was* there."

Curtis handed me the canteen. "How is that possible?"

"I don't know," I said. "But I think he came to convey a message, a message to *you*. When we saw him during his Life Review, he was agonizing because he had failed to wake up, to remember why he had been born. He was convinced that you were supposed to be a part of this group he mentioned. Can't you remember anything about that? I think he wanted you to know that violence won't stop these people. We have to do it another way, with this World Vision that David talked about."

He gave me a blank look.

"What about when the earth movement started," I asked, "and that fissure opened? I know I saw you roll in, yet you were lying at the edge when I got there."

He looked totally perplexed. "I'm not sure really. I couldn't hold on and was slipping into the hole. As I dropped down, this incredibly peaceful feeling came over me, and I was cushioned, like falling onto a soft mattress. All I could see was a white blur around me. The next thing I knew I was lying at the side of the fissure again and you were there. Do you think Dr. Williams could have done that?"

"I don't think so," I said. "I had a similar experience yesterday. I was almost crushed by stones and I saw the same white form. Something else is happening."

Curtis stared at me for a moment and then said something else, but I didn't respond. I was drifting into sleep.

"Let's turn in," he said.

Curtis was already up when I climbed out of my tent. The morning was clear, but a ground fog covered the forest floor. Instantly I knew he was angry.

"I can't stop thinking about what they're doing," he said. "And they aren't going to give up." He took a breath. "By now they've figured out what a mess they made on the hill. They'll spend some time recalibrating, but not for long, and then they'll try again. I can stop them but we have to find out where they are."

"Curtis, violence just makes it worse. Didn't you understand the information coming from Dr. Williams? We have to discover how to use the Vision."

"No!" he shouted with deep emotion. "I've tried that before!"
I looked at him. "When?"
His expression changed to confusion. "I don't know."
"Well," I stressed, "I think I do."
He waved me off with his hand. "I don't want to hear it. This is too crazy. Everything that's happening is my fault. If I hadn't

worked on this technology, they might not be doing this. I'm going to handle it my way." He walked over and began packing.

I hesitated, then started taking down my own tent, trying to think. After a moment I said, "I've already sent for some help. A woman I met, Maya, thinks she can persuade the Sheriff's Department to investigate this. I want you to promise me you'll give me some time."

He was kneeling beside his backpack, checking a bulging side pocket. "I can't do that. I may have to act when I can."

"You have explosives in your pack?"

He walked toward me. "I told you before I'm not going to hurt anyone."

"I want some time," I repeated. "If I can reach Wil again, I think I can find out about this World Vision."

"Okay," he said. "I'll give you as long as I can, but if they start experimenting again, and I think I'm out of time, I'll have to do something."

As he spoke, I saw Wil's face again in my mind's eye, surrounded by a rich emerald color. "Is there another high-energy location near here?" I asked.

He pointed south. "Somewhere up the big ridge, there's a rock overhang I've heard about. But that's private land that was recently sold. I don't know who owns it now."

"I'm going to look for it. If I can find the right place, then maybe I can locate Wil again."

Curtis finished packing and helped me tie up my own gear and spread leaves and branches where the tents had been. Toward the northwest we could hear the faint sound of vehicles.

"I'm heading east," he said.

I nodded as he walked away, then pulled my pack onto my shoulders and started up the rocky slope to the south. I traveled over several small hills and then tackled the steep incline of the main ridge. About halfway up I began to look through the dense forest for an overhang but found no sign of an opening.

After climbing several hundred more yards I stopped again. Still no outcropping, and I could see none at the crest of the ridge above. I was confused about which way to go and decided to sit down and attempt to raise my energy. After a few minutes I felt better, and was listening to the sounds of birds and tree frogs in the thick limbs over my head, when a large golden eagle fluttered from its nest and flew east along the top of the ridge.

I knew the presence of the bird had meaning, so, as with the hawk before, I decided to follow. Gradually the slope became more rocky. I crossed a small spring flowing from the rocks and refilled my canteen and washed my face. Finally, a half mile farther, I pushed my way through a grove of small fir trees, and there before me lay the majestic overhang. Almost half an acre of the slope was covered with huge terraces of thick limestone, and at the farthermost edge, a twenty-foot-wide shelf jutted out at least forty feet from the ridge, providing a spectacular view of the valley below. For an instant I detected a dark emerald highlight around the lower shelf.

I took off my pack and pushed it out of sight under a pile of leaves and then walked out and sat on the ledge. As I centered myself, the image of Wil came easily to mind. I took one more deep breath and began to move.

A HISTORY
OF
AWAKENING

W hen I opened my eyes, I was in an area of rich blue light, feeling the now-familiar sense of well-being and peace. I could detect Wil's presence to my left.

As before, he looked enormously relieved and happy that I had returned. He moved closer and whispered, "You are going to love it here."

"Where are we?" I asked.

"Look more closely."

I shook my head. "I have to talk to you first. It's imperative that we find this experiment and stop them. They've destroyed a hilltop. God knows what they're about to do next."

"What will we do if we find them?" Wil inquired.

"I don't know."

"Well, neither do I. Tell me what happened."

I closed my eyes and tried to center, then described the experience of seeing Maya again, particularly her resistance to my suggestion that she was part of the group.

Wil nodded without comment.

I went on to describe meeting Curtis, communicating with Williams, and surviving the effects of the experiment.

"Williams spoke to you?" Wil asked.

"Not really. The communication wasn't mental, as with you and me. He seemed to be influencing the ideas that were coming to us in some way. It felt like information I already knew at some level; yet both of us seemed to be saying what he was trying to communicate. It was odd, but I know he was there."

"What was his message?"

"He confirmed what you and I saw with Maya; he said we could remember beyond our individual birth intentions to a broader knowledge of human purpose and how we could complete this purpose. Apparently, remembering this knowledge brings in an expanded energy that can end the Fear . . . and this experiment. He called it a World Vision."

Wil was silent.

"What do you think?" I asked.

"I think all this is just more of the Tenth Insight knowledge. Please understand: I share your sense of urgency. But the only way we can help is to continue exploring the Afterlife until we find out about this larger Vision that Williams was trying to communicate. There must be an exact process for remembering what it is."

In the distance a movement caught my eye. Eight or ten very distinct beings, only partially out of focus, moved to within fifty feet. Behind them were dozens more, blended together in the usual amber-colored blur. All of them exuded a particular feeling of sentiment and nostalgia that was distinctly familiar.

"Do you know who these souls are?" Wil asked, smiling broadly.

I looked out at the group, sensing kinship. I did know, but I didn't. As I looked upon the soul group, the emotional connection continued to grow more intense, beyond anything I could remember ever experiencing. Yet, at the same time, the closeness was recognizable; I had been *here* before.

The group moved within twenty feet of me, increasing the euphoria and acceptance even more. I gladly let go, turning myself over to the feeling, wishing only to bask in it—content— perhaps for the first time in my life. Waves of acknowledgment and appreciation filled my mind.

"Have you figured it out?" Wil asked again.

I turned and looked at him. "This is my soul group, isn't it?"

With that thought came a flood of memories. Thirteenth-century France, a monastery and courtyard. All around me a group of monks, laughter, closeness, then walking alone on a wooded road. Two ragged men, ascetics, asking for help, something about preserving some secret knowledge.

I shook off the vision and looked at Wil, gripped by a perverse fear. What was I about to see? I attempted to center, and my soul group edged four feet closer.

"What is happening?" Wil asked. "I couldn't quite understand."

I described what I had observed.

"Probe further," Wil suggested.

Immediately I saw the ascetics again, and somehow knew they were members of a secret order of Franciscan "Spirituals" who had recently been excommunicated, after Pope Celestine V had resigned.

Pope Celestine? I glanced at Wil. "Did you get that? I never knew there were popes by that name."

"Celestine V was late thirteenth century," Wil confirmed.

"The ruins in Peru, where the Ninth Insight was ultimately found, were named after him when first discovered in the 1600s."

"Who were the Spirituals?"

"They were a group of monks who believed that a higher awareness could be achieved by extracting themselves from human culture and returning to a contemplative life in nature. Pope Celestine supported this idea and, in fact, lived in a cave himself for a while. He was deposed, of course, and later, most sects of the Spirituals were condemned as Gnostics and excommunicated."

More memories surfaced. The two ascetics had approached me asking for help, and I had reluctantly met with them deep in the forest. I had had no choice, so entrancing were their eyes and the fearlessness of their demeanor. Old documents were in great danger of being lost forever, they told me. Later I had smuggled them back to the abbey and had read them by candlelight in my chambers, the doors closed and locked securely.

These documents were old Latin copies of the Nine Insights, and I had consented to copy them before it was too late, working every moment of my spare time to painstakingly reproduce dozens of the manuscripts. At one point I was so enthralled by the Insights that I sought to persuade the ascetics to make them public.

They adamantly refused, explaining that they had held the documents for many centuries, waiting for the correct understanding to emerge within the church. When I questioned the meaning of this latter phrase, they explained that the Insights would not be accepted until the church reconciled what they referred to as the *Gnostic dilemma*.

The Gnostics, I somehow remembered, were early Christians

who believed that followers of the one God should not merely revere Christ but strive to emulate him in the spirit of Pentecost. They sought to describe this emulation in philosophical terms, as a method of practice. As the early church formulated its canons, the Gnostics were eventually considered willful heretics, opposed to turning their lives over to God as a matter of faith. To become a true believer, the early church leaders concluded, one had to forgo understanding and analysis and be content to live life through divine revelation, adhering to God's will moment by moment, but content to remain ignorant of his overall plan.

Accusing the church hierarchy of tyranny, the Gnostics argued that their understandings and methods were intended to actually facilitate this act of "letting go to God's will" that the church was requiring, rather than giving mere lip service to the idea, as the churchmen were doing.

In the end the Gnostics lost, and were banished from all church functions and texts, their beliefs disappearing underground among the various secret sects and orders. Yet the dilemma was clear. As long as the church held out the vision of a transformative spiritual connection with the divine, yet persecuted anyone who talked openly about the specifics of the experience—how one might actually attain such an awareness, what it felt like—then the "kingdom within" would remain merely an intellectualized concept within church doctrine, and the Insights would be crushed anytime they surfaced.

At the moment, I listened with concern to the ascetics and said nothing, but inwardly I disagreed. I was sure the Benedictine Order of which I was a part would be interested in these writings, especially at the level of the individual monk. Later, without telling the Spirituals, I shared a copy with a friend who was the closest adviser to Cardinal Nicholas in my district. Reaction came swiftly. Word arrived that the cardinal was out of the country, but I was asked to cease any discussion of the subject and to depart at once for Naples to report my findings to the cardinal's superiors. I panicked and immediately dispensed the manuscripts as widely as possible throughout the order, hoping that I might garner support from other interested brothers.

In order to postpone my summons, I faked a severe ankle injury and wrote a series of letters explaining my disability, delaying the trip for months while I copied as many manuscripts as I could in my isolation. Finally, on the night of a new moon, my door was kicked down by soldiers and I was beaten severely and taken blindfolded to the castle of the local noble, where I later languished at the stock for days before being decapitated.

The shock of remembering my death cast me into fear again and created a powerful tingling in my injured ankle. The soul group continued to move several feet closer until I managed to center myself. Still, I was left with a degree of confusion. A nod from Wil told me he had seen the entire story.

"This was the beginning of my ankle problem, wasn't it?" I asked.

"Yes," Wil replied.

I caught his eye. "What about all the other memories? Did you understand the Gnostic dilemma?"

He nodded and squared up to face me directly.

"Why would the church create such a dilemma?" I asked.

"Because the early church was afraid to come out and say that Christ modeled a way of life that each of us could aspire to, although that is what is clearly said in the Scriptures. They feared that this position would give too much power to individuals, so they perpetrated the contradiction. On the one hand the churchmen urged the believer to seek the mystical kingdom of God within, to intuit God's will, and to be filled with the Holy Spirit. But on the other hand they condemned as blasphemous any discussion of how one might go about achieving these states, often resorting to outright murder to protect their power."

"So I was a fool for trying to circulate the Insights."

"I wouldn't say a fool," Wil mused, "more like undiplomatic. You were killed because you tried to force an understanding into culture before its time."

I looked into Wil's eyes for another moment, then drifted back into the knowledge of the group, finding myself at the scene of the nineteenth-century wars again. I was back at the meeting of chiefs in the valley, holding the same packhorse, apparently just before departing. A mountain man and trapper, I was friends with both the Native Americans and the settlers. Almost all the Indians wanted to fight, but Maya had won the hearts of some with her search for peace. Remaining silent, I listened to both sides, then watched as most of the chiefs had left.

At one point Maya walked up to me. "I suppose you're leaving too."

I nodded affirmatively, explaining that if these Native medicine chiefs didn't understand what she was doing, I surely didn't.

She looked at me as though I must be kidding, then, turning, she directed her attention to another person. Charlene! I suddenly recalled that she had been there; she was an Indian woman of great power, but often ignored by the envious male chiefs because of her gender. She seemed to know something important about the role of the ancestors, but her voice was falling on deaf ears.

I saw myself wanting to stay, wanting to support Maya, wanting to reveal my feelings for Charlene, yet in the end I walked away; the unconscious memory of my mistake in the thirteenth century was too close to the surface. I wanted only to run away, avoid any responsibility. My life pattern was set: I trapped for furs, I got along, and I didn't stick my neck out for anyone. Perhaps I would do better next time.

Next time? My mind raced forward, and I saw myself looking outward toward the Earth, contemplating my present incarnation. I was watching my own Birth Vision, seeing the full possibility of resolving my reluctance to act or to take a stand. I envisioned how I might utilize my early family to its greatest potential, learning spiritual sensitivity from my mother, integrity and fun from my father. A grandfather would provide a connection with the wilderness, an uncle and aunt would provide a model for tithing and discipline.

And being placed with such strong individuals would bring my tendency to be aloof quickly into consciousness. Because of their ego and strong expectation, I would at first retreat from their messages, and try to hide, but then I would work through this fear and see the positive preparation they were giving me, clearing this tendency so that I could fully follow my life path.

It would be a perfect preparation, and I would leave that upbringing looking for the details of spirituality I had seen in the Insights centuries before. I would explore the psychological descriptions of the Human Potential Movement, the wisdom of Eastern experience, the mystics of the West, and then eventually I would run into the actual Insights again, just at the time they were surfacing to be brought finally into mass awareness. All this preparation and clearing would then allow me to further explore how these Insights were changing human culture and to be a part of Williams' group.

I pulled back and looked at Wil.

"What's wrong?" he asked.

"It hasn't exactly gone the ideal way for me either. I feel as if I've wasted the preparation. I haven't even cleared myself of the aloofness. There were so many books I didn't read, so many people that could have given me messages that I ignored. When I look back now, it seems as though I missed everything."

Wil almost laughed. "None of us can follow our Birth Visions exactly." He paused and stared. "Do you realize what you're doing at this moment? You just remembered the ideal way you wanted your life to go, the way that would have given you the most satisfaction, and when you look at how you actually lived, you are filled with regrets, just the way Williams felt after he died and saw all the opportunities he had missed. Instead of having to wait until after death, you're experiencing a Life Review *now*."

I couldn't quite understand.

"Don't you see? This has to be a key part of the Tenth. Not only are we discovering that our intuitions and our sense of destiny in our lives are remembrances of our Birth Visions. As we understand the Sixth Insight more fully, we're analyzing where we have been off track or failed to take advantage of opportunities, so that we can immediately get back on a path more in line with why we came. In other words, we're bringing more of the process into consciousness on a day-to-day basis. In the past we had to die to engage in a review of our lives, but now we can wake up earlier and eventually make death obsolete, as the Ninth Insight predicts."

I finally understood. "So this is what humans came to the Earth to do, to systematically remember, to gradually awaken."

"That's right. We're finally becoming aware of a process that has been unconscious since human experience began. From the start, humans have perceived a Birth Vision, and then after birth have gone unconscious, aware of only the vaguest of intuitions.

At first, in the early days of human history, the distance between what we intended and what we actually accomplished was very great, and then, over time, the distance has closed. Now we're on the verge of remembering everything."

At that moment I was drawn back into the knowledge of the soul group. In an instant my awareness seemed to increase another level, and all that Wil had said was confirmed. Now, finally, we could look at history not as the bloody struggle of the human animal, who selfishly learned to dominate nature and to survive in greater style, pulling himself from life in the jungle to create a vast and complex civilization. Rather, we could look at human history as a spiritual process, as the deeper, systematic effort of souls, generation after generation, life after life, struggling through the millennia toward one solitary goal: to remember what we already knew in the Afterlife and to make this knowledge conscious on Earth.

As from a great height, a large holographic image opened up around me and I could somehow see, in one glance, the long saga of human history. Without warning I was drawn into the image, and I felt myself being swept forward into the story, reliving it somehow in fast-forward, as if I had really been there, experiencing it moment by moment.

Suddenly I was witnessing the dawn of consciousness. Before me was a long, windswept plain, somewhere in Africa. Movement caught my eye; a small group of humans, unclothed, was foraging on a field of berries. As I watched, I seemed to pick up on the consciousness of the period. Intimately connected to the rhythms and signals of the natural world, we humans lived and responded instinctively. The routines of daily life were oriented toward the challenges of the search for food and toward membership within our individual band. Levels of power flowed downward from one physically stronger, attuned individual, and within this hierarchy we accepted our place in the same way we accepted the constant tragedies and difficulties of existence: without reflection.

As I watched, thousands of years passed by and countless generations lived and perished. Then, slowly, certain individuals began to grow restless with the routines they saw before them. When a child died in their arms, their consciousness expanded and they began to ask why. And to wonder how it might be avoided in the future. These individuals were beginning to gain *self-awareness*—beginning to realize that they were here, now, alive. They were able to step back from their automatic responses and glimpse the full scope of existence. Life, they knew, endured through the cycles of the sun and moon and seasons, but as the dead around them attested, it also had an end. What was the purpose?

Looking closely at these reflective individuals, I realized I could perceive their Birth Visions; they had come into the Earthly dimension with the specific purpose of initiating humanity's first existential awakening. And, even though I couldn't see its full scope, I knew that in the back of their minds was held the larger inspiration of the World Vision. Before their birth, they were aware that humanity was embarking on a long journey that they could already see. But they also knew that progress along this journey would have to be earned, generation by generation—for as we awakened to pursue a higher destiny, we also lost the calm peace of unconsciousness. Along with the exhilaration and freedom of knowing we were alive came the fear and uncertainty of being alive without knowing why.

I could see that humanity's long history would be moved by these two conflicting urges. On the one hand, we would be moved past our fears by the strength of our intuitions, by our mental images that life was about accomplishing some particular goal, of moving culture forward in a positive direction that only we, as individuals, acting with courage and wisdom, could inspire. From the strength of these feelings we would be reminded that, as insecure as life appeared, we were, in fact, *not* alone, that there was purpose and meaning underlying the mystery of existence.

Yet, on the other hand, we would often fall prey to the opposite urge, the urge to protect ourselves from the Fear, at times losing sight of the purpose, falling into the angst of separation and abandonment. This Fear would lead us into a frightened self-protection, fighting to retain our positions of power, stealing energy from each other, and always resisting change and evolution, regardless of what new, better information might be available.

As the awakening continued, millennia passed, and I watched as humans gradually began to coalesce into ever-larger groups, following a natural drive to identify with more people, to move into more complex social organizations. I could see that this drive came from the vague intuition, known fully in the Afterlife, that human destiny on Earth was to evolve toward unification. Following this intuition, we realized that we could evolve beyond the nomadic life of gathering and hunting and begin to cultivate the Earth's plants and harvest them on a regular basis. Similarly we could domesticate and breed many of the animals around us, ensuring a constant presence of protein and related products. With the images of the World Vision deep within our unconscious, driving us archetypically, we began to envision a shift that would be one of the most dramatic transformations in human history: the leap from nomadic wandering to the establishment of large farming villages.

As these farming communities grew more complex, surpluses of food prompted trade and allowed humanity to divide into the first occupational groups—shepherds and builders and weavers, then merchants and metalworkers and soldiers. Quickly came the invention of writing and tabulation. But the whims of nature and the challenges of life still pierced the awareness of early humanity, and the unspoken question still loomed: why were we alive? As before, I watched the Birth Visions of those individuals who sought to understand spiritual reality at a higher level. They came into the Earth dimension to specifically expand human awareness of the divine source, but their first intuitions of the divine remained dim and incomplete, taking polytheistic form. Humanity began to acknowledge what we supposed was a multitude of cruel and demanding deities, gods that existed outside of ourselves and ruled the weather, the seasons, and the stages of the harvest. In our insecurity we thought that we must appease these gods with rites and rituals and sacrifice.

Over thousands of years the multitude of farming communities coalesced further into large civilizations in Mesopotamia, Egypt, the Indus Valley, Crete, and northern China, each inventing its own version of the nature and animal gods. But such deities could not long forestall the anxiety. I watched generations of souls come into the Earthly dimension intending to bring a message that humanity was destined to progress by sharing and comparing knowledge. Yet, once here, these individuals succumbed to the Fear and distorted this intuition into an unconscious need to conquer and dominate and impose their way of life on others by force.

So began the great era of the empires and tyrants, as one great leader rose up after another, uniting the strength of his people, conquering as much land as possible, convinced that the views of his culture should be adopted by all. Yet, throughout this era, these many tyrants were always, in turn, conquered themselves and pressed under the yoke of a larger, stronger cultural view. For thousands of years different empires bubbled up to the top of humanity's consciousness, disseminating their ideas, rising for a time with a more effective reality, economic plan, and war technology, only to be later deposed by a stronger and more organized vision. Ever so slowly, through this method old, outdated ideas were replaced.

I could see that, as slow and bloody as this process was, key truths were gradually making their way from the Afterlife into the physical dimension. One of the most important of these truths—a new ethic of interaction—began to surface in various places around the globe, but ultimately found clear expression in the philosophy of the ancient Greeks. Instantly I could see the Birth Visions of hundreds of individuals born into the Greek culture, each hoping to remember this timely insight.

For generations they had seen the waste and injustice of mankind's unending violence upon itself, and knew that humans could transcend the habit of fighting and conquering others and implement a new system for the exchange and comparison of ideas, a system that protected the sovereign right of every individual to hold his unique view, regardless of physical strength—a system that was already known and followed in the Afterlife. As I watched, this new way of interaction began to emerge and take form on Earth, finally becoming known as *democracy*.

In this method of exchanging ideas, communication between humans still often degenerated into an insecure power struggle, but at least now, for the first time ever, the process was in place to pursue the evolution of human reality at the verbal rather than the physical level.

At the same time, another watershed idea, one destined to completely transform the human understanding of *spiritual reality,* was surfacing in the written histories of a small tribe in the Middle East. Similarly I could also see the Birth Visions of many of the proponents of this idea as well. These individuals, born into the Judaic culture, knew before birth that while we were correct to intuit a divine source, our description of this source was flawed and distorted. Our concept of many gods was merely a fragmented picture of a larger whole. In truth, they realized, there was only one God, a God, in their view, that was still demanding and threatening and patriarchal—and still existing outside of ourselves—but for the first time, personal and responsive, and the sole creator of all humans.

As I continued to watch, I saw this intuition of one divine source emerging and being clarified in cultures all over the world. In China and India, long the leaders in technology, trade, and social development, Hinduism and Buddhism, along with other Eastern religions, moved the East toward a more contemplative focus.

Those who created these religions intuited that God was more than a personage. God was a force, a consciousness, that could only be completely found by attaining what they described as an enlightenment experience. Rather than just pleasing God by obeying certain laws or rituals, the Eastern religions sought connection with God on the inside, as a shift in awareness, an opening up of one's consciousness to a harmony and security that was constantly available.

Quickly my view shifted to the Sea of Galilee, and I could see that the idea of one God that would ultimately transform Western cultures was evolving from the notion of a deity outside of us, patriarchical and judging, toward the position held in the East, toward the idea of an inner God, a God whose kingdom lay within. I watched as one person came into the Earth dimension remembering almost all of his Birth Vision.

He knew he was here to bring a new energy into the world, a new culture based on love. His message was this: the one God was a holy spirit, a divine energy, whose existence could be felt and proven experientially. Coming into spiritual awareness meant more than rituals and sacrifices and public prayer. It involved a repentance of a deeper kind; a repentance that was an inner psychological shift based on the suspension of the ego's addictions, and a transcendent "letting go," which would ensure the true fruits of the spiritual life.

As this message began to spread, I watched as one of the most influential of all empires, the Roman, embraced the new religion and spread the idea of the one, inner God throughout much of Europe. Later, when the barbarians struck from the north, dismembering the empire, the idea survived in the feudal organization of Christendom that followed.

At this point I saw again the appeals of the Gnostics, urging the church to focus more fully on the inner, transformative experience, using Christ's life as an example of what each of us might achieve. I saw the church lapse into the Fear, its leaders sensing a loss of control, building doctrine around the powerful hierarchy of the churchmen, who made themselves mediators, dispensers of the spirit to the populace. Eventually all texts related to Gnosticism were deemed blasphemous and excluded from the Bible.

Even though many individuals came from the Afterlife dimension intending to broaden and democratize the new religion, it was a time of great fear, and efforts to reach out to other cultures were distorted again into the need to dominate and control.

Here I saw the secret sects of the Franciscans again, who sought to include a reverence for nature and a return to the inner experience of the divine. These individuals had come into the Earth dimension intuiting that the Gnostic contradiction would eventually be resolved, and were determined to preserve the old texts and manuscripts until that time. Again I saw my ill-fated attempt to make the information public too soon, and my untimely departure.

Yet I could see clearly that a new era was unfolding in the West. The power of the church was being challenged by another social unit: the nation-state. As more of the Earth's peoples were becoming conscious of each other, the era of the great empires was coming to a close. New generations arrived able to intuit our destiny of unification, working to promote a consciousness of national origin based on common languages and tied more closely to one sovereign area of land. These states were still dominated by autocratic leaders, often thought of as ruling by divine right, but a new human civilization was unfolding, one with recognized borders and established currencies and trade routes.

Finally, in Europe, as wealth and literacy spread, a wide renaissance began. As I watched, the Birth Visions of many of the participants came into my view. They knew that human destiny was to develop an empowered democracy, and they came hoping to bring it into being. The writings of the Greeks and Romans were discovered, stimulating their memories. The first democratic parliaments were established, and calls were issued for an end to the divine right of kings and the bloody reign of the church over spiritual and social reality. Soon came the Protestant Reformation, which held the promise that individuals could go directly to important Scriptures and conceive a direct connection to the divine.

At the same time, individuals seeking greater empowerment and freedom were exploring the American continent, a landmass symbolically lying between the cultures of the East and the West. As I watched the Birth Visions of the Europeans most inspired to enter this new world, I could see that they came knowing that this land was already inhabited, aware that communication and immigration should be undertaken only by invitation. Deep inside, they knew that the Americans were to be the grounding, the road back, for a Europe quickly losing its sense of sacred intimacy with the natural environment and moving toward a dangerous secularism. The Native American cultures, while not perfect, provided a model from which the European mentality could regain its roots.

Yet, again because of the Fear, these individuals were able to intuit only the drive to move to this land, sensing a new freedom and liberty of spirit, but bringing with them the need to dominate and conquer, and to pursue their own security. The important truths of the Native cultures were lost in the rush to exploit the region's vast natural resources.

Meanwhile, in Europe, the Renaissance continued, and I began to see the full scope of the Second Insight. The power of the church to define reality was diminishing, and Europeans were feeling as though they were awakening to look at life anew. Through the courage of countless individuals, all inspired by their intuitive memories, the scientific method was embraced as a democratic process of exploring and coming to understand the world in which humans found themselves. This method—exploring some aspect of the natural world, drawing conclusions, then offering this view to others—was thought of as the consensus-building process through which we would be able, finally, to understand mankind's real situation on this planet, including our spiritual nature.

But those in the church, entrenched in Fear, sought to squelch this new science. As political forces lined up on both sides, a compromise was reached. Science would be free to explore the outer, material world, but must leave spiritual phenomena to the dictates of the still-influential churchmen. The entire inner world of experience—our higher perceptual states of beauty and love, intuitions, coincidences, interpersonal phenomena, even dreams—all were, at first, off limits to the new science.

Despite these restrictions, science began to map out and describe the operation of the physical world, providing information rich in ways to increase trade and utilize natural resources. Human economic security increased, and slowly we began to lose our sense of mystery and our heartfelt questions about the purpose of life. We decided it was purposeful enough just to survive and build a better, more secure world for ourselves and our children. Gradually we entered the consensus trance that denied the reality of death and created the illusion that the world was explained and ordinary and devoid of mystery.

In spite of our rhetoric, our once-strong intuition of a spiritual source was being pushed farther into the background. In this growing materialism, God could only be viewed as a distant Deist's God, a God who merely pushed the universe into being and then stood back to let it run in a mechanical sense, like a predictable machine, with every effect having a cause, and unconnected events happening only at random, by chance alone.

Yet here I could see the birth intent of many of the individuals of this time period. They came knowing that the development of technology and production was important because it could eventually be made nonpolluting and sustainable and could liberate humankind beyond all imagination. But in the beginning, born into the milieu of the time, all they could remember was the general intuition to build and produce and work, holding tightly to the democratic ideal.

The vision shifted, and I could see that nowhere was this intuition stronger than in the creation of the United States, with its democratic Constitution and its system of checks and balances. As a grand experiment, America was set up for the rapid exchange of ideas that was to characterize the future. Yet below the surface, the messages of the Native Americans, and the Native Africans, and other peoples on whose back the American experiment was initiated, all cried out to be heard, to be integrated into the European mentality.

By the nineteenth century we were on the verge of a second great transformation of human culture, a transformation that would be built on the new energy sources of oil and steam and finally electricity. The human economy had developed into a vast and complicated field of endeavor that supplied more products than ever before through an explosion of new techniques. In great numbers people were moving from rural communities to great urban centers of production, shifting from life on the farm to involvement in the new, specialized *industrial revolution*.

At the time, most believed that a democratically founded capitalism, unfettered by government regulation, was the desired method of human commerce. Yet, again, as I picked up on individual Birth Visions, I could see that most people born into this period had come hoping to evolve capitalism toward a more perfect form. Unfortunately the level of Fear was such that all they managed to intuit was a desire to build individual security, to exploit other workers, and to maximize profits at every turn, often entering into collusive agreements with competitors and with governments. This was the great era of the robber barons and of secret banking and industrial cartels.

However, by the early twentieth century, because of the abuses of this freewheeling capitalism, two other economic systems were set to be offered as alternatives. Earlier, in England, two men had posed an alternative "manifesto" which called for a new system, run by workers, that would eventually create an economic utopia, where the resources of the whole of humanity would be made available to each person according to his needs, without greed or competition.

In the horrible working conditions of the day, the idea attracted many supporters. But I quickly saw that this materialistic workers' "manifesto" had been a corruption of the original intention. When the Birth Visions of the two men came into view, I realized that what they were intuiting was that human destiny was eventually to achieve such a utopia. Unfortunately they failed to remember that this utopia could only be accomplished through democratic participation, born of free will and slowly evolved.

Consequently the initiators of this communist system, from the first revolution in Russia, erroneously thought that this system could be created through force and dictatorship, an approach that failed miserably and cost millions of lives. In their impatience the individuals involved had envisioned a utopia but had created communism and decades of tragedy.

The scene shifted to the other alternative to a democratic capitalism: the evil of fascism. This system was designed to enhance the profits and control of a ruling elite, who thought of themselves as privileged leaders of human society. They believed that only through the abandonment of democracy, and the union of government with the new industrial leadership, could a nation reach its greatest potential and position in the world.

I saw clearly that in creating such a system, the participants were almost totally unconscious of their Birth Visions. They had come here wishing only to promote the idea that civilization was evolving toward perfectibility and that a nation of people, totally unified in purpose and will, striving to attain their fullest potential, could reach great heights of energy and effectiveness. What was created was a fearful, self-serving vision wrongly claiming the superiority of certain races and nations, and the possibility of developing a supernation whose destiny was to rule the world. Again the intuition that all humans were evolving toward perfection was distorted by weak, fearful men into the murderous reign of the Third Reich.

I watched as others—who had likewise envisioned the perfectibility of mankind, but who were in greater touch with the importance of an empowered democracy—intuited that they must stand up against both alternatives to a freely expressed economy. The first stand resulted in a bloody world war against the fascist distortion, won finally at extreme cost. The second resulted in a long and bitter cold war against the communist bloc.

I suddenly found myself focusing on the United States during the early years of this cold war, the decade of the fifties. At this time, America stood successfully at the apex of what had been a four-hundred-year preoccupation with secular materialism. Affluence and security had spread to include a large and growing middle class, and into this material success was born an enormous new generation, a generation whose intuitions would help lead humanity toward a third great transformation.

This generation grew up constantly reminded that they lived

in the greatest country in the world, the land of the free, with liberty and justice for all its citizens. Yet, as they matured, members of this generation found a disturbing disparity between this popular American self-image and actual reality. They found that many people in this land—women and certain racial minorities—were, by law and custom, definitely *not free.* By the sixties the new generation was inspecting closely, and many were finding other disturbing aspects of the United States' self-image—for instance, a blind patriotism that expected young people to go into a foreign land to fight a political war that had no clearly expressed purpose and no prospect of victory.

Just as disturbing was the culture's spiritual practice. The materialism of the previous four hundred years had pushed the mystery of life, and death, far into the background. Many found the churches and synagogues full of pompous and meaningless ritual. Attendance seemed more social than spiritual, and the members too restricted by a sense of how they might be perceived and judged by their onlooking peers.

As the vision progressed, I could tell that the new generation's tendency to analyze and judge arose from a deep-seated intuition that there was more to life than the old material reality took into account. The new generation sensed new spiritual meaning just beyond the horizon, and they began to explore other, lesser known religions and spiritual points of view. For the first time the Eastern religions were understood in great numbers, serving to validate the mass intuition that spiritual perception was an inner experience, a shift in awareness that changed forever one's sense of identity and purpose. Similarly the Jewish Cabalist writings and the Western Christian mystics, such as Meister Eckehart and Teilhard de Chardin, provided other intriguing descriptions of a deeper spirituality.

At the same time, information was surfacing from the human sciences—sociology, psychiatry, psychology, and anthropology—as well as from modern physics, that cast new light on the nature of human consciousness and creativity. This cumulation of thought, together with the perspective provided by the East, gradually began to crystallize into what was later called the *Human Potential Movement,* the emerging belief that human beings were presently actualizing only a small portion of their vast physical, psychological, and spiritual potential.

I watched as, over the course of several decades, this information and the spiritual experience it spawned grew into a *critical mass* of awareness, a leap in consciousness from which we began to formulate a new view of what living a human life was all about, including, ultimately, an actual remembrance of the Nine Insights.

Yet, even as this new view was crystallizing, surging through the human world as a contagion of consciousness, many others in the new generation began to pull back, suddenly alarmed at the growing instability in culture which seemed to correspond to the arrival of the new paradigm. For hundreds of years the solid agreements of the old worldview had maintained a well-defined, even rigid, order for human life. All roles were clearly defined, and everyone knew his place: for instance, men at work, women and children at home, nuclear and genetic families intact, a ubiquitous work ethic. Citizens were expected to discover a place in the economy, to find meaning in family and children, and to know that the purpose of life was to live well and create a more materially secure world for the succeeding generation.

Then came the sixties wave of questioning and analysis and criticism, and the unwavering rules began to crumble. No longer was behavior effectively governed by powerful agreements.

Everyone now seemed empowered, liberated, free to chart his or her own course in life, to reach out for this nebulous idea of potential. In this climate what others thought ceased to be the real determinant of our action and conduct; increasingly our behavior was being determined by how we felt inside, by our own inner ethics.

For those who had truly adopted a more lived, spiritual point of view, characterized by honesty and love toward others, ethical behavior was not a problem. But of concern were those who had lost the outer guidelines for living, without yet forming a strong inner code. They seemed to be falling into a cultural no-man's-land, where now anything seemed to be permissible: crime and drugs and addictive impulses of all kinds, not to mention a loss of the work ethic. To make matters worse, many seemed to be using the new findings of the Human Potential Movement to imply that criminals and deviates weren't really even responsible for their own actions, but were, instead, victims of an oppressive culture that shamelessly allowed the social conditions that shaped this behavior.

As I continued to watch, I understood what I was seeing: a polarization of viewpoint was quickly forming around the planet, as those who were undecided now reacted against a cultural viewpoint they saw leading to runaway chaos and uncertainty, perhaps even to the total disintegration of their way of life. In the United States especially, a growing number of people were becoming convinced they were now facing what amounted to a life-and-death struggle against the permissiveness and liberalism of the past twenty-five years—a culture war, as they called it— with nothing short of the survival of Western civilization at stake. I could see that many of them even considered the cause already near lost, and thus advocated extreme action.

In the face of this backlash, I could see the advocates of Human Potential moving into fear and defensiveness themselves, sensing that many hard-earned victories for individual rights and social compassion were now in danger of being swept away by a tide of conservatism. Many considered this reaction against liberation an attack by the embattled forces of greed and exploitation, who were pushing forth in one last attempt to dominate the weaker members of society.

Here I could clearly see what was intensifying the polarization: each side was thinking the other to be a conspiracy of evil.

The advocates of the old worldview were no longer considering the Human Potentialists as misguided or naive, but were, in fact, considering them to be part of a larger conspiracy of *big government* socialists, holdout adherents of the communist solution, who were seeking to accomplish exactly what was occurring: the erosion of cultural life to the point where an all-powerful government could come in and straighten everything out. In their view this conspiracy was using fear of increasing crime as an excuse to register guns and systematically disarm the public, giving ever-greater control to a centralized bureaucracy that would finally monitor the movement of cash and credit cards through uplinks into the Internet, rationalizing the growing control of the electronic economy as crime prevention, or as a necessity to collect taxes or prevent sabotage. Finally, perhaps under the ploy of an impending natural disaster, *big brother* would step forward and confiscate wealth and declare martial law.

For the advocates of liberation and change, just the opposite scenario seemed more likely. In the face of the conservatives' political gains, all that they had worked for seemed to be crashing before their eyes. They, too, observed the increasing violent crime and the degenerating family structures, only for them the cause was not too much government intervention, but too little, too late.

In every nation capitalism had failed a whole class of people, and the reason was clear: for poor people there existed no opportunity to participate in the system. Effective education wasn't there. The jobs weren't there. And instead of helping, the government seemed ready to back away, throwing out the antipoverty programs with all the other hard-won social gains of the last twenty-five years.

I could see clearly that, in their growing disillusionment, the reformers were beginning to believe the worst: that the rightward swing in human society could only be the result of increased manipulation and control by the moneyed, corporate interests in the world. These interests seemed to be buying governments, buying the media, and ultimately, as in Nazi Germany, they would slowly divide the world into the haves and the have-nots, with the largest, richest corporations running the small entrepreneurs out of business and controlling more and more of the wealth. Sure there would be riots, but that would just play into the hands of the elite as they strengthened their police control.

My awareness suddenly jumped to a higher level and I finally understood the polarization of Fear completely: great numbers of people seemed to be gravitating to one perspective or the other, with both sides raising the stakes to that of war, of good vs. evil, and both visualizing the other as the perpetrators of a grand conspiracy.

And in the background I now understood the growing influence of those people who claimed to be able to explain this emergent evil. These were the *end-times* analysts to whom Joel had referred earlier. In the growing turmoil of the transition, these interpreters were beginning to increase their power. In their view the Bible's prophecies were to be understood literally, and what they saw in the uncertainty of our time was the long-awaited apocalypse preparing to descend. Soon would come the outright holy war in which humans would be divided between the forces of darkness and armies of light. They envisioned this war as a real physical conflict, fast and bloody, and for those who knew it was coming, only one decision was important: be on the correct side when the fighting began.

Yet simultaneously, just as with the other landmark turns in human history, I could see beyond the Fear and retrenchment to the actual Birth Visions of those involved. Clearly everyone on both sides of the polarization had come into the physical dimension intending that this polarization not be so intense. We wanted a smooth transition from the old materialistic worldview to the new spiritual one, and we wanted a transformation in which the best of the older traditions would be recognized and integrated into the new world that was emerging.

I could clearly see that this growing belligerence was an aberration, coming not from intention, but from the Fear. Our original vision was that the ethics of human society would be maintained at the same time that each person could be fully liberated and the environment protected; and that economic creativity would be at once conserved and transformed by introducing an overriding spiritual purpose. And further, that this spiritual purpose could descend fully into the world and initiate a utopia in a way that symbolically fulfilled the end-times Scriptures.

My awareness amplified even further, and just as when I had watched Maya's Birth Vision, I could almost glimpse this higher spiritual understanding, the full picture of where human history was intended to go from here, how we could achieve this reconciliation of views and go on to fulfill our human destiny. Then, as before, my head began to spin, and I lost concentration; I couldn't reach the level of energy needed to grasp it.

The vision began to disappear, and I strained to hold on, seeing the current situation one last time. Clearly, without the mediating influence of the World Vision, the polarization of Fear would continue to accelerate. I could see the two sides hardening, their feelings intensifying, as both began to think the other to be not just wrong, but hideous, venal . . . in league with the devil himself.

After a moment of dizziness and a sense of rapid movement, I looked around and saw Wil beside me. He glanced my way, then gazed out at the dark gray environment, a concerned expression on his face. We had traveled to a new location.

"Were you able to see my vision of history?" I asked.

He looked at me again and nodded. "What we just saw was a new spiritual interpretation of history, somewhat specific to your cultural view, but amazingly revealing. I've never seen anything like that before. This has to be part of the Tenth—a clear view of the human quest as seen in the Afterlife. We're understanding that everyone is born with a positive intention, trying to bring more of the knowledge contained in the Afterlife into the physical. All of us! History has been a long process of awakening. When we are born into the physical, of course, we run into this problem of going unconscious and having to be socialized and trained in the cultural reality of the day. After that, all we can remember are these gut feelings, these intuitions, to do certain things. But we constantly have to fight the Fear. Often the Fear is so great we fail to follow through with what we intended, or we distort it somehow. But everyone, and I mean everyone, comes in with the best of intentions."

"So you think a serial killer, for instance, really came here to do something good?"

"Yes, originally. All killing is a rage and lashing out that is a way of overcoming an inner sense of Fear and helplessness."

"I don't know," I said. "Aren't some people just inherently bad?"

"No, they just go crazy in the Fear and make horrible mistakes. And, ultimately, they must bear the full responsibility of these mistakes. But what has to be understood is that horrible acts are caused, in part, by our very tendency to assume that some people are naturally evil. That's the mistaken view that fuels the polarization. Both sides can't believe humans can act the way they do without being intrinsically no good, and so they increasingly dehumanize and alienate each other, which increases the Fear and brings out the worst in everyone." He seemed distracted again, looking away.

"Each side thinks the other is involved in a conspiracy of the greatest sort," he added, "the embodiment of all that's negative."

I noticed he was looking out toward the distance again, and when I followed his eyes, and also focused on the environment, I began to pick up an ominous sense of darkness and foreboding.

"I think," he continued, "that we can't bring in the World Vision, or resolve the polarization, until we understand the real nature of evil and the actual reality of Hell."

"Why do you say that?" I asked.

He glanced at me one more time, then gazed out again into the dull gray. "Because Hell is exactly where we are."

AN
INNER
HELL

A chill surged through my body as I looked out on
the gray environment. The ominous feeling I perceived earlier
was turning into a clear sense of alienation and despair.

"Have you been here before?" I asked Wil.

"Only to the edge," he replied. "Never out here in the middle.
Do you feel how cold it is?"

I nodded as a movement caught my eye. "What is that?"

Wil shook his head. "I'm not sure."

A swirling mass of energy seemed to be moving in our direction.

"It must be another soul group," I said.

As they came closer, I tried to focus on their thoughts, feeling
an even greater sense of alienation, even anger. I tried to shrug it
off, open up more.

"Wait," I vaguely heard Wil say. "You're not strong enough."
But it was too late. I was suddenly pulled into an intense blackness and then beyond it into a large town of some kind. In terror

I looked around, struggling to keep my wits, and realized that the architecture indicated the nineteenth century. I was standing on a street corner full of people walking by, and in the distance was the raised dome of a capitol building. At first I thought I was actually in the nineteenth century, but several aspects of the reality were wrong: the horizon faded out to a strange gray color, and the sky was olive green, similar to the sky above the office construction that Williams had created when he was avoiding the realization that he had died.

Then I became aware of four men watching me from the opposite street corner. An icy-cold feeling swept my body. All were well dressed and one cocked his head and took a puff from a large cigar. Another checked a watch and returned it to his vest pocket. Their look was sophisticated but menacing.

"Anyone who has raised their ire is a friend of mine," a low voice spoke from behind me.

I turned to see a large, barrel-shaped man, also well dressed and wearing a wide-brimmed felt hat, walking toward me. His face seemed familiar; I had seen him before. But where?

"Don't mind them," he added. "They're not so hard to outsmart."

I stared at his tall, stooped posture and shifting eyes, then remembered who he was. He had been the commander of the federal troops I had seen in the visions of the nineteenth-century war, the one who had refused to see Maya and had ordered the battle against the Native people to begin. This town was a construction, I thought. He must have re-created his later life situation in order to avoid realizing he was dead.

"This is not real," I blurted. "You're . . . uh . . . deceased."

He seemed to ignore my statement. "So what have you done to piss off that bunch of jackals?"

"I haven't done anything."

"Oh yes, you've done something. I know that look they're giving you. They think they run this town, you know. In fact, they think they can run the whole world." He shook his head. "These people never trust fate. They think they're responsible for seeing that the future turns out exactly as they plan. Everything. Economic development, governments, the flow of money, even the relative value of world currencies. All of which is not a bad idea, really. God knows the world is full of peons and idiots, who will ruin everything if left to their own devices. The people have to be herded and controlled as much as possible, and if one can make a little money along the way, why not?

"But these nuts tried to run *me*. Of course, I'm too smart for them. I've always been too smart for them. So what did you do?"

"Listen," I said. "Try to understand. None of this is real."

"Hey," he replied, "I would suggest that you take me into your confidence. If they're against you, I'm the only friend you have."

I looked away, but I could tell he was still eyeing me suspiciously.

"They're treacherous people," he went on. "They'll never forgive you. Take my situation, for example. All they wanted was to use my military experience to quash the Indians and open up their lands. But I was onto them. I knew they couldn't be trusted, that I would have to look out for myself." He gave me a wry look. "It's harder for them to use you and throw you away if you're a war hero, right? After the war I sold myself to the public. That way, these characters had to play ball with *me*. But let me tell you: never underestimate these people. They are capable of anything!"

He backed away from me a moment, as if pondering my appearance.

"In fact," he added, "they may have sent you as a spy."

At a loss as to what to do, I started to walk away.

"You bastard!" he yelled. "I was right."

I saw him reach into a pocket and pull a short knife. Petrified, I forced my body to move, running down the street and into an alleyway, his footsteps heavy behind me. On the right was a door, partially open. I ran through it and slid the bolt into the locked position. My next breath drew in the heavy odor of opium. Around me were dozens of people, their faces staring absently up at me. Were they real, I wondered, or part of the constructed illusion? Most quickly turned back to their muted conversation and hookah pipes, so I started to walk through the dirty mattresses and sofas to another door.

"I know you," a woman slurred. She was leaning against the wall by the door, her head hanging forward as if too heavy for her neck. "I went to your school."

I looked at her in confusion for a moment, then remembered the young girl in my high school who had suffered from repeated episodes of depression and drug use. Resisting all intervention, she had finally overdosed and died.

"Sharon, is that you?"

She managed a smile, and I glanced back at the door, concerned that the knife-bearing commander might have found a way inside.

"It's okay," she said. "You can stay here with us. You'll be safe in this room. Nothing can hurt you."

I walked a step closer and as gently as possible said, "I don't want to stay. All this is an illusion."

As I said that, three or four people turned and looked at me angrily.

"Please, Sharon," I whispered. "Just come with me."

Two of the closest stood up and walked over beside Sharon. "Get out of here," one told me. "Leave her alone."

"Don't listen to him," the other said to Sharon. "He's crazy. We need each other."

I stooped slightly so I could look directly into Sharon's eyes. "Sharon, none of this is real. You're dead. We have to find a way out of here."

"Shut up!" another person screamed. Four or five more people walked toward me, hate in their eyes. "Leave us alone."

I began to back toward the door; the crowd moved toward me. Through the bodies I could see Sharon turning back to her hookah hose. I turned and ran through the door, only to realize that I wasn't outside. I was in an office of some kind, surrounded by computers, filing cabinets, a conference table—modern, twentieth-century furniture and equipment.

"Hey, you're not supposed to be in here," someone said. I turned around to see a middle-aged man looking at me over his reading glasses. "Where's my secretary? I don't have time for this. What do you want?"

"Someone's chasing me. I was trying to hide."

"Good God, man! Then don't come in here. I said I don't have time for this. You haven't the slightest idea what I have to do today. Look at these case files. Who do you think will process them if I don't?" I thought I saw a look of terror on his face.

I shook my head and looked for another door. "Don't you know you're dead?" I asked. "This is all imagined."

He paused, the look of terror shifting to anger, then asked, "How did you get in here? Are you a criminal?"

I found a door that led outside and ran out. The streets were now completely empty except for one carriage. It pulled up to the hotel across from me, and a beautiful woman, dressed in evening attire, got out and glanced over toward me, then smiled. There was something warm and caring about her demeanor. I dashed across the street toward her, and she paused to watch me approach, her smile coy and inviting.

"You're alone," she said. "Why don't you join me?"

"Where are you going?" I asked tentatively.

"To a party."

"Who's going to be there?"

"I have no idea."

She opened the door to the hotel and motioned for me to come with her. I followed aimlessly, trying to think of what to do. We walked into the elevator and she pushed the button for the fourth floor. As we rode up, the sensation of warmth and caring increased with each floor. Out of the corner of my eye I saw her staring at my hands. When I looked, she smiled again and pretended to have been caught.

The elevator opened and she led me down the hall to a particular door and knocked twice. After a moment the door was unlocked and a man opened it. His face lit up at the sight of the woman.

"Come in!" he said. "Come in!"

She invited me to enter ahead of her, and as I walked in, a young woman reached over and took my arm. She was dressed in a strapless gown and was barefooted.

"Oh, you're lost," she said. "Poor thing. You'll be safe in here with us."

Past the door I could see a man without a shirt. "Look at those thighs," he commented, staring at me.

"He has perfect hands," another said.

In a state of shock I realized the room was crowded with people in various stages of nudity and lovemaking.

"No, wait," I said. "I can't stay."

The woman on my arm said, "You would go back out there? It takes forever to find a group like this. Feel the energy in here. Not like the fear of being alone, huh?" She moved her hand across my chest.

Suddenly there was the sound of a scuffle on the other side of the room.

"No, leave me alone!" someone shouted. "I don't want to be here."

A young man no older than eighteen pushed several people away and ran out the door. I used the distraction to run out behind him. Not waiting for the elevator, he bounded down the adjacent stairs and I followed. When I reached the street, he was already on the other side.

I was about to shout for him to stop when I saw him freeze in terror. Ahead on the sidewalk was the commander, still holding the knife, but this time facing the group of men who had watched me earlier. They were all talking at the same time, posturing angrily. Abruptly one of the group pulled a gun, and the commander rushed toward him with the knife. Shots rang out, and the commander's hat and knife flew backward as the bullet pierced his forehead. He dropped to the ground with a thud, and as he did, the other men stopped in midmotion and began to fade away until they disappeared completely. Just as quickly the man on the ground also disappeared.

Across from me, the young man sat wearily down on the curb and put his head in his hands. I rushed up to him, my knees shaking.

"It's okay," I said. "They're gone."

"No, they're not," he said in frustration. "Look over there."

I turned and saw the four men who had disappeared standing

across the street in front of the hotel. Unbelievably they were in
the exact position they had been in when I had first seen them.
One puffed his cigar and the other checked his watch.

My heart skipped a beat as I also spotted the commander,
standing across from them again, staring menacingly.

"This keeps happening over and over," the young man said.
"I can't stand this anymore. Someone's got to help me."

Before I could say anything, two forms materialized to his
right, but remained obscured, out of focus.

The young man stared at the forms for a long time, then, with
a look of excitement on his face, said, "Roy, is that you?"

As I watched, the two forms moved toward him until he was
completely hidden by their weaving shapes. After several minutes
he had completely disappeared, along with the two souls.

I stared at the empty curb where he had been sitting, feeling
remnants of a higher vibration. In my mind's eye I saw my soul
group again and felt their deep caring and love. Concentrating
on the feeling, I was able to shake off the blanketing anxiety and
to amplify my energy in increments until finally I began to open
up inside. Immediately the environment shifted to lighter shades
of gray and the town disappeared. As my energy increased, I was
able to image Wil's face, and instantly he was beside me.

"Are you okay?" he asked, turning to embrace me. His expression showed immense relief. "Those illusions were strong,
and you willed yourself right into them."

"I know. I couldn't think, couldn't remember what to do."

"You were gone a long time; all we could do was send you
energy."

"Who do you mean by we?"

"All these souls." Wil's hand gestured outwardly.

When I looked fully, I could see hundreds of souls stretching as far as I could see. Some were looking directly at us, but most appeared to be focused in another direction. I looked to see where they were staring, following their gaze to several large swirls of energy far in the distance. When I concentrated my focus, I realized that one of the swirls was in fact the town from which I had just escaped.

"What are those places?" I asked Wil.

"Mental constructions," he replied, "set up by souls who in life lived very restrictive control dramas and could not wake up after death. Many thousands of them exist out there."

"Were you able to see what was happening when I was in the construction?"

"Most of it. When I focused on the souls nearby, I could pick up on their view of what was happening to you. This ring of souls is constantly beaming energy into the illusions, hoping someone will respond."

"Did you see the teenage boy? He was able to wake up. But the others didn't seem to pay attention to anything."

Wil turned to face me. "Do you remember what we saw during Williams' Life Review? At first he couldn't accept what was happening, and he began to repress his death to the extent that he created a mental construction of his office."

"Yes, I thought of that when I was down there."

"Well, that's how it works for everyone. If we die and we have been so immersed in our control drama and routine as a way to repress the mystery and insecurity of life, to such a degree that we can't even wake up after death, then we create these illusions or trances so we can continue the same way of feeling safe, even after we enter the Afterlife. If Williams' soul group had not reached him, he would have entered one of the hellish places where you were. It's all a reaction to Fear. The people there would be paralyzed with Fear if they didn't find some way to ward it off, to repress it below consciousness. What they're doing is repeating the same dramas, the same coping devices, they practiced in life, and they can't stop."

"So these illusional realities are just severe control dramas?"

"Yes, they all fall within the general styles of the control dramas, except that they are more intense and nonreflective. For example, the man with the knife, the commander, was no doubt an intimidator in the way he stole energy from others. And he rationalized this behavior by assuming that the world was out to get him, and of course, in his life on Earth these expectations drew just those kinds of people into his life, so his mental vision was fulfilled. Here he just created imaginary people to be after him so he could reproduce the same situation.

"If he were to run out of people to intimidate and his energy were to fall, anxiety would begin to seep into consciousness again. So he has to keep up the intimidator role constantly. He has to keep this particular kind of action going, the action he learned long ago, the only action he knows that will preoccupy his mind sufficiently to kill the Fear. It is the action itself—the compulsive, dramatic, high-adrenaline nature of the action—that pushes the anxiety so far into the background that he can forget about it, repress it, and feel half at ease in his existence, at least for a little while."

"What about the drug users?" I asked.

"In this case, they were taking passivity, the 'poor me,' to the extreme of projecting nothing but despair and cruelty on the entire world, rationalizing a need to escape. Obsessively pursuing drugs still serves the function of preoccupying the mind and repressing anxiety, even in the Afterlife.

"In the physical dimension drugs often produce a euphoria

quite like the euphoria that comes from love. The problem with this false euphoria, however, is that the body resists the chemicals and counteracts them, which means that, as the drug is repeatedly used, it takes an increasingly larger dose to reach the same effect, which eventually destroys the body."

I thought of the commander again. "Something really strange happened down there. The man who was chasing me was killed, and then he seemed to come back to life and start the drama all over again."

"That's how it works in this self-imposed Hell. All these illusions always play out and blow up in the end. If you had been with someone who had repressed the mystery of life by eating great amounts of fat, a heart attack might have ended it. The drug users eventually destroy their own bodies, the commander dies over and over, and so on.

"And it works the same way in the physical dimension: a compulsive control drama always fails, sooner or later. Usually it happens during the trials and challenges of life; routines break down and the anxiety rushes in. It is what's called hitting bottom. This is the time to wake up and handle the Fear in another way; but if a person can't, then he or she goes right back into the trance. And if one doesn't wake up in the physical dimension, one might have difficulty waking up in the other as well.

"These compulsive trances account for all horrible behavior in the physical dimension. This is the psychology of all truly evil acts, the motivation behind the inconceivable behavior of child molesters, sadists, and serial monsters of all kinds. They're simply repeating the only behavior they know that will numb the mind and keep away the anxiety that comes from the lostness they feel."

"So you're saying," I interjected, "that there is no organized, conspiratorial evil in the world, no satanic plot to which we fall prey?"

"None. There is only human fear and the bizarre ways that humans try to ward it off."

"What about the many references in sacred texts and scriptures to Satan?"

"This idea is a metaphor, a symbolic way of warning people to look to the divine for security, not to their sometimes tragic ego urges and habits. Blaming an outside force for everything bad was perhaps important at a certain stage in human development. But now it obscures the truth, because blaming our behavior on forces outside ourselves is a way of avoiding responsibility. And we tend to use the idea of Satan to project that some people are inherently evil so we can dehumanize the ones we disagree with and write them off. It is time now to understand the true nature of human evil in a more sophisticated way and then to deal with it."

"If there is no satanic plot," I said, "then 'possession' doesn't exist."

"That's not so," Wil said emphatically. "Psychological 'possession' does exist. But it is not the result of a conspiracy of evil; it is just energy dynamics. Fearful people want to control others. That's why certain groups try to pull you in and convince you to follow them, and ask you to submit to their authority, or fight you if you try to leave."

"When I was first drawn into that illusory town, I thought I had been possessed by some demonic force."

"No, you were drawn in because you made the same mistake you made earlier: you didn't just open up and listen to those souls; you gave yourself over to them, as if they automatically had all the answers, without checking to see if they were connected and motivated by love. And unlike the souls who are divinely connected, they didn't back away from you. They just pulled you into their world, the same way some crazy group or cult might do in the physical dimension if you don't discriminate."

Wil paused as if in thought, then continued. "All this is more of the Tenth Insight; that's why we're seeing it. As communication between the two dimensions increases, we'll begin to have more encounters with souls in the Afterlife. This part of the Insight is that we must discern between those souls who are awake and connected with the spirit of love and those who are fearful and stuck in an obsessive trance of some kind. But we must do so without invalidating and dehumanizing those caught in such fear dramas by thinking they are demons or devils. They are souls in a growth process, just like us. In fact, in the Earth dimension those who are now caught up in dramas from which they can't escape are often the very souls who were the most optimistic in their Birth Visions."

I shook my head, not following his meaning.

"That is why," he continued, "they chose to be born into such drastic, fearful situations that necessitate such intense, crazy coping devices."

"You're talking about coming into abusive and dysfunctional families, that sort of situation?"

"Yes. Intense control dramas of all kinds, whether they are violent or just perverse and strange addictions, come from environments where life is so abusive and dysfunctional and constrictive, and the level of Fear is so great, that they spawn this same rage and anger or perversion over and over, generation after generation. The individuals who are born into these situations choose to do so on purpose, with clarity."

The idea seemed preposterous to me. "Why would anyone want to be born into a place like that?"

"Because they were sure they had enough strength to break out, to end the cycle, to heal the family system in which they would be born. They were confident that they could awaken and work through the resentment and anger at finding themselves in these deprived circumstances, and see it all as a preparation for a mission—usually one of helping others out of similar situations. Even if they are violent, we have to see them as having the potential to break free of the drama."

"Then the liberal perspective on crime and violence, the idea that everyone can change and be rehabilitated, is the desirable one. The conservative approach is without merit?"

Wil smiled. "Not exactly. The liberals are right to see that people who have grown up in abusive and oppressive situations are a product of their environments, and the conservatives are out of touch to the extent they believe stopping a life of crime or public dole is just a matter of making a conscious choice.

"But the liberal approach is superficial as well, to the degree they believe people can change if offered different circumstances, better financial support, or education, for instance. Usually intervention programs focus only on helping others to better their decision making and economic choices. In the case of violent offenders, rehabilitation attempts have always offered, at best, superficial counseling and, in the worst cases, excuses and leniency, which is precisely the wrong thing to do. Every time someone with a disturbed control drama is slapped on the hand, turned loose with no consequences, it enables the behavior to continue and reinforces the idea that this behavior is not serious, which just sets up the circumstances that guarantee it will occur again."

"Then what can be done?" I asked.

Wil seemed to be vibrating with excitement. "We can learn to intervene spiritually! And that means helping to bring the whole process into consciousness, as these souls here are doing for those caught in the illusions."

Wil was staring at the souls in the ring, then looked at me and shook his head. "I can get all the information I've just relayed to you from these souls, but I still can't see the World Vision clearly. We haven't learned how to build enough energy yet."

I focused on the souls in the ring but could get no information other than what Wil had conveyed. Clearly the soul groups held a greater knowledge and were projecting this knowledge toward the fear constructions, but like Wil, I still couldn't quite understand anything more.

"At least we have another piece of the Tenth Insight," Wil said. "We know that no matter how undesirable the behavior of others is, we have to grasp that they are just souls attempting to wake up, like us."

I was suddenly jolted backward by a blast of dissonant noise, images of whirling colors seizing my mind. Wil lunged forward and caught me at the last moment, pulling me into his energy and again holding me back firmly. For a moment I seemed to shake violently and then the discord passed.

"They've started the experiment again," Wil said.

I shook off the dizziness and looked at him. "That means Curtis will probably try to use force to stop them. He's convinced that's the only way."

As soon as I spoke those words, I saw a clear picture of Feyman in my mind, the man David Lone Eagle thought had something to do with the experiment. He was somewhere overlooking the valley. Glancing at Wil, I realized that he had seen the same image. He nodded in agreement and we instantly began to move.

When we stopped, Wil and I were facing each other. Around us was more gray. Another loud, disharmonious sound shattered the silence, and Wil's face began to lose focus. He continued to hold onto me, and after several moments the sound ended.

"These sound bursts are coming more frequently now," Wil said. "We may not have much time left."

I nodded, fighting the dizziness.

"Let's look around," Wil said.

As soon as we focused on our surroundings, we saw what appeared to be a mass of energy several hundred yards away. Immediately it closed to within forty or fifty feet.

"Be careful," Wil cautioned. "Don't identify completely with them. Just listen and find out who they are."

I focused warily, and immediately saw souls in motion and an image of the town from which I had escaped.

I recoiled in fear, which actually made them come closer to us.

"Stay centered in love," Wil instructed. "They can't pull us in unless we act as though we want them to save us. Try to send them love and energy. It'll either help them or make them run away."

Realizing the souls were more afraid than I was, I found my center and beamed them love energy. Immediately they moved rapidly away from us to their original position.

"Why can't they accept the love and wake up?" I asked Wil.

"Because when they feel the energy and it raises their consciousness a degree, their preoccupation lifts somewhat and doesn't fend off the anxiety of their aloneness. Coming into awareness and breaking free of a control drama always feels anxious at first, because the compulsion has to lift before the inward solution to the lostness can be found. That's why a 'dark night of the soul' sometimes precedes increased awareness and spiritual euphoria."

A movement to the right caught our attention. When I focused, I realized that other souls were in the area; they came closer and the others moved away. I strained to pick up on what the group was doing.

"Why do you think this group is here?" I asked Wil.

He shrugged. "They have something to do with this guy Feyman."

In the space around the group I began to see a moving image, a scene of some kind. When I brought it clearly into focus, I realized it was the image of an expansive industrial plant somewhere on Earth, with large metal buildings and rows of what looked like transformers and pipes and miles of interlinking wire. At the center of the complex, atop one of the largest buildings, was a command center of pure glass. Inside I could see rows of computers and gauges of all descriptions. I glanced at Wil.

"I see it," he said.

As we continued to survey the complex, our perspective expanded so that we could now view the plant from above. From here we could see miles of wire leaving the plant in all directions, feeding huge towers containing some sort of laser beams shooting energy out to other local stations.

"Do you know what all this is?" I asked Wil.

He nodded. "It's a centralized energy-generating plant."

Movement at one end of the complex attracted our attention. Emergency vans and fire trucks were arriving at one of the larger buildings. An ominous glow radiated from the third-floor windows. At one point the glow brightened and then the ground under the entire building seemed to crack. In an explosion of dust and debris the building shuddered and then slowly collapsed. To the right another building burst into flames.

The scene moved to the command center, where inside, technicians moved frantically. From the right a door opened and a man entered with an arm full of charts and blueprints. He laid them out on a table and worked with what appeared to be determined confidence. Walking with a limp to one side of the room, he began to adjust switches and dials. Gradually the ground stopped shaking and the fires were brought under control. He continued to work hastily and to instruct the other technicians.

I looked at the individual now in charge more closely and then turned to Wil. "That's Feyman!"

Before Wil could respond, the scene shifted into fast-forward. Before our eyes the plant was saved, then, quickly, workers began to dismantle it, building by building. At the same time, on a site nearby, a new, smaller facility was being constructed that would manufacture more compact generators. Finally most of the complex had been returned to its natural, wooded state, and the new facility was turning out small units that we could see behind each house and business throughout the countryside.

Abruptly our perspective backed away until we could see a single individual in the foreground watching the same scene we were. When we could see his profile, I realized that it was Feyman, before his current birth, contemplating what he could achieve in life.

Wil and I looked at each other. "This is part of his Birth Vision, isn't it?" I asked.

Wil nodded. "This must be his soul group. Let's see how much more we can find out about him."

We both focused on the group, and another image formed in front of us. It was the nineteenth-century war camp; the head-quarters tent again. We could see Feyman together with the commander, the man I had seen again in the illusional town. Feyman was the other aide who had been there with Williams. He was the one who limped.

As we watched their interaction, we began to pick up on the story of their association. A bright tactician, Feyman was in charge of strategy and technological developments. In advance of the attack the commander had ordered smallpox-laden blankets covertly traded to the Native Americans, a tactic Feyman ada-mantly opposed, not so much because of its effect on the indige-nous people as because he felt that it was politically indefensible.

Afterward, even as the success of the battle was being hailed in Washington, the press found out about the use of smallpox, and an investigation was launched. The commander and his cro-nies in Washington set Feyman up as the scapegoat and his ca-reer was ruined. Later the commander set forth on a glorious political career and national stature, before he was also treacher-ously double-crossed by the same Washington insiders.

Feyman, for his part, never recovered; his own political ambi-tions had been totally destroyed. Over the years he became in-creasingly more embittered and resentful, trying desperately to marshal public opinion to challenge his commander's account of the battle. For a while several journalists pursued the story, but soon public interest faded completely and Feyman remained in a state of disgrace. Later, toward the end of his life, he languished in the realization that his political goals would never be reached, and, blaming his old commander for his humiliation, he attempted to assassinate the ex-politician at a state dinner and was shot dead by bodyguards.

Because Feyman had cut himself off from his inner security and love, he could not fully awaken after death. For years he believed he had escaped his ill-fated attempt to kill his old commander, and had lived in illusional constructions, holding on to his hate and doomed to the repeated horror of planning and attempting another assassination, only to be shot, over and over.

As I watched, I realized that Feyman could have been trapped in the illusions for a much longer period of time had it not been for the determined efforts of another man who had been at the military encampment with Feyman. I could see an image of his face, and I recognized his expression.

"That's Joel again, the journalist I met," I said to Wil without losing my focus on the image.

Wil nodded in response.

After death, Joel had become a member of the outer soul ring and became totally dedicated to waking up Feyman. His intention during the lifetime with Feyman had been to expose any cruelty or treachery on the part of the military toward the Native Americans, but even though he had known about the smallpox contamination, he had been persuaded to keep quiet by a combination of bribes and threats. After death he had been devastated by his Life Review, but had remained conscious, and had vowed to help Feyman, who he felt had been ruined because of his failure to intervene.

After a long period of time, Feyman finally responded and underwent a long and painful Life Review himself. He had originally intended in the nineteenth-century life to become a civil engineer, involved in the peaceful development of technology. But he had been beguiled by the prospect of becoming a war hero, like the commander, and of developing new war strategies and devices.

In the years between lives, he had been involved in helping others on Earth with the proper use of technology, when he slowly began to receive a vision of another life approaching. Slowly at first and then with great conviction, he realized that soon mass-energy devices would be discovered that had the potential of liberating humankind, but these devices would be extremely dangerous.

As he felt himself being born, he knew that he would come to work with this technology, and he was well aware that in order to succeed, he would have to again face his tendency to crave power and recognition and status. Yet he saw that he would have help; there would be six other people. He visualized the valley, working together somewhere in the dark, the falls in the background, utilizing a process to bring in the World Vision.

As he began to fade from view, I could make out aspects of the process he was seeing. First the group of seven would begin to remember past experiences with each other and to work through the residual feelings. Then the group would consciously amplify its energy, using the Eighth Insight techniques, and each would express his or her particular Birth Vision, and finally the vibration would accelerate, unifying the soul groups of the seven individuals. Out of the knowledge gained would come the full memory of our intended future, the World Vision, the view of where we're going and what we have to do to reach our destiny.

Suddenly the whole scene disappeared, along with Feyman's group. Wil and I were left there alone.

Wil's eyes were animated. "Do you see what was happening?" he asked. "This means that Feyman's original intention was actually to perfect and decentralize the technology he's working on. If he realizes this fact, he will stop the experiment."

"We've got to find him," I said.

"No," Wil replied, pausing to think. "That won't help, not yet. We've got to find the rest of this group of seven; it must take the pooled energy of a group to bring in the memory of the World Vision, a group that can work through the process of re-membering and energize themselves."

"I don't understand this part about clearing residual feelings."

Wil moved closer. "Remember the other mental images you've been having? The memories of other places, other times?"

"Yes."

"The group that is forming to deal with this experiment has been together before. There will be residual feelings that *must* be worked through! Everyone will have to deal with them."

Wil looked away for a moment, then said, "This is more of the Tenth Insight. Not just one group is coming in; there are many others. We'll all have to learn to clear these resentments."

As he spoke, I thought about the many group situations I'd experienced, where some members of the group liked each other immediately, while others seemed to fall into instant discord, for no apparent reason. I wondered: was human culture now ready to perceive the distant source of these unconscious reactions?

Then, without warning, another shrill sound reverberated through my body. Wil grabbed me and pulled me closer, our faces almost touching. "If you fall again, I don't know if you can get back while the experiment is operating at this level," he shouted. "You'll have to find the others!"

A second blast ripped us apart, and I felt myself release into the familiar swirling colors, knowing that I was heading back, as before, into the Earth dimension. Yet this time, instead of tumbling quickly into the physical, I seemed to linger momentarily; something was pulling at my solar plexus, moving me laterally. As I strained to focus, the surging environment calmed, and I began to sense the presence of another person, without actually seeing the individual's form. I could almost remember the character of the feeling. Who makes me feel this way?

At last I began to discern a blurry figure thirty or forty feet away, which moved closer, gradually, until I recognized who it was. Charlene! As she closed to within ten feet, I sensed a shift in my body, as though I was suddenly relaxing more completely. Simultaneously I noticed a pinkish-red energy field that encircled Charlene. Seconds later, to my amazement, I noticed an identical field around myself. When we were about five feet from each other, the relaxation in my body grew into an increased sensualness and finally into a wave of orgasmic love. I suddenly couldn't think. What was happening?

Just as our fields were about to touch, the shrill dissonance returned and I was jolted backward again, twisting out of control.

FORGIVING

As my head cleared, I gradually became aware of something cold and wet against my right cheek. Slowly I opened my eyes, the rest of my body frozen in place. For a moment the half-grown wolf looked at me and sniffed hard, his tail bristling, then he dashed into the woods as I jerked back and sat up.

In a tired stupor I retrieved my pack in the fading light and walked into the thick trees and raised my tent, afterward virtually collapsing into the sleeping bag. I struggled to stay awake, intrigued by my strange meeting with Charlene. Why had she been in the other dimension? What had drawn us together?

The next morning I awoke early and made oatmeal, wolfing it down, and then made my way carefully back to the small creek I had passed on my way up the ridge to wash my face and fill my canteen. I still felt tired, but I was also anxious to find Curtis.

Suddenly I was jolted to my feet by the sound of an explosion toward the east. That had to be Curtis, I thought, as I ran to the tent. A wave of fear passed through me as I quickly packed and headed toward the sound of the blast.

After about a half mile the woods ended abruptly at what appeared to be an abandoned pasture. Several strands of rusty barbed wire hung loosely between the trees in my path. I surveyed the open field and the line of trees and dense bush a hundred yards beyond. At that moment the bushes parted and Curtis burst through and headed in a dead run straight toward me. I waved, and he immediately recognized who I was and slowed to a fast walk. When he reached me, he carefully climbed through the barbed wire and collapsed against a tree, breathing rapidly.

"What happened?" I asked. "What did you blow up?"

He shook his head. "I couldn't do much. They're running the experiment underground. I didn't have enough explosives, and I . . . I didn't want to hurt the people inside. All I could do was blow up an outside dish antenna, which hopefully will delay them."

"How did you get close enough to do that?"

"I set the charges last night after dark. They must not expect anyone to be up here, because they have very few guards outside."

He paused for a moment as we heard the sound of trucks in the distance. "We'll have to get out of this valley," he continued, "and find some help. We don't have any choice now. They'll be coming."

"Wait a minute," I said. "I think we have a chance to stop them, but we've got to find Maya and Charlene."

His eyes widened. "Are you talking about Charlene Billings?"

"That's right."

"I know her. She used to do some contract research for the

corporation. I hadn't seen her for years, but I saw her last night going into the underground bunker. She was walking with several men, all of them heavily armed."

"Were they holding her against her will?"

"I couldn't tell," Curtis said distractedly, his ears tuned to the trucks, which now seemed to be heading in our direction. "We've got to get out of here. I know a place where we can hide until dark, but we'll have to hurry." He looked back toward the east. "I set a false trail, but it won't sidetrack them for long."

"I've got to tell you what happened," I said. "I found Wil again."

"Right, tell me on the way," he said, walking quickly. "We've got to move."

I looked out of the mouth of the cave and across the deep gorge to the opposite hillside. No movement. I listened carefully but could hear nothing. We had walked in a northeasterly direction for about a mile, and as quickly as I could, I had told Curtis what I had experienced in the other dimension, stressing my belief that Williams had been correct. We could stop this experiment if we could find the rest of the group and remember the larger Vision.

I could tell that Curtis was resisting. He had listened for a while, but then began rambling about his past association with Charlene. I was frustrated that he knew nothing that might explain what she had to do with this experiment. He also told me how he had come to know David. They had become friends, he explained, after a chance meeting had revealed many common experiences in the military.

I told him it was significant that he and I both had an association with David and that we knew Charlene.

"I don't know what it means," he had said distractedly, and I had dropped it, but I knew it was further proof that we had all come to this valley for a reason. Afterward we had walked in silence as Curtis searched for the cave. When we had found it, he backtracked and erased our tracks with dead pine branches and then had lingered outside until he was convinced we hadn't been seen.

"This soup is ready," Curtis said from behind me. I had used my camp stove and water to cook the last of my freeze-dried food. Walking over, I made us both a bowl and then sat down again at the mouth of the cave, looking out.

"So how do you think this group can build enough energy to have an effect on these people?" he asked.

"I'm not sure exactly," I replied. "We'll have to figure it out."

He shook his head. "I don't think anything like that is possible. Probably all I did with my little bit of explosives was to irritate them and put them more on guard. They'll bring more people in, but I don't think they will stop. They would have had a replacement antenna close by. Maybe I should have taken out the door. God knows I could have. But I just couldn't bring myself to do that. Charlene was inside and who knows how many others. I would have had to shorten the timer, so they would have gotten me . . . but maybe it would have been worth it."

"No, I don't think so," I said. "We're going to find the other way."

"How?"

"It'll come to us."

We heard the faint sound of the vehicles again, and simultaneously I noticed a movement on the downslope below us.

"Someone's out there," I said.

We crouched down and looked closely. The figure moved again, partially obscured by the underbrush.

"That's Maya," I said, disbelieving.

Curtis and I stared at each other for a long moment, then I moved to get up. "I'll go get her," I said.

He grabbed my arm. "Stay low, and if the vehicles close in, leave her and come back here. Don't risk being seen."

I nodded and ran carefully down the hill. When I was close enough, I stopped and listened. The trucks were still moving closer. I called out to her in a low voice. She froze for an instant, then recognized me and climbed up a rocky slope to where I stood.

"I can't believe I found you!" she said, hugging my neck.

I led the way back to the cave and helped her through the opening in the rock. She appeared exhausted and her arms were covered with scratches, some of them still bleeding.

"What happened?" she asked. "I heard an explosion, and then those trucks were everywhere."

"Did anyone see you come this way?" Curtis asked with irritation. He was up and looking outside.

"I don't think so," she said. "I was able to hide."

I quickly introduced them. Curtis nodded and said, "I think I'll take a look." He slipped out through the opening and disappeared.

I opened my pack and took out a first-aid kit. "Were you able to find your friend with the Sheriff's Department?"

"No, I couldn't even get back to town. There were Forest Service agents along all the paths back. I saw a woman I knew and gave her a note to take to him. That's all I could do."

I applied some antiseptic to a long gash across Maya's knee.

"So why didn't you leave with the woman you saw? Why did you change your mind and come back out here?"

She took the antiseptic and silently began applying it herself. Finally she spoke: "I don't know why I came back. Maybe because I kept having these memories." She looked up at me. "I want to understand what's happening here."

I sat down facing her and gave her a sketchy summary of everything that had happened since we parted, particularly the information Wil and I had received about the group process of moving past the resentment to find the World Vision.

She looked overwhelmed but seemed to accept her role. "I noticed your ankle no longer seems to be bothering you."

"Yeah, I guess it cleared up when I remembered where the problem came from."

She stared at me for a moment, then said, "There are only three of us. You said Williams and Feyman had both seen seven."

"I don't know," I replied, "I'm just glad you're here. You're the one who knows about faith and visualization."

A look of terror crossed her face.

A few moments later Curtis came back through the opening and told us he had seen nothing out of the ordinary, then sat down away from us to finish his meal. I reached over and served another plate and gave it to Maya.

Curtis leaned back and handed her a canteen. "You know," he said, "you took a hell of a risk walking around in the open like that. You could have led them right to us."

Maya glanced at me and then said defensively, "I was trying to get away! I didn't know you were up here. I wouldn't even have come this way if the birds hadn't—"

"Well, you've got to understand how much trouble we're in!" Curtis interrupted. "We still haven't stopped this experiment."

He got up and stepped outside again and sat behind a large rock near the opening.

"Why is he so mad at me?" Maya asked.

"You said you were having memories, Maya. What kind?"

"I don't know . . . of another time, I guess, of trying to stop some other violence. That's why all this is so eerie to me."

"Does Curtis seem familiar to you?"

She struggled to think. "Maybe. I don't know. Why?"

"Do you remember when I told you about seeing a vision of all of us in the past, during the Native American wars? Well, you were killed, and someone else was with you who seemed to be following your lead, and he was killed too. I think it was Curtis."

"He blames me? Oh God, no wonder he's so mad."

"Maya, can you remember anything about what you two were doing?"

She closed her eyes and tried to think.

Suddenly she looked at me. "Was a Native American also there? A shaman?"

"Yes," I said. "He was killed too."

"We were thinking about something . . ." She looked me in the eye. "No, we were visualizing. We thought we could stop the war . . . That's all I can get."

"You've got to talk to Curtis and help him work through his anger. It's part of the process of remembering."

"Are you kidding? With him this angry?"

"I'll go speak with him first," I said, standing up.

She nodded slightly and looked away. I moved to the cave's opening, crawled out, and sat down beside Curtis.

"What do you think?" I asked.

He looked at me, slightly embarrassed. "I think there's something about your friend that makes me mad."

"What are you feeling, exactly?"

"I don't know. I felt angry as soon as I saw her out there. I got the sense she might pull some blunder and expose us, or get us captured."

"Maybe killed?"

"Yeah, maybe killed!" The force in his voice surprised both of us, and he took a breath and shrugged.

"Remember when I told you about the visions I saw, of a time during the nineteenth-century Native American wars?"

"Vaguely," he muttered.

"Well, I didn't tell you then, but I think I saw you and Maya together. Curtis, you were both killed by soldiers."

He looked at the ceiling of the cave. "And you think that's why I'm angry at her?"

I smiled.

At that moment a light dissonance filled the air and we both heard the hum.

"Damn," he said. "They're firing it up again."

I grabbed his arm. "Curtis, we've got to figure out what you and Maya were trying to do back then, why you failed, and what you intended to happen differently this time."

He shook his head. "I don't know how much of all this I even believe; I wouldn't know where to begin."

"I think if you just talk with her, something will come up."

He just looked at me.

"Will you try?"

Finally he nodded and we crawled back into the cave. Maya smiled awkwardly.

"I'm sorry I've been so angry," Curtis offered. "It seems maybe I'm mad about something that occurred a long time ago."

"Forget it," she said. "I just wish we could remember what we were trying to do."

Curtis looked hard at Maya. "I seem to remember you're into healing of some kind." He glanced at me. "Did you tell me that?"

"I don't think so," I replied, "but it's true."

"I'm a physician," Maya said. "I use positive imaging and faith in my work."

"Faith? You mean you treat people from a religious perspective?"

"Well, only in a general sense. When I said faith, I meant the energy force that comes from human expectation. I work at a clinic where we're trying to understand faith as an actual mental process, as the way we help create the future."

"And how long have you been into all this?" Curtis asked.

"My whole life has prepared me to explore healing." She went on to tell Curtis the same story of her life that she had told me earlier, including her mother's tendency to worry that she would get cancer. As Maya discussed all that had happened to her, both Curtis and I asked questions. As we listened and gave her energy, the fatigue that had shown on her face began to ease, her eyes brightened, and she began to sit up straight.

Curtis asked, "You believe your mother's worry and negative vision of her future affected her health?"

"Yes. Humans seem to help draw into their lives two particular kinds of events: what we have faith in and what we fear. But we're doing it unconsciously. As a physician, I believe much can be gained by pulling the process fully into consciousness."

Curtis nodded. "But how is that done?"

Maya didn't answer. She stood up and stared straight ahead, a panicked look on her face.

"What's wrong?" I asked.

"I was just . . . I . . . see what happened during the wars."

"What was it?" Curtis asked.

She looked at him. "I remember we were there in the woods. I can see it all: the soldiers, smoke from the gunpowder."

Curtis seemed to be pulled into deep thought, obviously picking up on the memory. "I was there," he mumbled. "Why was I there?" He looked at Maya. "You brought me to that place! I knew nothing; I was just a congressional observer. You told me we could stop the fighting!"

She turned away, obviously struggling to understand. "I thought we could . . . There's a way . . . Wait a minute, we weren't alone." She turned and stared at me, an angry expression appearing on her face. "You were there, too, but you abandoned us. Why did you leave us?"

Her statement stirred the memory I had brought back earlier and told them both what I had seen, describing the others who were also there: the elders of several tribes, myself, Charlene. I explained that one elder voiced strong support of Maya's efforts, but believed the time was not right, arguing that the tribes had not yet found their correct vision. I told them another chief had exploded with rage at the atrocities perpetrated by the white soldiers.

"I couldn't stay," I told them, describing my memory of the experience with the Franciscans. "I couldn't shake the need to run. I had to save myself. I'm sorry."

Maya seemed lost in thought, so I touched her arm and said, "The elders knew it couldn't work; and Charlene confirmed that we hadn't yet remembered the ancestors' wisdom."

"Then why did one of the chiefs stay with us?" she asked.

"Because he didn't want the two of you to die alone."

"I didn't want to die at all!" Curtis snapped, looking at Maya. "You misled me."

"I'm sorry," she said. "I can't remember what went wrong."

"I know what went wrong," he said. "You thought you could stop a war just because you *wanted* to."

She gazed at him for a long moment, then looked at me. "He's right. We were visualizing that the soldiers must stop their aggression, but we had no clear picture of how that could happen. It didn't work because we didn't have all the information. Everyone was visualizing from fear, not faith. It works just like the process of healing our bodies. When we remember what we're really supposed to do in life, it can restore our health. When we're able to remember what all of humanity is supposed to do, starting right now, from this moment, we can heal the world."

"Apparently," I said, "our Birth Vision contains not only what we individually intended to do in the physical dimension but also a larger vision of what humans have been trying to do throughout history, and the details of where we are going from here and how to get there. We just have to amplify our energy and share our birth intentions, and then we can remember."

Before she could respond, Curtis jumped to his feet and moved to the cave's opening. "I heard something," he said. "Someone's out there."

Maya and I crouched beside him, straining to see. Nothing moved; then I thought I detected the rustling sound of someone walking.

"I'm going to check this out," Curtis said, moving through the opening.

I glanced at Maya. "I had better go with him."

"I'm coming too," she said.

We followed Curtis down the slope to an outcropping where we could look straight down at the gorge between the two hills. A man and a woman, partially obscured by the underbrush, were crossing the rocks below us, heading toward the west.

"That woman's in trouble!" Maya said.

"How do you know that?" I asked.

"I just know. She looks familiar."

The woman turned once and the man pushed her menacingly, exposing a pistol held in his right hand.

Maya leaned forward, looking at both of us. "Did you see that? We've got to do something."

I looked closely. The woman had light hair and was dressed in a sweatshirt and green fatigues with leg pockets. As I watched, she turned and said something to her captor, then glanced toward us, giving me a clear look at her face.

"That's Charlene," I said. "Where do you think he's taking her?"

"Who knows?" Curtis replied. "Look, I think I can help her but I have to go alone. I need both of you to stay here."

I protested but Curtis would have it no other way. We watched him as he walked back to the left and down the slope through a section of woods. From there, he crept quietly to another outcropping of rock just ten feet above the bottom of the gorge.

"They'll have to pass right by him," I told Maya.

We observed anxiously as they moved closer to the rocks. At the precise moment they had passed, Curtis bounded down the hill and leaped upon the man, knocking him to the ground and holding his throat in a peculiar fashion until he stopped moving. Charlene jumped back in alarm and gathered herself to run.

"Charlene, wait!" Curtis called. She stopped and took a cautious step forward. "It's Curtis Webber. We worked together at Deltech, remember? I'm here to help you."

She obviously recognized him and moved closer. Maya and I made our way carefully down the hill. When Charlene saw me, she froze and then ran toward my embrace. Curtis rushed up and pushed us to the ground.

"Keep down," he said. "We could be seen here."

I helped Curtis tie up Charlene's guard with a roll of tape we found in his pocket and pulled him up the slope into the forest.

"What did you do to him?" Charlene asked.

Curtis was checking his pockets. "I just knocked him out. He'll be okay."

Maya bent down to check his pulse.

Charlene turned her attention to me, reaching out for my hand. "How did you get here?" she asked.

Taking a breath, I told her about the call from her office informing me of her disappearance and about finding the sketch and coming to the valley to look for her.

She smiled. "I made that sketch intending to call you, but I left so suddenly I didn't have time . . ." Her voice trailed off as she looked deeply into my eyes. "I think I saw you yesterday, in the other dimension."

I pulled her to the side, away from the others. "I saw you too, but I couldn't communicate."

As we stared at each other, I felt my body grow lighter, a wave of orgasmic love sweeping across me, centered not in my pelvic region, but somehow around the outside of my skin. Simultaneously I seemed to be falling into Charlene's eyes. Her smile grew and I realized she must be feeling much the same way.

A movement from Curtis broke the spell, and I realized both he and Maya were staring at us.

I looked back at Charlene. "I want to tell you what's been happening," I said, then described seeing Wil again, learning about the polarization of Fear, and the group coming back, and the World Vision. "Charlene, how did you get into the Afterlife dimension?"

Her face fell. "All this is my fault. I didn't know the danger until yesterday. I'm the one who told Feyman about the Insights. Shortly after receiving your letter, I found out about another group that knew of the nine Insights, and I studied with them intensely. I had many of the same experiences you talked about. Later I came with a friend to this valley because we had heard that the sacred locations here were connected somehow with the Tenth Insight. My friend didn't experience much, but I did, so I stayed to explore. That's when I met Feyman, who employed me to teach him what I knew. From that moment forward he was with me every minute. He insisted I not call my office, for security reasons, so I wrote letters rescheduling all my appointments, only, as it turned out, I guess he was intercepting my letters. That's why everyone thought I was missing.

"With Feyman I explored most of the vortexes, especially the ones at Codder's Knoll and The Falls. He couldn't sense the energy personally, but I found out later that he was tracking us electronically and getting some sort of energy profile on me as we tuned into the locations. After that he could hone in on the area and find the exact location of the vortex electronically."

I glanced at Curtis and he nodded knowingly.

Tears filled Charlene's eyes. "He had me completely fooled. He said that he was working on a very inexpensive source of energy that will liberate everyone. He sent me to remote areas of the forest during much of the experimentation. Only later, after I confronted him, did he admit the dangers of what he was doing."

Curtis turned to face Charlene. "Feyman Carter was a chief engineer at Deltech. Do you remember?"

"No," she said, "but he's totally in control of this project. Another corporation is now involved; and they have these armed men. Feyman calls them operatives. I finally told him I was leaving, and that's when he put me under guard. When I told him he would never get away with this, he just laughed. He bragged about having someone in the Forest Service working with him."

"Where was he sending you?" Curtis asked.

Charlene shook her head. "I have no idea."

"I don't think he intended to let you live," Curtis said. "Not after telling you all that."

An anxious silence fell over the group.

"What I can't understand," Charlene said, "is why he's here in this forest in the first place. What does he want with these energy locations?"

Curtis and I met eyes again, then he said, "He's experimenting with a way of centralizing this energy source he's found by focusing on the dimensional pathways in this valley. That's why it's so dangerous."

I became aware that Charlene was staring at Maya and smiling. Maya returned the gaze with a warm expression.

"When I was at the falls," Charlene said, "I moved through into the other dimension, and all these memories rushed in." She looked at me. "After that, I was able to go back several times, even when I was under guard, yesterday." She looked at me again. "That's where I saw *you* . . ."

Charlene paused and looked back at the group. "I saw that we're all here to stop this experiment, if we can remember everything."

Maya was watching her closely. "You understood what we

wanted to do during the battle with the soldiers, and supported us," she said. "Even though you knew it couldn't work."

Charlene's smile told me she had remembered.

"We've remembered most of what happened," I said. "But so far we haven't been able to recall how we planned to do it differently this time. Can you remember?"

Charlene shook her head. "Only parts of it. I know we have to identify our unconscious feelings toward one another before we can go on." She looked into my eyes and paused. "This is all part of the Tenth Insight . . . only it hasn't been written down anywhere yet. It's coming in intuitively."

I nodded. "We know."

"Part of the Tenth is an extension of the Eighth. Only a group that's operating fully in the Eighth Insight can accomplish this kind of higher clearing."

"I'm not following you," Curtis said.

"The Eighth is about knowing how to uplift others," she continued, "knowing how to send energy by focusing on another's beauty and higher-self wisdom. This process can raise the energy level and creativity of the group exponentially. Unfortunately, many groups have trouble uplifting each other in this manner, even though the individuals involved are able to do it at other times. This is especially true if the group is work-oriented, a group of employees, for instance, or people coming together to create a unique project of some kind, because so often these people have been together before, and old, past-life emotions come up and get in the way.

"We are thrown together with someone we have to work with, and we automatically dislike them, without really knowing why. Or perhaps we experience it the other way around: the person doesn't like us, again for reasons we don't understand. The emotions that come up might be jealousy, irritation, envy, resentment, bitterness, blame—any of these. What I intuited very clearly was that no group could reach its highest potential unless the participants seek to understand and work through these emotions."

Maya leaned forward. "That's exactly what we've been doing: working through the emotions that have come up, the resentments from when we were together before."

"Were you shown your Birth Vision?" I asked.

"Yes," Charlene replied. "But I couldn't get any further. I didn't have enough energy. All I saw was that groups were forming and that I was supposed to be here in this valley, in a group of seven."

Presently the sound of another vehicle far to the north attracted our attention.

"We can't stay here," Curtis said. "We're too exposed. Let's go back to the cave."

Charlene finished the last of the food and handed me the plate. Having no extra water, I placed it in my pack dirty and sat down again. Curtis slipped through the mouth of the cave and sat down across from me beside Maya, who smiled faintly at him. Charlene sat to my left. The operative had been left outside the cave, still bound and gagged.

"Is everything okay outside?" Charlene asked Curtis.

Curtis looked nervous. "I think so, but I heard some more sounds to the north. I think we need to stay in here until dark."

For a moment we all just looked at each other, each of us obviously trying to raise our energy.

I looked at the others and told them about the process of

reaching the World Vision I had seen with Feyman's soul group. When I had concluded, I looked at Charlene and asked, "What else did you receive about this clearing process?"

"All I got," Charlene replied, "was that the process couldn't begin until we come totally back to love."

"That's easy to say," Curtis said. "The problem is doing it."

We all looked at each other again, then simultaneously realized the energy was moving to Maya.

"The key is to acknowledge the emotion, to become fully conscious of the feeling, and then to share it honestly, no matter how awkward our attempts. This brings the emotion fully into present awareness and ultimately allows it to be relegated to the past, where it belongs. That's why going through the sometimes long process of saying it, discussing it, putting it on the table, clears us, so that we're able to return to a state of love, which is the highest emotion."

"Wait a minute," I said. "What about Charlene? There may be residual emotions toward her." I looked at Maya. "I know you felt something."

"Yes," Maya replied. "But only positive feelings, a sense of gratitude. She stayed and tried to help . . ." Maya paused, studying Charlene's face. "You tried to tell us something, something about the ancestors. But we didn't listen."

I leaned toward Charlene. "Were you killed too?"

Maya answered for her. "No, she wasn't killed. She had gone to try to appeal to the soldiers one more time."

"That's right," Charlene said. "But they were gone."

Maya asked, "Who else feels something toward Charlene?"

"I don't feel anything," Curtis said.

"What about you, Charlene?" I asked. "What do you feel toward us?"

Her gaze swept across each member of the group. "There don't seem to be any residual feelings toward Curtis," she said. "And everything is positive toward Maya." Her eyes settled on mine. "Toward you I think I feel a bit of resentment."

"Why?" I asked.

"Because you were so practical and detached. You were this independent man who wasn't about to get involved if the timing wasn't perfect."

"Charlene," I said, "I'd already sacrificed myself for these Insights as a monk. I felt it would have been useless."

My protests seemed to irritate her and she looked away.

Maya reached over and touched me. "Your comment was defensive. When you respond that way, the other person doesn't feel heard. The emotion she harbors then lingers in her mind because she continues to think of ways to make you understand, to convince you. Or it goes unconscious and then there's ill feeling that dulls the energy between you two. Either way the emotion remains a problem, getting in the way. I suggest you acknowledge how she could be feeling that."

I looked at Charlene. "Oh, I do. I wish that I had helped. Maybe I could have done something, if I had had the courage."

Charlene nodded and smiled.

"How about you?" Maya asked, looking at me. "What do you feel toward Charlene?"

"I guess I feel some guilt," I said. "Not so much guilt about the war, but about now, this situation. I had been withdrawn for several months. I think if I had talked to you immediately after returning from Peru, maybe we could have stopped the experiment earlier and none of this would be happening."

No one replied.

"Are there any other feelings?" Maya asked.

We only looked at each other.

At this point, under Maya's direction, each of us focused on connecting inside, with building as much energy as we could. As I focused on the beauty around me, a wave of love swept through my body. The muted color of the cave walls and floor began to brighten and glow. Each person's face began to appear more energized. A chill ran up my spine.

"Now," Maya said, "we're ready to figure out what we intended to do this time." She again appeared to be in deep thought. "I . . . I knew this was going to happen," she said finally. "This was part of my Birth Vision. I was to lead the amplification process. We didn't know how to do this when we tried to stop the war on the Native Americans."

As she spoke, I noticed a movement behind her against the cave wall. At first I thought it was a reflection of light, but then I detected a deep shade of green exactly like the one I witnessed earlier, when observing Maya's soul group. As I struggled to focus on the foot-square blob of light, it swelled into a full holographic scene, receding into the wall itself, full of fuzzy, humanlike forms. I glanced at the others; no one seemed to see the image except me.

This, I knew, was Maya's soul group, and as soon as I had this realization, I began to receive an inflow of intuitive information. I could see her Birth Vision again, her higher intention of being born to her particular family, her mother's illness, the resulting interest in medicine, particularly the mind/body connection, and now this gathering. I clearly heard that "no group can reach its full creative power until it consciously clears and then amplifies its energy."

"Once free of the emotions," Maya was now saying, "a group can more easily move past power struggles and dramas and find its full creativity. But we have to do it consciously by finding a higher-self expression in every face."

Curtis' blank look provoked more explanation. "As the Eighth Insight reveals," Maya continued, "if we look closely at another person's face, we can cut through any facades, or ego defenses, that may be present, and find the individual's authentic expression, his or her *real* self. Ordinarily most people don't know what to focus on when talking to another. Should it be the eyes? It's hard to focus on both. So which one? Or should it be on the feature that most stands out, such as the nose or mouth?

"In truth, we are called upon to focus on the whole of the face, which with its uniqueness of light and shadow and alignment of features is much like an inkblot. But within this collection of features, one can find an authentic expression, the soul shining forth. When we focus in love, love energy is sent to this higher-self aspect of the person, and the person will seem to change before our eyes as his or her greater capabilities shift into place.

"All great teachers have always sent this kind of energy toward their students. That's why they were great teachers. But the effect is even greater with groups who interact this way with every member, because as each person sends the others energy, all of the members rise to a new level of wisdom which has more energy at its disposal, and this greater energy is then sent back to everyone else in what becomes an amplification effect."

I watched Maya, attempting to find her higher expression. No longer did she appear tired, or reluctant in any way. Instead, her features revealed a certainty and genius she had not expressed before. I glanced toward the others and saw that they were similarly focused on Maya. When I looked at her again, I noticed that she seemed to be taking on the green hue of her soul group. She was not only picking up on their knowledge; she seemed to be moving into a kind of harmony with them.

Maya had stopped speaking and was taking a deep breath. I could feel the energy shifting away from her.

"I've always known that groups could acquire a higher level of functioning," Curtis said, "especially in work settings. But I haven't been able to experience this until now . . . I know I came into this dimension to be involved in transforming business, and shifting our view of business creativity, so that we can ultimately utilize the new energy sources in the correct way and implement the Ninth Insight automation of production."

He paused in thought, then said, "I mean, business is too often labeled as the greedy villain, out of control, with no conscience. And I guess it's been exactly that in the past. But I've felt as though business, too, was moving into a spiritual awareness, and that we needed a new kind of business ethic."

At that moment I saw another movement of light, directly behind Curtis. I watched for a few seconds, then realized I was seeing the formation of his soul group as well. As with Maya's group, when I focused on the emerging image, I was again able to pick up on their collective knowledge. Curtis was born in the peak of the industrial revolution occurring just after World War II. Nuclear power had been the final triumph and shocking horror of the materialist worldview, and he had entered with a vision that technological advancement could now be made conscious and moved, in full awareness, toward its destined purpose.

"Only now," Curtis said, "are we ready to understand how to evolve business and the resulting new technology in a conscious manner; all the measures are now in place. It's not an accident that one of the most important statistical categories in economics is the productivity index: the record of how many goods and services are produced by each individual in our society. Productivity has steadily increased because of technological discoveries and the more expansive use of natural resources and energy. Through the years the individual has found ever-greater ways to create."

As he spoke, a thought came to me. At first I decided to keep it to myself, but then everyone looked my way. "Doesn't the environmental damage that economic growth is causing form a natural limit to business? We can't go on like we have, because if we do, the environment will literally fall apart. Many of the fish in the ocean are already so polluted we can't eat them. Cancer rates are increasing exponentially. Even the AMA says that pregnant women and children should not eat commercial vegetables because of the pesticide residue. If this keeps up, can you imagine what kind of world we'll be leaving our children?"

As soon as I had said this, I recalled what Joel had said earlier about the collapse of the environment. I could feel my energy falling as I felt the same Fear.

Suddenly I was hit with a burst of energy, as each of the others stared in an effort to find my authentic expression again. I quickly reestablished my inner connection.

"You're right," Curtis said, "but our response to this problem is already occurring. We've been advancing technology with a kind of unconscious tunnel vision, forgetting that we're here on an organic planet, an energy planet. But one of the most creative areas of business is the field of pollution control.

"Our problem has been trying to depend on government to police the polluters. Polluting has been against the law for a long time, but there will never be enough government regulation to prevent the illegal dumping of waste chemicals or the midnight venting of smokestacks. This polluting of the biosphere won't completely stop until an alarmed citizenry pulls out their video recorders and takes it upon themselves to catch these people in the act. In a sense, business and the employees of business must regulate themselves."

Maya leaned forward. "I see another problem with the way the economy is evolving. What about all the displaced workers who are losing their jobs as more of the economy is automated? How can they survive? We used to have a large middle class and now it is diminishing rapidly."

Curtis smiled and his eyes brightened. The image of his soul group swelled behind him. "These displaced people will survive by learning to live intuitively and synchronistically," he said. "We all have to understand: there's no going back. We're already living in the information age. Everyone will have to educate themselves the best they can, become an expert in some niche, so that they can be in the right place to advise someone else or perform some other service. The more technical the automation becomes, and the more quickly the world changes, the more we need information from just the right person arriving in our lives at just the right time. You don't need a formal education to do that; just a niche you've created for yourself through self-education.

"Yet, for this flow to be optimally established, across the economy, the stated purposes of business must shift into higher awareness. Our guiding intuitions become most clear when we approach business from an evolutionary perspective. Our questions must change. Instead of asking what product or service I can develop to make the most money, we're beginning to ask, 'What can I produce that liberates and informs and makes the world a better place, yet also preserves a delicate environmental balance?'

"A new code of ethics is being added to the equation of free enterprise. We have to come awake wherever we are and ask, 'What are we creating and does it consciously serve the overall purpose for which technology was invented in the first place: to make everyday subsistence easier, so that the prevailing orientation of life can shift from mere survival and comfort to the interchange of pure spiritual information?' Each of us has to see that we have a part in the evolution toward lower and lower subsistence costs, until finally the basic means of survival is virtually free.

"We can move toward a truly enlightened capitalism if, instead of charging as much as the market will bear, we follow a new business ethic based on lowering our prices a specified percentage as a conscious statement of where we want the economy to go. This would be the business equivalent of engaging in the Ninth Insight force of tithing."

Charlene turned to face him, her face luminous. "I understand what you're saying. You mean, if all businesses reduce prices ten percent, then everyone's cost of living, including the raw materials and supplies to the businesses themselves, will also go down."

"That's right, although some prices might go up temporarily as everyone takes into account the true cost of waste disposal and other environmental effects. Overall, though, prices will systematically decline."

"Doesn't this process already happen at times," I asked, "as a result of market forces?"

"Of course," he replied, "but it can be accelerated if we do it consciously—although as the Ninth Insight predicts, this process will be greatly enhanced by the discovery of a very inexpensive energy source. It appears as if Feyman has done that. But the energy has to be made available in the most inexpensive way possible if it is to have its most liberating impact."

As he spoke, he seemed to grow more inspired. Turning, he looked straight into my eyes. "This is the economic idea I came here wanting to contribute," he said. "I've never seen it so clearly. That's why I wanted to have the life experiences I've had; I wanted to be prepared for delivering this message."

"Do you really think enough people will reduce prices to make a difference?" Maya asked. "Especially if it takes money out of their own pockets? That seems to fly in the face of human nature."

Curtis didn't answer. Instead he looked at me, along with the others, as if I had the answer. For a moment I was silent, feeling the energy shift.

"Curtis is right," I said finally. "We'll do it anyway, even though we may give up some personal profit in the short run. None of this makes any sense at all until we grasp the Ninth and Tenth Insights. If one believes that life is just a matter of personal survival in an essentially meaningless and unfriendly world, then it makes perfect sense to focus all one's wits on living as comfortably as possible and seeing to it that one's children have the same opportunities. But if one grasps the first nine Insights and sees life as a spiritual evolution, with spiritual responsibilities, then our view completely changes.

"And once we begin to understand the Tenth, then we see the birth process from the perspective of the Afterlife, and we realize that we're all here to bring the Earth dimension into alignment with the Heavenly sphere. Besides, opportunity and success are very mysterious processes, and if we operate our economic life in the flow of the overall plan, we synchronistically meet all the other people who are doing the same thing, and suddenly prosperity opens up for us.

"We'll do it," I continued, "because individually that's where the intuition and coincidences will take us. We'll remember more about our Birth Visions and it will become clear that we intended to make a certain contribution to the world. And most important, we'll know that if we don't follow this intuition, not only will the magic coincidences and the sense of inspiration and aliveness stop, but eventually we may have to look at our actions in an Afterlife Review. We'll have to face our failure."

I stopped abruptly, noticing that Charlene and Maya were both staring wide-eyed at the space behind me. Reflexively I turned around; there was the hazy outline of my own soul group, dozens of individuals fading into the distance, again as though the walls of the cave weren't there.

"What are all of you looking at?" Curtis asked.

"It's his soul group," Charlene said. "I saw these groups when I was at the falls."

"I've seen a group behind both Maya and Curtis," I said.

Maya twisted around and looked at the space behind her. The group there flickered once, then came fully into focus.

"I don't see anything," Curtis said. "Where are they?"

Maya continued to stare, obviously seeing all of the groups. "They're helping us, aren't they? They can give us the vision we're looking for."

As soon as she made that comment, all of the groups moved away from us dramatically and became less clear.

"What happened?" Maya asked.

"It's your expectation," I said. "If you look to them for your energy, as a replacement for your own inner connection to divine energy, they leave. They won't allow a dependence. The same thing happened to me."

Charlene gave me a nod of agreement. "It happened to me too. They're like family. We're connected to them in thought, but we have to sustain our own connection with the divine source beyond them before we can link to them and pick up on what they know, which is really your own higher memory."

"They hold the memory for us?" Maya asked.

"Yes," Charlene replied, looking directly at me. She started to say something else, then stopped herself, appearing to drift off in thought. Then she said, "I'm beginning to understand what I saw in the other dimension. In the Afterlife each of us comes from a particular soul group, and these groups each have a particular angle or truth to offer the rest of humanity." She glanced at me. "For instance, you come from a group of facilitators. Do you know that? Souls that help evolve our philosophical understanding of what life is about. Everyone who belongs to this particular soul group is always trying to find the best and most comprehensive way of describing spiritual reality. You struggle with complex information, and because you're so dense, you keep pushing and exploring until you find a way to express it clearly."

I looked at her askance, which made her burst out laughing.

"It's a gift you have," she said reassuringly.

Turning to Maya, she said, "And you, Maya, your soul group is oriented toward health and well-being. They think of themselves as solidifiers of the physical dimension, keeping our cells operating optimally and full of energy, tracing and removing emotional blocks before they manifest in disease.

"Curtis' group is about transforming the use of technology, as well as our overall understanding of commerce. Throughout human history this group has been working to spiritualize our

concepts of money and capitalism, to find the ideal conceptual-
ization."

She paused, and I could already see an image of light flickering behind her.

"What about you, Charlene?" I asked. "What is your group
doing?"

"We're journalists, researchers," she replied, "working to help
people appreciate and learn from each other. What journalism is
really all about is looking deeply at the life and beliefs of the
people and organizations we cover, at their true substance and
higher expression, just the way we're looking at each other now."

I again remembered my conversation with Joel, specifically
his jaded cynicism. "It's hard to see journalists doing that," I said.

"We're not," she replied. "Not yet. But this is the ideal toward
which the profession is evolving. This is our true destiny, once
we become more secure and break free from the old worldview
in which we need to 'win' and bring energy and status our way.

"It makes perfect sense why I wanted to be born to my family.
They were all so inquisitive. I picked up on their excitement,
their need for information. That's why I was a reporter for so
long, and then joined the research firm. I wanted to help work
out the ethics of reporting and then come together with all of . . ."
She drifted away again, staring at the floor of the cave, then her
eyes widened and she said, "I know how we're bringing in the
World Vision. As we remember our Birth Visions and integrate
them together as a group, we *merge* the power of our relative soul
groups in the other dimension, which helps us remember even
more, so we finally get to the overall vision of the world."

We all stared at her, puzzled.

"Look at the whole picture," she explained. "Each person on
Earth belongs to a soul group, and these soul groups represent

the various occupational groups that exist on the planet: medical people, lawyers, accountants, computer workers, farmers, every field of human endeavor. Once people find their right work, the job that really fits them, then they are working with other members of their soul group.

"As each of us wakes up and begins to remember our Birth Vision—why we're here—the occupational groups to which we belong come more into alignment with the members of our groups in the other dimension. As this happens, each occupational group on Earth moves toward its true soul purpose, its role of service in human society."

We all continued to be spellbound.

"It's like with us journalists," she continued. "Throughout history we have been the individuals most inquisitive about what others in the culture were doing. And then a few centuries ago, we became conscious enough of ourselves to form a defined occupation. Since then we've been busy broadening our use of the media, reaching more and more people with our newscasts, that sort of thing. But like everyone else, we suffered from insecurity. We felt that to get attention and energy from the rest of humanity we had to create increasingly more sensational stories, thinking that only negativity and violence sell.

"But that's not our true role. Our spiritual role is to deepen and spiritualize our perception of other people. We see and then communicate what the various soul groups, and individuals within these groups, are doing, and what they stand for, making it easier for everyone to learn the truth others provide.

"It's the same for every occupational group; we're all awakening to our true message and purpose. And as this happens all over the planet, we're then able to go further. We can form close spiritual associations with people outside of our particular soul group, just the way we're doing here. We all shared our Birth Visions and raised our vibration together, and that transforms not only human society but the culture in the Afterlife as well.

"First, each of our soul groups comes closer into vibration with us on Earth and we with them, the two dimensions opening into each other. Because of this closure, we can begin to have communication between the dimensions. We are able to see souls in the Afterlife and pick up on their knowledge and memory more readily. That's happening with increasing frequency on the Earth."

As Charlene was speaking, I noticed the soul groups behind each of us widening and spreading out until each touched the others, forming a continuous circle around us. The convergence seemed to jolt me into an even higher awareness.

Charlene seemed to feel it too. She took a breath and then with emphasis continued. "The other thing that happens in the Afterlife is that the groups themselves come closer into resonance with each other. That's why the Earth is the primary focus of the souls in Heaven. They can't unite on their own. Over there, many soul groups remain fragmented and out of resonance with each other because they live in an imaginary world of ideas that manifests instantly and disappears just as quickly, so reality is always arbitrary. There is no natural world, no atomic structure, as we have here, that serves as a stable platform, a background stage, that is common to all of us. We affect what happens on this stage, but ideas manifest much more slowly and we must reach some agreement on what we want to happen in the future. It's this agreement, this consensus, this unity of vision on the Earth, that also pulls the soul groups together in the Afterlife dimension. That's why the Earth dimension is deemed so important. The physical dimension is where the true unification of souls is taking place!

"And it's this unification that's behind the long historical journey that humans have been taking. The soul groups in the Afterlife understand the World Vision, the vision of how the physical world can evolve and the dimensions can close, but this can only be accomplished by individuals who are born into the physical, one at a time, hoping to move the consensus Earth reality in that direction. The physical arena is the theater upon which evolution has been playing out for both dimensions, and now we're bringing it all into culmination as we remember consciously what's going on."

She pointed to us with a sweeping motion of her finger. "This is the awareness that we're remembering together, right now—and it's the awareness that other groups, just like us, are remembering all over the planet. We all have a piece of the complete Vision, and when we share what we know, and unify our soul groups, then we're ready to bring the whole picture into consciousness."

Suddenly Charlene was interrupted by a slight tremor that ran through the earth under the cave. Specks of dust fell from the ceiling. Simultaneously we heard the hum again, but this time the dissonance had disappeared; it sounded almost harmonious.

"Oh God," Curtis said. "They almost have the calibrations right. We have to go back to the bunker." He made a movement to get up, as the energy level of the group plummeted.

"Wait," I said. "What are we going to do there? We agreed that we would wait here until dark; there's still hours of daylight out there. I say we stay here. We achieved a high level of energy, but we haven't moved through the rest of the process yet. We seem to have cleared our residual emotions and amplified our energy and shared our Birth Visions, but we haven't seen the World Vision yet. I think we can do more if we remain where it's safe, and try to go further." Even as I spoke, I saw an image of all of us back in the valley again, together in the darkness.

"It's too late for that," Curtis said. "They're ready to complete the experiment. If anything can be done, we've got to go there and do it now."

I looked hard at him. "You said they were probably going to kill Charlene. If we're caught, they'll do the same to us."

Maya held her head in her hands and Curtis looked away, trying to shake off the panic.

"Well, I'm going," Curtis said.

Charlene leaned forward. "I think we should stay together."

For an instant I saw her in Native American clothing, again in the virgin woods of the nineteenth century. The image quickly faded.

Maya stood up. "Charlene is right," she said. "We have to stay together, and it might help if we can see what they're doing."

I looked out through the cave's entrance, a long, deep-seated reluctance rising in my gut. "What are we going to do with this . . . operative . . . outside?"

"We'll drag him into the cave and leave him here," Curtis said. "We'll send someone for him in the morning, if we can."

I met eyes with Charlene, then nodded agreement.

REMEMBERING
THE
FUTURE

We knelt at the top of the hill and looked carefully down at the base of a larger ridge. I could see nothing out of the ordinary in the fading light; no movement, no guards. The hum, which had persisted for most of the forty-minute walk, had now completely disappeared.

"Are you sure we're at the right place?" I asked Curtis.

"Yes," he said. "Do you see the four large boulders about fifty feet up the slope? The doorway is right beneath them, hidden in the bushes. To the right, you can just make out the top of the projection dish. It looks functional again."

"I see it," Maya said.

"Where are the guards?" I asked Curtis. "Maybe they've abandoned the site."

We observed the doorway for almost an hour, waiting for signs of activity, hesitant to move or talk much until darkness had fallen across the valley. Suddenly we heard movement behind us. Flashlights clicked on, flooding us in light, and four armed men rushed in, demanding that we raise our hands. After spending ten minutes going through our gear, they searched each of us, then moved the group down the hill and up to the bunker's entrance.

The door of the bunker swung open and Feyman charged out, loud and angry. "Are these the ones we've been looking for?" he shouted. "Where did you find them?"

One of the guards explained what had happened as Feyman shook his head and stared at us through the beams of light. He walked closer and demanded, "What are you doing here?"

"You've got to stop what you're doing!" Curtis retorted.

Feyman was struggling to recognize him. "Who are you?" The guards' flashlights settled, illuminating Curtis' face.

"Curtis Webber . . . I'll be damned," Feyman said. "You blew up our dish, didn't you?"

"Listen to me," Curtis said. "You know this generator is too dangerous to operate at these levels. You could ruin this entire valley!"

"You were always an alarmist, Webber. That's why we let you go at Deltech. I've been working on this project for too long to give up at this point. It's going to *work*—exactly as I planned."

"But why are you taking the chance? Concentrate on the smaller, house-size units. Why are you trying to increase the output so much?"

"That's none of your business. You need to keep quiet."

Curtis edged toward him. "You want to centralize the generating process so you can control it. That's not right."

Feyman smiled. "A new energy system has to be phased in. Do you think we can go overnight from energy being a substantial part of household and business costs to practically nothing? The sudden disposable income throughout the world would cause hyperinflation and then probably a massive reaction that would cast us into a depression."

"You know that's not true," Curtis replied. "Reduced energy costs would increase the efficiency of production tremendously, supplying more goods at lower costs. No inflation would occur. You're doing this for yourself. You want to centralize the production so you can control its availability and price, despite the dangers."

He stared angrily at Curtis. "You're so naive. Do you think the interests that act to control energy prices now would allow a sudden, massive shift to an inexpensive source? Of course not! It has to be centralized and packaged to work at all. And I'm going to be known for having done this! It's what I was born to do!"

"That's not true!" I blurted. "You were born to do something else, to help us."

Feyman swung around to face me. "Shut up! Do you hear me? All of you!" His eyes found Charlene. "What happened to the man I sent with you?"

Charlene looked away without responding.

"I don't have time for this!" Feyman was shouting again. "I'd suggest you worry about your personal safety right now." He paused to look us over, then shook his head and walked to one of the armed men. "Keep them here in a group until this is over. All we need is another hour. If they try to escape, shoot them."

The operative spoke briefly to the other three and they formed a perimeter encircling us at a distance of about thirty feet. "Sit down," one of them said.

We sat facing each other in the darkness. Our energy was almost totally deflated. There had been no sign of the soul groups since we left the cave.

"What do you think we should do?" I asked Charlene.

"Nothing's changed," she whispered. "We've got to build our energy again."

The darkness was now almost total, broken only by the operatives' lights sweeping back and forth across the group. I could barely make out the outlines of the others' faces, even though we were sitting in a tight circle, eight feet apart.

"We have to try to escape," Curtis whispered. "I think they will kill us."

Then I remembered the image I'd seen in Feyman's Birth Vision. He envisioned being with us in the woods, in the dark. I knew there was also another landmark in the scene, but I couldn't remember what it was.

"No," I said. "I think we need to try again here."

At that moment the air was filled with a high-pitched sound, a sound similar to the hum but, again, more in harmony, almost pleasing to the ear. Again a perceptible shimmer swept through the ground under our bodies.

"We have to increase our energy *now*!" Maya whispered.

"I don't know if I can do it here," Curtis responded.

"You have to!" I said.

"Focus on each other the way we did before," Maya added.

I tried to screen out the ominous scene around us and return to an inner state of love. Ignoring the shadows and the flickering beams of light, I focused on the beauty of the faces in the circle. As I struggled to locate the others' higher-self expression, I began to notice a shift in the light pattern around us. Gradually I could see every face and expression very clearly, as though I was looking through an infrared viewer.

"What do we visualize?" Curtis asked in desperation.

"We have to get back to our Birth Visions," Maya said. "Remember why we came."

Suddenly the ground shook violently and the sound from the experiment again took on a dissonant, grating quality.

We moved closer together and our collective thought seemed to project the image of fighting back. We knew that somehow we could marshal our forces and push back the negative and destructive attempts of the experiment. I even picked up a picture of Feyman being pushed backward, his equipment blowing up and burning, his men fleeing in terror.

Another surge in the noise disrupted my focus; the experiment was continuing. Fifty feet away, a huge pine tree snapped in half and thundered to the ground. With a ripping sound and a cloud of dust, a fissure, five feet wide, opened up between us and the guard on the right. He reeled back in horror, the beam of his flashlight swinging wild in the night.

"This isn't working!" Maya screamed.

Another tree crashed to the ground on our left as the earth slid four or five feet, knocking us flat.

Maya looked horrified and jumped to her feet. "I've got to get away from here!" she yelled, then began to run north into the darkness. The guard on that side, lying where he had been thrown by the earth's movement, rolled to his knees and caught her form in the beam of his flashlight, then raised his gun.

"No! Wait!" I screamed.

As she ran, Maya looked back, spotting the guard who was now aiming directly at her, preparing to fire. The scene seemed to shift into slow motion, and as the gun discharged, every line in her face revealed an awareness that she was about to die. But instead of the bullets ripping into her side and back, a wisp of white light darted in front of her and the bullets bore no effect. She hesitated momentarily, then disappeared into the darkness.

At the same time, sensing the opportunity, Charlene leaped

up from her position to my right and ran to the northeast, into the dust, her movement unnoticed by the guards.

I started to run but the guard who had fired at Maya turned his weapon toward me. Quickly Curtis reached out and grabbed my legs, dragging me to the ground.

Behind us, the bunker door swung open and Feyman ran to the dish antenna and furiously adjusted the keyboard. Gradually the noise began to diminish and the earth movements slowed to mere tremors.

"For God sakes!" Curtis yelled toward him. "You've got to stop this!"

Feyman's face was covered with dust. "There's nothing wrong that we can't fix," he said with eerie calm. The guards were on their feet, dusting themselves off and walking toward us. Feyman noticed that Maya and Charlene were missing, but before he could say anything, the noise returned with ear-shattering volume and the earth under us seemed to leap upward several feet, rolling everyone to the ground once more. The splintering limbs from a falling tree sent the guards scurrying toward the bunker.

"Now!" Curtis said. "Let's go!"

I was frozen. He jerked me to my feet. "We've got to move!" he yelled in my ear.

Finally my legs worked and we ran northeast in the same direction that Maya had fled.

Several more tremors reverberated under our feet and then the movements and sounds ceased. After making our way through the dark woods for several miles, our path lighted only by the rays of the moon filtering through the foliage, we stopped and huddled in a grove of small pines.

"Do you think they'll follow us?" I asked Curtis.

"Yes," he said. "They can't allow any of us to get back to

town. I would guess that they still have people stationed along the paths back."

While he was talking, a clear picture of the falls entered my mind. It was still pristine, undisturbed. The falling water, I realized, was the landmark in Feyman's vision that I had been trying to remember.

"We have to go northwest to the falls," I said.

Curtis nodded toward the north, and as silently as possible we headed in that direction, crossing the stream and carefully making our way toward the canyon. Periodically Curtis would stop and cover our tracks. During a rest, we could hear the low rumbling of vehicles from the southeast.

After another mile we began to see the moonlit canyon walls rising up into the distance. As we approached the rocky mouth, Curtis led the way across the creek. Suddenly he jumped backward in fright as someone walked around a tree from the left. The person screamed and recoiled, almost losing balance, teetering at the edge of the creek bank.

"Maya!" I yelled, realizing who it was.

Curtis recovered and lunged forward and pulled her back as rocks and gravel slid into the water.

She hugged him intensely and then reached out to me. "I don't know why I ran like that. I just panicked. I could only think to head toward the falls you told me about. I just prayed that some of you would get away too."

Leaning back against a larger tree, she took a deep breath, then asked, "What happened when the guard fired back there? How did those bullets miss me? I saw this strange streak of light."

Curtis and I looked at each other.

"I don't know," I said.

"It seemed to calm me," Maya continued, ". . . in a way I've never experienced before."

We looked at each other; no one spoke. Then, in silence, I heard the distinct sound of someone walking up ahead.

"Wait," I said to the others. "Someone's up there." We crouched down and waited. Ten minutes went by. Then, from the trees ahead, Charlene walked up and dropped to her knees.

"Thank God I found you," she said. "How did you get away?"

"We were able to run when a tree fell," I said.

Charlene looked deep into my eyes. "I thought you might head toward the falls so I walked in this direction, although I don't know if I could have found them in the dark."

Maya motioned for us, and we all moved out to a clearing where the creek went through the mouth of the canyon. Here the full light of the moon illuminated the grass and the rocks to each side.

"Maybe we're going to have another chance," she said, urging us with her hands to sit down and face each other.

"What are we going to do?" Curtis said. "We can't stay here long. They'll be coming."

I looked at Maya, thinking we should go on to the falls, but she seemed so energized that, instead, I asked, "What do you think went wrong before?"

"I don't know; maybe there are too few of us. You said there were supposed to be seven. Or perhaps there's too much Fear."

Charlene leaned toward the group. "I think we have to remember the energy we achieved when we were in the cave. We have to connect at that level again."

For several long minutes we all worked on our inner connection. Finally Maya said, "We have to give each other energy, find the higher-self expression."

I took several deep breaths and watched the faces of the others again. Gradually they became more beautiful and luminescent, and I caught sight of their authentic soul expression. Around us, the surrounding plants and rocks lit up even more, as though the moon's rays had suddenly doubled. A familiar wave of love and euphoria swept through my body and I turned to see the shimmering figures of my soul group behind me.

As soon as I saw them, my awareness seemed to expand even more and I realized that the soul groups of the others were in similar positions, although they had not yet merged.

Maya caught my eye. She was looking at me in a state of complete openness and honesty, and as I watched her, it seemed as though I could see her Birth Vision as a subtle expression on her face. She knew who she was and it beamed outward for everyone to observe. Her mission was clear; her background had prepared her perfectly.

"Feel as if the atoms in your body are vibrating at a higher level," she said.

I glanced at Charlene; on her face was the same clarity. She represented the information bearers, identifying and communicating the vital truths expressed by each person or group.

"Do you see what's happening?" Charlene asked. "We're seeing each other as we really are, at our highest level, without the emotional projections of old fears."

"I can see that," Curtis said, his face again full of energy and certainty.

No one spoke for several minutes. I closed my eyes as the energy continued to build.

"Look at that!" Charlene suddenly said, pointing at the soul groups all around us.

Each soul group was beginning to blend with the others, just as they had done at the cave. I glanced at Charlene and then at Curtis and Maya. I could now see on their faces an even fuller expression of who they were as participants in the long movement of human civilization.

"This is it!" I said. "We're reaching the next step; we're seeing a more complete vision of human history."

Before us, in a huge hologram, appeared an image of history that seemed to stretch out from the very beginning to what appeared to be a distant end. As I strained to focus, I realized that this was an image very similar to the one I had observed earlier while with my soul group—except that in this instance the story was beginning much earlier, with the birth of the universe itself.

We watched as the first matter exploded into being and gravitated into stars that lived and died and spewed forth the great diversity of elements that ultimately formed the Earth. These elements, in turn, combined in the early terrestrial environment into ever-more-complex substances until they finally leaped into organic life—life that then also moved forward, into greater organization and awareness, as if guided by an overall plan. Multicelled organisms became fishes, and fishes progressed into amphibians, and amphibians evolved into reptiles and birds and ultimately into mammals.

As we watched, a clear picture of the Afterlife dimension opened up in front of us, and I understood that an aspect of each of the souls there—in fact, a part of all of humanity—had lived through this long, slow process of evolution. We had swum as fishes, boldly crawled upon the land as amphibians, and struggled to survive as reptiles, birds, and mammals, fighting every step of the way to finally move into human form—all with intention.

We knew that through wave after wave of successive generations, we would be born into the physical plane, and no matter how long it took, we would strive to wake up, and unify, and evolve, and eventually implement on Earth the same spiritual culture that exists in the Afterlife. Certainly the journey would be difficult, even torturous. With the first intuition to awaken, we would sense the Fear of aloneness and separation. Yet we would not go back to sleep; we would fight through the Fear, relying on the dim intuition that we weren't alone, that we were spiritual beings with a spiritual purpose on the planet.

And, following the urge of evolution, we would gravitate together into larger, more complex social groupings, differentiating into more diverse occupations, overcoming a need to defeat and conquer each other, and eventually implement a democratic process through which new ideas could be shared and synthesized and evolved into ever-better truths. Gradually our security would come from inside us, as we progressed from an expression of the divine in terms of nature gods to the divine as one father God outside ourselves to a final expression as the Holy Spirit within.

Sacred texts would be intuited and written, offering heartfelt symbolic expression of our relationship and future with this one deity. Visionaries from both East and West would clarify that this Holy Spirit was always there, always accessible, waiting only for our ability to repent, to open, to clear the blocks that prevent a full communion.

Over time, we knew, our urge to unify and share would expand until we sensed a special community, a deeper association with others who shared a particular geographical location on the planet, and the human world would began to solidify into political nation-states, each holding a unique viewpoint. Soon after would come an explosion of trade and commerce. The scientific method would be instituted, and the resulting discoveries would initiate a period of economic preoccupation and the great secular expansion known as the Industrial Revolution.

And once we developed a web of economic relationships around the globe, we would begin to further awaken and to remember our full spiritual nature. The Insights would gradually permeate human consciousness and we would evolve our economy into a form compatible with the Earth, and, finally, begin to move beyond the last fearful polarization of forces toward a new spiritual worldview on the planet.

Here I momentarily glanced at the others. Their faces told me that they had shared this vision of Earth's history. In one brief revelation we had grasped how human consciousness had progressed from the beginning of time right to the present moment.

Suddenly the hologram focused on the polarization in great detail. All humans on the Earth were migrating into two conflicting positions: one pushing toward a vague but ever-clearer image of transformation, and the other resisting, sensing that important values contained in the old view were being lost forever.

We could see that in the Afterlife dimension, it was known that this conflict would be our greatest challenge to the spiritualization of the physical dimension—particularly if the polarization grew extreme. In this case, both sides would entrench into an irrational projection of evil onto the other, or worse, might believe the literal interpreters of the end-times prophecies and begin to think the coming future was beyond their influence and therefore give up completely.

To find the World Vision and resolve the polarization, we could see that our Afterlife intention was to discern the deeper truths of these prophecies. As with all the Scriptures, the visions in Daniel and Revelation were divine intuitions coming from the

Afterlife into the physical plane, and so must be understood as draped in the symbolism of the seer's mind, much like a dream. We would focus on the symbolic meaning. The prophecies envisioned an eventual end to the human story on Earth; but an "end" that, for *believers,* would be quite different from the one experienced by nonbelievers.

Those in the latter group were seen to experience an end of history that would begin with great catastrophes and environmental disasters and collapsing economies. Then, at the height of the fear and chaos, a strong leader would emerge, the Antichrist, who would offer to restore order, but only if individuals would agree to give up their liberties and carry the "mark of the beast" upon their bodies in order to participate in the automated economy. Eventually this strong leader would declare himself a god and take by force any country that resisted his rule, at first making war on the forces of Islam, then on the Jews and Christians, ultimately casting the whole world into a fiery Armageddon.

For believers, on the other hand, the scriptural prophets predicted a much more pleasant end to history. Remaining true to the spirit, these believers would be given spiritual bodies and be raptured into another dimension called the New Jerusalem, but would be able to go back and forth into the physical. Eventually, at a certain point in the war, God would fully return to end the fighting, restore the Earth, and implement a thousand years of peace where there would be no sickness or death, and everything would be transformed, even the animals of the world, who would no longer eat meat. Instead, "The wolf shall dwell with the lamb . . . and the lion shall eat straw like the ox."

Maya and Curtis caught my eye, and then Charlene looked up; we all seemed to sense, at once, the core meaning of the prophecies. What the end-times seers were receiving was an intuition that in our time, two distinctive futures would be opening before us. We could choose either to languish in the Fear, believing that the world is moving into a Big Brother style of automation and social decay and ultimate destruction . . . or we could follow the other path and consider ourselves the believers who can overcome this nihilism and open to the higher vibrations of love, where we are spared the apocalypse and can enter a new dimension in which we invite the spirit, through us, to create just the utopia the scriptural prophets envisioned.

Now we could see why those in the Afterlife felt that our interpretation of these prophecies was key to resolving the polarization. If we decide that these Scriptures mean that the destruction of the world is inevitable, written unalterably into God's plan, the effect of such a belief would be to create this very outcome.

Clearly we had to choose the path of love and believing. As I had seen earlier, the polarization was not intended to be so severe. It was known in the Afterlife that each side represented a part of the truth that could be integrated and synthesized into the new, spiritual worldview. Further, I saw that this synthesis would be a natural outgrowth of the Insights themselves, especially the Tenth Insight, and of the special groups that would begin to form all over the world.

Suddenly the hologram raced forward and I felt another expansion of consciousness. I knew that we were now moving into the next step of the process: the actual remembrance of how we intended to become believers and accomplish this prophesied utopian future. We were finally remembering the *World Vision*!

As we watched, we first saw the Tenth Insight groups forming all over the planet, reaching a critical mass of energy, and then learning to project this energy in such a way that the entrenched sides of the polarization immediately began to lighten and ease, overcoming the Fear. Especially affected would be the technological controllers, who would remember themselves and give up their last efforts to manipulate the economy and seize power.

The result of the projected energy would be an unprecedented wave of awakening and remembrance and cooperation and personal involvement, and a virtual explosion of newly inspired individuals, all of whom would begin to fully recall their Birth Visions and follow their synchronistic path into exactly the right positions within their culture.

The scene shifted to images of decaying inner cities and forgotten rural families. Here we could see a new consensus forming on how to intervene in the cycle of poverty. No longer would intervention be conceived in terms of government programs or merely in terms of education and jobs; the new approach would be deeply spiritual, for the structures of education were already in place; what was missing was the ability to break free from the Fear and to overcome the hellish diversions set up to ward off the anxiety of poverty.

In this regard I saw a sudden surge of private outreach surrounding each family and each child in need. Waves of individuals began to form personal relationships, beginning with those who saw the family every day—merchants, teachers, police officers on the beat, ministers. This contact was then expanded by other volunteers working as "big brothers," "big sisters," and tutors—all guided by their inner intuitions to help, remembering their intention to make a difference with one family, one child. And all carrying the contagion of the Insights and the crucial message that no matter how tough the situation, or how entrenched the self-defeating habits, each of us can wake up to a memory of mission and purpose.

As this contagion continued, incidents of violent crime began mysteriously to decrease across human culture; for, as we saw clearly, the roots of violence are always frustration and passion and fear scripts that dehumanize the victim, and a growing inter-action with those carrying a higher awareness was now beginning to disrupt this mind-set.

We saw a new consensus emerging toward crime that drew from both traditional and human-potential ideas. In the short run, there would be a need for new prisons and detention facili-ties, as the traditional truth was recognized that returning offend-ers to the community too soon, or leniently letting perpetrators go in order to give them another chance, reinforced the behavior. Yet, at the same time, we saw an integration of the Insights into the actual operation of these facilities, introducing a wave of pri-vate involvement with those incarcerated, shifting the crime cul-ture and initiating the only rehabilitation that works: the contagion of remembering.

Simultaneously, as increasingly more people awakened, I saw millions of individuals taking the time to intervene in conflict at every level of human culture—for we all were reaching a new understanding of what was at stake. In every situation where a husband or wife grew angry and lashed out at the other, or where addictive compulsions or a desperate need for approval led a youthful gang member to kill, or where people felt so restricted in their lives that they embezzled or defrauded or manipulated others for gain; in all these situations, there was someone per-fectly placed to have prevented the violence but who had *failed* to act.

Surrounding this potential hero were perhaps dozens of other friends and acquaintances who had likewise failed, because they didn't convey the information and ideas that would have created the wider support system for the intervention to have taken place. In the past perhaps, this failure could have been rationalized, but no longer. Now the Tenth Insight was emerging and we knew that the people in our lives were probably souls with whom we had had long relationships over many lifetimes, and who were now counting on our help. So we are compelled to act, compelled to be courageous. None of us wants to have failure on our conscience, or have to bear a torturous Life Review in which we must watch the tragic consequences of our timidity.

As the scenes rushed past, we saw this burgeoning awareness motivating activity toward other social problems as well. We could see an image of the world's rivers and oceans, and again I observed a synthesis of the old and new which, while admitting the often capricious behavior of government bureaucracy, also raised to a new level of priority the human desire to safeguard the environment, initiating a surge of private intervention.

The wisdom was emerging that, as with the problem of poverty and violence, the crime of pollution always has compliant bystanders. People who would never consciously pollute the environment themselves worked with or knew about others whose projects or business practices damaged the planet's biosphere.

These were the people who in the past had said nothing, perhaps because of job insecurity or because they felt alone in their opinion. Yet now, as they awakened and realized they were in exactly the right position to take action, we watched them rally public opinion against the polluters—whether it was the dumping of industrial wastes into the ocean in the dead of night, venting excess oil from a tanker far at sea, secretly using banned insecticides on commercial vegetable plots, leaving the scrubbers off at an industrial plant between inspections, or faking the research on the dangers of a new chemical. No matter what the crime, now there would be *inspired* witnesses who would feel the support of grassroots organizations offering rewards for such information, and who would take their camcorders and expose the crime themselves.

Similarly we observed the environmental practices of governments themselves being exposed, especially regarding policies toward public lands. For years, it would be discovered, governmental agencies had sold mining and logging rights on some of the most sacred places on Earth, at below-market rates, as political favors and paybacks. Majestic, cathedral forests, belonging to the public, had been unbelievably pillaged and clear-cut in the name of proper forest management—as though planting rows of pine trees would replace the diversity of life, and energies, inherent in a hardwood forest that had matured for centuries.

Yet it would be the emerging spiritual awareness that would finally force an end to such disgrace. We watched a new coalition forming, made up of old-view hunters and nostalgic history buffs and those who perceived the natural sites as sacred portals. This coalition would finally sound the alarm that would save the few remaining virgin forests in Europe and North America, and begin to protect on a larger scale the essential rain forests in the tropical regions of the world. It would be commonly understood that every remaining site of beauty must be saved for the benefit of future generations. Cultivated plant fibers would replace the use of trees for lumber and paper, and the remaining public land would all be protected from exploitation and used to supply the exploding demand to visit such unspoiled and energizing areas of nature. At the same time, as intuition and awareness and remembering expanded, the developed cultures would finally turn to the native peoples of the world with a new respect and appreciation, eager to integrate a mystical redefinition of the natural world.

The holographic scene moved forward again, and I could see the wave of spiritual contagion permeating every aspect of culture. Just as Charlene had foreseen earlier, every occupational group was beginning consciously to shift its customary practice toward a more intuitive and ideal level of functioning, finding its spiritual role, its vision of true service.

Medicine, led by individual practitioners who focused on the spiritual/psychological genesis of disease, was moving from the mechanical treatment of symptoms toward prevention. We could see the legal profession moving from the self-serving methods of creating conflict, and obscuring truth in order to win, into its true role of resolving conflict in the most "win-win" manner possible. And just as Curtis had seen, everyone involved in business, industry by industry, was shifting into an enlightened capitalism, a capitalism oriented not just to profits, but to filling the evolving needs of spiritual beings, and making these products available at the lowest possible prices. This new business ethic would produce a grassroots deflation, initiating a systematic evolution toward an eventual full automation—and ultimately the free availability—of the basic necessities of life, liberating humans to engage in the spiritual "tithe" economy envisioned in the Ninth Insight.

As we continued to watch, the scenes accelerated forward, and we could see individuals remembering their spiritual missions at increasingly younger ages. Here we could see the precise understanding that would soon embody the new spiritual worldview. Individuals would come of age and remember themselves as souls born from one dimension of existence into another. Although memory loss during the transition would be expected, recapturing pre-life memory would become an important early goal of education.

As youths, our teachers would first guide us through the early experience of synchronicity; urge us to identify our intuitions to study certain subjects, to visit particular places, always looking for higher answers as to why we were pursuing these particular paths. As the full memory of the Insights emerged, we would find ourselves involved with certain groups, working on particular projects, bringing in our full vision of what we had wanted to do. And finally we would recover the underlying intention behind our lives. We would know that we came here to raise the vibratory level of this planet, to discover and protect the beauty and energy of its natural sites, and to ensure that all humans had access to these special locations, so that we could continue to increase our energy, ultimately instituting the Afterlife culture here in the physical.

Such a worldview would especially shift the way we looked at other people. No longer would we see human beings merely in the racial dress or national origin of one particular lifetime. Instead, we would see others as brother or sister souls, engaged, like us, in a process of coming awake and of spiritualizing the planet. It would become known that the settling of certain souls into various geographical locations on the planet had occurred with great meaning. Each nation was, in fact, an enclave of specific spiritual information, shared and modeled by its citizens, information waiting to be learned and integrated.

As I watched the future unfold, I could see that a world political unity, envisioned by so many, was finally being achieved—not by forcing all nations into subservience to one political body, but rather through a grassroots acknowledgment of our spiritual similarities while treasuring our local autonomy and cultural differences. As with individuals interacting in a group, each member of the family of nations was being recognized for this culture truth represented to the world at large. Before us, we saw Earth's political struggles, so often violent, shifting into a war of words. As the tide of remembrance continued to sweep the planet, all humans began to understand that our destiny was to discuss and compare the perspectives of our relative religions and, while honoring the best of their individual doctrines at the personal level, ultimately to see that each religion supplemented the others and to integrate them into a synthesized global spirituality.

We could see clearly that these dialogues would result in the rebuilding of a grand temple in Jerusalem, jointly occupied by all the major religions—Jewish, Christian, Islamic, Eastern, even the de facto religion of secular idealism, represented by those economic enclaves in China and Europe who thought primarily in terms of a pantheistic economic utopia. Here, ultimate spiritual perspective would be debated and discussed. And in this war of words and energy, at first the Islamic and the Jewish perspectives would hold center stage, then the Christian perspective would be compared and integrated, along with the inner vision of the Eastern religions.

We saw the awareness of humanity entering another level, with the collective human culture progressing from primarily the sharing of economic information to the synchronistic exchange of spiritual truths. As this occurred, certain individuals and groups would begin to reach levels approaching that of the Afterlife dimension and would disappear to the larger majority remaining on Earth. These select groups would walk intentionally into the other dimension, yet would learn to go back and forth—just as the Ninth Insight predicts and the scriptural prophets saw. Yet, after this Rapture began, those left on Earth would understand what was occurring and accept their role in remaining in the physical, knowing that they would soon follow.

Now it was time for the secular idealists to proclaim their truths on the temple steps. At first their energetic thrust into Jerusalem would come from Europe with its primarily secular vision, with one strong leader proclaiming the spiritual importance of secular matters. This perspective would be met strongly by the determined "otherworldly" spiritualism of the Muslims and the Christians. But then this conflict of energy would be mediated and later synthesized into one by the inner spiritual emphasis of the Eastern perspective. By then, the last attempts of the controllers, who had once conspired to create a tyrannical society of chips and robots and forced compliance, would have been won over by the contagion of awakening. And this last synthesis would open everyone to the final infusion of the Holy Spirit. We saw clearly that through this Middle Eastern dialogue of energy integration, history had fulfilled the scriptural prophecies in a *symbolic and verbal* manner, avoiding the physical apocalypse expected by the literalists.

Suddenly our focus shifted to the Afterlife dimension, and here we could see with great clarity that our intention all along was not merely to create a New Earth, but a New Heaven as well. We watched as the effect of the World Vision remembrance transformed not only the physical dimension but also the Afterlife. During the raptures on Earth, the soul groups would also have been rapturing toward the physical, completing the transfer of energy into the expanded physical dimension.

Here the full reality of what was happening in the historical process became apparent. From the beginning of time, as our memory opened, energy and knowledge had systematically moved from the Afterlife dimension into the physical. At first, the soul groups in the Afterlife had borne full responsibility for maintaining the intention and envisioning the future, helping us to recall what we wanted to do, giving us energy.

Then, as consciousness on Earth progressed and the population increased, the balance of energy and responsibility had slowly shifted toward the physical dimension, until, at this point in history, when enough energy had shifted and the World Vision was being remembered, the full power and responsibility for believing and creating the intended future would be shifting from the Afterlife to the souls on Earth, to the newly forming groups, to us!

At this point, we have to carry the intent. And that's why it now fell to us to resolve the polarization and to help shift the particular individuals, right here in this valley, who were still caught in the Fear and who felt justified in manipulating the economy for their own purposes, justified in seizing control of the future.

At exactly the same time, all four of us glanced at each other in the darkness, the hologram still surrounding us, the soul groups still merged in the background, glowing brightly. Then I noticed a huge hawk fly onto a limb ten feet above the group and gaze down at us. Beneath it, less than five feet away, a rabbit hopped to within three feet of my right elbow and stopped, followed seconds later by a bobcat, who sat directly beside it. What was happening?

Abruptly a silent vibration tingled my solar plexus; the experiment had been reactivated!

"Look over there!" Curtis yelled.

Fifty yards away, barely distinguishable in the moonlight, was a narrow fissure, shaking the bushes and small trees, extending slowly in our direction.

I looked at the others.

"It's up to us now," Maya shouted. "We have enough of the Vision now; we can stop them."

Before we could act, the earth under us shook violently and the fissure accelerated toward us. Simultaneously several vehicles pulled to a stop in the underbrush, their lights shining through fuzzy silhouettes made by the trees and dust. Unafraid, I maintained my energy and focused again on the hologram.

"The Vision will stop them," Maya yelled again. "Don't let the Vision go! Hold it!"

Embracing the image of the future before us, I again felt the group marshal energy toward Feyman, as if holding our intention like a giant wall against his intrusion, imaging his group being pushed back by the energy, fleeing in terror.

I glanced at the crevice still racing toward us, confident it would soon stop. It accelerated instead. Another tree fell. Then another. As it sped into the group, I lost my concentration and rolled backward, choking on the dust.

"It's still not working!" I heard Curtis yell.

I felt as if it was all happening again. "Up this way," I shouted, struggling to see in the sudden darkness. As I ran, I could barely make out the dim outlines of the others; they were veering away from me to the east.

I climbed up the stony ridge that formed the left wall of the canyon and didn't stop until I was a hundred yards away. Kneeling in the rocks, I looked out into the night. Nothing moved, but I could hear Feyman's men talking at the canyon entrance. Quietly I made my way farther up the slope, angling northwest, still watching carefully for any sign of the others. Finally I found a way to climb down to the canyon floor again. Still no movement anywhere.

Then, as I began to walk north again, someone suddenly grabbed me from behind.

"What—" I yelled.

"Shssssssss," a voice whispered. "Be quiet. It's David."

HOLDING
THE
VISION

I turned and looked at him in the moonlight, observing the long hair, the scarred face.

"Where are the others?" he whispered.

"We were separated," I replied. "Did you see what happened?"

He moved his face closer. "Yes, I was watching from the hill. Where do you think they'll go?"

I thought for a moment. "They'll head toward the falls."

He motioned for me to follow and we started in that direction. After several minutes had passed, he glanced back as he walked and said, "When you were sitting together at the entrance back there, your energy pooled, and then swelled far out into the valley. What were you doing?"

In an attempt to explain, I summarized the whole story: finding Wil and entering the other dimension; seeing Williams and running into Joel and Maya; and especially meeting Curtis and trying to bring in the World Vision to defeat Feyman.

"Curtis was back there with you at the mouth of the canyon?" David asked.

"Yes, and Maya and Charlene, although I think there are supposed to be seven of us . . ."

He gave me another quick glance, almost chuckling. All of the tense, pent-up anger he had displayed in town seemed to have completely disappeared. "So you found the ancestors too, didn't you?"

I hurried up to walk beside him. "You reached the other dimension?"

"Yes, I saw my soul group and witnessed my Birth Vision, and just as you, I remembered what happened before, that we've all come back to bring in the World Vision. And then—I don't know how—when I was watching all of you back there in the moonlight, it was as if I was with you, was part of your group. I saw the World Vision around me." He had stopped in the shadow of a large tree that blocked the moon, his face rigid and cast back.

I turned to face him. "David, when the group of us were together back there, and we brought in the World Vision, why didn't it stop Feyman?"

He moved forward into the light and immediately I recognized him as the angry chief who had rebuked Maya. Then his rock-hard expression shifted and he burst out laughing.

"The key aspect of this Vision," he said, "is not the mere experience of it, although that's hard enough. It's how we *project* this Vision of the future, how we *hold it* for the rest of humanity. That's what the Tenth Insight is really all about. You didn't hold the Vision for Feyman and the others in a way that would help them wake up." He looked at me a moment longer, then said, "Come on, we have to hurry."

After we had traveled perhaps half a mile, a bird of some kind cried out toward our right, and David stopped abruptly.

"What was that?" I asked.

He cocked his head as the cry again filled the night. "That's a screech owl, signaling the others that we are here."

I gave him a blank expression, remembering how strange the animals had been acting ever since I arrived in the valley.

"Does anyone in that group know the animal signs?" he asked.

"I don't know; maybe Curtis?"

"No, he's too scientific."

I then remembered that Maya had mentioned following the sounds of birds when she had found us in the cave. "Perhaps Maya!"

He looked at me questioningly. "The physician you mentioned, who uses visualization in her work?"

"Yes."

"Good. That's perfect. Let's do what she does and pray."

I turned and looked at him as the owl cried out again. "What?"

"Let's . . . visualize . . . that she remembers the gift of the animals."

"What is the gift of the animals?"

A trace of anger flashed across his face, and he paused for a moment, closing his eyes, obviously trying to shake off the emotion. "Haven't you understood that when an animal shows up in our lives, it is a coincidence of the highest order?"

I told him about the rabbit and the flock of crows and the hawk, which had shown up as I had first entered the valley, and then about the bobcat cub, the eagle, and the young wolf that had appeared later. "Some of them even showed up when we saw the World Vision."

He nodded expectantly.

"I knew something significant was happening," I said, "but I didn't know exactly what to do except to follow some of them. Are you saying that all these animals had a message for me?"

"Yes, that's exactly what I'm saying."

"How do I know what the message is?"

"It's easy. You know because of the particular *kind* of animal you are attracting at any one time. Each species that crosses our paths tells us something about our situation, what part of ourselves we must call upon to handle the circumstances we face."

"Even after everything that's happened," I said, "that's hard to believe. A biologist would say animals are primarily robots, operating on dumb instinct."

"Only because animals reflect our own level of consciousness and expectation. If our level of vibration is low, the animals will merely be there with us, performing their usual ecological functions. When a skeptical biologist reduces animal behavior to mindless instinct, he sees the restriction that he himself has put upon the animal. But as our vibration shifts, the actions of the animals that come to us become ever more synchronistic, mysterious, and instructional."

I just stared.

Squinting, he said, "The hare that you saw was pointing out a direction for you both physically and emotionally. When I talked to you in town, you seemed depressed and fearful, as though you were losing faith in the Insights. If you watch a wild rabbit for a long time, you can perceive that it models how to really face our fear, so that we can later move past it into creativity and abundance. A rabbit lives in close proximity to animals that feed on it, but it handles the fear and stays there and is still very fertile and productive and upbeat. When a rabbit appears in our lives, it is a signal to find the same attitude within ourselves. This was the message to you; its presence meant you had the opportunity to remember the medicine of rabbit and to fully look at your own fear and move beyond. And because it occurred during the beginning of your trip, it set the tone of your whole adventure. Hasn't your trip been both fearful and abundant?"

I nodded.

He added, "Sometimes it means that the abundance can be of a romantic nature too. Have you met anyone?"

I shrugged, remembering the new energy I had felt with Charlene. "Maybe, in a way. What about the crows I saw and the hawk that I followed when I found Wil?"

"Crows are the holders of the laws of spirit. Spend time with crows and they will do amazing things that always increase our perception of spiritual reality. Their message was to open up, to remember the spiritual laws that were presenting themselves to you in this valley. Seeing them should have prepared you for what was to come."

"And the hawk?"

"Hawks are alert, and observant, ever vigilant for the next bit of information, the next message. Their presence means that it is important at that time to increase our alertness. Often they signal that a messenger is close." He cocked his head.

"You mean, it was foretelling the presence of Wil?"

"Yes."

David went on to explain why the other animals I had seen had been drawn my way. Cats, he told me, implore us to remember our ability to intuit and to self-heal. The bobcat cub's message, arriving as it did, just before meeting Maya, was to signal that an opportunity to heal was near. Similarly an eagle soars to great heights, and represents an opportunity to actually *venture* into the higher realms of the spirit world. When I saw the eagle on the ridge, David said, I should have prepared for seeing my soul group and for understanding more of my own destiny. Lastly, he told me, the young wolf was there to energize and awaken my latent instinct for courage and my ability to teach, so that I might find the words to help bring together the other members of the group.

"So the animals represent," I said, "parts of ourselves we need to get in touch with."

"Yes, aspects of ourselves that we developed when we were those animals during the course of evolution, but have lost."

I thought of the vision of evolution I had witnessed at the canyon entrance with the group. "You're speaking of the way life progressed forward, species by species?"

"We were there," David continued. "Our consciousness moved through each animal as it represented the end point of life's development and then leaped to the next. We experienced the way each species views the world, which is an important aspect of the complete spiritual consciousness. When a particular animal comes around, that means we're ready to integrate its consciousness into our waking awareness again. And I'll tell you something: there are some species that we aren't even close to catching up with. That's why it's so important to preserve every life-form on this Earth. We want them to endure not just because they are a part of the balanced ecosphere, but because they represent aspects of ourselves that we're still trying to remember."

He paused for a moment, looking out into the night.

"This is also true of the rich diversity of human thought, represented by the various cultures around the planet. None of us knows exactly where the current truth of human evolution re-sides. Each culture around the world has a slightly different worldview, a particular mode of awareness, and it takes the best of all cultures, integrated together, to make a more ideal whole."

An expression of sadness crossed his face. "It's too bad that four hundred years had to pass before the real integration of the European and Native cultures could begin. Think of what has happened. The Western mind lost touch with the mystery and reduced the magic of the deep woods to lumber and the mystery of wildlife to pretty animals. Urbanization has isolated the great majority of people, so we now think a journey into nature is a stroll on the golf course. Do you realize how few of us have expe-rienced the mysteries of the wilderness?

"Our National Parks represent all that is left of the great ca-thedral forests and rich plains and high deserts that once charac-terized this continent. There are too many of us now for the wild areas that still exist. In many parks there are waiting lists over a year long. And still, the politicians seem bent on selling off more and more of the public lands. Most of us are forced to draw from decks of animal cards to see what animal signs are coming into our lives, instead of being able to take quests into the truly wild areas of the world to experience the real thing."

Suddenly the screech owl's cry erupted so close that the sound made me jump involuntarily.

David was squinting impatiently. "Can we pray now?"

"Listen," I said, "I don't know what you mean. Do you want to pray or visualize?"

He tried to calm his voice. "Yes, I'm sorry. Impatience seems to be a residual emotion I have with you." He took a breath. "The Tenth Insight—learning to have faith in our intuitions, remembering our birth intention, holding the World Vision—all of it is about understanding the essence of real *prayer*.

"Why does every religious tradition assume a form of prayer? If God is the one, all-knowing, all-powerful God, then why would we have to beseech his help or impel him to do something? Why wouldn't he just set up commandments and covenants and judge us accordingly, taking direct action when *he* wanted to, not us? Why would we have to ask for his special intervention? The answer is that when we pray in the correct fashion, we are not asking God to do something. God is inspiring us to act in his place to enact his will on the Earth. We are the emissaries of the divine on this planet. True prayer is the method, the visualization, that God expects us to use in discerning his will and implementing it in the physical dimension. His kingdom come, his will be done, on Earth, as it is in heaven.

"In this sense, every thought, every expectation—all of what we visualize happening in the future—is a prayer, and tends to create that very future. But no thought or desire or fear is as strong as a vision that is in alignment with the divine. That's why bringing in the World Vision, and holding it, is important: so we will know what to pray for, what future to visualize."

"I understand," I said. "How do we help Maya become aware of the owl?"

"What did she say to do when she talked to you about healing?"

"She said we should visualize patients remembering what they intended to do with their lives but still hadn't done. She said that real healing springs from a renewed sense of what one wants to do once health is regained. When they remember, then we can also join them in holding this more specific plan."

"Let's do the same now," David said. "Hopefully, her original intention was to follow the sound of this bird."

David closed his eyes, and I followed his lead, trying to visualize an image of Maya awakening to what she was supposed to do. After a few minutes I opened my eyes and David was staring at me. The owl screamed again right above our heads.

"Let's go," he said.

Twenty minutes later we were standing on the hill above the falls. The owl had followed, calling out periodically, and had stationed itself fifty feet to our right. In front of us, the pool glistened in the moonlight, muted only by wisps of fog that drifted along its surface. We waited for ten or fifteen minutes without speaking.

"Look! There!" David said, pointing.

Among the rocks to the right of the pool I could make out several figures. One of them looked up and saw us; it was Charlene. I waved and she recognized me. Then David and I made our way down the rocky slope to where they were standing.

Curtis was ecstatic at seeing David, grabbing his arm. "We'll stop these people now." For a moment they looked at each other in silence, then Curtis introduced Maya and Charlene.

I met eyes with Maya. "Did you have any trouble finding your way here?"

"At first, we were confused and lost in the darkness, but then I heard the owl and I knew."

"The presence of an owl," David said, "means that we have the opportunity to see through any possible deception by others, and if we avoid the tendency to harm or lash out, we can, like the owl, cut through the darkness to hold a higher truth."

Maya was watching David closely. "You look familiar," Maya said. "Who are you?"

He looked at her questioningly. "You were told my name. It's David."

She grabbed his hand gently. "No, I mean who are you to me, to us?"

"I was there," he said, "during the wars, but I was so full of hatred for the whites that I didn't support you; I didn't even listen to you."

"We're doing it differently now," I said.

David glared at me reflexively, then caught himself and softened, as he had before. "Back in that war, I had even less respect for you than the others. You wouldn't take a stand. You ran away."

"It was fear," I replied.

"I know."

For several more minutes everyone talked with David about the emotions we were feeling, discussing everything we could remember about the tragedy of the war on the Native Americans. David went on to explain that his soul group was made up of mediators and that he had come this time to work through his anger at the European mentality, and then to work for the spiritual recognition of all indigenous cultures and the inclusion of all people.

Charlene glanced at me, then turned to David. "You're the fifth member of this group, aren't you?"

Before he could answer, we felt a vibration racing through the ground under our feet; it sent irregular ripples across the surface of the pool. Accompanying the tremor was another eerie melodious whine that filled the forest. Out of the corner of my eye I saw flashlights moving on the hill fifty feet above us.

"They're here!" Curtis whispered.

I turned to see Feyman at the edge of an overhang directly above our heads; he was adjusting a small dish antenna on what looked like a portable computer.

"They're going to focus on us and try to fine-tune the generator that way," Curtis said. "We've got to get out of here."

Maya reached over and touched his arm. "No, please, Curtis, maybe it will work this time."

David moved closer to Curtis, then said lowly, "It can work."

Curtis stared at him for a moment, then finally nodded his agreement, and we began to raise our energy again. As in the two previous attempts, I began to see higher-self expressions on every face, and then our soul groups appeared and merged into a circle around us, including for the first time the members of David's group. As the memory of the World Vision returned, we were again pulled into the overall intent to transfer energy and knowledge and awareness into the physical dimension.

Also, as before, we saw the fearful polarization occurring in our time, and the panoramic vision of the positive future that would succeed it once the special groups formed and learned how to intercede, how to *hold the Vision*.

Suddenly another tremor shook the ground violently.

"Stay with the Vision," Maya shouted. "Hold the image of how the future can be."

I heard a fissure tear through the ground to my right, but I kept my concentration. In my mind I again saw the World Vision as a force of energy that was emanating outward from our group in all directions and pushing Feyman back away from us, defeating the energy of his Fear vision. To my left, a huge tree ripped from its roots and crashed to the ground.

"It's still not working," Curtis shouted, jumping to his feet.

"No, wait," David said. He had been deep in thought, and now he reached out and grabbed Curtis, pulling him down beside him. "Don't you see what's wrong?! We're treating Feyman and the others as if they are enemies, trying to push them back. Doing that actually strengthens them, because they have something to fight against. Rather than fighting them with the Vision, we have to include Feyman and the operatives in what we're visualizing. In reality, there are no enemies; we're all souls in growth, waking up. We have to project the World Vision toward them as though they are just like us."

I suddenly recalled seeing Feyman's Birth Vision. Now it all made perfect sense: the view of Hell, understanding the obsessive trance states that humans use to ward off fear, seeing the ring of souls as they tried to intervene. And then observing Feyman's original intention.

"He *is* one of us!" I shouted. "I know what he intended to do! In actuality, he came to break through his need for power; he wanted to prevent the destruction that could be caused by the generators and the other new technology. He saw himself meeting with us in the darkness. He's the sixth member of this group."

Maya leaned forward. "This works just like in the process of healing. We have to image him remembering what he is really here to do." She glanced at me. "That helps break the fear block, the trance, at every level."

As we began to concentrate on including Feyman and his men, our energy leaped forward. The night became illuminated and we could clearly see Feyman and two men on the hill. The soul groups seemed to move more closely into focus, appearing more humanlike, while at the same time we became more luminescent, like them. From the left, more soul groups seemed to be joining.

"It's Feyman's soul group!" Charlene said. "And the soul groups of the two men with him!"

As the energy increased, the massive hologram of the World Vision again encircled us.

"Focus on Feyman and the others the way we focused on each other," Maya shouted. "Visualize that they remember."

I turned slightly and faced the three men. Feyman was still working furiously at his computer, the other two men looking on. The hologram encircled them as well, especially the image of each person awakening at this historical moment to his or her true purpose. As we watched, the forest was cast in a perceptible field of swirling, amber energy, which seemed to pass through Feyman and his associates. Simultaneously I saw the same wisps of white light that had protected Curtis and Maya and me hovering over the men, and afterward the white streaks of light grew in size and began to emanate outward in all directions, disappearing finally into the distance. After a few minutes the ground tremors and strange sounds stopped. A breeze blew the last of the dust toward the south.

One of the men stopped watching Feyman and eased away from us into the trees. For several seconds Feyman continued to work on his keyboard, then gave up in frustration. He looked down at us and picked up the computer, cradling it gently with his left arm. With the other hand, he pulled out a handgun and began to walk our way. The other man, armed with an automatic weapon, followed.

"Don't let go of the image," Maya cautioned.

When they were twenty feet away, Feyman set the computer down and punched at the keyboard again, keeping the pistol ready. Several large rocks, loosened earlier, broke free and crashed into the pool.

"You didn't come here to do this," Charlene said softly. The rest of us focused on his face.

The operative, keeping his weapon aimed at us, walked closer to Feyman and said, "We can't do anything else here. Let's go."

Feyman waved him off, then began to type angrily again.

"Nothing is working," Feyman yelled at us. "What are you doing?" He looked at the operative. "Shoot them!" he screamed. "Shoot them!"

For an instant the man looked at us coldly. Then, shaking his head, he backed away and disappeared into the rocks.

"You were born to prevent this destruction from happening," I said.

He dropped the gun to his side and stared at me. For an instant his face lightened, appearing exactly as I had seen it during his Birth Vision. I could tell he was remembering something. Seconds later a look of fright swept across his face, turning quickly into anger. He grimaced and held his stomach, then turned and retched onto the rocks beside him.

Wiping his mouth, he raised the gun again. "I don't know what you're trying to do to me, but it won't work." He took several steps forward, then seemed to lose energy. The gun fell to the ground. "It doesn't matter, you know? There are other forests. You people can't be at all of them. I'm going to make this generator work. Do you understand? You're not taking this away from me!"

He stumbled backward a few feet, then turned and ran into the darkness.

When we reached the hill above the bunker, a great wave of relief swept through the group. After Feyman had left, we had cautiously made our way back to the site of the experiment, not knowing what we would find. Now, as we looked, the bunker area was aglow with dozens of truck lights. Most of the vehicles bore the insignia of the Forest Service, although the FBI was represented, along with the local Sheriff's Department.

I crawled forward several more feet on the crest of the hill and looked closely to see if anyone was being interrogated or held in any of the cars. They all looked empty. The door of the bunker was open and officers seemed to be going in and out as if investigating a crime scene.

"They've all left," Curtis said, leaning forward on his knees and gazing past the trunk of a large tree. "We stopped them."

Maya turned and sat down. "Well, at least we stopped them here. They won't try the experiment again in this valley."

"But Feyman was right," David said, looking at the rest of us. "They can go to some other place, and no one will know." He stood up. "I've got to go in there. I'll tell them the whole story."

"Are you crazy?" Curtis said, walking up to him. "What if the government is part of this?"

"The government is just people," David replied. "Not all of them are involved."

Curtis stepped up closer. "There has to be another way. I'm not letting you go in there."

"There will be someone in one of those agencies who will listen to us," David said. "I'm sure of it."

Curtis was silent.

Charlene was leaning on a rock several feet away, and said, "He's right. Someone could be in just the right position to help."

Curtis shook his head, grappling with his thoughts. "That might be true, but you'll need someone with you who can accurately describe the technology . . ."

"That means you'll have to go too," David said.

Curtis managed to return a smile. "Okay, I'll go with you but only because we have an ace in the hole."

"What?" David asked.

"A guy that we left tied up back in a cave."

David put a hand on his shoulder. "Come on, you can tell me about it on the way. Let's see what happens."

After anxious good-byes to the rest of us, they moved away to the right to approach the bunker site from another direction.

Suddenly Maya whispered loudly for them to wait.

"I'm going too," she said. "I'm a physician; people know me in the area. You might need a third witness."

The three of them looked at Charlene and me, obviously wondering if we might join them as well.

"Not me," Charlene said. "I think I'm needed elsewhere."

I also declined and asked them not to mention us. They agreed and then walked away toward the lights.

Left alone, Charlene and I met eyes. I recalled the deep feeling I had experienced toward her in the other dimension. She was taking a step toward me, about to speak, when both of us detected a flashlight fifty yards to our right.

Carefully we moved deeper into the trees. The light changed position and headed right toward us. We kept still and low to the ground. As the light approached, I began to hear a lone voice, someone apparently talking to himself. I knew this person; it was Joel.

I caught Charlene's eye. "I know who it is," I whispered. "I think we should talk to him."

She nodded.

When he was twenty feet away, I called out his name.

He stopped and shined his light toward us. Recognizing me immediately, he walked over and crouched down where we were.

"What are you doing out here?" I asked.

"There's not much left back there," he replied, pointing toward the bunker. "There's an underground laboratory over there that has been completely cleaned out. I thought I would try to go to the falls; but when I got out there in the dark I changed my mind."

"I thought you were leaving the area," I said. "You were so skeptical."

"I know. I was going to leave, but I . . . well, I had a dream that disturbed me. I thought I'd better stay and try to help. The Forest Service people thought I was crazy, but then I ran into a deputy from the county Sheriff's Department. Someone had sent him a message, so we came out here together. That's when we found this laboratory."

Charlene and I looked at each other, then I briefly told Joel about the confrontation with Feyman and the eventual outcome.

"They were creating that much damage?" Joel asked. "Was anyone hurt?"

"I don't think so," I replied. "We were lucky."

"And how long ago did your friends go down there?"

"Just a few minutes ago."

He looked at both of us. "You're not going in yourselves?"

I shook my head. "I thought it would be better if we watched how the authorities handle all this, without their knowing."

Charlene's expression confirmed that she felt the same way.

"Good thinking," Joel said, looking back toward the bunker site. "I think I had better get back down there, though, just so they'll know the press is aware of those three witnesses. How can I get in touch with you?"

"We'll call *you*," Charlene said.

He handed me a card, nodded to Charlene, and headed toward the bunker.

Charlene caught my eye. "He was the seventh person in the group, wasn't he?"

"Yeah, I think so."

We were silent with our thoughts for a moment, then Charlene said, "Come on, let's try to get back to town."

We had walked for almost an hour when suddenly we heard the sound of songbirds, dozens of them, somewhere to our right. Dawn was just breaking and a cool mist rose from the forest floor.

"Now what?" Charlene asked.

"Look over there," I said. Through a break in the trees to the north was a huge, old poplar, perhaps eight feet in diameter. In the half-light of daybreak, the area around the tree appeared brighter somehow, as if the sun, still below the horizon, had been in position to burst through to radiate downward on that one spot.

I experienced the sense of warmth that had grown so familiar.

"What is it?" Charlene asked.

"It's Wil!" I said. "Let's go over there."

When we were within ten feet, Wil peeked around the tree, smiling broadly. He had changed; what was it? As I continued to study his body, I realized that his luminosity was the same, but he was now more clearly in focus.

He hugged us both.

"Were you able to see what happened?" I asked.

"Yes," he said. "I was there with the soul groups; I saw everything."

"You're in sharper focus. What did you do?"

"It wasn't what I did," he replied. "It was what you and the group did, especially Charlene."

"What do you mean?" Charlene asked.

"When the five of you increased your energy, and consciously remembered most of the World Vision, you lifted this whole valley into a higher vibratory pattern. It rose closer to the vibratory level of the Afterlife, which means that I now appear clearer to you, as you appear clearer to me. Even the soul groups will become more readily visible in this valley now."

I looked hard at Wil. "Everything we've seen in this valley, everything that has happened. It's all the Tenth Insight, isn't it?"

He nodded. "These same experiences are occurring to people all over the planet. After we grasp the first nine Insights, each of us is left at the same place—trying to live this reality day-to-day, in the face of what seems to be a growing pessimism and divisiveness all around us. But at the same time, we are continuing to gain a greater perspective and clarity about our spiritual situation, about who we really are. We know we are awakening to a much larger plan for planet Earth.

"The Tenth is about maintaining our optimism and staying awake. We're learning to better identify and believe in our own intuitions, knowing that these mental images are fleeting recollections of our original intention, of how we wanted our lives to evolve. We wanted to follow a certain path in life, so that we could finally remember the truth that our life experiences are preparing us to tell, and bring this knowledge into the world.

"We are now seeing our lives from the higher perspective of the Afterlife. We know that our individual adventures are occurring within the context of the long history of human awakening. With this memory, our lives are grounded, put into context; we can see the long process through which we have been spiritualizing the physical dimension, and what we have left to do."

Wil paused momentarily and moved closer to us. "Now we will see if enough groups like this one come together and remember, if enough people around the world grasp the Tenth. As we have seen, it is now our responsibility to keep the intention, to ensure the future.

"The polarization of Fear is still rising, and if we are to resolve it and move on, each of us must participate personally. We must watch our thoughts and expectations very carefully, and catch ourselves every time we treat another human being as an enemy. We can defend ourselves, and restrain certain people, but if we dehumanize them, we add to the Fear.

"We all are souls in growth; we all have an original intention that is positive; and we can all remember. Our responsibility is to hold that idea for everyone we meet. That's the true Interpersonal Ethic; that's how we uplift, that's the contagion of the new awareness that is encircling the planet. We either fear that human culture is falling apart, or we can *hold the Vision* that we are *awakening*. Either way, our expectation is a prayer that goes out as a force that tends to bring about the end we envision. Each of us must consciously choose between these two futures."

Wil seemed to drift into thought, and in the background, against the far ridge toward the south, I caught sight again of the streaks of white light.

"With all that was happening," I said, "I never asked you about these movements of white light. Do you know what they are?"

Wil smiled, and reached out and gently touched both of our shoulders. "They're the angels," he said. "They respond to our faith and vision and make miracles. They seem to be a mystery even to those in the Afterlife."

At that moment I was seized by a mental image of a community, somewhere in a valley much like this one. Charlene was there, and others, including many children.

"I think we are supposed to understand the angels next," Wil continued, gazing out toward the north as if seeing an image of his own. "Yes, I'm sure of it. Are you two coming?"

I gazed at Charlene, whose look confirmed that she had seen the same vision as I.

"I don't think so," she said.

"Not right now," I added.

Without speaking Wil pulled us into a brief embrace, then turned and walked away. At first, I was reluctant to let him go, but I remained silent. A part of me realized this journey was far from over. Soon, I knew, we would see him again.